I0629635

Return

To

Iran

******

By

Trish Clough

RETURN TO IRAN COPYRIGHT © 2025 BY PATRICIA (TRISH) CLOUGH. ALL RIGHTS RESERVED. NO PART OF THIS NOVEL MAY BE USED OR REPRODUCED WITHOUT WRITTEN PERMISSION EXCEPT IN THE CASE OF BRIEF QUOTATIONS EMBODIED IN CRITICAL ARTICLES AND REVIEWS.

PATRICIA CLOUGH HAS ASSERTED HER RIGHT TO BE IDENTIFIED AS THE AUTHOR OF THIS WORK IN ACCORDANCE WITH THE COPYRIGHT, DESIGNS AND PATENTS ACT 1988

ISBN 979-8-9871323-3-3 (PAPERBACK)

This novel is a work of fiction. In some cases, true-life figures are mentioned, but their actions and conversations are sometimes fictitious. All other characters are products of the author's imagination. Names of places and descriptions of events are based on historical information and the author's imagination.

Return

To

Iran

Part One

Chapter 1 - The Deadly Decision

Dr. Saeed Ardehali bent down and carefully opened the eyelid of his unconscious patient. She'd come into the hospital ER with a major head injury, and he had performed emergency surgery to release the pressure on her brain. She was a young, small-framed woman, likely in her early 20s.

The delay in getting the girl to the hospital, along with her severe blood loss, had added to the severity of her trauma. Even though the odds were stacked against her, Dr. Ardehali believed she could have a full recovery. The surgery had gone well, and her age and fitness boosted her chances of survival. Unbeknownst to the doctor, there was an additional threat to her life. The Khomeini government wanted his patient dead.

As he felt for her pulse, a soldier pushed open the door, "Dr. Ardehali?"

"Yes, I am he."

"I have instructions from the top. I mean our highest government officials," said Commander Zubin Rashidi.

Before he could continue, the doctor responded, "I'm not involved with the government. You must have the wrong person."

"You're involved. You just don't know it yet," the commander clarified.

"What exactly are you talking about?" asked Saeed, feeling more anxious and confused.

"This girl," said Rashdi as he pointed to Cindy, "her name is Cindy Stetson, and she is an American. Alive, she poses a threat to all of us. You need to eliminate her quietly."

"But…" Saeed protested.

"No buts," the commander stopped him. "We cannot have the Americans finding out that she was brutally beaten by one of my soldiers. We are going to tell them that she died of a drug overdose. Also, you need to incinerate the body. We need to destroy the evidence and have nothing to give the US authorities."

The doctor's eyes widened, and his mouth gaped slightly while he processed the soldier's instructions.

"I don't understand. I just spent hours in surgery trying to save her life; now you want me to end it."

"Yes," he answered gruffly. "I don't care how you do it; just get it done."

Dr. Ardehali took a deep breath and began to object once again.

"Sir, I... I..." stammered the doctor.

"You what?" asked the soldier angrily. "Do you understand what I'm telling you?"

Dr. Ardehali did not respond. Being a medical professional for over 30 years and a devout Muslim, he stood silently staring at the uniformed man. He was horrified at the thought of killing another human being. He believed in the sanctity of life, and what the soldier wanted him to do went against every fiber of his being. Not only was murder wrong, but he had sworn an oath to save lives, not take them.

Becoming impatient with the doctor's silence, the commander positioned himself two inches from the doctor's ear and whispered slowly, "You will do as I have instructed, yes?"

Obediently, Dr. Ardehali began to nod his head in compliance.

"Good," said the soldier before turning to leave.

"Wait!" said the doctor. "How do you expect me to cremate the body?"

Commander Rashidi looked back at him and said, "Burn it in the furnace downstairs. We're telling the Americans that embalming fluid caught on fire and burned several bodies beyond recognition. With the chaos happening at their embassy and the protests in Tehran, the US government shouldn't have a problem believing our story. Honestly, the Americans don't have a choice but to believe us."

The doctor desperately wanted to reject the man's orders. However, he also wanted to keep his freedom, and he knew that defying a commander in the military would, at a minimum, land him in prison. Besides that, he knew his pleas to save the young woman would be met with suspicion and anger. He had been ordered to kill the American girl by some high-ranking official in the newly formed government, and if he did not comply, he and his family would face severe consequences.

"Must it be done now?" asked the doctor.

"Yes, tonight," replied the commander impatiently. "We don't want to give the Americans another reason to retaliate. We already have the hostage crisis to deal with, and the news of an American woman bludgeoned into a coma by our forces could push Carter to go on the offense and attack us. We cannot risk going to war with the Americans over one young woman. Do you understand?"

"Yes, sir. I'll take care of it," Dr. Ardehali confirmed.

With his assignment accomplished, the soldier left the room with Saeed standing silently over his patient. He looked down at her swollen face and heavily bandaged head. Even with the blood transfusions, he thought her skin looked pale.

His operating team had done an excellent job of helping him through the surgery, and together, they had gotten her stabilized and into recovery. Now, he had orders to take the life they had worked so hard to save. His mind raced as he tried to reconcile with his decision to follow the government's demands.

"How can I do this? She's so young, and she's done nothing to deserve death," he thought anxiously to himself. "But I must think of my family. What will they do to them if I don't comply?" Dr. Ardehali walked over to the chair in the corner of the room and sat down. "If I don't do it, I will be putting myself and my family in danger. If I do it, I will have sold my soul to the regime." Then, he reasoned, "If I refuse, they'll just find another doctor to do it, and my refusal doesn't stop it from happening. It only hurts me and the people I love."

Finally, after arguing with himself for several minutes, the doctor got up and went to the supply room. As he prepared the lethal dose of morphine, sweat began to form on his lined forehead just above his salt-and-pepper eyebrows. He took out a cloth hanky and wiped the sweat away. Guilt and remorse weighed heavily on his emotions as he placed the full syringe deep within the large outside pocket of his white coat.

Dr. Ardehali slowly walked back to his patient's room while trying to convince himself that her death was inevitable and that he was just moving the process along. Begrudgingly, Saeed walked up to the bed and picked up Cindy's hand to disconnect the saline IV. When he did, the doctor paused momentarily to notice the unique birthmark on her forearm. It was in the shape of a triangle and was more pinkish than others of its type.

Returning to his task, the doctor pulled the syringe out of its hiding place. He took a deep breath before slowly pushing the lethal liquid into his patient's vein. Without warning, the young woman's arm jerked, and it caused Saeed to stop after only a tiny amount of morphine had entered her bloodstream.

"I can't do this," he said decisively to himself, "but I must do something."

He went to the door and checked to see who was nearby. Fortunately, it was late. All the visitors had gone home, and many staff members were already sleeping in their call rooms. The night nurse was the only one at the station.

Dr. Ardehali retrieved an unused gurney from the hallway and pushed it into Cindy's room. With his adrenaline surging, he heaved her limp body awkwardly onto the stretcher before unhooking the saline bag from its pole and laying it beside his patient. Next, he disconnected the ventilator and fitted a bag valve onto her breathing tube. Saeed vigorously squeezed the bag to begin pumping air manually into Cindy's lungs. Between the six-second intervals, he carefully covered Cindy's entire body with the bed sheet, making sure there was enough cloth on his side to hide the equipment. He quickly pushed the gurney towards the elevator, which was located directly across from the nurses' station.

"Dr. Ardehali, what are you doing? Do you need my help?" the nurse asked questioningly.

"No, thank you," he said in his calmest possible voice.

"Are you sure?" she probed further. "I'm not busy at the moment."

Knowing he needed to send more oxygen to Cindy's lungs, Saeed faked a loud cough to cover the deflating noise of the bag.

"Sorry," he said apologetically before explaining his actions. "I'm sure you saw the soldier who visited me earlier. Well, anyway, while he was speaking to me, my patient passed away. He instructed me to take care of the body personally. Therefore, I'm following his orders."

The nurse was about to respond when a patient buzzed her desk.

"I guess you're wanted elsewhere," he said overtly.

The nurse looked at the doctor subserviently before excusing herself and heading down the corridor. Dr. Ardehali gave the bag another squeeze just as the elevator door opened. He quickly maneuvered the gurney inside and pushed the button to close the door.

******

When the doctor arrived at his home just outside the main downtown area of Tehran, he knew every minute counted. He had been able to drive home one-handedly to administer oxygen to his patient, but getting her into the house would be difficult. He ran inside and got the gurney he used to move his wife, Delbar, from room to room in the last days before her death.

Once inside, the doctor moved Cindy onto the empty hospital bed in the room just off the main entrance to his home. It had been Delbar's bed during her illness. She had died three months earlier of cancer, and all of her medical equipment was still in the room, along with extra bags of saline and other lifesaving supplies. He had done all that he could to keep his wife alive, but it wasn't enough. Saeed could not save her from the cancer. In her honor, Dr. Ardehali looked down at Cindy and vowed to do everything possible to save this young, forsaken woman from an early, unwarranted death.

Saeed carefully adjusted Cindy's limp body to make sure her position was appropriate for her treatment and injuries. Next, he hooked her up to all the life-support equipment in the room.

"I'll get additional supplies when I return to the hospital," he told himself. "This should be sufficient for now."

Once he felt that Cindy was settled, Saeed called his subordinate to cover for him until the morning. Next, he telephoned his brother.

"Kaveh, I have a situation here," he said fretfully. "Is your wife still at her mother's house?"

Hearing the intensity in his brother's voice, Kaveh sat up in his bed.

"Yes, she'll be there for another week. Why?"

"I rescued an American woman from our hospital. Khomeini's regime wanted me to kill her so that they didn't have to explain her head injury to the Americans, but I couldn't do it. She's in a coma, and I don't know if she'll survive, but right now, she's stable. If they find out I didn't do it, I could be imprisoned or killed."

"Are you at home?" asked Kaveh.

"Yes," he said. "I have her stabilized and resting in Delbar's bedroom. I still have all the equipment and supplies that were left over after she passed. I wasn't emotionally ready to remove it yet."

"Do you have help?" his brother asked.

"My housekeeper will be here in a couple of hours," responded Saeed. "Hopefully, she will assist me."

"Can you trust her to keep your secret?" Kaveh inquired.

"Yes, I think so. She has been with me for 23 years. However, my patient will need 24-hour care, and I can't ask her to work more than ten hours a day. Are you able to come and help, at least until I can figure out a plan?"

"I need to get some things in order first. I can be there tonight. Are you going to be okay without me until then?" probed Kaveh.

"Yes, I can manage. As I said, she's stable for now, and I can get additional supplies from the hospital. I plan to head back to work later this morning to check on my other patients. After I finish my rounds, I will tell my team I am taking a few days off," said Saeed.

"I will be there as soon as I can," said Kaveh. "Do you need me to bring anything?"

"No, but..." he paused questioningly. "Do you think I've made the right decision?"

"Well..." Kaveh began.

"Honestly," Saeed interrupted, "it doesn't matter what anyone thinks. I can't kill her. I just can't do it."

"Of course, you can't," said Kaveh supportively. "Besides, Delbar would have been very disappointed in you. She would have wanted you to save her."

With a weepy voice, the doctor softly responded, "I know. She was a good woman."

"Yes," concurred Kaveh before moving the conversation forward. "Tell your housekeeper the woman is with me. I brought her to your home because I wanted your expert supervision, and I didn't like the care she was getting at one of the smaller hospitals outside the city. Tell her I had to leave momentarily. If she questions my motives, tell her it's none of her business," Kaveh said gruffly.

"She won't ask questions," responded Saeed. "She knows her place in my home. However, I will tell her it's a very sensitive matter, and she must not disclose it to anyone. I must go now. I will see you tonight."

The doctor hung up the phone and immediately returned to the bedroom. He looked down at the young woman's face and gently stroked her cheek.

"I will take care of you. Everything is going to be okay," he whispered.

When Dr. Ardehali's housekeeper arrived, he vaguely explained why he had a patient in his home and that he needed her help. When she looked at him questioningly, the doctor announced that he planned to increase her wages substantially. Once her exuberance subsided, he politely yet sternly told her that her silence about the situation was paramount. She nodded her understanding and asked no other questions.

Finally, the doctor mentioned that his brother would arrive later that night to assist them with the woman's recovery. He told his housekeeper he needed to return to work and expected her to watch over his patient while he was away. Knowing she had recently helped him care for his deceased wife, Dr. Ardehali quickly reviewed the nursing protocol he expected. Once he felt confident that she could attend to his patient appropriately, he left for the hospital.

While making his rounds, Dr. Ardehali struggled to be present and interested in his other patients' care. Feeling nervous and distracted, he deliberately questioned his residents about his follow-up care and instructions while planning his early exit.

When he was ready to leave, Saeed cautiously made his way to the supply room, where he filled his medical bag with the items needed for Cindy's care.

Meanwhile, in Shiraz, Kaveh worked diligently to prepare for his unscheduled trip to Tehran. Once ready, he hurriedly wrote a vague note and a check to his wife.

Dear Nahid,

I need to go to Tehran. I am not sure how long I will be gone. It could be several weeks. However, included with this note is a check to pay for your extended stay with your mother and sisters. There is no reason for you to return to Shiraz at this time. I will call you in a couple of days to ensure you have received this letter and the check.

Your husband, Kaveh

Chapter 2 - New York

Paula's mother, Mary Ann Williams, sat alone in the dark. She couldn't sleep, so she got up and fixed herself a drink. Normally, she was not much of a drinker. Having two drinks at a party would be unusual for her, and she never drank at home unless she and her husband were entertaining guests. This night was different; earlier in the day, she had attended the funeral of her daughter's best friend.

As Mary Ann sipped her vodka and tonic, she thought back to how it all started. Paula, her friend Cindy, and the Iranian boys, Shahin and Kamal, had gone together on a trip into the mountains of Iran to take rock samples to complete their independent study courses. What started as an innocent research project turned into a fight for their lives and freedom. Being in the remote regions of the country, the four were isolated from the current news for months. They had no idea that the Shah of Iran had abruptly left the country and his enemy, Ayatollah Khomeini, had taken over. By the time Paula and her friends found out they needed to leave Iran for safety reasons, it was too late. The four were forced to go into hiding. That was all Mary Ann knew until she was told Cindy had died and several days later that Paula, Shahin, and Kamal had been picked up by a Navy ship in the Strait of Hormuz.

Mrs. Williams took a sip of her drink and refocused on the events that had taken place earlier that day. She tried to imagine how she would feel if the US government had told her that she could not publicly express her anger and grief for her daughter's death. The State Department had "asked" Cindy's parents to avoid any interviews with the news media. The reason they gave had been two-fold. At the time of their request, Paula and her Iranian friends were still missing, and the government felt the announcement of Cindy's death could further

9

jeopardize their attempts to find and rescue the other students. Secondly, they believed that interviews and press coverage could hinder their negotiations to end the American hostage crisis happening inside the US Embassy in Tehran.

Cindy's parents had begrudgingly agreed and planned the small, private memorial that commemorated their daughter's life earlier that day. After all, they soberly concluded, they had no body to bury.

******

The news of Paula's rescue had come two days before the funeral, and Mrs. Williams had allowed her jubilation for her daughter's return to overshadow the sorrow she should have felt for the Stetsons and their loss. The contrast between their children's outcomes couldn't be more different, and May Ann felt intense guilt for being so happy.

Mrs. Williams was also troubled by the uncertainty about what to expect when Paula returned home after more than a year of hiding inside Iran. She had been warned that Paula could be traumatized by her experience. Mary Ann knew her daughter was a strong-willed woman and wasn't easily shaken. However, nothing could have prepared her for the events that had taken place during her time in Iran.

******

It was still early morning when the limousine pulled up to the Williams' hotel to drive them to La Guardia airport. They had flown to New York City the day before to greet Paula and celebrate her homecoming. Upon their arrival at the terminal, an FBI agent greeted Paula's parents and ushered the two onto a motorized vehicle that drove them through the concourse to a private room.

Similarly, Shahin Ali's parents drove up from Washington, DC, to welcome Shahin and Kamal. The Alis and the security staff were already waiting for the students to arrive when Paula's parents entered the meeting room.

As the four parents anxiously waited for the arrival of their children, Mr. and Mrs. Williams asked Shahin's parents about their current situation, and Mr. Ali gladly explained. When the Shah was overthrown, he and his wife were unable to return to Iran, so they decided to make Washington, D.C., their new home. Shahin's father took a position with the US government. His job title was once again vague, but it involved foreign relations and international politics, similar to his position in Iran under the Shah. Shahin's mother had decided to return to her profession as an architect and worked part-time for a local firm. After Mr. Ali described their lives, Mrs. Ali mentioned that the US authorities believed that Kamal's parents were still living in Tehran, Iran, with their grown daughter, Farah.

Next, the couples shared what they knew about their children's rescue. Mr. Ali began by explaining the steps taken by the US government after the American hostages were captured inside the US Embassy.

The Sultan of Oman wanted to show his country's support for the United States by allowing them to use its ports and airfields for military purposes. He believed the newly formed Islamic Republic of Iran should have released the hostages instead of siding with the militant students who took over the US Embassy in Tehran.

The Sultan's permission gave the US a strategic advantage, allowing it to guard and monitor the international waters in the Persian Gulf region. During one of the American battleship's patrols, they picked up Shahin, Kamal, and Paula from a small boat in the Strait of Hormuz. Luckily, even though the vessel was under heavy fire from an Iranian gunboat, the three students were rescued unharmed. Sadly, the man helping them escape was fatally wounded and died a few hours after boarding the Navy ship.

Paula's parents continued to ask more questions about the rescue, and Mr. Ali did his best to answer them. A medical team on board the ship checked out each student to ensure they had no immediate medical issues. Next, their children were taken into separate rooms and interviewed. When the battleship arrived back in the city of Muscat, Oman, the three students were flown to London, England. There, a second team of doctors conducted a more in-depth medical checkup, and a group of specialists questioned each student at length. They determined that the students were physically and mentally healthy and did not pose a national security risk. Therefore, the students were allowed to return to the United States promptly.

It surprised Mr. and Mrs. Williams to learn how much more Mr. Ali knew about their children's escape than they did. Moving past their minor concern, they expressed happiness in knowing that Paula was in good health and on her way home.

After their initial greeting and the discussion about the rescue, the parents talked about the long months they had spent waiting for any news about their children. They briefly discussed the death of Cindy, and the parents openly shared their regrets and sadness. The moms, especially, shared their stories of pain and anguish while waiting to hear something about their children's safety. All four concurred and acknowledged how lucky they were that their children were still alive. Despite this mutual understanding, the two couples still felt a palpable tension between them.

Finally, the head of security entered the small room and told the group that the three students had landed. Everyone clapped their hands enthusiastically and yelled their elation. The secure room was elevated above the tarmac, with large windows facing the asphalt. All four parents excitedly moved to stand in front of them to watch for their children's arrival. They saw an airline transport bus pull up outside the terminal, and within seconds, Paula, Shahin, and Kamal exited the bus holding their bags. Paula's mother waved frantically as they walked across the tarmac to the building. The movement caught Paula's eye, and when she saw it was her mother waving, she began to run towards the terminal door. Shahin and Kamal followed Paula's lead and jogged behind her. A security agent at the entrance led the students to the room where the parents eagerly awaited their arrival.

As the door opened, Paula dropped her bags and rushed to embrace her mom and dad. They hugged and kissed each other frantically, uttering apologies and expressing their love.

Shahin quickly went over to his parents and hugged them both, while Kamal stood close by, waiting quietly for them to acknowledge his presence. Within seconds, Mrs. Ali motioned for Kamal to join in, and all four hugged and greeted one another with love, happiness, and statements of relief. It was a jubilant occasion for everyone, and Paula's mother cried tears of joy.

After the initial reunion, the group headed to a quiet, secluded restaurant. Paula, Shahin, and Kamal took turns telling the parents funny stories about their time in Iran and a few of the less harrowing experiences of their ordeal. After a couple of hours of food, drinks, and discussions, the group decided it was time for a break, and everyone headed back to their respective hotel rooms.

The one topic the group did not discuss in detail at the restaurant was Cindy's death. No one felt it was appropriate to discuss it in a public place. Each family would be able to hear the story privately, allowing them to express their grief openly.

Once inside their room, Paula's parents were anxious to hear everything that had happened, not just the funny stories. She knew they expected a full report, and she graciously pushed through another lengthy explanation of her time hiding inside the safe houses and the rescue. She was tired and didn't want any more drama, so she purposely omitted the conflicts and intimate details about her relationships with Cindy and the guys. She knew it would cause numerous questions and complicate her friends' relationships with her parents.

Finally, Paula's parents asked her tentatively if she was ready to explain what had happened on the day Cindy died. She reluctantly agreed. Both parents sat in horror as Paula explained the moments leading up to and after Cindy's death. When Paula was finished, her parents sat silent, unable to think of something suitable to say.

The federal government had provided two rooms, one for Paula and another for her parents, even though both rooms had two double beds. It was still early when Paula's father announced it was time for him to go to bed. Mary Ann concurred; it was time for Paula to return to her room.

Paula slowly walked to the door. She opened it halfway before sheepishly turning to her parents and asking if she could sleep in one of their beds instead of in her private room. Surprised by her question, yet happy, Paula's mother immediately said, "Yes".

"I'll help you with your things," said Mrs. Williams.

"It's okay, Mom," said Paula. "All I have is two small bags."

"Well, I'll just keep you company, then," said her mother.

At that point, Paula knew that her mother wanted some time alone.

"I do have my stuff spread out on the bathroom counter. You can help me gather it up," she said, giving her mother another reason to accompany her to the room.

Paula waited for her mother to say something meaningful, but Mary Ann began talking about the new face products that had come out after Paula had left the US. They were about to leave Paula's room when Mrs. Williams gently grabbed her arm and said, "Paula, I need to apologize."

"No, Mom, you don't," Paula replied.

"Yes, it's about your fight with your father. I should have stood up to him. Especially when I knew you were right. Sometimes, I'm just afraid of making waves. I realize now that there are times when standing down is best and other times when I need to stand up and voice my opinion."

"I guess I learned the same thing while I was gone," said Paula. "I know now that being in a long-term relationship is hard, and consistently getting in the middle of arguments between your kids and your husband could damage your marriage."

"I appreciate your understanding, but I was wrong to stand aside during your argument. Things would have been very different between us if I had stood up to him," Paula's mother admitted.

The two women hugged and promised to evaluate each situation more carefully and support one another when needed. When they returned to the other hotel room, Mr. Williams was still in the shower.

Paula changed into a nightgown her mother had brought for her to use and got into bed. Paula's father exited the bathroom, fully dressed in his pajamas. He saw his daughter and went to her bedside.

"Good night, Babba," he said lovingly as he bent down to kiss her forehead.

Paula hadn't heard her nickname for over a year, and it overwhelmed her senses with an emotional flood of love and regret.

Without thinking, Paula lightly grabbed his wrist and whispered, "Dad, I'm sorry, I ..." but her father interrupted before she could finish her sentence.

"I know," he said softly, "me too, now get some sleep."

He smiled lovingly at his daughter before kissing her gently on the forehead a second time.

The following morning, Paula woke up early. She had gone to her room to shower and had just finished blow-drying her hair when the room phone rang. Shahin called to reassure Paula that he and Kamal would meet her at the airport. When it was time for Paula to leave, a flurry of mixed emotions flowed through her body. She was excited to go home but hesitant to leave Shahin. It would be the first time in 16 months that they would be apart for more than a day. Paula began having very mixed emotions. Along with a pang of unexpected anxiety, she felt both happy and sad at the same time. She allowed the feelings to linger momentarily but then dismissed them as impossible to reconcile.

Shahin and Kamal arrived at the airport and found Paula and her parents waiting at the gate to leave. First, Shahin, then Kamal, addressed Paula's parents, shaking their hands and wishing them well.

An awkward silence followed before Kamal turned his attention to Paula. She mumbled positive words into his ear while hugging him goodbye. When they released one another, Paula smiled compassionately at him and promised Kamal she would keep in touch.

Then, it was time for Paula and Shahin to say goodbye. Silently, Paula took his hand and began to pull Shahin away from the others. He willingly followed Paula's lead and stopped when she turned back to look at him.

"This is so weird," Paula said softly. "When will we see each other again?"

"I'm not sure. It feels unreal. How are we supposed to go back to whatever normal is?"

"I don't know. I guess we'll just have to take it one day at a time," responded Paula. "Promise me you'll call tomorrow."

"I will, I promise. I love you, Paula," added Shahin.

"I love you too," Paula said, almost in tears.

Suddenly, Paula's father shouted, "Paula, dear, we need to go!"

"Okay, give me a minute," she yelled back.

"Well then, I guess this is it," said Paula, lifting her lips to Shahin's.

After a soft, lingering kiss, Paula slowly pulled away from Shahin, focusing intently on his facial expressions. Shahin stared back at Paula while gently holding her hand. As she moved farther away, his grasp began to hinder her ability to part company with him. Shahin gave Paula a solemn look of regret before reluctantly releasing his grip on her hand.

Chapter 3 - The Lie

It had been two months since Kaveh arrived at his brother's house to help Dr. Ardehali care for Cindy. Kaveh purposely avoided conversations with the housekeeper about his relationship with the young woman, and she did not ask him. She spent her days doing chores and sitting with Cindy when needed. To make their time with the unconscious woman less boring, Dr. Ardehali installed a TV in his patient's room. Not only would it help them pass the time, but he also hoped it would stimulate the mind of his coma patient.

In addition to the TV, Kaveh would read to Cindy from the local newspaper. It was his way of staying up-to-date with current events and providing Cindy's brain with something to process. He hoped the articles would cause her brain to respond and wake her from the coma. He didn't only read the positive news. Instead, he shared the controversial sections and political decisions that might spark anger. Unfortunately, the stories didn't elicit any response from Cindy.

As the days passed, the swelling on Cindy's face subsided, and Kaveh could see her beauty returning. On his own, he decided to add physical stimulation to his daily care for Cindy. He began by carefully combing her hair, ensuring he did not touch the areas where the injury had occurred. Her hair had grown longer since she arrived, and her bangs were now well below her eyelids. He took the comb and then his finger to move the strands of hair off her face. The smooth skin of her forehead made something stir inside him that he hadn't felt in a very long time.

The following day, Kaveh's physical engagement with Cindy became more intimate. He began to stroke Cindy's arms and legs, telling himself he was helping her circulation. He had watched his brother and the housekeeper reposition Cindy to help prevent bed sores from forming, and he related his massage of her extremities as just another way to protect her from the adverse side effects of being bedridden. It was innocent enough at first, but soon, his massages were moving to her neck and shoulders, then down to Cindy's waist and back. He hadn't touched her breasts or buttocks, but his massage of her legs had moved closer and closer to her torso.

He rationalized his actions by telling himself that the sponge baths given to Cindy by the housekeeper were not stimulating her muscles sufficiently. So, it was up to him to provide her with the additional care she deserved.

Kaveh became increasingly infatuated with Cindy, and he began to imagine himself caressing her large breasts and exploring every part of her body.

One day, while sitting at Cindy's bedside, Kaveh came up with an idea that would allow him the opportunity to spend time with her even after she had recovered from her injury. Knowing his brother was struggling with what he would do once Cindy awakened, Kaveh created a plan to help him.

✳✳✳✳✳✳

Saeed smiled as he entered the kitchen just before dinner, "I think the young woman will be waking soon, so I removed the feeding tube," he told his brother. "Today, her fingers twitched during my examination. If she wakes in the next couple of days, I won't have to re-insert the tube."

"That's excellent news, but then we're going to have another problem," said Kaveh. "You know what I'm talking about. We have to come up with a strategy to get her safely out of Iran." Before Saeed could respond, Kaveh continued, "I've been thinking about it and formulated a plan. I will take time away from my business and help her leave the country. Of course, it would be after she has fully recovered. She can pose as my second wife. I will tell the authorities I am taking her to Turkey for a vacation. I think it's a good cover."

"I can't ask you to do that. It's too dangerous," responded Saeed.

"I know it has risks, but how else are you and I going to get her out of the country?"

"I'm not sure; I only know I cannot do it. If I suddenly take more vacation time, it could raise suspicion. I've spent so much time away from my duties as it is. I've heard people at the hospital occasionally mention her death, and I've been asked if I'm okay. A couple of the doctors have told me I seem edgy and distracted. I guess I'm not a very good actor. Anyway, let's talk about it more tomorrow morning. The hospital called, and they need me to come in tonight. I'll be leaving here in a few minutes."

******

Kaveh had just sat down to begin his work for the day when the housekeeper entered the room.

"Please, sir, you must come. The young woman has awakened. She is afraid. I told her she had been in an accident, and she told me she did not remember anything of her past."

"How do you know this?" he asked nervously. "Do you speak English?"

"What? I do not understand," said the housekeeper in Farsi.

Kaveh paused momentarily while formulating his next question, "Did she speak to you in Farsi?"

"Yes..." she answered with a puzzling look on her face. "Why would you ask me such a question?"

"I'm sorry, I misspoke. Of course, she talked to you in Farsi," Kaveh said apologetically. "It's silly of me to think she would still be speaking English. Let me explain. You see, several days before the accident happened, she was fervently studying for an English exam, and for many days leading up to it, she spoke only in English." The housekeeper gave him a bewildered look but said nothing. To fill the awkward silence, Kaveh continued, "You don't need to concern yourself with this issue. I will talk to her alone and explain what has happened."

******

Terrified, Cindy looked around the room. It seemed like the woman had told her the truth. She was hooked up to an IV and oxygen. Her body felt stiff and ached, but it was nowhere near as painful as her head. She carefully felt her forehead. It was lightly bandaged, and she could feel the pain emanating from the area.

Suddenly, Cindy panicked. She hastily moved her hand to feel her face. Her eyes, nose, cheeks, lips, and chin felt normal, and no pain was associated with her touch. Happy that her face seemed unscathed by the accident, Cindy let out a sigh of relief and turned her attention to her mind.

"What's wrong with you?" she asked herself in the third person syntax. "Why can't you remember?" she continued. "The woman said you were in an accident, but that's not a reason to forget who you are! Remember, you idiot! Remember," she demanded, but her insistence was useless; she could not recall her identity.

A new thought popped into her mind, "I need to get out of here. Maybe it's this place that I don't recognize."

Then, it hit her. If she left, where would she go? She had no recollection of where she was or how she had gotten there. She would immediately be lost. With that realization, Cindy decided to lie back down and wait for the woman to return.

******

Kaveh took a deep breath and walked prominently into the room where Cindy lay awake and confused.

"I am so happy you are finally awake," he said lovingly in Farsi. "The housekeeper told me you do not remember anything about your past. Is that true? Are you unable to remember or recall anything up until now?"

"Well... Yes, it's true. I do not know who or where I am," responded Cindy.

Kaveh saw his opening, and he made a reckless decision.

"You do not need to worry," he said comfortingly. "I am your husband, and I will help you recover."

"Oh..." Cindy said with surprise. "We're married?"

"Yes, newlyweds. We were on our honeymoon here in Tehran when you fell down a flight of stairs," he said convincingly.

"Can you tell me my name?" Cindy asked humbly.

Kaveh panicked slightly before choosing an appropriate name for his new wife.

"My dearest, your name is Yasmin," he said convincingly. "You took an awful fall, and we were worried that you would not survive. However, here you are, alert and better."

"You are my husband?" Cindy said with uncertainty, still trying to process this news. "I do not remember. I'm sorry. Please forgive me." A moment later, a sharp pain cut through Cindy's forehead. She gasped and put her hand to her head.

"Are you okay? What happened?" asked Kaveh nervously.

"A twinge, but I'm okay," said Cindy. "How long was I unconscious?"

"It's only been a week," he lied. "We were married on January 7th," Kaveh said, wanting to avoid any further questions. "You must be hungry. I will have the housekeeper fix something simple for you to eat. I will return shortly and stay with you. Please, don't be afraid."

Kaveh left the room and found the housekeeper. He instructed her to make Cindy something easy to digest, and then he dialed the hospital.

******

"What's going on?" asked Dr. Ardehali. "The nurse said it was urgent."

"She's awake!" Kaveh blurted.

"How's she doing?" Saeed asked excitedly.

"She seems fine except for one thing. She can't remember who she is or anything about her past," his brother added.

"What? She has amnesia. Well, this complicates things," said Saeed.

"Don't worry, I have it handled," his brother assured him.

"We'll figure this out when I get home. Right now, try and get her to eat something," the doctor told him. "Make sure it's soft and bland."

"I have already instructed your housekeeper to prepare something," Kaveh responded. "Also, there is something else," he said hesitantly. "I told her she is my wife and that she's only been unconscious for a week. I thought distancing her from the November takeover was a good idea."

Saeed quickly glanced around to see who might be able to hear him respond to his brother. When he saw no one close, he whispered forcefully into the receiver.

"You did what? Are you crazy? This is an absurd idea, Kaveh," insisted Saeed. "I'm on my way home. We'll talk about it when I get there."

Dr. Ardehali quickly assigned a resident to take over for him and left the hospital.

******

Saeed opened his front door and walked directly into his study, where his brother was waiting.

"I know, brother," pleaded Kaveh. "It was a snap decision, but it is done."

"What were you thinking? You already have a wife," whispered Saeed angrily. "You have no right to lie to this woman."

Whispering, Kaveh explained, "Listen to me. Nahid has been pleading with me to hire a housekeeper. She says her back is bothering her, and she can no longer clean the house without pain. Also, she asked me to allow her to go on a vacation with her mother and sisters starting next week. I said *no* because I wouldn't have anyone to cook and clean for me when I returned. Remember, I am going to Shiraz on business in two days."

"Yes, I know," said the doctor.

"Anyway, now, with this new situation, I will hire a full-time housekeeper. Nahid will be angry about another woman at first, but happy that she no longer has to cook and clean."

"No," said the doctor. "This is wrong! We cannot lie to her about her past. It's not right, Kaveh."

"But she is so young and beautiful," pleaded Kaveh. "Plus, you know that Nahid cannot give me children. I have already mentioned to her that I am considering taking a second wife who can. She wasn't totally opposed to it. Besides, she hasn't been interested in sex with me for a few years."

"Those aren't valid reasons," said Saeed. "You have no right to lie to this young woman. We have to help her escape, not force her into a life she did not choose."

"What are you going to tell her? She doesn't remember anything. She doesn't even know that she's American."

Confused, Saeed asked, "What do you mean she doesn't know she's American? Does she think she's British? Her accent should make her realize that she's not British."

"Brother, listen to me; when your maid asked her how she felt in Farsi, she answered in Farsi. Since her mind awakened, all she has heard is Farsi; it's the language she's using and understanding. Besides, I think it's safer for Yasmin to only speak in Farsi. It will help her blend in with the local people and make it harder for them to find out who she really is."

"Yasmin?" asked Saeed.

"Yes, that is the name I gave her," said Kaveh.

"This is very risky," said the doctor. "Plus, it's not fair to her. I'm sure she would want to know the truth."

"The truth is that she doesn't know anything about her past," said Kaveh. "What good will it do her to send her home to strangers?"

"But her memory could return at any moment. You have to understand how dangerous this is for all of us," responded the doctor.

"I don't care about that," said his brother. "I want to take her as my wife. I will make her love me, and then if she remembers her past, she will not care because she will be in love with me."

"Nahid will never go for this," said Saeed.

"She doesn't have a choice," Kaveh retorted. "The laws under the Shah have been repealed. I can take another wife if I choose."

"Just because Khomeini has implemented a form of Sharia law that allows a man to have multiple wives, doesn't make it right," replied Saeed, "and what makes it worse is that many are just young girls."

"It also disgusts me that Khomeini is, once again, allowing girls as young as nine to be married, but Yasmin is an adult woman."

"Well..." Saeed began, but Kaveh interrupted.

"She's not a child," he said defensively. "She's a wanted American woman, and I am only trying to protect her."

"Enough," said the doctor. "I need to examine my patient."

"What will you say to her?" asked Kaveh anxiously. "Are you going to tell her the truth?"

"I should, but no, at least not yet," the doctor barked before leaving the room.

Chapter 4 - Back in the USA

Paula and her parents arrived home from New York in the late afternoon to a small group of Paula's close friends and family. Seeing everyone, she quickly mustered the energy and poise to share the details of her time trapped inside Iran. It was the fourth time she had to relive the drama, and she was becoming weary. During the festivities, Cindy's parents called Paula and asked her to come to their home the following afternoon. Paula kindly agreed, feeling too overwhelmed to argue or postpone the visit.

Finally, the party ended. Exhausted from all the attention, Paula slowly ascended the stairs to her room. Mechanically, she got ready for bed, allowing the tiredness to dull her senses. She felt confident she would fall asleep as soon as her head hit the pillow.

Once in bed, the silence and the lack of physical activity allowed Paula's inner feelings to surface. Tears began to flow, and she wept for several minutes. The pent-up emotions had finally been unleashed. Not surprisingly, she cried tears of joy and sorrow simultaneously. Paula was happy and relieved to be home but crushingly sad about Cindy's demise. The grief was raw, yet the reality of her friend's passing was still impossible to comprehend. She still couldn't process the thought of her best friend being gone forever.

Paula was still in bed when her mother called up the stairs the following morning.

"Shahin is on the phone for you," she yelled.

"I'll take it up here," Paula yelled back and raced to the upstairs extension.

"Hi," Shahin said awkwardly before abruptly asking Paula how she was doing.

She mechanically replied, "Fine, just tired."

Feeling uneasy, Shahin quickly began telling Paula about Washington, DC. Minutes after he and Kamal arrived at the apartment, Shahin's mother began searching for a larger place.

"She assumed Kamal and I would be moving in with them. We both went along with it. Neither of us wanted to argue with my mom on our first day back," Shahin explained.

"Yeah, I felt the same way; just go with the flow for now," added Paula.

"Our bedroom is small, but there's enough space in their apartment for all four of us," Shahin reasoned. "Anyway, we spent our first day back at the mall shopping for clothes. My mom wanted to go along, but I convinced her to let us go alone."

Paula and Shahin's conversation became relaxed, comfortable, and positive until she told him about Cindy's parents' call. Shahin could hear the change in Paula's voice as she expressed her concern about the visit. She couldn't stop herself from telling him how anxious they sounded to hear everything that had happened to Cindy, including details about her death. Shahin understood both Paula's and the Stetsons' positions and tried to make Paula understand their need to know more.

A few hours later, after Paula and Shahin had hung up, Paula stood in front of the Stetsons' front door. She took a deep breath and knocked. The door opened quickly, and Cindy's mother led Paula into their family room. Paula could already feel the stress building, and she hadn't even begun to explain anything about Iran. To add to her emotional discomfort, one of Cindy's brothers, whom Paula did not know, had come to hear about his sister's death.

Paula gave him a fake smile as she sat down in an armchair facing the sofa and a second oversized chair. She began her story by detailing the first portion of their trip and tried to emphasize how happy Cindy had been. She also discussed Cindy's natural ability to learn Farsi, using the correct accent and dialect of northern Iranians. Paula purposely mentioned that she did not possess the same talent, hoping they would feel some additional pride in their daughter's accomplishments. Finally, she made sure it was clear to Cindy's family that this part of their trip was a positive experience for all of them.

Knowing it was going to be uncomfortable, Paula winced when Cindy's older brother brought up the day of his sister's death. She felt a slight panic run through her and quickly decided to talk about their experiences in the safe houses first.

Paula glossed over Cindy's relationship with Kamal throughout her stories and provided little detail about their affection for one another. She also left out several other bits of information that she felt would be unnecessarily hurtful to Cindy's family. She didn't think of it as lying, just leaving out parts of the story that would be difficult for Cindy's family to accept.

The hours passed, and by the time Paula finished telling them about Cindy's encounter with the soldiers in front of the embassy, she felt mentally weary and physically exhausted from the emotional upset. As she drove away from the Stetsons' house, Paula took solace in the fact that the event was over, and now she and Cindy's family could move on from the painful memories surrounding her death.

When Paula returned home, she immediately went to the phone and dialed Shahin's number.

"I don't care if it's expensive," she told herself. "I need to hear his voice and tell him what it was like."

Shahin was getting ready to go out to dinner. His parents wanted him and Kamal to meet their friends. He only had a few minutes to talk with Paula before he had to leave with them for the restaurant.

Shahin listened to Paula and did his best to convey his appreciation for her sacrifice and the immense emotional toll it had taken on her well-being. He quickly thanked her for explaining it all to Cindy's family and then hurriedly excused himself from their conversation, saying he had to go. Paula wasn't ready to conclude their discussion and felt annoyed that Shahin couldn't give her more of his attention. As she hung up the phone, Paula, feeling slightly jolted, did her best to try to understand that Shahin had other responsibilities and needed to end their call.

Chapter 5 - David

The US government wanted to keep the details of the students' escape from Iran as quiet as possible. Like the news of Cindy's death, they were concerned it could escalate the tensions between the two countries. They were worried that more negative news about the Khomeini government would undermine their negotiations to release the American hostages.

Unfortunately, the government knew it would be impossible to hide the news completely. All they could hope was that the students understood the gravity of the situation and would decline all media interviews until the hostages were released. Paula, Shahin, and Kamal all agreed that it would be easy for them to comply. None of them wanted to talk publicly about what had happened. Not only was the pain too new and raw, but on some level, they all felt some guilt for the decisions they had made in Iran.

******

Within a few days after Shahin and Kamal arrived in Washington, DC, Shahin's mother proudly announced that she had found a house to rent. They would be moving to their new place in a week. It was a large five-bedroom home just outside the center of the city. There were three bedrooms on the second floor, and the master and maid's quarters were on the first floor of the small mansion. Mrs. Ali made an extra effort to say that she felt the home was spacious enough for the four of them to live comfortably together in the long term.

Excited about more space, Shahin quickly called Paula to share the news. The phone rang several times before an answering machine picked up the call. Shahin left Paula a message to call him when she got home.

Later in the afternoon, Paula's little sister, Amy, was opening the kitchen entry door when she heard the telephone ring. She ran to it and snapped up the receiver.

"Hello, Williams' residence, Amy speaking," she said, breathing heavily.

The answering machine clicked on, and Amy accidentally hit the delete button while trying to stop the machine from interrupting the current call. It stopped, and Amy waited for the person on the other end of the line to speak.

"Amy, this is David, Paula's old boyfriend. Is your sister there?" he asked politely.

"I know who you are," said Amy matter-of-factly. "But, sorry, she's not here. My mom told me she went shopping with Karen."

"Okay, well, I'm at my parents' house. Will you tell her to call me when she gets home?"

"Sure, I'll tell her," replied Amy.

When Paula returned home, Amy was doing her homework at the kitchen table.

"Did anyone call for me?" asked Paula.

"Yeah, David, your old boyfriend. He said he was at his parents' house and wants you to call him."

"Okay, thanks," said Paula as she put her purchases on the dining room table. "Shahin didn't call?"

"No, just David," answered Amy.

Bewildered, Paula walked into the living room and plopped down on the sofa.

"Why is David calling me? We've been broken up now for over two years. Maybe he just wants to say hi or tell me he's sorry to hear about Cindy," thought Paula. "I guess it couldn't hurt for me to call him back. It's not like Shahin is jealous or anything. Plus, it would be rude not to."

After assuring herself that she was doing nothing wrong, she walked over to the telephone and dialed David's number.

"Hello," answered David.

"Hi... David, this is Paula," she said hesitantly. "Amy told me you called."

"Yeah, thanks for calling me back."

"Sure," Paula said, still sounding uncertain of herself.

"Well, first, are you okay?" he asked caringly. "I heard about the whole Iran thing and Cindy."

"I'm doing okay, but it's hard. I really miss her," Paula admitted.

"I'm sorry. It must be difficult for you to deal with your grief as well as all of the family stuff, hers and yours."

"Yeah, it's been tough," Paula sighed.

"Well... that isn't the only reason I called," David said cautiously. "I was wondering if I could interview you. You know, about what happened to you in Iran."

"Interview me?" Paula questioned.

"Yeah, I changed my major to journalism, and I need to interview someone who has traveled internationally. You're the only one I know."

"But I'm not supposed to talk to the media. I gave my word," Paula told him.

"Oh...well... I'm not the media, not yet, anyway. It's just something for my final project. I can tell my professor that he can't publish it or give it to anyone," David added.

"Well, I guess I can talk about the first part of my trip before the Shah left Iran. That's still a pretty interesting story," Paula conceded.

"Okay then, I'll pick you up tomorrow at 3:00. I've set up a room in my parents' basement. It has pretty good sound quality, and there won't be any distractions. Oh! It will be a video interview, so you might want to dress a little nicer than just jeans, or not..., it's up to you. Actually...," David said awkwardly, "jeans would be great; I want you to look like a student. Forget I said anything. Dress however you want."

Paula chuckled slightly, "Okay, I'll pick something casual but a little nicer than my workout clothes."

She hung up the phone and pondered the idea of seeing David again. "It sounds like he's doing well. Maybe he's changed?" she thought curiously. Then she asked, "Have I changed?" Immediately, she responded to her question. "Of course, I have. Everything has, and it won't ever be the same again."

******

Shahin called the next day at 3:30 PM, and again, Amy answered the call.

"Hello, Williams' residence, Amy speaking."

"Hello, this is Shahin. I left a message for Paula yesterday but didn't hear back from her, so I'm calling again."

"Sorry, she's not here. She left a few minutes ago with David."

"Oh," said Shahin, slightly surprised, "do you know if she's going to be gone long?"

"I don't know. She looked like she was going out on a date. She had her hair all done and wore the new top she bought yesterday."

Shahin felt a pang of jealousy run through his veins, but remained positive.

"Well, I'm sure your sister is a very popular person these days," he said understandingly.

"No, not really. She doesn't get that many phone calls, just David and her friends."

"Okay, well, please let her know that I called again. She can call me back anytime," Shahin added.

"Okay, I'll tell her," responded Amy. Then, without warning, she blurted out, "Bye!" and hung up the phone.

"It's no big deal," Shahin mumbled to himself. "What did I expect, that she'd never see David again? She has the right to hang out with whomever she chooses, even if that person is her old boyfriend."

Shahin sighed softly while trying to convince himself that it was no big deal.

******

The interview with David took much longer than Paula had anticipated. Even though they were not finished, Paula told David that she needed to continue the interview the next morning. She had already made dinner plans with her friends.

"Is it okay if I call Karen and have her pick me up here? I'm ready, and your house is on the way to the restaurant."

"Sure, the phone is still in the same spot upstairs," David responded.

Paula ran to Karen's car as she pulled up to David's house.

David hollered, "Remember, I'll pick you up at 10:30 tomorrow morning!"

"Okay, see you in the morning!" Paula yelled back.

After they had dinner, Paula and her friends drove to the local movie theater. *The Rose*, starring Bette Midler, had just been released nationwide. The first show was sold out, so they walked around the mall until the 10 p.m. movie began.

Meanwhile, Shahin waited for Paula to call. Kamal was studying at the library, so Shahin decided to watch TV in his room to help take his mind off her and David together. A show came on, and it caused Shahin to relive the night Charles died. As he replayed it over again in his head, he saw Charles lying in a pool of blood, telling him to run. The feeling that he had abandoned Charles returned as Shahin recalled glancing back at him just before he closed the closet door. The remembrance only added to Shahin's sadness. Deep down, he still loved Charles and worked daily to forgive him.

Shahin felt he finally understood what Charles had gone through and how romantic love could alter a person's perspective. He realized that love could cause a person to be dishonest and ultimately do disgraceful things. He, himself, he thought, had kept the worsening security situation in Iran from his friends for the same reason. No, he hadn't betrayed them like Charles had betrayed him, but Shahin knew he hadn't been completely honest with them either. Shahin recalled using his skewed reasoning to justify his bad behavior. Remembering how it all happened helped Shahin to accept Charles's failings even though he couldn't accept his own. Thinking about it further, Shahin considered Charles's declaration to him as they were about to leave the bunker. With a greater understanding of how romantic love can manipulate a person, Shahin finally accepted that even though Charles betrayed him, he did love him. Coming to this conclusion helped to ease the anger and pain Shahin felt against the elderly man.

As Shahin continued to think about that night, another thought surfaced. He remembered his shock when Kamal fired his gun at the soldier who had just shot Charles.

"Without his quick reaction," thought Shahin, "all three of us would most likely be dead."

Thinking about Kamal's actions, Shahin suddenly realized that he hadn't ever discussed the shooting with Kamal. He had thanked him at the time for saving his life, but he hadn't asked him if the event had negatively affected him. Shahin decided that he needed to talk to Kamal about it when the time was right, but he knew it wouldn't be an easy conversation for either of them. They were guys, Shahin reasoned, and even though he and Kamal had been through a lot together, they struggled to communicate their inner feelings to one another. Concluding that he would address the issue with Kamal another day, Shahin returned his thoughts to Paula.

"Why hasn't she called? Is she still out with him? Why am I letting it bug me so much?" Then, Shahin had an idea. "I know. I'll plan a surprise visit to Michigan. I can fly there this weekend. I will call the travel agent in the morning and arrange a flight and a car."

It was after midnight when Paula got home. The first thing she did was search for a note. Often, her mother would leave a message on the kitchen counter if someone had called for her, but the counter was empty. She quietly snuck upstairs, trying not to wake her family. Lying in bed that night, Paula wondered why Shahin had not called. She told herself that she had to give him time to adjust to his new surroundings and that she should not expect him to call her daily. Paula had hoped, however, that he would call her at least every other day.

"Maybe he's just as busy as I am," thought Paula as she got into bed. "I'll try to call him tomorrow when I get back from the interview."

Chapter 6 - Time to Leave

Kaveh left Tehran to interview women for housekeeping and cooking in Shiraz one week after Cindy had awakened. That first night, Cindy felt very alone. She lay awake, desperately trying to remember her past; everything felt foreign and wrong. Kaveh had told her about her childhood and how she had lost her family when she was just seven years old.

After losing her family, Kaveh further explained, Cindy was sent to the orphanage in Mashhad. The children who might have known Cindy when she was young were now grown, and their files were confidential. This would make it impossible for Cindy to find them.

To make Cindy's quest for more answers even more complicated, Kaveh told her the unhappy news about her last employment. She had been a nanny for a family who abruptly left the country. The parents of the children she tended were labeled as dissidents, and fleeing Iran was the only way to avoid imprisonment. They departed without telling anyone, even Kaveh, a family friend, their destination or contact information.

Kaveh told Cindy that he was at his friend's home during the chaos of their departure, helping them prepare their business records and documents to take with them. During this visit, Cindy implored Kaveh to marry her, saying she had nowhere else to go. Driven by his affection for her and his desire for more children, Kaveh agreed. He concluded his explanation with the news that they had married just three weeks earlier, reinforcing his narrative that Cindy had been the one who desired to wed, and all he had done was graciously accept her proposal.

Finally, Kaveh told Cindy that his first wife, Nahid, had only recently been informed of their marriage.

"She took it well," he said positively.

Sadly, Kaveh's reassurances about his first wife's acceptance did little to quell Cindy's growing apprehension. The thought of meeting Nahid and the uncertainty of her place in Kaveh's home, particularly her sexual role, weighed heavily on Cindy's mind.

When Kaveh wasn't by her side, Cindy pressed Dr. Ardehali's housekeeper for more information about her past. Unfortunately, the woman had little knowledge to share with Cindy.

Equally, Dr. Ardehali had very little to add to Kaveh's story. Cindy noticed that Saeed became surprisingly evasive and uncomfortable whenever she brought up the subject. Cindy concluded that he disapproved of their marriage and stopped asking him for more details.

Cindy's efforts to remember her past were futile and disheartening. Finally, she decided to accept her current circumstances and make the best of her situation. She would do her best to make her husband happy and to become friends with his first wife.

The following morning, Cindy woke up feeling surprisingly strong. Still wearing one of the oversized hospital gowns, Cindy carefully got up and wrapped the large cloth around her slender body. Next, she used the cloth belt given to her by the housekeeper to secure the garment in place. Once she completed the knot, she decided to make her bed. She slowly pulled the bed covers up and carefully arranged her pillow. When finished, she looked proudly down at her accomplishment.

Suddenly, Cindy heard someone pounding on Dr. Ardehali's front door. It startled her, and she instinctively raced to the closet. She parted the hanging clothes and stepped inside the dark room. Luckily, a large basket of loosely folded linens was positioned on the left side of the closet.

Cindy shimmied around the full basket and crouched down in the corner. Once settled, she listened intently for more sounds from outside. She could hear someone jiggling the door handle, trying to open it. A moment later, Cindy heard Dr. Ardehali's voice.

"Who is it?" he asked.

A loud voice boomed, "This is Commander Zubin Rashidi. Open this door immediately!"

Cindy heard the door squeak open. She intuitively knew that this man posed a danger to her. She grabbed a black chador hanging on a hook beside her and pulled it over her entire body before crouching further onto the closet floor. She could hear the commander yell out orders to at least two other men. As she continued to listen, she heard the sound of boots running up the steps to the second floor.

Moments later, the door to her bedroom swung open and slammed against the doorstop positioned on the wall. Cindy couldn't see what was happening, but she could hear heavy boots clattering on the hardwood floor, followed by a much lighter noise, which she determined were most likely Dr. Ardehali's dress shoes.

"I can explain…" the doctor blurted before stopping abruptly. Cindy thought he probably noticed she was gone, and the bed was made.

"This was my late wife's room. I haven't been able to get rid of her things since her passing. It's only been a few months, and I am still grieving," the doctor explained in a much more even tone.

The commander ignored Dr. Ardehali's comments and began searching the room. As he inspected the surroundings, he and the doctor could hear the soldiers upstairs tromping through the space above them.

"I didn't realize how much noise from upstairs can be heard down here," said Dr. Ardehali, trying to make small talk with the incensed commander.

Still disregarding the doctor's statements, Commander Rasidi walked over to the closet and swung open the door. He parted the hanging clothes and surveyed the garments.

"They are my wife's clothes," offered Saeed. "She was a full-bodied woman before she became ill."

Knowing the woman he was searching for was significantly shorter and thinner, the commander growled at the doctor's explanation. He glanced over the basket into the dark enclosure. All he saw was the blackness of the unlit corner. He was about to search further when one of his men came in, pulling Dr. Ardehali's housekeeper with him.

"I found this one in the kitchen," he said proudly.

Before the commander could interrogate the woman, another soldier yelled down from the second floor.

"Hold her," he said to the man, grasping the arm of the housekeeper.

Commander Rashidi walked past the three of them and headed to the stairs. Saeed immediately followed him as he walked up the stairs and into one of the bedrooms.

"I found these, Sir," said the soldier, holding several silky nightgowns out for the commander to inspect. "There are other women's items in here as well."

"These are also my wife's clothes," explained the doctor nervously. "She used to sleep in this bedroom with me until she became ill. It was too much for her to walk up the stairs, so she stayed in our downstairs guest bedroom towards the end."

The commander took one of the gowns and held it out with both hands. He sighed disappointedly as a large gown unfolded. It was evident that the garment would not fit the girl.

"This isn't what we're looking for," he growled to his subordinate. "Have you found any clothes that would fit a smaller, thinner woman?"

"No, sir, this is all, no girl either," added the soldier. "There isn't anyone else up here."

"Okay, let's go," said the commander angrily.

He turned toward the stairs, followed by the doctor and the two soldiers.

Commander Rashidi approached the housekeeper and began his interrogation, "Where's the girl?" he asked gruffly.

The housekeeper glanced briefly at the doctor and then responded to the inquiry, "I'm not sure who you are referring to, Sir."

"Is there a girl living here, a small, slender woman with a head injury?"

"No, sir," she said shyly.

"You're sure?" he asked again.

She nodded and looked down at her feet, intimidated by his presence and questioning.

Exasperated, the commander begrudgingly addressed his corporal, "Let her go. The rumors must not be true."

"What rumors?" asked the doctor. "What are you referring to?"

"There's some speculation going around the hospital about the night…" The commander stopped in mid-sentence and pulled the doctor aside. Under his breath, he said, "There's talk about the death and disposal of the American woman. I needed to make sure the rumors weren't true. You did burn the body in the furnace as I instructed, correct?"

"Yes," Saeed whispered. "I did just as you told me."

The commander returned to his men and said, "The allegations must be stories and gossip. We don't need to bother the doctor further."

The commander apologized to Dr. Ardehali, and the four men left the house.

When the doctor was sure the men were gone, he thanked his housekeeper for her discretion and went back into the bedroom, "Yasmin… are you in here?" he whispered.

Cautiously, Cindy emerged from the closet, "Who was that man? Was he looking for me?"

"It was a misunderstanding," Saeed said reassuringly. "There's no need to worry."

"I'm glad I hid, even if it wasn't me he was looking for. He seemed very angry and agitated," Cindy added.

"Yes, he seems to be a very unhappy person," agreed Dr. Ardehali. "You need to return to your bed and rest. The stress isn't good for your head injury."

Saeed walked her to the bed and helped Cindy get under the covers before returning to his study. He sat at his desk, contemplating what to do next. It was apparent, he determined, that the American woman's presence in his house put all of them in danger.

"I'm going to have to allow Kaveh to take her home even if she's not fully healed," Saeed concluded. He thought further about her future and how to protect her identity. "I'll tell Kaveh to make her wear an additional face covering when she's out in public. It shouldn't be too long, maybe six months, before this whole thing disappears."

Saeed called his brother and told him about the search and his decision to send Yasmin with him to Shiraz.

******

When Cindy and Kaveh arrived at his home in Shiraz, Bahar, their new housekeeper and cook met them at the door. She was a fairly tall woman who appeared to be in her late forties. She introduced herself to Cindy and quickly assisted her into the dining room for a refreshing fruit drink.

Kaveh had explained that Bahar's job was housekeeping and cooking. Food shopping, however, would be a shared responsibility between her and his first wife, Nahid. This way, they could occasionally choose the particular foods they liked.

Kaveh told Cindy that Nahid would return to the house in a week. This would give the two of them the privacy to continue with their honeymoon. He quietly whispered to Cindy that she had been a very explosive and passionate lover before her injury. Cindy cringed at the thought of having sex with Kaveh but realized that it was her obligation as his wife.

******

Cindy sat upright in the bed and pulled the covers up over her naked body. Kaveh had retreated to the bathroom to clean himself up after their latest sexual encounter. Nahid would return from her trip to her mother's house the following morning. Cindy hoped Nahid's presence would limit the time she had to spend with Kaveh. He seemed to have an insatiable sexual appetite, and the twice-daily episodes of passion pushed Cindy further into despair.

Cindy believed Kaveh was trying to be a good and thoughtful lover, but she felt empty and unfulfilled after each sexual interlude. She wasn't in love with Kaveh, and all the attention and gifts he bestowed upon her hadn't changed her feelings for him. Cindy wanted to love him, but the passion just wasn't there.

******

The contracted driver arrived mid-day with Nahid and all four pieces of her luggage. Cindy waited in the bedroom while Kaveh helped Nahid into the living room.

"Please sit down. In a minute, I will introduce you to Yasmin, my new wife, and Bahar, our new housekeeper," he told Nahid. "You are going to like both of them. Bahar will do the housework and cooking, allowing you and Yasmin time to redecorate our home. I know how much you like to decorate. I have budgeted money for you to redo the house in whatever décor you please. Yasmin will assist you with your shopping. However, the design of the main areas of our house will be your decision."

"What about the rest of the shopping?" she asked.

"Both of you may choose some weekly food items from the markets for yourselves, but, as usual, I will decide the main course for our dinners."

Kaveh brought Yasmin and Bahar in and sat them down across from Nahid.

Nahid looked intensely at Cindy for a moment while ignoring Bahar's presence. Frowning, she turned her gaze to Kaveh and announced, "I will begin with my bedroom. "She can be in charge of your bedroom. I won't be spending time in there anyway." Nahid gave Kaveh an indignant smirk, this time ignoring Cindy's presence and obvious shock. "I will be in my bedroom unpacking. What time will dinner be ready?" she asked Bahar as she got up.

"Dinner is planned for 7:00 PM," responded Bahar softly.

"Good," Nahid said curtly, "in the meantime, I would like a cup of tea and sweet bread delivered to my room."

Bahar shyly acknowledged her request.

Enjoying her new power and freedom, Nahid looked at all three of them snootily before turning and heading down the hall to her new bedroom.

******

The following morning, Kaveh left for his office early. The latest developments in Tehran had trickled down into all the businesses in Iran, and Shiraz was no exception. President Carter had broken all diplomatic ties with Iran, and US warships patrolled the Persian Gulf. This development had hurt his company, and he needed to spend long hours at his office trying to circumvent the fallout and find new avenues to keep his company profitable.

In addition to his profits falling, Kaveh had become paranoid about Cindy's true identity, and his obsession grew with each passing day. As his brother suggested, Kaveh had ordered Cindy to wear a scarf over her face, allowing only her eyes to be seen. Unfortunately, his paranoia continued to grow, and he decided to make Cindy wear a hijab that covered all of her hair and forehead under the full-length black chador. Only a small opening for her eyes was allowed to be uncovered. Cindy was baffled by this demand but followed his orders and covered her face. Nahid was jealous of Cindy's youth and beauty, and she liked that Cindy had to wear the additional face covering. With her face mostly covered, no one could see Cindy's pouty lips, high cheekbones, and petite nose, characteristics Nahid wished she possessed.

Chapter 7 - The Bar

Shahin was still obsessing over Paula and David the following morning when he found his mother crying at the kitchen table. He cautiously questioned why she was upset, but she told him it was unimportant. He pressed her further, and she finally admitted that she missed their home in Tehran and felt a deep sense of sadness for the entire country of Iran.

Shahin felt his mother's sadness and remorse and wondered if it might be associated with Charles's death and her role in his feeling of abandonment. Usually, she would ensure that everyone around her had the emotional support they needed to confront any personal and troubling issues that affected them. Mrs. Ali did this by openly analyzing and discussing the matter at hand with the persons involved. Oddly, she had chosen to remain silent about Charles, which made Shahin reluctant to bring up the subject. The whole situation felt weird and uncomfortable, so Shahin hadn't initiated any conversation with his parents that mentioned Charles or his role in the revolution.

Seeing his mother so distraught, Shahin decided to delay telling her about his planned trip to Michigan. Instead, he excused himself by stating that he needed to call Paula. For the third time in less than 24 hours, Shahin tried to reach Paula.

"Williams residence, Amy speaking."

"Hi Amy, it's me again, Shahin. Is Paula there?"

"No, I think she left with David again. Just a minute," Amy held the receiver away from her mouth and yelled to Paula's mother. "Mom! Is Paula here, or did she go with David?"

Mrs. Williams responded, and Amy relayed the message to Shahin.

"Yeah, she's with David."

"Well… could you let her know that I called again?" asked Shahin, trying to remain polite as his jealousy rose.

"Yeah, I will," said Amy.

"Thanks, it's important that she call me. She has my phone number."

The call ended, and Shahin tried to defend Paula's actions to himself.

"Of course, she's busy. Unlike Kamal and me, Paula is back in her hometown, where everyone knows her, including ex-boyfriends like David."

Shahin sat thinking about how different his family's situation was from Paula's. His parents had made a few friends in DC, but he and Kamal knew no one. Feeling sorry for himself, Shahin allowed his anger and resentment to take over his rationale.

"First, she was with David all day yesterday, and now she's gone with him again this morning. For being my girlfriend, she certainly seems to be hanging out a lot with her ex-boyfriend," Shahin brooded. "Things will be better once I get to Michigan," he assured himself.

Shahin looked up the travel agent's number and asked her to make a flight reservation for him on Friday.

******

That afternoon, David and Paula completed the interview. To celebrate, David asked Paula to join him at their local hangout for happy hour. Reluctant at first, Paula decided to say "yes".

Paula had worked at the bar her first two summers out of high school. At the time, the legal drinking age in Michigan was 18. However, in December 1978, the voters changed the drinking age back to 21. Luckily, she and David had turned 21 the previous year, and the new law didn't affect them.

The bartender was aware of Paula's ordeal and was happy to see that she was back home with her family. He hadn't heard any details about her experience, but he knew she had been missing in Iran for almost a year.

It felt like old times to Paula. When she was eighteen, she and David often sat at the bar after her shift. After hanging out for a few hours, Paula told David it was time for her to go home. He paid their bill, and they got up to leave. Just before he opened the door for Paula to walk out into the parking lot, he gently pulled her away from the door and into his arms. He paused briefly, then gently leaned down and kissed her.

Without thinking, Paula kissed him back. The alcohol had gone to her head, and for a moment, she had forgotten all about Iran and her current circumstances. What she felt was something safe and familiar. However, that feeling didn't last long. She came to her senses and pulled away.

"David, I can't. I'm sorry. I should never have kissed you back. I..." David wasn't looking for an apology. He was looking for more. He leaned down to kiss Paula again, only this time, she stopped him.

"It's okay," said David lovingly. "I know you've been through a lot."

"No," Paula said. "It's not that. I'm in love with someone else. He's one of the guys I was with in Iran."

"I understand," said David. "He was there, and you needed to be loved, but now you're home, and I'm here."

"No, it wasn't just convenient. I loved him well before my trip. I just didn't do anything about it. It's actually why I broke up with you. I felt guilty for secretly wanting someone else."

Paula immediately saw the disappointment in David's eyes. He hung his head for a second or two, trying to accept what Paula had told him. When he looked up, Paula could see the resignation on his face. He understood that he and Paula would not be getting back together. Her heart belonged to another man.

******

While Paula was out with David, Shahin had become even more frustrated and impatient with his current situation. A little after 2:00 p.m., Shahin called Paula's house again. This time, Paula's mother answered the telephone. Feeling uncomfortable, he politely asked to speak with Paula. Mrs. Williams promptly told him she wasn't home but offered no information about where she might be. Shahin briefly thought about telling her that he had booked a flight to Detroit, but quickly abandoned the idea. Instead, he asked her to please have Paula call him as soon as she arrived home. Mrs. Williams agreed, and the call ended.

Shahin's mother entered the apartment just as he hung up the phone.

He took one look at her face and knew something was terribly wrong. "President Carter has ordered all Iranian assets held in the United States to be frozen," she said angrily. "It's going to have serious consequences for the entire Iranian population living here in the US. Many students and government-supported diplomats will be heavily impacted. They will no longer have access to the government money set aside to pay for their housing, education, or salaries."

"But we're okay, right?" asked Shahin.

"Yes, but the other families, how are they supposed to pay their bills?" she lamented.

"I'm sure it will be temporary. Carter will probably make an exception for those families affected," Shahin said confidently.

"I hope so," said his mother. "You know it's different for us because we have our own money, but many families here rely on those funds."

"Yeah, I understand," agreed Shahin. He paused and then cautiously introduced his plans. "Because we have plenty of money, it's okay for me to go to Michigan this weekend, right?"

Mrs. Ali stared at him disbelievingly, "What? You're planning to leave?"

"Well, yeah, I want to go and see Paula," he responded.

"No! I don't want you to leave," said his mother, sounding desperate.

At first, Shahin thought it was about the cost and tried to reassure her that the plane ticket and hotel had already been paid for with his money. He tried to explain why he hadn't asked her first, but it sounded like he reacted impulsively without considering anyone else or their plans. His mother became even more upset when he admitted that he hadn't told Paula yet.

"You planned a trip to see Paula this weekend, and you haven't even asked her if it's okay!"

"Well, I... I tried, but she's never home," Shahin said in his defense.

"Well, you're not going," his mother ordered. "Besides, if she doesn't know you're coming, you won't disappoint her."

"But, mom..." Shahin began.

"Please, Shahin, I'm afraid," she begged.

The last phrase of his mother's sentence confused Shahin.

"What? You're afraid?" repeated Shahin.

"Yes, the Americans are angry with us. Not us personally, all Iranians. Who knows what they might do next?" responded Mrs. Ali.

"But..." Shahin tried to argue.

"No!" Shahin's mother cried out. "I don't want you to go! I thought I lost you once, and I cannot bear it if something were to happen to you in Michigan."

Shahin had never seen his mother act like this before. She had always been the calm and levelheaded one of the family. Both he and his father had lost their tempers in the past, but never his mother. At that moment, it became clear to Shahin how hard it had been for his mother to wait and hope that he would escape Iran unharmed. He hadn't thought about the stress and pressure on her. He knew his mother would worry about him, but he hadn't put that worry into real feelings. Now, he saw the terror in his mother's eyes for the first time.

Immediately, Shahin decided to back down and cancel his trip. The last thing he wanted was to cause his mother to worry because of his petty insecurities. She had already gone through so much because of him.

******

It was early evening when Shahin finally spoke with Paula. Oddly, he felt a strange distance between them. Paula seemed uneasy and aloof about what she had been doing since they spoke last. He tried to continue their conversation about her meeting with Cindy's parents, but Paula acted disinterested. Instead, Paula gave him a vague overview of her visit and then expressed her thankfulness that it was over.

Not knowing what to say next, Shahin decided to ask about David. Paula immediately responded with a question of her own.

"David, what about him? I guess you know he interviewed me."

"What?" asked Shahin. "He interviewed you! But you know we're not supposed to talk to anyone about what happened."

Paula winced at his statement and then proceeded to defend herself.

"Well, I didn't tell him anything about our escape or the safe house. I just told him about the first part of our trip. You know, the sampling and the…"

"I don't think what you said matters!" exclaimed Shahin. "You weren't supposed to say anything!"

Not wanting to fight, Paula tried to calm the situation.

"I know we need to get the hostages home. Please, believe me. I didn't say anything to compromise their safety." Unfortunately, Paula knew her comment had come too late. Shahin was already upset.

"Shahin, I..." Paula began.

"Don't, Paula!" yelled Shahin. "It's too late to apologize."

At that moment, Paula realized that she may have said more than she should have to David, but she didn't understand why Shahin was so emotional about it.

Overhearing the conversation as she entered the room, Paula's mother approached Paula and asked, "Is everything okay? You sound upset."

"Yeah, Shahin and I are just talking about the hostages," Paula said, trying to convince her mother that everything was fine.

"It's very upsetting, I agree," responded Paula's mother. "However, right now, I need you to go and pick up your sister. It's started to rain, and I don't want her walking home. Can you call him back later?"

Feeling relieved she had an excuse to end the conversation, Paula excused herself, "Shahin, sorry, I need to go. My mom needs me to pick up my sister. Let's talk after dinner, okay?"

Shahin could hear Paula's mother in the background, and even though he wanted to ask more about David, he reluctantly agreed.

"Okay," he said. "Call me later."

Shahin slowly hung up the phone, feeling a weird uneasiness that had come between him and Paula. Minutes after the call, Shahin's mother told him that he and Kamal needed to go out to dinner with them that evening. She had arranged for an immigration attorney and his wife to meet them at the restaurant to discuss their statuses and futures in America. After his earlier conversation with his mother, Shahin immediately agreed without any argument.

When Paula called Shahin, no one answered the telephone. She tried a second time, and still, he didn't answer. She told herself it was no big deal and left a message on his answering machine asking him to call her in the morning.

Chapter 8 - Kamal

Kamal yearned to see his family. It had been over a year since he saw them last. He thought back to the day he left for the sampling trip. He had given his sister, Farah, a quick hug before heading to Shahin's house. He had told her he would call when he got to Kish Island. She had returned his embrace and jokingly made a snide remark about him getting fat and lazy since he was the guy going along for the ride.

Kamal's thoughts jumped ahead to the sea rescue. Shortly after boarding the Navy ship, Kamal remembered asking the captain if he had any information about his family, especially Farah. She should have been in London, England, attending school.

The captain contacted the US State Department to get some answers for Kamal. He was told that Farah had flown back to Iran a few weeks prior to the Shah's departure. As far as the US authorities knew, she never returned to England, and they surmised that she was still in Iran with the rest of Kamal's family.

The thought of Farah living under the repressive Khomeini regime enraged Kamal, and Shahin and Paula could do little to quell his anger and guilt.

"I know you're trying to help," he told them, "But your words don't change the fact that she's stuck in Iran! I wish I'd known that she was there. Somehow, I would have gotten her out with us."

In the days that followed, Kamal's anger waned, and sadness took over. "I was really hoping to see her when we arrived in London," he had admitted to Paula and Shahin. "It may sound dumb, but I miss my little sister a lot."

"Me too," Shahin told him. "She was like the little sister I never had."

In London, the US government informed Kamal that they would assist him in contacting his family in Iran. However, after hearing his harrowing stories about killing at least two Khomeini soldiers, the US government changed its mind. They said they feared that the Islamic Republic might detain and torture Kamal's family if they were suspected of helping their criminal son. Sadly, Kamal had no choice but to accept their rationale.

******

For the first couple of days in the DC apartment, Kamal did his best to cope with Cindy's death and the forfeiture of communications with his family. Unfortunately, the reality of losing these people pushed Kamal into an unrealistic and unhealthy state. Some days, he didn't even want to try to move on. He just wanted to wallow in self-pity and sorrow.

"It's not fair!" Kamal told himself.

He had shot the soldier in self-defense. Besides, it was the Iranian government that started the whole thing, and all he did was try to protect himself and his friends. But he knew that's not how they saw it. The regime saw him as a cold-blooded murderer fighting against the new government.

Kamal tried desperately to suppress these angry feelings, but he couldn't stop the frustration from resurfacing. He began taking out his aggression on Shahin and the other people around him. These hostilities were passive and non-violent, so it was initially difficult for them to recognize his behavior as rage.

Kamal's actions were deemed acceptable under the circumstances, and he was given considerable latitude to continue his negative behavior by the people around him.

Shahin's mother did her best to make Kamal feel like he was part of the family, but it wasn't enough to stave off his feelings of being an outsider. In addition, she was too eager to help him, and her efforts were often unwanted. One afternoon, Kamal inadvertently complained to Mrs. Ali that Washington, D.C., had a six-month waiting list to take the CPA exam. In response, Mrs. Ali went to great lengths to get him a spot on the upcoming exam schedule. Kamal hadn't wanted to wait six months; that was true, but the next test was scheduled for mid-December, and he didn't feel he would be ready to take it by then. Frustrated and angry, he called the testing place and canceled his reservation.

That evening, Kamal felt overwhelmed by his grief and loneliness. Without considering the consequences of his actions, Kamal impulsively called his old girlfriend, Nousha. Immediately, her answering machine began the recorded message.

"This is Nousha. Please leave me a message."

 Rattled by the quickness with which he needed to speak, Kamal abruptly said, "Hi, this is Kamal. I'm back in the United States. I hope you're doing okay." Then he hung up without sharing his new phone number or any details about his situation.

When Nousha returned home and heard the message, she looked up Paula's home phone number.

"Hello," answered Paula.

"Hi, Paula, this is Nousha."

"Oh... Hi, how are you?" asked Paula in surprise.

"I'm doing well. I've heard a little about your return, but I didn't want to cause any additional problems for Kamal. However, he called me and left a message on my answering machine. Unfortunately, he didn't leave his number. Do you have it?"

"Yes," said Paula, "he lives with Shahin and his parents in Washington, DC. Honestly, I haven't spoken to him since we got back. It's been hectic here, and I've hardly talked to Shahin either."

"I understand," said Nousha. "I'm sure you have a lot of catching up to do. Anyway, can you please give me the number?"

Paula gave Nousha the number, and they ended their conversation politely.

Kamal had just returned to the apartment after a day of studying at the library when Nousha called. Mrs. Ali handed the receiver to Kamal with a curious grin.

 At first, Kamal felt awkward and embarrassed talking to Nousha. It had been hard enough for him to write her about his romantic relationship with Cindy and his decision to break up. Now, having to discuss it directly with Nousha made it even more difficult and uncomfortable.

In the first part of their conversation, Kamal apologized to her for his behavior. She accepted his apology and politely shifted the conversation away from Cindy and onto the present. So much time had passed since they had seen each other, she told him, that it would be a waste of time for them to harbor ill feelings towards one another. She also acknowledged her mistake in going to Indonesia for months without him. She suggested that they had both made bad decisions that strained their relationship and contributed to its end.

After some hesitation, Kamal agreed to start a new friendship with Nousha. He was happy to hear her voice when she called him the following day, and he realized that her familiarity made him feel more comfortable than he had in weeks.

By the third phone call, Kamal had begun to open up to Nousha about what had happened in Iran. He mentioned his relationship with Cindy and voiced his frustrations regarding his family. He had been warned not to contact them, fearing retaliation by the Iranian government against them.

In addition, he told Nousha that he felt weirdly disconnected from Shahin and his parents. He felt isolated, despite their efforts to include him.

"It happened almost immediately after I moved in with them," he admitted. "It's strange because I've spent so much time with them over the years, and I never felt like this."

******

Kamal knew his feelings were unwarranted, yet he couldn't shake them off. Because of his continued uneasiness, Kamal didn't share much with Shahin about his rekindled friendship with Nousha. He mentioned she had called a few times, but he made it sound like it was no big deal. Shahin didn't give Kamal's renewed relationship with Nousha much thought because he was caught up in his own drama with Paula and his mother.

Both men knew outside factors had strained their friendship, but they ignored the warnings. Instead of sharing their frustrations, they bottled up their emotions, which only worsened the situation and created an even greater wedge between them.

******

After a few weeks, Nousha noticed a new irritation in Kamal's voice. His anger about Cindy and his family had been redirected toward Shahin. Nousha hadn't experienced the death of someone close to her, and therefore, she did not know the stages of grief.

Kamal began to grumble that Shahin had suffered minimal consequences for the bad decisions he had made in Iran. Kamal pointed out that Shahin still had his family and his girlfriend. He, on the other hand, Kamal lamented, had lost pretty much everything in comparison. This new attitude worried Nousha, and she decided that Kamal needed to leave DC, at least for a little while.

Nousha devised a plan for Kamal to visit her in Michigan and presented the "vacation" to him once everything was in place. To her delight, he welcomed the escape, and a week later, Nousha picked him up from the Lansing airport and drove him to a hotel near her apartment. It was a bit awkward at first, but they soon fell into a familiar, comfortable pattern. Nousha convinced Kamal that she had forgiven him for his past behavior and was ready to move forward with their new relationship. Within a couple of days, the two became romantically involved once again.

Things moved quickly after the couple were reunited, and Nousha's parents stepped in to help Kamal relocate to East Lansing by offering him an interest-free loan. He accepted their financial assistance and immediately signed up to take his CPA exam there in the first week of February.

When Kamal told Shahin he was moving back to East Lansing to be with Nousha, Shahin was not surprised. It was very apparent to him and his parents that Kamal was unhappy in DC and needed a change.

Chapter 9 - The Secrets

Cindy's mother called and asked Paula to come to their home a second time on Tuesday before Thanksgiving. Two more of her children were coming for the holiday and wanted to hear directly from Paula about Cindy.

Paula willingly accepted the invitation, understanding it was difficult for Cindy's family to accept her death. However, after she arrived, it became clear that Cindy's siblings wanted more than an explanation of her and Cindy's harrowing experiences in Iran. They wanted the reason why it happened and someone to blame. The mood in the house had changed from grief to anger, and Cindy's family was looking to Paula for answers.

The day after Thanksgiving, Paula was summoned to the Stetsons a third time to meet with another of Cindy's brothers, who couldn't attend her previous two visits. Paula became increasingly frustrated and impatient with Cindy's family. She wanted to tell them how traumatizing it was for her to relive the events before and after her friend's death, but she decided against it. Sharing intimate and gruesome details about her experiences might upset the family even further, knowing that many of the events she was describing would have been equally traumatic for Cindy. Even though Paula withheld the most frightening incidents from Cindy's relatives, her mind continued to re-create the actual experiences. At one point, Paula had to excuse herself. She stayed in the Stetsons' restroom for 15 minutes, splashing water on her face to wash away the tears. What made these family meetings even worse was the increasingly aggressive allegations they began to make against her friends.

"It sounds to me like you should have realized that the embassy had been compromised and retreated to Shahin's house," said the oldest brother.

"Yeah, why didn't you turn around and go back?" asked the younger one.

"You weren't there. You don't understand. They had been protesting for days, and no one knew they would storm the compound," replied Paula.

"Couldn't you see the soldiers?" asked the oldest sister. "That's when you should have turned around."

"No, there were so many people," Paula upheld her position. "Plus, Cindy and I had on our chadors. You can't see very well when you're trying to hide your face under a hood."

"The men didn't have any head coverings," the older brother argued. "Why didn't they say or do something?"

"We all thought we were doing the right thing," Paula said defensively. "Even your sister agreed that going to the embassy was the safest bet. Looking back, maybe we should have tried to get out another way. There is no way to know. We could have all ended up dead by staying in the bunker!"

The youngest brother heard Paula's anger and frustration and decided to stop his brothers and sister from continuing their harassment.

"Okay, everybody," he said calmly. "It's not fair to hypothesize about the best way to escape. No one knows the answer, and accusing Paula and Cindy's other friends isn't going to bring her back or change what happened."

"Thank you for understanding," said Paula. "We are all grieving the loss of Cindy, and you are blaming the wrong people for her death."

Paula stood up and politely bid Cindy's family farewell before walking to the front door. Mrs. Stetson followed her and gave her a heartfelt hug while murmuring her apologies. As Paula walked to her car, she vowed never to return for another meeting. Paula got in the car and desperately wanted to reach out to Shahin. She didn't want to tell him what Cindy's family had said about him because she thought it might further damage him emotionally, but she wanted to hear his voice.

Paula anxiously drove home and immediately called Shahin upon her arrival. When describing her visit, she was purposely vague about her conversation with the Stetsons. It didn't fool Shahin, and he openly voiced his concerns. To avoid telling him the truth, Paula kept the conversation brief by making an excuse to end the call.

That evening, Paula was haunted by an unspoken truth shared between her and her friends. When in Iran, all four of them were aware of the growing danger within the country, yet they chose to ignore it. All knew that if they had openly recognized the perilous political situation, they would be obligated to cancel the rest of their trip. In addition, Paula and Cindy would have had to leave immediately.

✱✱✱✱✱✱

"Now," Paula thought, "as she hung up the phone, I have two secrets I'm keeping from Shahin."

Hiding the truth only amplified her guilt, making Paula's conversations with Shahin even more awkward and uncomfortable. Their discussions became riddled with complaints, and his voice always had an underlying tone of anger. Paula kept waiting for the right moment to tell him about David, but there was no "right time".

A few more weeks passed, and both Paula and Shahin had moved into the anger stage of their grief. Their relationship had become so strained that a confrontation was inevitable. After weeks of hiding David's kiss from Shahin, Paula finally found the courage to tell him.

"Why, Paula!" yelled Shahin. "Why did you kiss him back? Are you in love with him?"

"I don't know why I kissed him! I guess because it felt safe and familiar. But I don't love him. I love you!"

"I understand, Paula," Shahin said flatly. "I get it. I make you feel afraid and uncomfortable."

"What? No, I didn't mean that! What I meant was, well, you know, it's just being home..." Paula stammered.

"I know Paula. You need to move on with your life without me," Shahin said categorically.

"But Shahin, you can't mean that."

"I do," Shahin barked. "Things have changed. Iranians aren't wanted here anymore. We are treated like we are the ones who took the hostages. David has always treated you well. He's who you belong with, not me."

Shahin slammed the receiver down hard, physically cracking the plastic on his new telephone.

"I don't need her anyway!" he said through gritted teeth. "It was never going to work. She's better off with him."

There was a knock on Shahin's bedroom door, followed by his mother's voice, "Shahin, honey, are you okay?"

"Yeah, Mom, I'm fine," he said in a much calmer voice.

"I just wanted to let you know that dinner will be ready in 10 minutes," she added. "Are you sure that you're okay?" Mrs. Ali asked again.

"Yeah, I'll be down in just a few minutes," he assured her.

As Shahin sat at the dinner table, he wallowed in anger and despair. His parents noticed his silence and preoccupation with his thoughts but decided not to press him for information. The upheaval in their lives had elevated everyone's stress level, and no one was willing to discuss their inner feelings.

Returning to his bedroom, Shahin decided to analyze his conversations with Paula over the past several weeks. He wanted to find any indicators that Paula was having a romantic relationship with David.

Instead, Shahin recalled several vague, yet telling, phrases and comments made by Paula that led him to believe that the Stetsons thought he was accountable for Cindy's death. This realization put Shahin in an entirely different frame of mind.

"Why shouldn't they blame me?" Shahin asked himself. "After all, I'm the one who was responsible for their daughter's death. I know Paula and Kamal blame me, too. They both try to hide it, but I can see it." As he recalled the decisions he made on the sampling trip, Shahin continued his self-admonishment. "I was the one in charge, and even though I knew the violence was escalating, I kept going. If I hadn't been so selfish, Cindy would still be alive." Shahin's thoughts spiraled out of control before turning his emotions back to Paula and David. "Why would Paula want me instead of David? I'm the one who got her best friend killed and put the rest of us in grave danger."

Feeling worthless and guilty, Shahin came to a hasty, emotionally driven decision, "The best thing for me to do is to let Paula go. She deserves someone better than me. Plus, she'll be happier with David. He's not a fuck up like I am."

Once Shahin concluded that he and Paula did not belong together, he made another irrational decision. "I will end our relationship immediately," he murmured determinedly.

Then, Shahin turned his thoughts to Kamal. Shahin thought about all the years they had spent together as children and the closeness they shared with each other's families. He knew Kamal had the right to despise him for his inaction on their trip, but he also felt there was a chance that Kamal could forgive him; for that reason, Shahin wanted to try to keep his relationship with Kamal.

Chapter 10 - The Proposal

After Kamal moved to Michigan, he and Paula agreed to talk at least once a week. They both felt a deep-seated need to rekindle the friendship they had shared during their time in Iran. The scars from their ordeal could only be understood by those who had gone through it, and they felt the calls would give them the opportunity to share not only their grief but also their love and affection for their fallen friend and lover.

In early March, Kamal found out that he had passed his CPA exam. It was the news he needed to move ahead in his life. Unfortunately, his academic success could not fill the void left in him after Cindy's death. To heal his heart, Kamal decided to ask Nousha to marry him. She happily accepted his proposal, and they began planning a wedding for early autumn.

The news of Kamal's engagement didn't surprise Paula. She knew Kamal was ready to put the past behind him. Unfortunately, Paula often felt that many of Kamal's decisions had been impulsive and sometimes erratic. She mentioned it to him at the beginning, but found that he took it as a personal attack. She soon realized that her concerns for Kamal's well-being were best kept to herself, and when he announced his engagement, Paula immediately congratulated them both.

******

Even before Kamal moved to Michigan, he and Shahin had drifted apart. Their friendship became so strained that Kamal hadn't even told Shahin he planned to ask Nousha to marry him. It wasn't until after she had said "yes" that Kamal called Shahin to tell him the news. Shahin was initially speechless, but quickly recovered from his shock and offered his congratulations to Kamal. In his next breath, Shahin began to apologize.

"Hey man, I'm sorry. I know I've been a jerk. I should have called more often. Really, I'm happy for you and Nousha, and I promise to be a better friend."

"It's not just you," said Kamal. "I was looking for a fight when I got back. I wanted to blame everybody for my misery, and that included you. Anyway, let's forget about it."

"Yeah, that sounds good," Shahin replied happily.

There was a brief pause before Kamal asked cautiously, "Hey, will you be my best man?"

"Of course I will. I'd be honored, dude," responded Shahin before asking, "Does Paula know?"

"Yeah," Kamal confirmed. "I called her first. We've been talking more lately."

"Is she okay?" asked Shahin caringly. "I haven't taken any of her calls since I broke up with her. I'm afraid I'll cave and beg her to come back, and we both know that a life with me would be filled with snide remarks and even violent aggression from strangers. The Americans distrust me and wish that I'd get out of their country, but Paula, she would be ridiculed even more for choosing to, as they say, *sleep with the enemy*," he said flatly. "Knowing that, I just can't put her through it. Eventually, she'll thank me."

"Hey, let's stop talking about Paula and get back to my wedding," said Kamal, trying to avert a disagreement with Shahin.

"Sure, sorry I brought it up," Shahin said apologetically.

Kamal told Shahin what he knew about Nousha's plans for the ceremony, and then the two men discussed their future plans. Shahin told him he hadn't chosen a new research project yet for his master's thesis, and instead of narrowing his choices, Shahin said he had expanded his possibilities. He planned to live with his parents while he figured things out. He needed time, he told Kamal, to re-evaluate his life, especially now that he would have to start all over again. He even said that he was questioning his chosen career.

Kamal admitted that he, too, had reservations about his career choice. However, now that he is working in his field, he enjoys the job much more than he had expected.

Immediately after the call, Shahin's thoughts returned to Paula. His heart ached for her, and it was a constant struggle to fight the urge to call her and apologize.

Shahin wanted Paula to be safe and happy more than anything, and he thought again about her future without him. It meant a life free from the hate that surrounded him. The world had changed, and just being with an Iranian man could subject a person to ridicule and possibly violence. Many Americans treated the Iranians living in the US as if they were somehow responsible for the taking of the hostages at the US Embassy in Tehran. They showed their distrust and anger by verbally condemning innocent Iranians using numerous false accusations and racial slurs. Shahin was no exception, and he did not want Paula to suffer the verbal abuse he had endured since he returned to America.

Chapter 11 - The News

It had been five months since Paula returned home. After numerous visits and phone calls, Cindy's family members finally stopped contacting Paula to rehash their continued blame and accusations regarding Cindy's death. This cessation finally allowed Paula to pull herself out of her depression and move forward with her life.

By mid-April, Paula had submitted her alternative reports for her independent study courses, as allowed by her professors. Paula wrote about Iran's protected areas instead of turning in the rock sampling analysis. She also petitioned and was granted credits for learning a foreign language while enrolled in the independent study program, which made her months of confinement feel more productive.

Paula kept her promise to Kamal and called him weekly. Their conversations were usually brief, sharing only the latest highlights of their week. They intentionally avoided topics involving Shahin and refocused their discussions on their daily lives instead.

Paula was happy that Nousha was there for Kamal. She hoped Nousha could help mend his heart and encourage him to begin a new life. The craters created by Cindy's death and the loss of his family were vast.

Even with all of her progress, Paula still missed Shahin. After their fight, Paula was hopeful Shahin would accept her apology and understand that she loved him, not David. Sadly, after weeks of unsuccessful attempts to speak to him, Paula finally relinquished her quest to get back together with Shahin and moved on with her life.

******

On a warm afternoon in mid-April, Paula's mom handed her an envelope from the stack of mail she was reviewing. The letter was addressed to Paula, but did not have a return address. Curious about its origin, Paula quickly tore open the envelope. The letter inside was from Darian, a man who ended up hiding with her and her friends in Mashhad, the second safe house in Iran, where they waited for a rescue.

One night, after months of confinement, Darian made unwanted sexual advances toward Cindy. Feeling threatened by his aggressions, she forcefully rebuffed his desires and screamed for help. The incident ended at that moment, but it left everyone deeply upset, not just Cindy.

To express his regret and humiliation for his bad behavior, Darian secretly left the safe house early the following morning and never returned. Paula had not seen or heard from Darian since his abrupt departure from the house.

Now, after reading his correspondence, Paula dropped her hand holding the letter and sat stunned as she struggled to process the unbelievable statements written within it. After several more seconds of astonishment, Paula lifted the note and read it again.

Dear Paula,

I hope this letter finds you well. I saw through the media that you, Shahin, and Kamal escaped the clutches of Khomeini and his guards.

I, too, have left Iran. After leaving the safe house, I drove back to Shiraz. I looked up an old friend of mine and asked him if he would hide me. He agreed. I stayed with him for several months, helping him with his business. As time passed, I realized that my identity had not been compromised. My sister and brother-in-law were questioned, along with all the other store owners in the vicinity, but they were released. They assured me that the authorities knew nothing about me or my involvement in your escape. Even with these assurances, I still felt uncomfortable crossing the border. Then, I saw something in Shiraz that pushed me to risk leaving the country.

We must meet. I know my behavior at the safehouse was inexcusable, and I don't deserve your forgiveness. However, I want you to please accept my most humble apologies and find a way to put your anger and disgust for me aside. Please do not let my behavior at the safe house cause you to ignore my request.

I cannot fully explain what I have found out in this letter. That is why I am coming to Michigan. We need to meet in person. I think it is vital that Shahin and Kamal come with you to our meeting.

I will be in Detroit, Michigan, from April 25 through April 30, 1980. I am willing to meet you at any location of your convenience. Below is my contact information. Please write or call me as soon as you receive this letter. Cindy is ALIVE!

Sincerely,

Mohammed Darian Abed, 718-223-4678

"How can this be? How can Cindy still be alive? Could it really be true?" Paula considered the words Darian wrote over and over in her mind. She reread the last sentence again and again, ensuring she had not misread the words on the page. "I have to call him. I have to call him right now!" she told herself.

Paula walked over to the phone and dialed Darian's number. A man answered the phone, but it didn't sound like him.

"Darian?" she said questioningly.

"No, he's not here. He has a work conference starting today, and he said he may not be back until early May. He's hoping to go to Michigan after the conference ends. Can I take a message?" the man asked.

"Yes, tell him Paula called. The guys and I will meet him in Detroit on April 25th. If he can't reach me to tell me a time and place, he can leave a message with my parents. Paula gave him all of her contact information and Shahin's phone number before thanking him and ending the call.

Unable to think about anything else, Paula excitedly called Kamal to tell him about Darian's letter. She knew he would have numerous questions that she wouldn't be able to answer, but the news about Cindy was just too important to keep to herself.

With her heart pounding, Paula took a deep breath and sighed audibly before picking up the receiver.

"Hello," said Kamal casually.

"Hey, it's me. Do you have a couple of minutes to talk? Are you alone?"

"Yeah," he said cautiously, hearing the seriousness in her voice. "I'm alone. Is everything okay?"

"Well..." Paula paused. "I got this letter from Darian, and he wants all of us to meet. I mean you, me, him, and Shahin."

"Okay," said Kamal skeptically. "What's this about?"

"I don't know if it's true or if I believe it, but Darian says Cindy is alive!" Paula was silent and waited anxiously for Kamal's response. Finally, after hearing nothing, she asked impatiently, "Are you there? Did you hear what I said?"

"Yeah, I heard," Kamal confirmed. "I'm just trying to wrap my head around it... Cindy's not dead; he knows this for sure?"

"That's what Darian said in his letter. I tried to call him, but he wasn't home. I don't know how he knows this or where she is; I only know that he says she's alive. It's why he wants us to meet," replied Paula.

"When?" asked Kamal. "When does he want us to meet?"

"Any time between April 25 and the 30th in Detroit. You'll come, right? I can pick you up if you don't have a car. You can even stay at my house overnight. I will drive you back after the meeting or the next day. We have a guest bed in our basement," said Paula earnestly.

"Thanks, Paula," replied Kamal. "I don't need you to pick me up. I'll be there. What day do you want to meet? I'd say the sooner, the better. Have you talked to Shahin?"

"No, I was hoping you could call him. You know he won't take my calls," she conceded.

"It's been months now. I think he'll talk to you," insisted Kamal. "If not, I'll call him. I want him to hear it from you because you're the one who got the letter. Besides, you guys have to put aside your issues for Cindy's sake. Just call him and see if he can make it to Detroit."

"Okay," Paula relented. "I'll call you back and tell you what he says."

Paula hung up the phone and stared blankly out the window. Her mind began to race as she considered her call to Shahin. With numerous thoughts and scenarios running through her brain, Paula decided to get a root beer first. After several sips of her drink, Paula set the glass on the telephone stand and dialed Shahin's number.

"Hello," said Shahin solemnly.

"Oh, hi, it's Paula," she said sheepishly.

"Hi," he said modestly, not knowing what else to say.

"Well, I ah…" Paula hesitated. "I called because I have some news. Darian wrote to me and said Cindy was alive."

"What? What did you say?" asked Shahin excitedly.

"Cindy, she's not dead," Paula stated. "I don't have any more details than that. He wants us to meet him between April 25 and the 30th. I've already spoken to Kamal, and he said he can meet anytime, but he wants it to be as soon as possible. Can you make a meeting here in Detroit on the 25th?"

"Ah… Yeah," replied Shahin. "Maybe I'd better call and make sure I can get a flight."

"Sure, of course," said Paula. "Just let me know when you have the answer."

Finally breaking the formality, Shahin asked excitedly, "Paula, do you really think it's true? Could she be alive?"

"I hope so, but I'm trying to keep myself from getting too excited. It's been so long. I'm finally feeling a little more normal," said Paula cautiously. "I just don't want to be hurt again if it's not true."

"Yeah, I know what you mean," added Shahin.

"Call me back when you have your flight, and I'll let Kamal and Darian know our schedule," said Paula, trying to return their conversation to a more casual level.

"I'll call the travel agent right now to make my reservation," said Shahin. "Thanks for calling, Paula. It's good to hear your voice."

His words cut through Paula's façade, and she struggled to steady her voice. "You, too. I'll talk to you soon," she replied and quickly hung up the phone. She grabbed her drink, tipped the bottle, and took a large swig of her root beer.

******

Shahin stepped into his closet to find a suitcase to take to Detroit. He wasn't sure why, but he decided to pull out the duffel he had stuffed in the back corner after he returned from Iran. Opening the top, he noticed a corner of stationery paper sticking out from the inside pocket. Immediately, it brought back the memories and emotions associated with the note.

Feeling unsteady, Shahin sat down on the bed. The letter was a reminder of his grief, and he wanted nothing to do with the hurtful memories surrounding the note. It's why he had stuffed the paper into the pocket in the first place.

The letter was written the same day Charles had died, and Shahin was purposely trying to block the event from entering his consciousness. Now, seeing the words again had forced his memories to return.

Anxiously, Shahin reached in and pulled the note from its hiding place. Opening the message, he saw there was writing on the back of the letter that he hadn't noticed before. With his heart pounding, Shahin turned the letter over and began to read.

… I want you to know that I saved your family's jewels from being confiscated by the Khomeini government. When the Shah was overthrown, I realized the gems would not be safe inside the home, so I quickly journeyed to a much safer location to store them.

After months of waiting for you to return, I finally had a secret meeting with the young woman you call "Little Sis." I don't want to write her name in case this letter falls into the wrong hands. In our meeting, she agreed to help me, so I told her the name of the city where the safety deposit box is located. There is a key with the street address inscribed on it, but I did not have it with me when we met. To open the box, the person must have the key.

We made a date to meet again so I could give her the key. Then you called, and after our conversation, I decided to take a chance that you would return to the estate for your passport, and I could explain what I did and give you the key instead.

Unfortunately, as you know, our first interaction did not go well. In addition, I did not have the key with me at the time. Anyway, I have the key now. I hope we can have a proper conversation where I can clarify my actions and answer any questions you may have before I give you the key. It's important to me that I explain myself.

If I do not have the opportunity to see you again, I will give the key to Little Sis. I am being watched and will be unable to retrieve the jewelry myself.

There is a third tier of security, and you must know all three to find the valuables. Once you have arrived at the special place, look at the left side of the stone, and you will faintly see a rectangular seam. Push it in with medium pressure to…

Shahin stared blankly at the unfinished sentence before recalling why Charles had stopped writing mid-sentence.

"He was writing this letter to me in the bunker when we returned from the embassy," thought Shahin, "and before Charles could say anything or give it to me, I punched him in the face."

Now, looking back, Shahin knew he had been lashing out at Charles for Cindy's capture and their predicament. Even back then, Shahin regretted his behavior.

Trying to ignore the past and focus on the present, Shahin turned the letter over to reread the front page. He felt confident that he knew who Charles was referring to on the second page. However, he hoped some additional clues would help him confirm Little Sis's identity.

Instead of helping him solidify his conclusion, the words on the first page compounded Shahin's grief. It was sentence after sentence of Charles's deepest apologies for his unforgivable behavior and numerous statements from Charles declaring his unabashed parental love for Shahin.

Shahin's gut tightened, and his body stiffened as he tried to physically stop the images of that day from resurfacing. His contortions were futile. He could not stop the memories from reconstructing each scene inside the bunker and the house on that day. They played like a movie streaming across his mind's eye. Then came the final act. He saw himself ascending the stairs, going up into the house with Charles directly behind him. The memory made Shahin's entire body slump down in defeat as Charles's words pierced his heart.

"I don't expect you to forgive me, but I want you to know that I love you, son." Charles had voiced his love for him, and Shahin had remained stubbornly silent. Regret flooded Shahin's emotions again, knowing he had missed the opportunity to express his deep affection for Charles.

Knowing what was coming next, Shahin dropped onto the bed for support. In a flash, the scene changed to the area of the house just outside the stairway closet. Shahin closed his eyes as the visions of the confrontation between him, Charles,

Kamal, and the soldier unfolded. It happened so fast that Shahin couldn't actually recall hearing the fatal shot. All he could picture was the flash of a body blocking his vision for an instant. Charles had saved his life by taking the bullets meant for him.

Finally, Shahin saw his last moments with Charles before his friend demanded that Shahin run to the bunker. The moment still haunted Shahin. He recalled dropping to one knee to try and help Charles, but it was no use; blood was flowing quickly out of his body. Shahin looked affectionately into Charles's eyes, revealing his deep love and appreciation for him. It was a second chance to express his love verbally, but again, Shahin was silent. Now, all he could do was hope that his facial expressions had shown Charles his true feelings, but sadly, Shahin knew he would never know the answer to that question.

******

The day of the meeting finally arrived. Paula got to the restaurant first and chose a table in the back. Shahin had flown into Detroit the night before, and Kamal planned to pick him up from his hotel for the meeting.

Paula watched as Kamal and Shahin entered the restaurant. Immediately, a wave of anxiety flowed through her body. She hadn't seen Shahin in several months, and the anticipation of seeing him had caused her several sleepless nights and hours of imagining what the meeting would be like.

"Hi," said Paula as she stood and leaned in to hug Kamal. "I'm so glad you guys could make it." When the embrace finished, Paula turned and gave Shahin a very brief one-armed hug before motioning for the two men to sit down. "Darian should be here soon. He called me this morning and said he would be a few minutes late."

"Sounds like his bloody bullshit," said Kamal, "but... I still want to wait and hear what he has to say."

"How's Nousha?" asked Paula, trying to make small talk.

"Well…" he said flatly. "She broke up with me. She said we were through if I came to this meeting. I told her I had to come regardless of her threats. She accused me of still loving Cindy and said she would always be my second choice. I couldn't deny it, and so we ended it. Things weren't going all that well anyway. Trying to rekindle a love that wasn't really there was a bad idea. At least we found out before the wedding."

"Oh, Kamal, I'm sorry. I know you hoped Nousha and your new job would fill the void left after losing Cindy and your family."

"Yeah, well…" he said, trailing off.

"I'm sure one day your family will be able to leave Iran safely," Paula said reassuringly. "This crackdown can't last forever."

Feeling uncomfortable, Shahin quickly changed the subject to something more positive, "I heard from Amir and Laleh. They left Iran and are partnering with a group that owns a resort in Tahiti."

"What happened with their resort in the Gulf?" asked Paula.

"Oh, yeah, you probably don't know," recalled Shahin. "After the revolution, tourism plummeted, and they decided it was too risky to stay in Iran, at least for now. It's sad they never actually got to open. They were so close, but the timing wasn't right after the Shah left."

"I feel bad for them. All that work for nothing," added Kamal.

"It's awful. They were so excited," agreed Paula. "Hopefully, their new project will work out."

"Tahiti is a very popular tourist destination right now," explained Shahin. "The resort just opened a little over a year ago. They needed more help running it, and Amir and Laleh were the perfect fit. At least that's what I was told."

"I'm happy for them," Paula replied. "They are such a nice couple, not to mention hard workers."

"Hey, Kamal, the last time we talked, you were going to try to find out more about your sister, Farah? Have you heard anything new?" asked Paula.

"No, and they keep telling me it's too dangerous to call my family. I'm still not sure why they haven't left Iran. Who knows, maybe they're doing well. I honestly don't know," Kamal said sadly.

"It's too bad she's stuck in Iran. I liked hanging out with her when she visited you at school," Paula added.

Suddenly, there was an awkward pause in the conversation, which triggered Shahin to move to another topic.

"So, how's work going?" he casually asked Kamal.

Kamal perked up. He liked his job and began to describe his work and schedule to Shahin. Paula already knew the details and quickly let her thoughts drift off as the two continued to discuss accounting.

Silently, she refocused on her last conversation with Shahin. The one where he ended their relationship. She knew it by heart but couldn't help reviewing the exchange again. Her breakup with him had been abrupt, and she was still hurt and angry about it. She felt Shahin hadn't given her a chance to explain her platonic relationship with David, and he had unjustly concluded that she was romantically involved with him. It still bothered her a lot that Shahin insisted that her old boyfriend was the more appropriate person for her to love. His concern for her future and safety was admirable, thought Paula, but not what she had wanted to hear. Paula felt she should be the one to decide whether or not she wanted to put up with other people's judgment and ridicule if she remained romantically involved with Shahin, not him.

Just then, Darian walked into the restaurant, and all thoughts and conversation turned to him. He nervously stepped up and addressed the group. The tension between him and the guys was evident, and Paula felt the need to reduce the awkwardness.

"It's been a long time," she said politely, motioning for Darian to sit beside her. "Are you doing okay?"

Darian nodded positively before sitting down and answering her question, "Yeah, it's been a little rough, but I'm fine."

"We've all gone through quite a lot since we saw you last," said Paula, still trying to ease the tension.

"Yeah, it's been bloody hell for us," said Kamal.

Shahin added gruffly, "Not to mention how fucking awful it was for us after you left me and the girls with no car."

"Come on, guys," said Paula. "Let's not rehash the past. Remember, we're here to find out about Cindy." Shahin and Kamal mumbled their understanding and allowed Paula to continue. "So, tell us what you know. You've been so secretive with me."

"It's because I wanted to wait until we were all together to explain what I saw," Darian replied.

"Okay, then," said Paula. "We're all here."

"Well, I know it sounds crazy, but I saw her," Darian insisted.

"How do you know it was her?" asked Kamal skeptically.

"I first saw her at the open market. Yousif and I were looking for a specific type of squash to cook for dinner. He's a pretty big guy and loves to eat," explained Darian.

"His name sounds familiar. Did you mention him when you lived in the safe house with us?" Paula asked.

"I'm not sure. He's got brown hair and a bushy gray and brown beard. I may have mentioned his love of sour cherry jelly when you talked about your lodge-owner friend," Darian expounded.

"Stop talking about jelly and get to the point!" insisted Kamal.

"Sorry," said Paula, "I was the one who distracted him."

"Well, anyway," Darian continued. "I saw this woman, and her eyes looked so much like Cindy's that I couldn't stop looking at her. Unfortunately, I couldn't see the rest of her face because she wore a scarf across her nose and mouth. She was with another woman who, unlike her, had her face on display," he added. "She was a lot older and seemed to be with Cindy, but not really her friend."

"Okay, so you saw her eyes. I don't think that's enough to determine who she is," said Paula.

"I know. I'm getting to the rest of it," said Darian. "As I watched her, she removed her right arm from under her chador to reach for a head of cabbage. When she did, I saw her birthmark! You know, the pink triangular one on the inside of her forearm. It was Cindy's birthmark. I just know it! My heart raced excitedly, and I wanted to say something, but I couldn't get close enough. The other woman was standing right next to her the whole time."

"So, you didn't talk to her?" asked Shahin.

"No, not at this first meeting. After she purchased the cabbage, the two women left the market and got into a taxi waiting for them near the entrance. I ran to my car and followed them. Luckily, the taxi driver was taking his time driving them home. He drove them to a house in an upper-middle-class neighborhood in southeast Shiraz. I wrote down the address and then researched the records until I found the owner's name. It turns out that he's a pretty wealthy local businessman."

"Dude, you better have more than just this," said Kamal angrily.

"Yeah, you have more, right?" inquired Shahin.

"Yes," Darian responded defensively before taking a packet of photos from his pocket. "I was going to show these to you in the order that things happened, but, well... You seem so impatient that I might as well show them to you now. I took these pictures of Cindy just before I left for the US. I waited to get them developed here. Unfortunately, none of them are very good."

"Let me see them," said Paula as she grabbed the photos from his hand.

"Like I said, they're not very good," Darian reiterated as Paula thumbed through the stack.

Paula passed the photos around, and the lack of quality was evident by the disappointed looks on everyone's faces.

"Darian, you have to understand why we're questioning you," said Paula diplomatically. "We all want to believe that Cindy is alive, but what you're saying is not very convincing, and these photos are terrible. They don't prove anything. It sounds like you saw a woman in the market with a birthmark and eyes that kind of looked like Cindy's. That's it?"

"No, I have more," he said, arguably. "I watched the house every day for three weeks. Cindy and the other woman left every Tuesday and Saturday morning for the same open market near their house. On the other days, they did other shopping. I think they're redoing the inside of the house based on the kinds of stores they went to."

"That doesn't matter," said Shahin. "Did you ever talk to her?"

"Well," Darian paused, "the third time I saw her at the market, I tried. I waited for her to arrive with the intention of talking to her, but I think she's still mad at me. I don't blame her, of course. She has every right to be upset with me, and you should all know that if I had to do it over again, I would never have acted the way I did."

"We know," Paula said impatiently. "So, what happened? Did she yell at you or what?"

"No yelling, I wish she had. Instead, she just stared at me. Even though I could only see her eyes, I knew the look. It was fear that I saw. Her eyes were filled with fear," Darian said as he looked down at the table in shame.

"Then what?" demanded Kamal. "What happened next?"

"Did she say anything?" Paula pleaded.

"No, the woman she was with grabbed her arm and led her away. They went directly to the taxi waiting for them and left."

"Do you know any more than that?" asked Paula.

"Yes, listen to this. The guy she lives with only has one wife registered with the government. However, one of the vendors told me she was his second wife. It must be a cover for her, or they're holding her against her will."

"You're sure it's Cindy?" questioned Kamal again.

"Yeah, I know it's her," he insisted. "One time, when I was watching her, I heard her speaking to one of the vendors. It was Cindy's voice, all right, even though she spoke to him in Farsi."

"So, she sounds like Cindy and looks like her," said Paula. "Plus, she has the birthmark; that increases the odds that it's her."

"Well, it's not a lot to go on," said Shahin, "but it's pretty persuasive."

"I agree, all three together would be impossible for someone else to have," added Kamal, "and the fact that she's hiding her face and is pretending to be the guy's second wife sounds like she's hiding her identity."

"It does, doesn't it," said Paula excitedly. "I think it's her!"

Paula reached across the table and grabbed Shahin and Kamal's forearms. "I could only dream of something like this happening. Now, it seems to be real."

"We need to figure out how to get her back," Kamal said anxiously as he stood for no apparent reason. "She must be so scared."

"Yeah!" Shahin shouted as he joined Kamal. "We have to help her. She needs us!"

"I agree with you guys," said Paula. "So, sit back down, and let's get to work on a plan."

As the guys retook their seats, Darian asked, "Do you want me to stay and help?"

"No, I think we can take it from here," replied Paula. "We'll get the exact market location later after we figure out a few things."

"Can we keep the photos?" asked Shahin.

"Yeah, of course," replied Darian. "Call me anytime. I will do my best to help."

"We really appreciate you going to all the trouble for Cindy," added Paula. "We would never have known she was alive if it wasn't for you."

Knowing Paula was right, Shahin and Kamal reluctantly muttered their thanks, trying to put their animosity towards Darian aside.

"It's the least I could do after what happened between us," he said solemnly. "I still care a lot about Cindy, and I'm sorry for how I acted."

"Right now, let's focus on getting her out of Iran safely," said Paula diplomatically. "She needs all of us to cooperate with each other."

"Please keep me informed of your progress, and, of course, I'll help in any way I can."

Paula got up and gave Darian a light hug.

"I'll let you know," she whispered to him.

Following her lead, Shahin and Kamal begrudgingly stood and shook his hand. They thanked him again for his efforts before sitting back down to formulate a basic plan to get Cindy home.

Chapter 12 - Frustration

Paula, Shahin, and Kamal decided that Paula should contact the US State Department about Cindy's existence and circumstances. They reasoned that even though men were taken more seriously than women, Paula was a US citizen. Her higher status might justify and lend more gravity to her request.

It took a few weeks, but Paula finally scheduled a meeting with Special Agent Jackson. She was told that he had personal knowledge about Iran and the hostage crisis. Before the meeting, Shahin found out that Mr. Jackson was one of the people involved in the failed Delta Force mission a few weeks earlier and relayed the information to Paula.

The meeting began with Mr. Jackson asking Paula numerous questions about her source, insisting that the interrogation was needed to validate Paula's friend's claim. Paula understood his position and answered his queries to the best of her knowledge. The agent listened to each response and pointed out problems with each claim she presented.

First, the agent questioned Darian's conclusion that the woman he saw was, in fact, Cindy Stetson. He reasoned that physical identification was impossible without seeing most of her body and facial features. The birthmark was anecdotal at best, and the poor-quality photographs Paula showed him were insufficient identifiers for the federal government to initiate even a strategic, small-scale rescue mission.

Secondly, the agent concluded that the fact that Darian tried to speak with the woman and she refused to answer him suggested that she was not Cindy Stetson, but rather, another woman who looked similar to Cindy. Paula countered this statement by explaining that Cindy and Darian's relationship was complicated, and it wouldn't be abnormal for her to ignore him or be fearful. Her comment raised an eyebrow from the agent, and he asked her to explain further. Paula quickly told him about the incident at the safe house. She added that Darian had profusely apologized for his behavior and left the safe house of his own volition in disgrace.

When she finished explaining what had happened between Darian and Cindy, Paula pointed out that Darian could have ignored seeing Cindy; instead, he chose to risk his well-being by investigating his discovery further. Once he concluded that Cindy was alive and living in Shiraz, he traveled to the United States and spent hundreds of dollars to inform her of Cindy's existence. The agent applauded Darian's efforts but fell short of endorsing his claims.

Next, Agent Jackson explained additional complications that would greatly hinder a rescue operation for Cindy.

"Even if my bosses were convinced that Cindy Stetson was still alive, the current stalemate between the US government and the Islamic Republic makes it almost impossible for us to conduct an exaction deep within the Iranian borders without being noticed. The risk of exposure and failure is very high and could create an even bigger problem.

To prove his point, the agent reminded Paula of the US government's unsuccessful attempt, just weeks earlier, to rescue the American hostages being held inside the US Embassy in Tehran. The Delta Force Mission untaken by the US Marine Corp. was not only disastrous but tragic. Nine Marines died trying unsuccessfully to liberate the American captives.

Finally, Agent Jackson told Paula about the information he received from a CIA agent still embedded inside Iran.

"When I got your message stating the premise of our meeting, I reached out to someone we know in Iran, and he told me that the Iranian government believes Cindy is dead. Therefore, if she is still alive and we ask for her to be returned, it would pose a significant threat to Cindy and the person who rescued her from the hospital."

The agent concluded his reasons for denying Paula's request by stating one more example of the chaos that could occur if the US government accused the Iranians of lying to them about the status of an American citizen. It would significantly increase the likelihood that no negotiation would be reached to free the hostages still in custody. Putting the lives of 51 Americans in jeopardy for one unidentified person would be an irresponsible act by the US government. At the end of the meeting, Agent Jackson told Paula that his agency would not participate or initiate a covert action to rescue a woman who was presumed dead.

Feeling disappointed and overpowered, Paula thought she had no choice but to accept the government's decision. As she stood to leave, the agent added a caveat to explain the government's stance further. The Iranians were actively trying to undermine the heads of the US government by releasing the black and female hostages just days after taking over the US Embassy. They said the two groups had already been persecuted enough by the white men in power.

Paula tactfully, yet directly, made it clear to the white male agent that the Iranians hadn't been wrong about the sexism and racism that plagued US society, but the irony was laughable. The Islamic Republic of Iran was denouncing the USA's treatment of women while implementing new oppressive laws to subjugate their own women and severely limit many other freedoms of both their women and the Iranian Jews still living in Iran.

Paula thanked Agent Jackson for his time and returned to her hotel room. She felt rejected but not defeated. She was still confident that she would find another way to save her friend.

******

Paula called Shahin and Kamal to tell them the bad news. All three agreed that they needed to move on to the next step. That evening, Shahin approached his father and asked if he would present their case to the CIA. Shahin explained that Paula had been unsuccessful in securing their help.

Mr. Ali had already told Shahin it was unlikely that the US government would initiate a rescue plan under the current circumstances. The Carter administration was desperate to bring the hostages home, and any additional accusations or military operations that might undermine their diplomatic progress would not be an option. He told Shahin he was willing to speak with his colleague, but only after he spoke directly with Darian and was convinced Cindy was alive.

During their meeting with Darian, Mr. Ali felt that Darian's evidence was compelling but inconclusive. However, because of the serious nature of the allegation, he agreed to discuss the matter further with the CIA.

At the meeting, the agency's employee created a file and told Mr. Ali that he would present the evidence to his bosses. Several days later, the agent contacted Mr. Ali with the CIA's decision. Unfortunately, it was similar to Paula's outcome for the same reasons. At the end of the call, the agent did leave a sliver of hope for a possible evacuation sometime in the future without giving Mr. Ali any assurances or details of when that might be. Mr. Ali understood that it was the agency's way of nicely telling him "No".

******

When Paula, Shahin, and Kamal left the underground bunker under Shahin's estate in Tehran for the second time, Paula took Cindy's duffel bag with her as a sentimental gesture. On the way to Oman, after their rescue, she finally had the time to go through Cindy's stuff. Paula found Roxana's brother's business card, which Roxana had given to Cindy upon their arrival in Iran. Roxana had written her phone numbers on the back so that Paula and Cindy could contact her when they returned to Tehran or after they returned to the USA. Roxana had homes in both locations.

Seeing the card brought back Paula's memories of when she first met Roxana. She and Cindy had gone upstairs to the Boeing 747's first-class lounge on their way to Iran. She thought about how much fun it had been to meet Roxana and the others in this small, intimate bar.

Paula and Cindy had hoped to contact Roxana when they were finished with their sampling project and back in Tehran, but sadly, things had gone very wrong, and none of those plans materialized.

******

Paula was home for a month when she finally decided to call Roxana. She pulled out the business card and read the information about Roxana's brother more closely before turning the card over and dialing Roxana's number in the US. To her surprise, Paula felt unexpectedly comfortable talking to her about Cindy's death and all that had happened to her and her friends while hiding in Iran.

Roxana shared that she also had a tense and stressful time inside Iran after the Shah left the country. She was Jewish, and even though life wasn't perfect under the Shah, she had enjoyed a prosperous and satisfactory life. Now, under Khomeini, things had become worse, and Roxana decided to leave her home in Iran and resettle permanently in the US.

Toward the end of their conversation, Roxana conveyed her heartfelt condolences to Paula regarding Cindy's passing and offered to help Paula through the grieving process. Paula accepted Roxana's help, which opened up an avenue for both women to begin a friendship and share their emotions and personal views of the events unfolding around them.

The two began to speak twice a week, and a month after their first conversation, Paula visited Roxana. She had moved to Dearborn, Michigan, and it was just over an hour's drive from Paula's house. As their friendship grew, they began entrusting one another with more personal information about their lives and families.

When Paula visited Dearborn, Roxana mentioned her concerns for her brother, Caspar, and explained how things had changed so drastically for all Jews in Iran.

Caspar had decided to stay in Iran and give the new regime a chance. His business investments were tied to the Iranian economy, and he would lose everything if he fled. He and his remaining friends started to meet weekly to talk about what they could do legally to promote a more democratic and fair approach to governing. Sadly, the group quickly realized they would have to go underground and use new tactics if they wanted political change in Iran.

Most Muslims had been tolerant of the Jews under the Shah. This acceptance evaporated as tensions grew between Islamic fundamentalists and the Shah's supporters. Because of the increased friction, many Jews began to emigrate to other countries. After the Shah was overthrown, the migration exploded, and with their departure went their money.

Aware of the monetary capital being pulled out of his society, Khomeini promised to protect the Jews and their rights by issuing a "fatwa". Many of them believed he was sincere and stayed in Iran, but it soon became apparent that the decree wasn't being honored or enforced by the people running the government.

Because persecution and severe discrimination ensued, most Iranian Jews wanted to leave the country, but they were now prohibited from doing so. To keep them from fleeing, the new government stopped issuing valid passports to the Jews and other targeted individuals, making it impossible for them to exit Iran legally.

One day, Roxana told Paula in confidence that her brother had become part of an underground organization inside Iran. Their goal was to bring down the Khomeini regime and bring democracy to Iran. When Roxana learned of Paula's plans to rescue Cindy, she discreetly contacted Caspar to see if he could help them.

✱✱✱✱✱✱

When Mr. and Mrs. Ali heard about Kamal's breakup with Nousha, they insisted he move back in with them. Shahin lobbied hard for Kamal to make the move. He told Kamal he needed a friend in D.C. and argued that it would be much easier for them to plan Cindy's rescue. When Kamal hesitated, Shahin confided in Kamal that he had been experiencing irrepressible blame and guilt for Cindy's situation. After hearing Shahin's mindset, Kamal relented and agreed to make the move.

Shahin spent the rest of the day agonizing over what else he could do to help Cindy. Finally, he came up with an idea. Excitedly, he asked his parents for a meeting to discuss his plan.

"What's this all about, Shahin?" asked his mother. "Is Kamal having trouble getting all of his things in the car? If so, he can mail the boxes that don't fit."

"No, Mom," Shahin responded, "it's not about Kamal. He should be here in a couple of days."

"So, tell us why we're here," insisted his father. "I have to make a call in 15 minutes."

Shahin glanced at one parent and then the other before taking a deep breath, "I know you both have a lot of connections worldwide. You know, because of your knowledge and work in international affairs. Anyway, I was hoping that some of those companies might specialize in extractions. The type who employ private soldiers who are willing to risk their lives to rescue people from war zones or places like that for a price."

"What do you mean, exactly?" asked Mrs. Ali. "Are you speaking about mercenaries?"

"Yes, I'm talking about men who will go into dangerous situations for money," Shahin added.

"Son, is this about Cindy?" questioned his father.

"Yes, I'm asking you to pay mercenaries to rescue Cindy," Shahin blurted.

"Well, I guess it's something to consider. Your mother and I will need to talk more about this," said Mr. Ali. "However, it will have to be after my call."

"Okay, I can wait," said Shahin in desperation. "I think it's the only way we'll get her back." He added as he got up and kissed his mother on the cheek. "Can you let me know tonight?" he asked anxiously.

"How about tomorrow afternoon," said his mother. "I'll make some calls in the morning, and then your father and I can make a more informed decision."

"Yeah, that sounds good," Shahin said contentedly.

Shahin thought the discussion with his parents went well and was hopeful they would finance a mission to get Cindy back. Presumptively, he went to his room and used his private phone line to share his ideas with his friends.

The following morning, Shahin learned from the housekeeper that his mother and father had already left for an early morning meeting and that both would return in the afternoon. When they entered the foyer, Shahin eagerly asked, "Did you think about it? Did you find a group who'll do it?"

"Shahin, darling," said his mother, "it's not that we are unwilling to help your friend. Unfortunately, everyone we spoke to this morning said the same thing. They are unwilling to go into such a dangerous situation without having anyone who can identify Cindy. The details of her whereabouts are not very complete, and with her body being so disguised, they said it would be impossible for them to know if they had the right person or not. If they make a mistake and take the wrong girl, the entire international community could call for their heads."

"Then I'll go with them," insisted Shahin. "I can identify Cindy!"

"No," said Mrs. Ali, "I will not even consider that as an option."

"But, Mom!" Shahin yelled. "I have to go! Don't you see, it's my fault that she's there! I have to make this right and bring her home if I can!"

"I forbid it!" his mother yelled back, seemingly shaken by the prospect of her son returning to Iran.

"Okay, everyone, let's talk about this later," said Mr. Ali. "I'm sorry, Shahin. It's just too dangerous for you to go."

"But it's my fault! Don't you understand that I can't live with myself knowing that she's there! Please, let me help her!" begged Shahin.

Shahin's father shook his head "No", and the discussion ended. Shahin stormed out of the house and spent the next few hours sitting at a bar, feeling frustrated and depressed. Finally, he concluded that he would have to hire the mercenaries himself.

When he returned home, Shahin asked his father for the names and numbers of the companies they had contacted. Shahin told him he wanted to ask them to reconsider their decisions. Secretly, however, Shahin wanted to know how much it would cost and to offer himself as Cindy's identifier.

The answers from the companies were not what Shahin had expected. After telephoning the businesses, Shahin realized he could not pay for the mission with his own money. The mercenary's fees and expenses were well above the cash Shahin had access to in his savings, and all but one company opposed him going with them as part of the team. One man said he would consider taking Shahin to Iran with them, but there would be an extra cost to protect him.

Solemnly, Shahin called Paula and told her the bad news. Her reaction was a mixture of varied emotions, with anger and disappointment being the most prominent. Paula understood Shahin's parents' point of view, and even though she was extremely disappointed with their decision, she knew that protecting Shahin had to be their first priority.

Most of Paula's frustration was primarily due to the political mess preventing the US government from stepping in and saving her friend. It was something none of them could fix, and she asked Shahin to let her vent her anger and frustration instead of offering a flimsy excuse for it.

Kamal arrived at Shahin's parents' house the following day. Immediately, he asked about the mission to save Cindy. Shahin tried to put him off, but Kamal wouldn't wait. Begrudgingly, Shahin told him the disappointing news. Kamal's response was similar to Paula's. He, too, voiced his extreme dissatisfaction with the current state of affairs. For a second day in a row, Shahin listened patiently while his friends shouted, cussed, and swore at all governments and the power-hungry people responsible for screwing up the world. It didn't change anything, but it allowed them to vent their frustrations. Ultimately, the three felt helpless and defeated but were resigned to find a way to get to Iran and rescue Cindy.

Later that evening, during dinner, Kamal adamantly volunteered to be the mercenaries' identifier, telling Shahin's parents how important it was for him to go. Unfortunately, they told him the same thing as Shahin. They could not in good conscience allow him to go back to Iran, even if it was to save Cindy.

******

Weeks passed, and Mr. Ali watched as Shahin and Kamal struggled with their inability to save Cindy. During the fourth week, he overheard Kamal talking to Paula. Her voice was loud and boomed out of the receiver so anyone nearby could hear her words.

"Hey, Paula, it's me, Kamal. How're you doing?"

"I'm fucking miserable. Somehow, we need to get back to Iran. I honestly haven't slept since I found out Cindy's alive."

"Yeah, Shahin and I feel the same," said Kamal. "Plus, all these months, Shahin's been beating himself up about Cindy's capture and death. Now, he has a second chance to help her, but can't get anyone to listen. I'm worried about him. He's worse than ever."

"It's not right!" yelled Paula. "I don't know how any of us can go on, knowing she's a prisoner in Iran. We have to do something, but what, I'm not sure."

"Shahin and I have been trying to come up with new ideas, but so far, nothing seems good enough to work," grumbled Kamal.

"I think we need to go back to the mercenary plan," said Paula. "I'm not afraid to return to Iran, and you know I won't let my parents stop me," she added defiantly. "Tell Shahin's parents I will gladly be part of the rescue team."

"Paula, it's too dangerous. I know you can handle a gun, but I don't think you know what you're getting into. You could get yourself killed," said Kamal uneasily.

"Oh, so it's okay for you two to go, but not me," Paula blurted. "You know I'm a better shot than you or Shahin. Hitting that soldier at the estate in the head was a lucky shot, that's all. Then Paula padded her argument. "Plus, I am a woman, and I can hide my identity using a hijab and chador. I can get much closer to Cindy without anyone recognizing me."

"Yeah, you make a good point," replied Kamal, "but it won't matter to Mr. and Mrs. Ali."

Still frustrated, Paula added, "Even if you men wore the religious robes of the mullah, that still wouldn't make you easily accessible to Cindy. Approaching another man's wife would be considered very inappropriate, if not illegal, in public."

Having little choice but to agree with Paula's argument, Kamal promised Paula that he would speak with Shahin's parents about her willingness and ability to participate in Cindy's rescue.

Later, Kamal told Shahin about his conversation with Paula, and that night, he and Shahin presented their case once again to Mr. Ali. The answer was still "No" from Shahin's father, and both young men went to bed feeling frustrated and angry about their inability to help Cindy.

In the days that followed, Mr. Ali watched helplessly as Shahin plummeted into further depression, and several times a day, he replayed the haunting words spewing from Shahin's emotional state.

"I can't live with myself knowing that she's there, and I'm doing nothing to help her. Living like this is more than I can take."

One afternoon, Mr. Ali's fears escalated to a breaking point. He concluded that his son's self-admonishment had become so severe that he questioned whether Shahin could go on living with the guilt and remorse stemming from the decisions he made in Iran. He became convinced that allowing Shahin to return to Iran with the mercenaries outweighed the risk of losing his son to suicide.

Next, Mr. Ali looked deeper at Kamal's state of mind. He determined that Kamal was not much better emotionally than Shahin. He knew Kamal and Cindy had been in a serious relationship in Iran, so he tried to imagine himself in Kamal's position. When he did, Mr. Ali found it impossible to accept the circumstances and realized that he couldn't expect Kamal to feel differently than himself.

After analyzing the boys' issues, Mr. Ali considered his wife's current feelings. He already understood her previous fears; they had both lived for months, not knowing if their son and his friend were dead or alive. Now that they had safely returned, it was normal for her as a mother to be determined to keep both of them safe at any cost. However, Mr. Ali also recognized that they were no longer boys. Shahin and Kamal were grown men with their own lives and decisions to make.

Finally, after many agonizing minutes of indecision, Mr. Ali realized that the only way for him to help Shahin and Kamal move past their guilt was to relent and allow them to return to Iran.

Chapter 13 - The Rescue Plan

Mr. Ali kept his word and hired a team of mercenaries. On the day of their first meeting, the company owner came alone. He introduced himself as "Kegger" and said it was the name he used and preferred. The other two team members, Stevie and Jake, would be part of the subsequent meetings, where the whole team would work out the actual military-like operational details.

Paula was not part of the extraction team. However, Mr. Ali allowed her to join them in the meeting with the mercenaries. Everyone agreed that she had unique personal knowledge about Cindy and could provide them with vital information the team would otherwise lack. It could help the rescue mission be successful.

"I don't think we can risk flying into Iraq with the summer Shamal winds," said Shahin. "It may be easier to sneak across the Iraqi/Iranian border rather than risk a beach landing, but a sand storm that could last for days or weeks could completely screw up our plans."

"Yeah, I agree with Shahin," said Kamal. "We should leave by boat from Oman and head northwest into the Gulf to Bandar Siraf. The storms rarely come down that far. Plus, we know the roads and the layout of the land there. We drove it extensively during our rock sampling trip."

"The guys are right," said Paula. "Our whole plan could be scrubbed for weeks if we wait for the storms to end. Cindy could move somewhere else, and then we'd never find her. We have to go with a quicker plan, even if it's a little more difficult."

"We can probably exit Iran via the Iraqi border," said Kegger. "As I mentioned, I have a couple of contacts in that area who should be able to smuggle us through Iraq to Kuwait. They have small boats to maneuver through the river delta south of Khorramshahr to the Kuwaiti border. We won't need to go through the border checkpoints for either country. They've had this network for a few years, and so far, so good. Once we're inside Kuwait, we can wait for a clear day to fly back to Muscat, Oman."

"How far across is it?" asked Paula.

"It's around 45 km. It depends on what route they take to maneuver through the swamp," replied Kegger.

"That's under 30 miles, right?" she confirmed.

"Yes, it's not far," said Kegger. "Plus, I have a good friend who lives part-time in Kuwait. He's gone all summer but moves back in the fall after the Shamals are over. His winter business is flying rich Kuwaitis around the region. He's been a helicopter pilot for 20 years. I know he'll let us stay at his place even if he isn't there this summer. That way, we'll have a secure place to wait while we're arranging our flight to Muscat."

"Yes, you should be safe inside Kuwait," Mr. Ali agreed. "US relations with Kuwait are strong."

"So, we're all in agreement with this exit plan?" asked Kegger.

"Yes," said Mr. Ali. "It shouldn't be a problem getting their passports stamped to enter Oman from a private plane or helicopter."

"Now, let's talk about a tentative schedule and our entry into Iran. We won't be able to work out any details today, but we should at least get our basics down." The others concurred before Kegger proceeded. "We arrive on the beach at approximately midnight," he supposed. "The resistance group members will meet us there and supply us with the two vehicles they promised."

"Yes," Shahin agreed. "Caspar, that's Roxana's brother, said they can do it. All they need is the date and time. When we get close, we'll need to communicate our exact position to them. After that, they will not be involved. It's strictly a favor. Caspar told Roxana that they could not risk any further exposure."

"I think it's a good plan," said Kamal. "That way, we are closer to where Cindy is supposed to be."

"Yeah," said Paula, "it will cut our travel time to Shiraz and give the Iranians less time to discover that we're there."

"Paula, you keep saying *us* and *our* when you are talking. You do mean just the men, correct?" asked Mr. Ali. "I have not authorized you to go."

"I'm sorry, Mr. Ali, but I need to go. It's just as important to my well-being as it is to your son's and Kamal's, maybe more. Please don't keep me from helping my friend. You know I can be a great asset to this team. Why wouldn't you want the best people to go in after her?"

"Well… I…" He stammered.

"Dad, you have to let her go. She has to be a part of this, just like Kamal and I do," insisted Shahin.

Mr. Ali put his elbows on the table and his head in his hands, similar to Shahin's mannerisms when distressed. After a few moments of silence, he lifted his head.

"Your parents will never forgive me if I allow this," he said solemnly.

"With due respect, Mr. Ali, I'm going to Iran one way or another," said Paula unequivocally. "Hopefully, it will be the safer way as part of this team. Otherwise, I will have to go on my own and hope for the best."

Conceding his defeat, Mr. Ali grumbled, "I'm not going to agree to it, but I'm also not going to stop you."

"Okay then, it's settled. We land in Bandar Siraf towards the end of July or early August," said Kegger. "We can narrow it down at the next meeting."

"Mrs. Ali is not going to like this plan at all," added Mr. Ali. "A beach landing is much more complicated than slipping across the Iraqi border. However, I know you're right about the winds being very unpredictable this time of year. They often impact flying."

✶✶✶✶✶✶

The second meeting was a few days later, and this time, Jake and Stevie attended the gathering. Once again, the question of whether or not they should inform Cindy's parents came up.

"Are you sure you don't want to tell the Stetsons that Cindy could be alive?" asked Mr. Ali. "I think I would want to know."

Immediately, Paula spoke up, "No! What if we don't succeed or if we find out that the woman isn't Cindy; to lose her again a second time could destroy them. They're elderly, and we don't want any other deaths to be caused by our failures."

"I agree with Paula," said Shahin. "They've been through so much, and we all know this mission may not work."

"I plan on succeeding," said Kegger definitively, "but if the girl isn't your friend, then there's nothing I can do about that."

The six men and Paula continued their discussions and worked out more details of the rescue plan. They set the extraction date for August 2nd to give Kegger time to train Shahin, Kamal, and Paula for the rescue mission. He wanted the operation to be a success and as safe as possible. That meant that all members of his team must know how to use, clean, and manage many types of weapons, understand operational strategies, survival tactics, and emergency medical first aid.

Later that night, after the meeting and dinner had concluded, Shahin called Paula's hotel room. They spoke briefly before Shahin asked her to meet him in the hotel lounge for a drink. She agreed, and 10 minutes later, Paula entered the bar to see Shahin talking with the bartender. She made her way up to him and sat down on the barstool next to Shahin. The bartender mentioned he would be closing in 20 minutes before walking away to begin his cleanup.

"Thanks for joining me," he said tentatively. "I needed to talk to you alone, and our meeting and group dinner were the wrong places for what I have to say. By the way, Paula, it's really great to see you."

"Is that what you needed to tell me?" asked Paula curtly.

"No," Shahin admitted. "I asked you here because I think I owe you an apology,".

"You think so?" she said angrily. "You stopped calling me and wouldn't return my calls. You just completely dropped me as if I were an unimportant nobody. I'm still really mad about it, but I dealt with it, and on some level, I have forgiven you for it."

Shahin apologized for his behavior and tried his best to explain his actions. Paula listened to his argument while inserting snarky comments into his defense. When he finished, she told him that nothing he said made up for how he had treated her. Shahin conceded that he handled their breakup poorly and asked Paula again to forgive him. She said his behavior was inexcusable but acknowledged that his reasoning about the social injustices facing a mixed couple could be quite challenging, especially since the hostage crisis had happened.

The bartender gave them an extra 20 minutes but then announced that he was closing. He walked to the exit and held the door for them to leave. As they walked past him, Shahin handed him a generous tip, and both thanked him for staying late.

As the two waited for the elevator, Shahin slipped his hand into Paula's and squeezed it gently. She looked up and grinned at him. Seeing her smile was more than he could resist. He pulled her close and kissed her hungrily.

******

Breathing heavily and a bit sweaty, Paula rolled onto her back next to Shahin's naked body. It had been over seven months since they had made love, and Paula evaluated the sex as still very gratifying and comfortable. Lingering on the feeling, her mind returned to their time together in Iran and the intense feelings she once had about sharing her life with Shahin. Without thinking about it too much, she began to compare her past emotions to her present state of mind and realized something was different. She still loved him; that part was genuine, but not in the same way as before, she admitted to herself.

It had taken Paula months to recover from everything that had happened to her after she returned home. First, there was the need to figure out how to live with the devastating loss of her friend, Cindy. It turned out to be exceptionally hard for Paula to face. In addition, Paula had struggled overwhelmingly with Shahin's decision to end their relationship. Luckily, she had Kamal to confide in, and he helped her through it by giving her bits and pieces of information about Shahin's reasons for the abrupt breakup and updates on his state of mind. In addition, Paula needed to heal mentally from the stress and trauma caused by the months of hiding inside Iran and the many harrowing experiences they had experienced trying to escape.

Finally, there was the remorse for involving Zahra's brother, Rostam. It wasn't only his death that haunted Paula. Her inability to keep her promise to him added to her distress. She had vowed to get his wife, Kyra, out of Iran and into the US.

Returning to the present moment, Paula continued to think about how things were different between her and Shahin. She wasn't sure of his feelings, but she knew her outlook on life had changed since she returned home. Paula reasoned that if she and Shahin continued down the same path again, it would most certainly put her back into the role of his girlfriend or fiancée, and as of now, she wasn't sure she wanted either title.

Paula remembered back to a time when she believed she couldn't live without Shahin by her side, but those sentiments had been replaced with new feelings and aspirations. Her journey and progress through depression and grief had changed her state of mind. Now in recovery, Paula had a new outlook on life.

Oblivious to Paula's train of thought, Shahin unexpectedly leaned over and kissed Paula on the cheek.

"I'll be right back," he said before launching himself off the bed towards the bathroom. "Promise you won't leave while I'm gone," he said jokingly.

Thoughtlessly, Paula replied, "I promise."

Suddenly, a slight panic rose within her, and she was initially confused by the sensation. Looking for answers, Paula continued to re-evaluate her situation and reflected on her recent life-changing decisions. Not only had she chosen to switch her career choice, but she had also modified her overall life goals. She wasn't sure what the ramifications of these actions meant for her immediate future, but hearing herself say she wouldn't leave caused her some unintended anxiety.

It was then that Paula confirmed to herself that her new aspirations felt right. She was comfortable not having her whole life planned, and it inspired her sense of adventure.

Without thinking further, Paula murmured, "I guess this proves it. I'm not ready to be somebody's wife right now, not even if that somebody is Shahin."

Part Two

Chapter 14 - The Landing

Paula's eyes opened wide, and she stared blankly at the ceiling for a moment before her mind could catch up. Her heart was already racing with anticipation.

"It's finally here!" she said to herself.

Paula glanced over at her alarm clock and saw it was 6:30 AM. She still had 30 minutes before it went off, and normally, she'd roll over and try to go back to sleep, but not today. Today, she was on a mission, a mission to save her friend. She headed to the bathroom to shower, and as she washed her hair, waves of excitement and nervousness overtook her emotions. She tried to keep her emotions in check, but it was no use. In a few hours, she was flying back to Washington, DC. Only this time, she wasn't just going to strategize and train. It was happening, the time had come to execute the plan to save her friend.

The first leg of Paula's journey back to Iran would officially start in DC. The team would fly to London first and then on to Muscat, Oman, the following day.

Once there, they planned to take a day to recuperate from the time change and jet lag. The next morning, they would fly in a private seaplane to the small bay off the isolated village of Kumzar on the Musandam Peninsula. It was the perfect place to start their covert voyage.

After the water landing, the team would quickly transfer to a small private boat that would take them through the Strait of Hormuz and into the Persian Gulf. The voyage would end on the shore of Bandar Siraf, Iran. It was a long, convoluted way to reach their destination, but the mercenary team felt it was the safest strategy.

The plan was not without its dangers. Small boats navigating the shipping channel often faced large wakes and the risk of collision with the numerous barges and ships within the narrow waterway. Kegger, however, had been assured that Captain Amini's extensive experience navigating these treacherous waters made the risk of any major problems negligible.

The final leg of their journey to the Iranian mainland would begin a mile off the coast. The team would deploy a small inflatable raft to take them across the last mile of water and onto the beach near Bandar Siraf.

******

Just after 9 AM, the team took off in the seaplane from Muscat. The day was clear, with bright blue skies expanding to the horizon. At first glance, it looked like the perfect day. The wind, however, was stronger than usual, which caused the pilot to make some flight adjustments to land safely in the bay.

"That must be your ride," said the pilot as he skimmed across the water.

His six passengers carefully stepped onto the pontoons and transferred their belongings into the swaying boat.

"The water is a little choppy today," said Captain Amini. "Watch your step; the swells can be tricky."

The captain directed the team to load their gear into the bow of the boat underneath the hull. The load would offset the weight of the team, who were positioned on the stern of the boat. Next, he instructed his passengers to sit three on each side, doing his best to level the boat. When everyone was situated, the captain pulled slowly away from the plane and headed toward the Strait of Hormuz.

"I may need to speed up some," he said. "With this headwind, we are falling behind our anticipated arrival time."

"Do what you need to do," said Kegger. "We need to meet someone on the shore, and I don't want to be late."

"But we still want to be safe," Shahin said nervously.

"Don't worry, I've made this trip many times," replied the captain. "We shouldn't have a problem. I just wish the wind would calm down a little."

They reached the point where they needed to cross the shipping lanes. Unfortunately, the wind began to blow even harder, gusting strongly across the bow of the boat. The captain realized that navigating his boat through these waters was going to be more challenging than he expected, so he enlisted the help of his passengers.

The captain had Shahin, Kegger, and Jake help him maneuver through the choppy waters while Paula, Kamal, and Stevie strapped down their raft. It had jarred loose and begun to partially inflate.

Suddenly, something menacing caught Paula's eye.

"Captain!" she yelled over the wind, "do you see what's coming towards us on the left? I think it could be a Shamal."

The others quickly refocused their eyes in the direction that Paula was pointing. A wall of dust was bearing down on them. They only had a few minutes before the storm hit.

"Fuck! We're in trouble!" yelled Kegger. "Do you have the raft secured? That damn dust is going to be here in a minute."

"We're trying! The automatic inflate valve isn't working right. The fuckin' thing wants to blow up now!" Stevie responded angrily.

"Let me look at it!" demanded Paula after pulling a paperclip from her pack. "This might work to release the air."

She started to deflate the raft just as the storm consumed them.

"Take it!" she shouted to Stevie. "I'm getting our scarves."

The air had quickly become unbreathable. Luckily, the team had expected to encounter dusty roads, so they had packed a bag of face masks in their group duffel. Paula left the guys and headed down into the hull to retrieve them. Meanwhile, the other men continued to help the captain navigate.

Paula returned on deck just as a large water swell rocked the boat forcefully sideways. She quickly grabbed onto the door frame to prevent herself from being slammed into it. Her brace only stopped her for a split second, and then the reverse inertia forced her onto the deck. Luckily, she had enough time to protect her face from hitting the hard surface.

Most of the men were not so lucky. Shahin and Jake lost their grasp on the flimsy canopy and plummeted overboard. Kamal and Stevie had just stood up from strapping down the raft and hadn't taken hold of something sturdy. They stumbled backward across the stern and toppled over the side of the boat. All four men were in the water while the others left on board clung to anything they could as the boat rocked violently back and forth. Kegger had wanted to put one more strap on the raft and was sitting sideways with his elbows on the deck for leverage and his right hand around a secured strap when the force caused his entire body to wrench sideways, squeezing his secured hand until it was bruised.

Captain Amini gripped the steering wheel as tightly as he could, but couldn't hold on. He was thrown into the side shield of the canopy and then onto the deck. He had a gash on his head from the impact but was still conscious.

Paula quickly recovered from her fall and took action. She found the rescue float ring, secured the rope to it, and threw it out to the men. Shahin, Kamal, and Jake were close enough to the ring to swim to it. Stevie, however, had been hit by another large wave and was quickly drifting away from the boat and the rescue float.

Knowing Stevie couldn't swim against the wind and current back to the boat or the float, Paula looked around for something else to save him. She saw a rope curled up near the back corner of the stern and knew this was her only option. She took out her knife and cut the starboard anchor off before tying the end around her waist and diving into the water. When she popped up, Paula took a deep breath and swam hard and fast toward the struggling man. Stevie's life preserver had come apart, and he struggled to keep himself afloat. Soon, Paula was at the end of

the rope, and Stevie was still a yard away. He tried frantically to swim to her but couldn't make any headway. Instead, he had begun to drift away. In the background, Paula could hear them trying to start the engine, but it was flooded and would not turn over. Refusing to give up, Paula untied the rope from her waist and wrapped it tight around her wrist and hand. Then she yelled as loud as she could to Stevie.

"Grab my foot and climb over me to the rope!"

Paula lay flat with her arms, legs, and torso horizontal to the water surface. The extra length was just enough for Stevie to grab her ankle.

Immediately, he pulled Paula under the water. She had expected it and was ready. While on the swim team, she and three other students stayed late several evenings to learn life-saving skills from a traveling instructor.

The teacher taught the students to evaluate each situation quickly and to remember that no two rescues were alike.

"You must approach each situation differently," she recalled him saying. His words ran through Paula's thoughts as she decided what to do next. "If you see that the person in trouble is not panicking or acting desperate," he told them, "Give the person a chance to save him or herself. Even if you have to go underwater for a few seconds." Remembering his instructions, Paula held on and allowed Stevie to climb over her body to grab the rope. Then, as promised by her teacher, Stevie pulled Paula to the surface.

A moment later, Kegger yelled, "Get ready! I'm pulling you in!"

Fortunately, the wind paused for a few moments, which gave the crew time to regroup. When Paula and Stevie were safe inside the boat, Kegger looked at her and said, "You're lucky I noticed you out there. With the noise of the wind and my focus on the other three guys, I didn't know you went after Stevie. It wasn't until I started to look for him that I saw you stretch out so he could grab onto you."

"Yeah, Paula, that was fucking awesome," Stevie admitted. "You saved my life. I was heading the wrong way fast." Stevie smiled at Paula and held up his hand for a high-five, saying, "Thanks, man, I owe you one."

Paula slapped her palm to his and smiled back.

Captain Amini interrupted, "I hate to spoil your victory, but we won't be able to go on. You'll have to abort your mission until this storm passes."

"But that could take days!" blurted Kamal. "How far are we now? Maybe we can get out here and walk the coast to our rendezvous point."

"I agree with Kamal," said Paula. "Let's take a minute and evaluate our situation. Captain Amini, how close are we to the shore?"

"The mainland... it's way too far in this storm, but Kish Island is closer."

"Okay then," replied Paula. "I vote for heading to Kish."

"Me too," agreed Shahin

Kegger interjected, "Our raft won't make it in this storm. We have limited navigation equipment."

"Once we get the motor started, I can get you closer to the Kish shoreline, but I will not be able to anchor," he stated. "You'll have to use your raft to land."

The captain continued to try to start the engine. Finally, after several more turns of the key, it sputtered to life.

"Okay, I need to know where we're going," said the captain. "The storms way down here come and go in waves. We shouldn't waste this lull."

"Can you get word to my father if we alter our plans?" asked Shahin.

"Yes, of course," he replied. "I will contact him immediately upon my return to Oman."

"Okay," said Kegger. "I'll agree to this plan if we think we can still get assistance from Roxana's brother."

"As I said, I can get a message to Mr. Ali. I feel certain that he can relay your new pick-up point and schedule to your contacts in Iran. They should have plenty of time to move the vehicles to your new location," Captain Amini assured him. "From what I've been told, Mr. Ali is a very resourceful man."

Kegger asked his men if they were willing to continue the mission with him, knowing it would most likely be more dangerous than their original itinerary. The guys agreed to the change, so Kegger gave the captain the nod to set a course for Kish.

The wind had slowed further when the team was ready to deploy their raft. The dust had also diminished, and visibility had improved. The storm looked like it was continuing to rage to the northwest, but the southeastern half of the Gulf was clearing, at least for the time being.

Together, the team readied the raft for their journey. Kegger got in first and helped each member get into the boat safely. They thanked the captain and headed towards Kish Island.

Minutes later, the wind picked up, and dust enveloped them once again, reducing their visibility to less than ten feet. The motor started to take in dust, which caused it to sputter as they approached the beach. When the six were 100 yards from the shore, the motor stopped working altogether. Within seconds, each grabbed a paddle and propelled the inflatable forward onto the beach.

"Hurry, we need to get out of sight as quickly as possible!" yelled Kegger.

Luckily, the crew had landed at a very opportune time, in addition to the raging Shamal; it was a Friday, and most Muslims were attending congregational prayers inside their mosque or in their homes. Stevie, Jake, Shahin, and Kamal each grabbed a handle on the raft and dragged it to a small area of vegetation before taking defensive positions on the ground around it. Meanwhile, Paula and Kegger went inland to determine where, on the island, they had landed.

Coincidentally, the rescue party had temporarily considered landing on Kish Island because of an intelligence brief that stated the hotel, casino, and palace had been closed down and shackled after the revolution. The report also said that most of the expensive interior items had been auctioned off after the buildings were vacated, and what was left was stolen by the villagers and other opportunists before the government cracked down on their thievery. Now, the buildings stand vacant, waiting for the government to implement its intended plans for the island. Fortunately for the extraction team, the proposals had not yet been acted upon due to the lack of resources and conflicting views on how best to proceed.

******

The team had gone ashore near the hotel where Paula and her friends stayed when they visited Kish Island during the New Year celebration the year before. Unsolicited scenes of her first romantic night with Shahin penetrated Paula's focus. Knowing this wasn't the time to reminisce, she immediately pushed her memories aside to attend to the issues at hand.

As she and Kegger approached the hotel, it was evident, even with their limited vision, that their intel had been correct. The hotel sat dark and empty, and it was apparent that all outside maintenance had ceased. Luckily, Kegger had grabbed the compact bolt cutters out of their supply duffel before they headed out to investigate. He told Paula he never goes on a mission without them.

Kegger pulled the pair off of his utility belt and quickly sliced through the chains and padlocks holding the service entrance doors closed. Cautiously, he and Paula entered the building. The first room looked stripped of any items worth taking. The only things left were the long metal tables used to fold the linens, something most people couldn't fit in an Iranian home.

Together, Paula and Kegger cautiously made their way through the employees' hallway to the hotel lobby. It was devoid of furniture and other expensive items. When they felt comfortable that they were alone, they continued their search of the entire first floor. There were no signs of squatters or guards' quarters. When they came to the storage room near the manager's office, Kegger looked at Paula. She quickly confirmed that this was the room where her and Shahin's samples had been stored.

She stepped in behind Kegger, and there, piled orderly in the corner, were the sample tubes. Most were still covered with shrink wrap, and only a small section was ripped open. The cored rock had been dumped out of their containers and onto the floor. It was evident that something so precious to Shahin and Paula was worthless to others.

Paula bent down and picked up one of the vials.

"At one time, these samples were so important to Shahin and me. Now, they mean nothing," she said solemnly. Paula turned to Kegger and added, "It's weird how our priorities have changed since we collected these. So much of what Shahin and I valued so highly just isn't relevant anymore." Kegger grunted his acknowledgment of her insight while he panned the area for intruders. Paula put the sample back in its place before saying, "I'm ready. Let's move on."

******

Paula and Kegger quickly ascended the hotel's stairs to investigate the second, third, and fourth floors, briefly searching inside each room. When Paula came to the suite where she and Cindy had stayed, Paula was overtaken with emotion. She lowered her weapon and stood blankly, staring at the ransacked room. Sadly, her loving memories of the place were overshadowed by their current set of circumstances. She wiped a tear from her cheek before lifting her semi-automatic rifle back up to a ready position and headed to inspect the bedrooms.

Once Paula and Kegger had completed their room search, they stopped and listened again for any sounds of human activity. The only noises they heard were the winds and sand raging outside. Establishing that the hotel was vacant, they cautiously returned to the landing site.

"The hotel looks safe!" shouted Kegger over the wind to the rest of the team.

"Follow me," instructed Paula. "I'll show you the best way to get in."

Shahin and Kegger carried the boat motor while Paula, Kamal, Stevie, and Jake transported the raft. Once inside the laundry room, the four dropped the raft, but

Shahin and Kegger continued with the engine to the manager's office. The room would be their headquarters for the night. It was a central location and the best place to monitor the hotel's entrances.

Next, the group broke up into three teams. Two teams double-checked that they were alone and searched for any useful supplies left behind. Paula and Kegger went to the maintenance room first to see if they could restart the water.

When the crew considered landing on Kish, intel sources told them that Khomeini had the soldiers close down the hotel temporarily. They hoped the closure meant that the main water valve inside the hotel had been turned off, but the water supply was still available. Happily, their assumption had been correct, and with a turn of the valve, the water was turned on throughout the hotel.

Paula and Kegger continued their search for comfort items. They returned to the laundry room, hoping to find towels and other linens. Unfortunately, every cabinet was empty. As the two were leaving, Paula turned and hurried back to the large, built-in dryer. She opened the door and peered inside. There, hidden in the shadows, were three bath towels that the looters had missed. Beaming with satisfaction, she snatched them up and rejoined Kegger.

While Paula and Kegger were in the employee area, Shahin and Stevie searched the hotel's top two floors, and Kamal and Jake investigated the rest of the first floor and the second. Shahin found two blankets hidden on the top closet shelf in two adjacent rooms, and Kamal found some soap and shampoo that had dropped behind the large shelves in the supply closet. When the groups completed their search, they returned to the office to share the treasures they had discovered.

******

Kegger was already dismantling the boat motor when Paula walked out of the bathroom, toweling her hair.

"I feel a hundred percent better," she said. "Who's going next?"

"I'll go," said Shahin. "I don't need a towel."

"Take this," Paula said as she offered him her towel. "It's damp, but still better than nothing. It's not like we haven't shared one in the past."

Shahin gave Paula a loving grin before he accepted the towel and headed to the shower.

"It may be early, but it's going to be a long day tomorrow," Kegger told the others. "Everybody needs to eat their rations, and those who can need to get some rest." He paused momentarily and said, "Stevie, Jake, blockade the service door before you position yourselves to guard the side exits. Use those big tables and whatever else you can find. I'm close enough to the main entrance to hear if someone tries to break in through the lobby doors. Someone will relieve you when it's your turn for a shower. Also, rest as much as possible because you'll need to be at your best tomorrow. Nobody's going to get in here without making some noise."

After their showers and rations, Paula, Shahin, and Kamal sat with Kegger to take apart and clean the boat engine.

"What you did today was awesome, Paula," said Kamal. "I wouldn't have been able to keep my cool in the water like you did."

"Yeah, it was pretty spectacular," said Shahin.

"Swim team guys and lifeguard training," she replied spiritedly, trying to diminish the seriousness of the situation.

"The guys are right," added Kegger. "You're braver than I expected."

The praise from Kegger caught Paula off guard, and she blushed as she replied, "Thanks, it was no big deal."

The guys admonished her for making light of her feat, but soon moved on to talk about the other day's events. Finally, after a couple of hours, they finished fixing the engine and settled into sleep.

At 3:00 AM, the team got up and headed to the beach. The wind had quit blowing, and the weather suggested the sandstorm was over. The six quietly got into the inflatable and paddled out until they felt it was safe to start the motor.

The trip across the water to the mainland went well, and when they arrived, three members of the Iranian underground resistance were waiting for them.

"Roxana has spoken very highly of you, and as she is my sister, I trust her judgment," Caspar said to Paula as he reached out to shake her hand.

"Thank you, Caspar. We are very grateful for your help," replied Paula. "We couldn't have attempted this rescue without your assistance."

"I must do what I can to change the course of my country and help those being persecuted," he responded. "I may not be an American, but as a Jewish man, my future here is uncertain under this new regime. As of now, the assurances Khomeini gave us have all but disappeared."

Paula acknowledged his plight and was about to continue their conversation when Kegger interrupted, "Not to be rude, but we need to leave now if we're going to make it to Shiraz on time."

While they spoke, the rest of the team and the resistance fighters deflated the raft and stuffed it and the motor into Caspar's truck. Caspar wished them good luck before handing Paula the keys to the two vehicles he had brought for them to use. Paula thanked him and immediately gave the keys to Kegger, who, in turn, handed one key to Stevie.

Paula, Shahin, and Kamal continued to thank all of the resistance members for their help and assistance before climbing into the unmarked vehicles.

As Paula, Shahin, and Kegger drove away in one of the vehicles, Paula said, "I'm so happy Caspar came through for us. It was hard for me to put so much trust in a man I had never met."

"It's a good thing," said Kegger. "I would have hated to implement plan B."

"I guess this is it, guys," said Shahin. "This is the only help we can expect until we're at the Iraqi border."

"Yeah, we're on our own from here on out," agreed Kegger.

Chapter 15 - Marketplace

Paula and the others watched from a distance as two women exited their home. Both women cloaked themselves with full-length chadors to cover their heads as required by law. In addition to her outer garment, the second woman wore a scarf that hid all but her eyes from public view.

Paula focused first on the woman whose face was fully exposed. She immediately noticed that the woman had a very prominent nose, and her skin looked weathered, with a more olive hue. It was distinctly different from Cindy's pinkish tone.

Paula quickly shifted her gaze past the older woman to refocus on the new female figure entering her view. From what little Paula could see, the other woman looked younger, and her eyes could definitely be Cindy's. However, from her vantage point, Paula could only speculate whether or not this woman was, in fact, Cindy.

The two women walked up to the black sedan waiting in front of the house. The driver did not get out of the car. Instead, the younger woman opened the back door and allowed the older woman to enter first. The driver pulled away, and the rescue team followed in the SUV provided to them by the Iranian resistance.

When the car stopped, the two women got out and started walking towards the nearest vegetable stands. Kegger pulled over and parked 20 yards behind them. Paula and Kamal got out together and casually exited the vehicle as if it were part of their weekly routine. Paula wore a hijab to hide her blonde hair and a chador to cover her jeans and T-shirt. Kamal had on jeans and a button-up shirt.

Stevie and Jake were already inside the market, waiting for the targeted women and the rest of their team to arrive. They had the weapons ready in case of trouble and had combed the area for suspicious activities. So far, nothing seemed out of the ordinary to them.

Shahin and Kegger followed behind Paula and Kamal before stopping briefly at a newsstand to create additional space between them.

As Paula kept her eyes on the woman presumed to be Cindy, a mix of excitement and anxiety surged within her. She had anticipated this meeting for months, and to be so close to her best friend felt almost overwhelming. She had to fight back her emotions and work to keep herself focused.

The veiled women entered the bustling market and began shopping for produce. For the first several minutes, the older woman remained close by the younger one's side, but finally, she walked several yards away to another vendor's stall. The tension in the air was palpable as Paula and the team continued their vigil.

"This is my chance," Paula said to herself. "I need to make contact now." She walked up and stood casually beside the veiled woman before whispering, "Cindy, it's me, Paula."

The woman did not respond to her words. Instead, she continued looking at the produce she planned to purchase.

"Cindy, did you hear me? It's me, Paula," she whispered again.

This time, the young woman turned and looked directly at Paula. Baffled, she looked around to see if there was another person nearby. When she saw no one, she glanced back at Paula in bewilderment.

"We came to get you," Paula said, raising her voice slightly.

Unease entered Cindy's gaze, and Paula decided she needed to retreat. She pretended to have an appointment to keep and quickly walked to the predetermined meeting place. On the nearby side street, Paula found the men anxiously waiting for her to give them a positive or negative identification.

"It's her! I'm sure of it! She looked straight at me, but something's wrong!" Paula said worriedly. "She's acting like she doesn't know me. I don't get it. Why wouldn't she talk to me?"

"Maybe she's afraid," said Kegger.

"Yeah… but knowing Cindy, she would at least give Paula a sign," said Kamal.

"I agree, something's off," said Shahin.

"Well, whatever's going on, I don't like it," said Paula. "I understand she's been here for months in captivity, but you'd think she'd be excited to see me. Cindy's got to know I'm here for her," she added in desperation.

"It's the same way she acted with Darian," said Kamal.

"Yeah, it's weird," Paula agreed.

Stevie spoke up, "Maybe she has that syndrome. You know, the one where the captive starts having good feelings towards their kidnappers."

"He's right!" Paula said eagerly. "She could have Stockholm syndrome."

"What's Stockholm syndrome?" asked Kamal.

"It's a psychological response that some people have when they're in captivity for a long period. They begin to identify with their captors and often decide to join them. The kidnappee refuses help from the police, their friends, and even their family," Paula explained.

"Oh, I remember this happening a few years ago," said Shahin. "What was that girl's name?"

"Patty Hearst!" blurted Paula. "She became part of the terrorist group that kidnapped her."

"Well, if that's the case, what's our next step?" asked Kegger. "Should I just go in and grab her?"

"No!" said Kamal forcefully. "Let's just take a minute and think about this."

While the group discussed their options, they moved closer to watch Cindy and her companion shop.

They decided to send Kamal over to get a response from the woman they believed to be Cindy. He hesitated at first, waiting until she walked to the next vendor.

"Go, this is the perfect time," Kamal told himself before moving towards her position. Mustering the courage, he casually strolled up to the fruit bin next to where Cindy was standing and reached out to grab a piece of produce. He had been so focused on what he would say to her that he hadn't noticed what she was purchasing. To Kamal's surprise, Cindy was buying a bag of sour cherries. Unable to adequately change his approach, his mannerisms remained the same as he had planned. He awkwardly picked up a handful of cherries and began to examine each one for defects. Cindy momentarily glanced over at his odd behavior but quickly looked away.

Starting to panic, Kamal walked up beside her and whispered, "Cindy, it's me, Kamal. I'm so glad you're alive," he said, expressing his unbridled relief. "We're here to take you home, me, Paula, and Shahin."

Cindy's face expressed fear at the sound of a second person speaking the same foreign language within minutes of the first. She stared intently at Kamal for a long moment, trying to understand why he had spoken to her in this language. When she could not justify his behavior, she turned and quickly walked away. Stunned, Kamal just stood there, unable to respond appropriately to her departure. Without moving towards Cindy, Kamal retreated from the meeting and returned to the group.

"I don't understand!" Kamal said in frustration. "She acted afraid of me as if I were some type of criminal. Why is she pretending not to know us? Even if she has the syndrome you're talking about, you'd think she'd at least acknowledge that she recognizes me."

"It could be that they have threatened to kill her if she tries to run away or get help," said Shahin. "Maybe she's trying to protect us."

"I don't know what's going on, but she's not herself," said Paula.

"What are we going to do?" asked Kamal impatiently. "We can't just leave her here. We have to help her!"

"We need a new plan," said Shahin.

"I agree," said Paula. "Maybe we grab her and get the answers to our questions later. I know she'll want to be rescued once we have her safe with us."

"Let me know what you decide," said Kegger, "but it must be soon."

While the others debated, Jake and Stevie watched for any unexpected company.

Finally, Kegger became impatient, "Guys, we're wasting time. Are we taking the girl with us or not?"

"Yes, we may not have another opportunity," said Paula decisively. "Plus, she could tell somebody about us. I think we have to take action now." The others mumbled their agreement as Paula laid out the plan. "Kegger, you and I are the best ones to grab her. Please don't take this wrong, but being mixed-race might make it easier for you to blend into the crowd, much more so than Jake or Stevie."

"Yeah, the southern Iranians do have a little African and some Arab heritage, much more than the northerners," agreed Kegger.

"Why can't I get Cindy?" asked Kamal. "I'm Iranian."

"Because she already saw you and ran," Paula told him flatly.

Reluctantly, Kamal nodded his understanding and yielded to Kegger.

They were about to execute their plan when Stevie saw a group of Iranian soldiers lining up to flank them.

"Soldiers!" he voiced urgently under his breath while flinging the weapon's bag off his shoulder and unzipping it.

"How did they know we'd be here?" questioned Shahin as he grabbed a machine gun from the duffel.

No one responded. Instead, they pulled guns from the carrier and took cover behind the nearest structure. A moment later, gunfire rang out. The people in the marketplace panicked. To protect themselves, they either crouched down in place or ran. Cindy and her companion hunkered down near a vegetable stall several yards away.

After a minute of intense shooting, Paula noticed that Cindy's companion had stopped crouching and was trying to pull Cindy away from the fighting. Paula saw it and motioned for Kegger to follow her. They skirted around the gunfight and came up on the opposite side of the stand where Cindy was resisting the older woman's forceful insistence that they flee.

"We need to stop them!" shouted Paula over the noise and began to move towards them.

The two women had taken only a few steps when Paula intercepted them. The older woman immediately protested against Paula's blockade while holding her chador with one hand and tugging on Cindy's arm with the other. Luckily, the confrontation was hidden from the view of the firing soldiers.

Paula had stopped the women momentarily but hadn't moved in to take Cindy. Suddenly, Kegger pushed past Paula, saying, "I got her!"

He quickly tore Cindy's arm from the other woman's grasp. When he did, Cindy panicked and released the grip on her chador. As the garment fell away from her body, Cindy stood motionless, apparently unsure of what to do next.

During that brief moment, both Kegger and Paula paused to evaluate Cindy's condition. A second later, Kegger hoisted Cindy up into his arms while expressing his intentions to free her from her enslavers.

Cindy kicked and screamed wildly while hitting the mercenary with her fists. To stop her from yelling, Paula pulled a bandana out of her pocket and swiftly placed the cloth across Cindy's open mouth and tied it tight. As Kegger waited, he glanced back at his team to assess their situation. He saw Jake get hit just above his bulletproof vest. Jake crumpled to the ground, and at that moment, Kegger knew the wound was fatal.

"We need to move now!" he yelled to Paula.

Paula quickly responded to his instructions and headed to their alternate vehicle. With Cindy battling to escape his hold, Kegger ran close behind Paula. They continued through the marketplace to the other side. A soldier saw them and stepped out from behind a stall to block their path. He had his rifle drawn and was about to shoot when Paula lifted her weapon and fired two shots. Paula shot him once in each shoulder, rendering him helpless. The man dropped his rifle and fell to the ground. As she passed by him, Paula leaned over and grabbed his rifle and handgun. She carried the old rusty weapons until she was out of his sight and then threw them into a nearby stall. The owner was about to protest her actions when he saw Kegger following behind.

******

During Cindy's abduction, Kamal had glanced over just as her chador fell away. The shock caused him to pause his engagement with the enemy. He stood in astonishment as he watched the mercenary cradle Cindy in his arms before fleeing the scene with Paula leading the way.

"Kamal, get a hold of yourself!" yelled Shahin.

It took Kamal another moment to regain his composure before he could continue firing upon the combatants. Shahin, Kamal, and Stevie fought the soldiers for several more minutes. One of the bullets grazed Shahin's arm, only slightly impeding his ability to shoot. Then, Stevie got hit in the thigh with a high-caliber weapon. He glanced down at the wound but continued to fire.

Shahin looked around at their situation. Jake had been shot in the carotid artery, and the bullet had severely damaged his entire neck. He lay dead in a large pool of blood next to Shahin. Stevie had been shot in his upper thigh. Luckily, it looked only to be a flesh wound, but it was bleeding profusely. Shahin had been more fortunate; a bullet had only grazed him, cutting a 3-inch-long gash across the outside of his upper left arm. Kamal was the lucky one; as far as Shahin knew, he had gone unscathed so far in the firefight.

At this point, Shahin realized they were outgunned and outmanned. Knowing they couldn't escape, Shahin yelled to the other men.

"It's no use. We'll all be killed if we don't surrender."

Stevie concurred, "Yeah, I'm bleeding pretty bad. Even if we run, they'll be able to track us."

Kamal nodded his agreement and took out a white hanky. He placed it in the nozzle of his gun and raised the weapon into the air to signal their surrender.

The gunfire ceased, and a soldier yelled to the three men, "Drop your weapons!"

Shahin, Kamal, and Stevie did as instructed and then raised their arms. The Iranian soldiers walked up to them and immediately kicked their weapons out of reach. Next, the lieutenant motioned for Shahin to check and see if the fallen man was still alive. Shahin carefully knelt, keeping his hands raised. When he was in his squat, he lowered his blood-soaked arm and felt for a pulse. After several seconds, he looked up at the lieutenant and shook his head, "No".

"I need to get a tourniquet on my leg," said Stevie. "I'll bleed out if I don't. If I die, you'll have one less hostage. Your commanders are not going to be happy about that."

"Not now!" said the soldier. "All of you, get down on the ground, belly first, and put your hands on your backs."

Stevie groaned in agony as he tried to comply with his captor's orders. Immediately, Shahin and Kamal each took an arm to help him down. Instantly, the dust and dirt on the ground began to infiltrate Stevie's wound. The powdered earth helped stop the bleeding by soaking up the blood and blocking more fluid from escaping. However, the bacteria, fungus, and whatever else lived in it now had direct access to Stevie's inner body.

Chapter 16 - The Delivery

Paula could still hear the gunfire from the market in the distance when she neared the location where the Jeep Cherokee was parked. Paula feared the worst, expecting the vehicle to be seized or compromised. When she rounded the last corner before it came into view, Paula took a deep breath, preparing herself to fight or run if necessary.

The Jeep was still there, and Paula felt a calculated sense of relief. It looked untouched, and the people in the vicinity seemed uninterested in the car. They were focused on the firefight happening in the distance.

Unable to wait and see if it was a trap, Paula ran up and unlocked the front door. She quickly reached around and pulled the back lock up before slipping out of the Jeep to open the rear door. Within a few seconds, Kegger arrived. He wrestled Cindy into the backseat as carefully as possible while trying to avoid her punches. Paula closed the door behind them and jumped into the driver's seat. She turned the key, and the Cherokee roared to life. Hoping to avoid further attention, Paula moved slowly onto the busy street while Cindy struggled to free herself from Kegger's grip.

"Why didn't you tell us she was pregnant?" Kegger demanded as he fought to keep Cindy under control.

"We didn't know! Darian never mentioned anything about a baby!" added Paula.

As Cindy attempted to shout at Paula and Kegger, Paula tried to explain why they had abducted her from the market.

"Cindy! What's wrong with you? It's me, Paula! We're here to take you home!"

Paula's words fell flat, making no impact on Cindy's behavior. The fighting and yelling continued until suddenly, Cindy cried out in pain and doubled over, "Owoo!"

"Something's wrong with her, Paula! I can see blood on her dress!" Kegger exclaimed.

"Quick, take off the gag! We're close to the rendezvous point! We'll be able to check her out in just a minute!" Paula yelled back.

Seconds later, Paula pulled into a small, narrow side street and stopped in front of a vacant building. She exited the car and hurried to the side door of what looked like an old factory. The pain had quenched Cindy's desire to free herself, and she finally allowed Kegger to lift her into his arms. He carefully carried Cindy through the open doorway and into the building. Inside was a large room with remnants of heavy machinery scattered about.

Paula had run ahead to open an unmarked door at the end of the room. As Kegger entered the smaller chamber, Cindy let out another anguishing sound of pain. The blood on her dress was spreading, and Paula knew Cindy needed immediate attention.

"Put her on the bed!" Paula demanded. "I'll get some ties to hold her down!"

By the time Kegger and Paula got Cindy's arms loosely fastened to the bedposts, Cindy's pain had subsided once again, and she began to yell at Paula.

Paula moved to the foot of the bed and pulled up Cindy's dress to investigate the bleeding while Kegger watched.

"Oh no, it's coming from her vagina," said Paula despairingly.

"Maybe if she rests a bit, it'll stop," said Kegger fearfully. "I was a little forceful with her. I could have done something to hurt her without knowing it."

"It's not your fault," said Paula as she continued to examine other areas of Cindy's lower half. "We didn't know she was pregnant when we planned this rescue. Besides, how you carried her shouldn't have caused her to bleed."

Out of instinct, Paula looked up at Cindy and said in Farsi, "Cindy, I don't understand why you're acting this way, but we're here to help you. Please talk to me."

The look on Cindy's face was inexplicable. She immediately calmed down and studied Paula. Realizing she was finally listening, Paula quickly added, "You are safe with us. We want to help you. We are here to take you home."

Kegger interjected, "I'm going to check and make sure we weren't followed."

Paula nodded and refocused on Cindy.

In Farsi, Cindy asked, "How do you know me?"

"Cindy! We're best friends!" Paula replied in Farsi.

"I don't know you," Cindy responded blankly, "but I can't remember my past."

Hearing her statement, Paula began to analyze Cindy's previous behavior.

"What's the first thing you can recall?" implored Paula.

"I can only remember what's taken place since my accident. I fell down a flight of stairs and severely injured my head," explained Cindy.

"You have amnesia?" she asked animatedly, expressing more of a statement than a question. Then, more confidently, Paula concluded her analysis: "Yes, that's it! That's why you've been acting so strange."

Paula felt it was imperative that Kegger be updated. She looked at Cindy and asked, "Will you be okay for a minute? I need to tell my friend your situation."

Cindy quietly nodded.

"Okay then, I'll be right back," said Paula before hastily exiting the room.

Once Paula was gone, Cindy glanced around. She noticed the place had been remodeled into a makeshift studio apartment. For a moment, Cindy considered trying to escape, but she was hit with another pain and realized that she was in no shape to run even if they let her go.

Accepting her incarceration, Cindy worked on settling her emotions. She knew all of the stress was bad for the baby. As she considered the nature of her captors,

Cindy thought first of the large man named Kegger, who had stripped away her chador and physically kidnapped her from the market. Initially, she had felt only fear and anger towards him. However, after replaying the episode in her mind, Cindy acknowledged that the man had been willing to take a lot of abuse from her when he could have easily subdued her violent behavior by using more force. The realization that the man had exercised extreme restraint and respect for her welfare caused Cindy to reassess her opinion of him. Her fear subsided as she pondered the explanation given to her by the woman named Paula. She insisted that she and the others were there to help her, not hurt her.

Then, Cindy considered the actions taken by Paula and her statements about friendship and the rescue. Cindy recalled her initial reaction had been fear of the unknown, but now, she inexplicably felt at ease around this woman. She wasn't sure why, but the calmness and comfort were undeniable.

"Was this woman truly part of her past as she claims?" Cindy asked herself. "Maybe I should let her help me? Something is wrong with me. I can feel it."

Cindy concluded that she should cooperate with her captors, if not for herself, for the baby's sake.

Paula found Kegger intently guarding the door. Wasting no time, she hurried up to him. "She has amnesia," Paula said matter-of-factly. "That's why Cindy's been acting so crazy. She can't remember anything. I just thought I should tell you."

"Well, that explains a lot," Kegger acknowledged, "but it also complicates things."

"I know," said Paula as she stepped backward toward the bedroom, "I really need to get back to her, but now that we know what we're dealing with, we can save her without feeling guilty."

At that moment, Paula heard a muffled scream coming from behind the metal door to the studio. She glanced back at Kegger in concern and then ran to Cindy. Paula helped her through the pain, and afterward, she did another examination and discovered that Cindy was dilating.

"The baby is coming, and there is no way for us to stop it from happening," Paula told Cindy.

"But it's too early!" she responded. "I'm only six months pregnant!"

"I can't stop it. We'll do our best to save you and your baby," Paula said lovingly, "but there's no guarantee."

The blood flow had diminished, and it seemed Cindy had begun a regular labor pattern. Paula helped Cindy through the next pain cycle, and after it subsided, Paula explained why they had abducted her from the market.

Cindy listened with great interest, and between labor pains, she shared what her life had been like since she had awakened. The despair and stress she had been under for the last several months made Paula's heart ache, and the guilt of their rescue taking so long to save her made it worse.

The rounds of pain continued, and Paula tried her best to make Cindy feel safe and comfortable. To pass the time, Paula asked her more about her current life. Cindy honestly told her that the only positive thing was the baby. The prospect of being a mother had given her hope that she could still have a fulfilling life despite her circumstances.

Suddenly, Cindy began to hemorrhage again, but she was determined to keep pushing. On the last big push, she fell unconscious. The loss of blood and the energy exertion had finally overwhelmed her ability to keep fighting.

Paula wasn't about to give up. She had the infant's head and the top of the newborn's shoulders in her hands. While supporting the head, Paula forcefully slipped her fingers into the small crevices of the baby's armpits and pulled steadily until the rest of the infant's body slid through the birth canal and out onto the bed.

Paula grabbed the warm washcloth she had set by the bedside and wiped the baby off so that she could evaluate him better. It was a boy, she observed before feeling inside his mouth to clear any obstruction hindering his breathing. She patted him lovingly to make him cry, and within a second, he took his first breath.

Feeling confident that he was breathing successfully, Paula completed what tests she could recall from the post-natal checklist she was required to learn in her high school women's health class.

The infant responded positively to the tests, making Paula happy but slightly confused. She wasn't sure if her memory was accurate, but she recalled a six-month-old fetus being non-viable. It would be significantly smaller and would fail all of the newborn tests. This child, thought Paula, as she wrapped him in a pillowcase, weighed at least four or five pounds, comparable to a small full-term infant.

Paula put her curiosity aside and found a pair of scissors to cut the umbilical cord. The cord was much stronger and more challenging to cut than Paula had anticipated, but finally, she disconnected the baby from the placenta. She tied the cord as tight and as close to the newborn's tummy as she could before placing him next to Cindy.

Next came the afterbirth; Paula was much less qualified to deliver the placenta. She knew very little about it, only knowing it had to be dislodged from the uterine wall and come out of the birth canal, similar to how the baby was expelled.

Paula was able to get most, if not all, of the placenta out; however, Cindy's bleeding did not stop. It had slowed but continued to trickle out. Paula knew this was a big problem, and Cindy was in danger of dying. Paula left her momentarily to talk to Kegger.

"We need to get Cindy some help. Someone who knows what they're doing," she told Kegger in desperation, "but we can't risk taking her to the hospital. They may let her die just to cover their tracks," stressed Paula.

"Yeah, I agree, but we have to do something," he concurred.

"Think!" Paula commanded herself. "Who can help Cindy?"

As she struggled to devise a plan, a memory surfaced. Paula remembered that Zahra, an elderly lady who ran a hotel near Margoon Waterfall, was a seasoned midwife. Paula had stayed at her hotel during her first trip to Iran.

Hopeful, Paula declared, "I know what to do! There's a woman who lives about an hour and a half from here. She's experienced in delivering babies. We need to leave right now for her lodge."

Paula wrote an encrypted note to Shahin to tell him where they were headed. She taped it to the bedroom door at eye level to ensure that Shahin would see it. Once she was finished, Paula delicately picked up the tiny newborn while Kegger lifted Cindy's unconscious body.

Paula and Kegger were about to leave when Paula asked, "Should we take the first-aid kit?"

"No," responded Kegger, "it won't help Cindy, and the guys may need it."

Paula nodded and carefully opened the entry door. They carried mother and child carefully to the Jeep. Kegger laid Cindy down in the back seat while Paula got in the front seat with the infant. Paula considered calling Zahra along the way to prepare her for the shock and their arrival, but decided there was no time to locate a phone.

******

Upon arrival at Zahra's vineyard, Kegger stopped at the edge of the property. Paula got out while Kegger stayed with Cindy and the baby. She looked for any signs of trouble, but everything seemed normal. As Paula moved along the perimeter of the vineyard towards the main house, she saw that the once beautiful and heavily fruited grapevines were gone. Nothing was left but the burnt remains of a once vibrant and productive estate.

Paula thought back to when she, Shahin, and Kamal went to the lodge after Cindy had been captured by Khomeini's thugs over eight months earlier. While there, Zahra had heard that the new Islamic government had planned to ban all alcoholic beverages from being grown, sold, or allowed inside the country. They were planning a crackdown on all businesses producing alcohol, including winemakers. Just before she and her friends left the Lodge, Zahra heard Khomeini had given the official directive. He had ordered all of the country's vineyards to be burned. To ensure his decree was followed, Khomeini sent out groups of arsonists to destroy all viable vineyards.

At that time, Shahin had been optimistic that Zahra's vineyards would survive the elimination, but Zahra knew better. She told her three guests that she believed the arsonists would find her vineyard, and sadly, Zahra was right.

Paula's heart ached as she thought about the loss of a 7,000-year-old tradition and culture because of one person's beliefs, the oppressive and authoritarian ruler Ayatollah Khomeini.

Returning to the present, Paula cautiously continued her trek towards the back door of the lodge. She wanted to avoid the main entrance in case it was being watched by soldiers surveilling the area. When she arrived at the door, Paula had a decision to make; should she knock first or quietly slip inside? She chose to go in unannounced and quietly tried the doorknob. It was locked.

Paula remembered that a key was stored under the potted plant beside the door frame. She lifted the container carefully and removed the key from its hiding place. Paula disengaged the deadbolt and cautiously entered the short hallway to the kitchen. Her heart raced in anticipation of the unknown. Instantly, she could smell the familiar aroma of lamb roasting in the oven.

Paula stopped at the doorway and peered inside the kitchen. There, standing at the sink, was Zahra and another woman. They had their backs to Paula, and she could not see their faces.

"Do I say something now or wait for Zahra to be alone?" Paula asked herself.

She thought of Cindy's condition and knew the answer.

"Zahra, hi, it's me, Paula Williams. I need your help."

131

Both women turned abruptly. Shock briefly covered Zahra's face, but her expression turned to concern once she processed Paula's request.

"Cindy is alive!" exclaimed Paula. "And she's hurt."

Paula's presence and words stunned Zahra momentarily, and she dropped the utensil she was holding before rushing to embrace Paula. As she did, Zahra made a slight whimpering sound of either happiness or concern; Paula wasn't sure which.

While they hugged, Paula looked at the other woman in the kitchen. Now, it was Paula's turn to be astonished. She recognized the woman's expressive facial features from a photo she had received from Rostam. Here, in front of her, stood his wife, Kyra.

Before Paula could speak, Zahra pushed herself away from Paula's embrace and began questioning her about Cindy.

"You say Cindy's alive?"

"Yes, and there's more. She was in labor when we found her, and she has delivered her baby. The infant is okay, but Cindy is still bleeding. It's been a couple of hours, and we need your help!" explained Paula. "She's waiting in the car with the man we hired to help rescue her."

Without responding to Paula, Zahra headed towards the door.

"Where are they?" she asked frantically as she looked around outside.

"They're in the vehicle not too far from here," said Paula.

"Quickly, show me where she is," said Zahra.

"Wait! I'll get them. It'll be faster," said Paula before she took off running.

******

Kegger carried Cindy into Zahra's bedroom and laid her on the bed. Once she was in place, Kegger returned to their vehicle and drove it back to their hiding place about a quarter-mile from the house. Paula remained in the room, cradling the infant and explaining what had happened after the birth.

Zahra and Kyra listened to her explanation while focusing on Cindy. Zahra pulled up a chair while Kyra cut Cindy's blood-soaked garment from her belly.

"A piece of the placenta must still be attached to the uterus. That's what's causing the bleeding. We need to dislodge it from the uterine wall," explained Zahra.

The situation was so critical that Zahra had not bothered introducing Paula to her sister-in-law. Zahra manipulated Cindy's abdomen, trying to force any afterbirth left inside to dislodge. After several minutes of massage, the last piece of placenta separated from Cindy's womb.

"Now, all we can do is wait and hope that she has not lost too much blood," said Zahra. "We need to keep her warm. Her body will not be able to generate the heat necessary to survive. We'll heat blankets on the wood stove and then rotate them often to supply her body with new warmth."

"Is it okay if I lay her little boy down by her side? Maybe if she feels him next to her, she will fight harder to live," said Paula.

"Yes, the warmth of his body and presence may help her," said Zahra. "No one knows what types of outside stimulation can help bring someone out of unconsciousness."

Paula laid the newborn carefully down in the crevice between Cindy's arm and chest. The infant was content at first, but soon fussed to suckle. This was going to be their next problem. Where were they going to get breastmilk or formula? The small village market sometimes carried formula, but buying it would raise questions that could alert the soldiers to their presence. They were able to get the baby to drink some water, but he needed nutrition. Milk from a goat might work, but it could also cause additional problems for him.

The other women had gone to clean themselves up, leaving Paula alone in the room with Cindy and her son. Feeling powerless, Paula lay down beside Cindy and spoke softly to her friend.

"Cindy," she whispered, "please wake up. You need to feed your boy. We all need you to be strong. He needs you, and so do I."

Paula lay with them for several minutes, listening to the baby's suckling noises. Soon, the infant started to cry. The sound caused Paula's heart to break. What could she do to soothe him? She knew he needed his strength to survive, and crying would only drain him further of his energy. Paula made a decision. She carefully lifted him and placed him in the bend of her left arm. She unbuttoned her blouse and pulled up her bra. Carefully, she maneuvered the newborn's head to her breast. His little mouth found her nipple and began to nurse. Even though there was no milk, the intimacy comforted the child. After a few minutes, he fell asleep. When Kyra knocked softly on the open door, Paula was quietly rocking the infant in an old wooden chair.

"Excuse me, how's Mama and Baby doing?"

"Cindy's about the same, and as you can see, the child is finally asleep. How about you?" asked Paula.

"Okay, the shower helped. By the way, I'm Kyra, Zahra's sister-in-law. With everything happening so fast, Zahra forgot to introduce us."

"I know who you are," said Paula. "I have a picture of you. Rostam gave it to me before we headed out into the Gulf to meet the US warship. I'm so sorry about what happened to him. He was a hero, you know. If he hadn't taken control of the steering wheel, my friends and I would have been killed, too. He gave his life helping us escape."

Paula watched as Kyra's bottom lip began to quiver, and her face contorted in anguish. Then, she put her face in her hands and began to cry. At that moment, Zahra walked in; she had been listening from the hallway. Paula glanced over at her with a confused look on her face. Zahra gently put her arms around her sister-in-law and whispered comforting words in her ear. Kyra collapsed onto Zahra's shoulder, now sobbing uncontrollably. Paula observed the two women quietly as they consoled one another. Hearing some of Zahra's statements, it became apparent to Paula that they had not fully known what had happened to Rostam. Paula realized that her description of the events leading up to her rescue finally confirmed what they had feared most. Rostam was dead.

Paula laid the infant on the bed and retreated to the living room. She snuggled into a ball in an old wingback chair in the corner to reflect on their current situation and Rostam's demise. A few minutes later, Zahra came in.

"Sorry, we needed some time alone. We still held out hope that he had made it to the US," she said. "Even though we knew it was unlikely he had survived."

"Again, I'm so sorry..." Paula began before hearing the baby cry out. She and Zahra returned to the bedroom to address the issue at hand. They needed to devise a way to feed the infant breastmilk or risk him having an adverse reaction to goat's milk. With Cindy unconscious, she wasn't able to hold him to breastfeed. The three brainstormed how best to feed him. Buying baby items, including formula, would compromise their safety. There seemed to be only one option left.

Zahra got two more pillows and propped them up behind Cindy's head. With Paula on one side and Kyra on the other, they awkwardly, yet gently, pulled Cindy's torso up onto the pillows. Once she looked comfortable, Kyra carefully cut two breast flaps in her maternity dress.

Paula knelt on the bed beside Cindy while Zahra brought the infant over to his unconscious mother. Kyra lifted the left flap, allowing Paula to raise the infant to Cindy's breast. The little boy easily latched on to Cindy's large breast and finally began receiving the nutrition he needed.

******

It was late when Paula walked out to the porch. Kegger was standing at the railing, smoking a cigarette. He offered Paula one from his pack, but she declined.

"You know those things can kill you," she said comically.

"Yeah, let's hope so. That means my career choice didn't," he said satirically.

"I hope Shahin and Kamal are okay," said Paula. "They should have been here by now. That's if they could get away and back to the car."

"They probably didn't return to the car. It was most likely compromised," replied Kegger. "We were set up. Those soldiers knew we were coming. Who besides the rebel group, your families, and the guy who told you about Cindy knew our schedule?"

"I'm not sure if anyone else knew. I guess Darian could have told his roommate in Shiraz about it. He may have thought he could help us somehow," reasoned Paula.

"Do you know him?" asked Kegger.

"No, I've never met him," she replied. "I do know he's desperate for money. Darian mentioned it in one of our conversations. If they offered a reward in return for information, I suppose he could have taken the money and told them our plans."

"Well, it's done, whoever did it," said Kegger. "As for our guys, they probably had to head to our rendezvous point on foot. Even if they made it there the same day, it might take them a few days to figure out how to get here. We're not even sure they understood your encrypted message."

"Oh, they understood my message, but you're right, it's not going to be easy to get here quickly," agreed Paula. "Besides, it's not like we can go anywhere anyway. Cindy has to get better first."

"Not to change subjects, but..." Kegger paused. "Ya know, you're pretty good at this stuff."

"What do you mean exactly?" questioned Paula.

"When I saw you at the training exercises for this mission, I knew you had good reflexes. Your instincts, however, are better than I expected. We could use someone like you on our team. Especially now that Jake is...," Kegger stopped short of saying what he thought, just in case he was wrong. "He always said that being alone in this business would make it easier for his friends."

"How does him being alone make it easier for you guys?" asked Paula.

"You know, not having a family, we don't have to worry about contacting anyone. He's single, and his parents are both gone. He does have a brother, but they're not close. It won't matter if I tell him months from now."

"If Jake is ... gone, will you miss him?"

"Yeah, of course," said Kegger. "He wasn't just my co-worker. He was a good friend."

"Then he did have family who cared, just not blood-related," Paula said warmly.

"I guess that's true," Kegger agreed.

"You know," said Paula, "after seeing what you do firsthand, I realize just how dangerous your job actually is, but I guess you guys know that."

"Yeah, we know," responded Kegger.

They spoke for a few more minutes about Jake's presumed passing, and then Paula said goodnight and went back inside to check on Cindy.

Chapter 17 - At the Camp

After several minutes of waiting, the lieutenant finally reached the commander on the CB radio.

"Sir, we have three hostages and one man who was fatally wounded by our team of soldiers."

"Where are the rest?" he asked angrily.

"Unfortunately, sir, the women, and an unknown man got away. He's most likely a mercenary," the soldier reasoned. "The good news is that we think one of the men we have in custody is Shahin Ali, and the other is his friend Kamal Ahmad. The third man we have and the dead man look like mercenaries, most likely hired by the Ali boy's father."

"Have you questioned them about the others?" asked Commander Rashidi.

"Yes, sir, they're not talking," the soldier replied.

"Eventually, I want them brought up here to my base near Tehran, but for now, I want you to take them to the camp near Yasuj. My interrogator is on his way there now. Do what he says and get him anything he needs. Also, another crucial thing you need to do is search them for a key. Not their car key, but something small, most likely to open a small box. It's vitally important that you secure the key and bring it to me along with the hostages when my interrogator is finished with them."

"Yes, Sir!" said the lieutenant before clicking off the radio.

The man walked over to Shahin and began to pat down his body. He felt every inch of Shahin's clothes, but he was clean. Annoyed, he walked over and searched Kamal, Stevie, and the dead man.

After finding nothing on them, he forcefully asked, "So, where are you hiding it?"

Shahin, Kamal, and Stevie looked at the soldier in bewilderment.

"Hiding what?" asked Shahin.

"You're supposed to be carrying a key. Where is it?"

Shahin and Kamal looked at each other, shrugged at one another, and then looked at Stevie.

"Don't look at me," he said innocently. "I don't know what this guy is talking about."

The three returned to stare back at the soldier.

"We don't know anything about a key except the one for the Land Rover, and you already have that," said Shahin. "I saw a soldier take it from Stevie's pocket and give it to your soldiers to search our vehicle."

A moment later, two soldiers ran up to the lieutenant and said, "Sir, we have checked out the car, and there's nothing inside it. Raja is driving it to our base now for further inspection."

Frustrated, the lieutenant barked out his next orders, "I've had enough. Load the prisoners into the transport truck."

In response, Shahin spoke up, "Please, my friend is going to die if we don't stop his leg from bleeding! Then, you'll only have two prisoners."

Rolling his eyes, the lieutenant motioned to one of his privates to unlock Shahin's handcuffs so that he could attend to the wounded mercenary.

"I'm glad Kegger gave you some first aid training," said Stevie as Shahin removed his belt and wrapped it around Stevie's thigh to slow the bleeding.

Next, Shahin took off his shirt and rolled it lengthwise to use as a bandage. He placed the cloth on the wound first and then tied the ends around Stevie's leg. When he was finished, the lieutenant ordered his subordinate to re-cuff Shahin before loading the three men into the middle seat of a military transport truck.

Kamal got in first, followed by Shahin. Stevie was last in. He solicited the help of the private to step up into the vehicle while moaning loudly throughout the event.

The three prisoners watched as the soldier monitoring them struggled to lock the car door next to Stevie. He pushed and shoved on the latch, but it would not stay securely fastened. Finally, the man decided it was good enough, especially with an injured man sitting beside the door. He quickly walked around to the driver and told him the prisoners were loaded and ready for transport. Then, he opened the door to the bench seat behind the three captives and got in.

The lieutenant finished his conversation with another of his soldiers and stepped into the front seat next to the driver, who was busily buttoning down a heavy, clear plastic separator to muffle the sound between the front and back seats. Once his work was complete, he started the engine and put the truck in gear.

Anxious to discover who was behind their capture, Kamal tilted his head back and asked the guard, "So, how did you know we'd be at the market? It's obvious someone set us up."

"Yeah, you need to pick better friends," the soldier joked.

"What do you mean by that?" asked Shahin.

"You Shah lovers screw each other like the Shah screwed us," the man boasted. "He told us you'd be there sometime this week to find an American woman. So, we set up an ambush and waited for you to walk into it."

"Darian! That bastard! I'm going to kill him when I see him," Kamal raged.

"Darian? No, that wasn't the guy's name," said the soldier. "I think he said his name was Yousif."

"You saw him? He was here in Iran?" asked Kamal disbelievingly.

"Yeah," said the soldier, sounding confused and uncertain as to why Kamal sounded so surprised, "about two weeks ago."

"What did the guy look like?" asked Shahin.

"You know, fat guy with brown hair and a full beard," he replied before bragging about how much he knew about the meeting. "I heard he was paid handsomely for the intel."

Shahin leaned over and whispered to Kamal.

"That sounds like Darian's friend. You know, the guy he lived with after he left me and the girls. Plus, Darian's in New York."

"Yeah, so maybe it wasn't him," Kamal relented, "but he shouldn't have told anyone about our mission, not even his old roommate."

"I'm sure Darian didn't know he would stab us in the back," said Shahin. "He was probably excited to share the news that we were finally going to do something to help Cindy."

"Yeah, but he should never have trusted him," added Kamal.

As the truck rumbled down a jarring portion of the city streets, Stevie observed that the door was becoming looser. He nudged Shahin and nodded slightly before averting his eyes towards the door. Shahin acknowledged his understanding by returning the gesture. Shahin elbowed Kamal softly before giving him a sideways glance. Kamal returned an expression of confusion and uncertainty. Shahin's green eyes made contact with Kamal's gaze a second time, and he led Kamal's attention to the jiggling door. It took a moment, but soon, Kamal gave Shahin a slight nod, relaying his understanding of what was coming next.

They entered an urban slum filled with homeless people lying openly on the street or in makeshift shelters to keep the blistering sun off of them. To add to the disorder and confusion, many vendors were selling items from small carts and dilapidated stalls. Those who had permanent lodging had laundry covering most of their balconies. All of these things created an area that could easily conceal a person. A few seconds later, the vehicle made a sharp left turn, and the centrifugal force caused the door to fly open. Stevie saw his opportunity and immediately jumped out and rolled to a stop.

Ignoring his injured leg, Stevie jumped up and began to run into the crowded encampment. Shahin and Kamal followed him as the truck screeched to a halt. At the time, the commander was talking to the lieutenant on his walkie-talkie.

"What's happening!" yelled the lieutenant to his guard as he turned to look behind him. When he saw the prisoners escaping, he shouted, "Get them!"

The guard jumped out and quickly headed towards the prisoners.

"What the hell is going on there!" insisted Commander Rashidi.

"Sir, the prisoners jumped out!" He shouted before dropping the walkie-talkie and grabbing his weapon.

The wounded mercenary had jumped out fifty yards back and was already out of sight. Shahin and Kamal were much closer because it had taken them longer to scoot to the edge of the seat before leaping onto the street below. The lieutenant and the guard were upon them a second later with their guns drawn. Holding them at gunpoint, the lieutenant quickly ordered Shahin and Kamal to return to the vehicle. The commander was still on the radio, barking out orders and demanding to know what had happened.

"Do you have them back in custody?" he yelled.

The driver grabbed the radio and spoke calmly to the commander while the lieutenant and his subordinate forced Shahin and Kamal to get in the vehicle.

"Yes, we have two of them," he reported, "but the wounded man escaped into the streets."

"Why didn't the escort truck go after him?" the officer bellowed.

"Sir, he stopped to let a crippled woman get across the road. He'll be here shortly," the driver explained.

"He's not with you?" questioned the commander. "You idiots! Radio them now and tell them to search the area. He's injured, right?" he bellowed. "It shouldn't take long to find him."

"Yes, sir," said the man obediently. "I'll call them now."

"Listen to me first! I want the other two prisoners brought here as soon as the interrogator gets the information out of them," Commander Rashidi barked. "Now call the escort!"

"Yes, sir," the man said and clicked off the signal.

He radioed the second truck just as it pulled up behind him. He quickly explained what had happened and told them to find the escapee as ordered by the commander himself. When they were clear about their mission, he pointed to the location where the mercenary disappeared.

******

When they arrived at the camp, Shahin and Kamal noticed it looked hastily built. The buildings were tent-like structures, except for a few permanent ones peppered throughout the encampment. The fencing was better, but it also looked temporary. Shahin and Kamal quickly found out that one of the concrete buildings near the entrance had been converted into a jail.

The air inside the interrogation room was thick with moisture and smelled like musty swamp water. In the corner of the room, a short stack of water tubs rested next to a hose and faucet. Next to them were some pieces of cut-up rope.

In the center of the room, a single light bulb hung from the ceiling, and four feet on either side of it were heavy ropes dangling down from wooden beams. On the end of each rope was a large, heavy hook. Two small windows allowed yellowish rays of the setting sun to radiate into the otherwise dimly lit room.

Two soldiers brought Shahin and Kamal into the room while a guard with a machine gun stood by to make sure their prisoners didn't cause any trouble. Two wooden chairs were sitting under each hook. The first soldier grabbed Kamal by the arm and led him to the far chair while the other took Shahin to the closer seat. They ripped open the men's shirts and pulled them down to their wrists. Next, they stripped the men down to their underwear and removed their socks and boots. One of the men picked up all of the items and threw them in the corner of the room. The other soldier forced Shahin down on the chair before slipping his tied wrists behind the back of the chair. He did the same thing to Kamal and told his comrade that the men were ready. The other soldier nodded and left the room.

For over an hour, Shahin and Kamal waited for something else to happen. Finally, the soldier returned with a tall, lanky man dressed in a white doctor's coat.

"Sorry," the thin man said to Shahin and Kamal. "I was delayed. You can address me as Dr. Sway. I got the name because I am excellent at persuasion."

"You're British?" Kamal stated in the form of a question.

"Yes, does that surprise you?" wondered the doctor.

"Well, yeah," responded Kamal. "How come you're helping Khomeini?"

"My dear boy, money, of course," Dr. Sway replied arrogantly, "but I digress. Shall we get started?"

The soldiers patiently waited for the doctor to address them. Finally, he turned and spoke to the three men. "You," he said to the larger soldier, "I may need your help. It's all going to depend on how much cooperation I get." He paused momentarily and then said to the more petite man, "There's no need for you to stick around. We have this handled."

"Yes, sir," he replied before saluting and leaving the room.

"You can stand back here," he said to the guard with the machine gun. "I don't want you to get in my way."

Dr. Sway refocused his attention on Shahin and Kamal. He smiled an evil grin before saying, "This can be easy and only slightly unpleasant, or it can be excruciatingly painful. You boys need to make a choice." He approached Shahin first and asked cooly, "Tell me, where are the others in your group hiding out?"

Shahin looked at him in defiance and said, "I'm not telling you anything."

The doctor turned around and motioned for his assistant to come over.

"Give him your best shot," he said politely.

"Yes, sir," said the soldier and stepped up to Shahin.

"Last chance before the unpleasantness begins," Dr. Sway announced.

"As I said, I'm not telling you anything," Shahin said boldly.

The large man looked back at the doctor, who nodded his go-ahead. The man hurled around and planted his fist into Shahin's jaw. Shahin's head flew back and to one side. His chair rocked backward, almost tipping over from the force. Blood quickly began to seep out of the corner of Shahin's mouth as his head returned to its center position.

"That's just a preview of what's to come if you don't tell me what I want to know," said the torturer.

"Go to hell!" yelled Shahin. "I'll never give up my friends."

Dr. Sway looked at the soldier and gave him another nod. He punched Shahin again, this time hitting him with an uppercut to the abdomen. Shahin grunted and bent over in pain before gasping for air. When his lungs refilled, Shahin responded gruffly, "No, I won't tell you."

"Again," said the doctor.

The soldier took a deep breath and targeted Shahin's gut a second time.

Shahin groaned loudly but offered no response to his request.

"Again, and this time, make it a double punch to his gut," said Sway.

When Shahin recovered enough to be able to speak, the torturer asked, "Now, don't you have something you want to tell me?"

Shahin was silent. Instead, he looked defiantly up at the doctor.

Annoyed with Shahin's insolence, Sway walked over to Kamal.

"You've seen what happened to your friend. It will be just as bad or worse for you," he said calmly. "So, I'm going to ask you. Where are the women?"

"Like Shahin, I'm not talking," said Kamal smugly.

Doctor Sway looked over at his assistant and gave him the green light. Again, without saying a word, the soldier landed a strike squarely on Kamal's jaw. The force was extreme, and it caused Kamal's chair to tip sideways. So much so that instead of the chair returning to the ground like Shahin's, it tipped over on its side. Kamal's shoulder hit the floor with a resounding thud, but luckily, he kept his head from striking the concrete.

The doctor noticed the thick, chiseled abdomen of Kamal and knew he would be able to sustain many punches to the gut before it would really hurt him. Irritated, he said, "I don't have time for this," and motioned to the guard holding the gun. "Help him pick up the prisoner."

Both soldiers bent down and lifted the chair upright with Kamal still in it.

"So, we have two strong, virtuous men. Is that it?" he said sarcastically. "We'll see how self-righteous and determined you really are if you don't tell me what I want to know."

Suddenly, Shahin yelled, "Only two people know our meeting place. It's the leader of the mercenaries and his second-in-command. Your soldiers already killed the head guy, and the other one got away."

Playing along with Shahin's lie, Kamal added, "Yeah, we're not the professionals. We just follow their orders. They actually said that we would squeal if we got caught, and that's why they weren't going to tell us any details."

Disbelievingly, the doctor said, "Okay, I've had enough of this. Corporal, bring in the machine."

The soldier promptly obeyed the command, and within minutes, he and another man were wheeling in an electric shock machine.

Shahin gave Kamal an alarming look, and Kamal worriedly returned the stare.

Doctor Sway smiled menacingly at the two men before giving them an ultimatum.

"Well, boys, tell me the truth, or we begin this new form of persuasion," he said coolly.

Kamal and Shahin sat silent, neither willing to give up the location of their friends.

After waiting only a few seconds, the torturer ordered his helper to prepare the prisoners.

"Retie their hands in front and use the pieces rope to bind their feet together."

"This isn't very secure," said the soldier after tying Shahin's ankles. I can't get it very tight."

"It's not important," said the doctor. "Now stand them up and place their wrist ties over the hooks. Make sure the height is right. I want his arms to be taut and both men on their toes."

"Yes, sir," said the helper.

Kamal's rope height was good, but the soldier needed to adjust the height of Shahin's rope due to his taller stature. While he did so, the doctor put on rubber boots and said, "You need to be careful around water and electricity. Make sure you stand back when I'm persuading our guests to talk."

"I will, sir," he replied.

"While I test the paddles, I want you to hose them down," the doctor told his assistant. "The water adds an extra bit of conductivity and makes the current travel throughout their body better," he explained. "It usually speeds up the interrogation." His description, while directed at the soldier assisting him, caused the guard with the machine gun to feel uncomfortable.

"Sir, I should monitor the outside door," he said authoritatively. "Someone could sneak into the small lobby, and we'd never know it." He added boldly, "Plus, the other guys might come in to see what's going on if they hear a lot of screaming."

"Are you sure it's about the other guys?" laughed the doctor. "Or is it that you don't want to watch?"

"Maybe both, sir," the guard sheepishly admitted.

"Then, go!" Sway insisted. "I don't want you vomiting or passing out. I have enough things to worry about."

The man thanked him, and he quickly exited the room.

"This machine is acting up again," Dr. Sway complained as he tried to regulate the voltage. "If I shock them with the power this high, I'll kill them both right away. When you're done hosing them down, I want you to come over and adjust the dial. It's finicky, but I will tell you when to stop turning it."

"Yes, sir," responded the assistant. "I just have to get this one's chest again and then I'll be right there."

Suddenly, a violent tremor rocked the temporary camp. The powerful jolt caused the doctor to lurch forward while still holding the electrified paddles. He stumbled a few steps before falling hands-first into the puddles of water surrounding Shahin and Kamal. Immediately, the electricity surged up the arms of the doctor and into his body, causing him to stiffen and jerk uncontrollably. A split second later, the current moved through the puddles and up the water stream to the hose.

The soldier holding the nozzle teetered at the puddle's edge but did not step into the water. Unfortunately for him, he had gripped the metal fitting of the tube with his hand to force the jet of water to lengthen. When the electricity that had traveled up the stream came in contact with his fingers, it quickly continued into the soldier's body. Searing pain caused the man to step forward into the water as he tried to regain his balance. Now, both men were encircled by the electrical currents. They heaved and grunted from the agonizing pain as the electricity coursing through their bodies eventually caused their hearts to stop.

Simultaneously, when the tremors hit, Shahin and Kamal were yanked slightly upward as the building's movement caused their ropes to swing and lift them away from the ground. Instinctively, they lifted their feet, fortuitously avoiding the electricity surging through the doctor and his assistant. The guard outside heard the commotion and came running into the room.

Seeing his friend and the doctor in pain, he ignorantly rushed over to help them. As he did, the guard tripped on the electrified cables and fell into the water beside the doctor. Instantly, he, too, was engulfed in the high-voltage currents.

Luckily for Shahin and Kamal, the doctor's rigid fingers were still gripping the electrical paddles when the guard tripped, causing the shock machine to fall onto the hard concrete floor. The impact caused the housing to crack open slightly, but the machine continued to send high volts of electricity through the lines and into the water and men.

"Hang on, Kamal!" yelled Shahin while holding his feet up and slowly swinging back and forth. "Don't touch the water!"

"I'm not!" Kamal yelled back as he swung in the same direction as Shahin. "Try and get your feet released. The rope is pretty loosely tied."

Shahin and Kamal pulled their legs up and down, working their ropes loose. A minute more went by, and Shahin's abdomen was fatiguing. "I don't know how much longer I can keep my feet up!" he announced worriedly. "Those punches to the gut really weakened my stomach muscles."

"You have to!" Kamal fervently insisted. "Sooner or later, it'll stop! You've got to hang on!"

"I'm trying!" Shahin yelled back.

"I'm going to try and swing to you," said Kamal. "When I get close, use what energy you have left to wrap your legs around me. It will rest your stomach muscles and make your legs work instead."

Kamal rocked his body back and forth, making his rope move toward Shahin.

"Can you swing closer to me?" Kamal pleaded. "I'm not sure if my rope will go all the way to you. Plus, it'll make it easier for you to lift your legs to me."

The oscillating movement caused by the quake was almost gone, and Shahin did not have the strength to swing himself closer to his friend.

"I can't!" Shahin shouted discouragingly. "I don't have the strength!"

"You swore to your mother you'd come home!" shouted Kamal. "Remember, you vowed to do everything possible to survive!"

Kamal's statements made Shahin think about the promise to his mother and the grief he would cause her if he didn't keep his word. The thought of it moved something inside of him that was stronger than pain or weakness itself, and he found the strength to maneuver toward Kamal. He began to swing his legs back and forth, using his arms and upper body to assist his damaged abdomen.

"I will keep my promise," he repeated silently to himself as he forced his body to perform.

The two men were almost close enough for Shahin to wrap his legs around Kamal when the shock machine suddenly stopped. Finally, enough water had seeped in through the cracked casing to short-circuit the electrical wiring.

Shahin and Kamal looked at one another and smiled broadly. Relief flooded through them, and for a moment, their problems had disappeared. A second later, the reality of their situation came back into focus, and they knew the danger was not over. They agreed to wait another few seconds before letting their feet touch the ground.

Once Kamal's toes contacted the hard concrete surface, he pushed himself toward his chair, which was lying on its side just a few feet away. He hooked the rung of the chair with the top of his foot and pulled it closer. Next, he awkwardly stood on top of it to gain extra height. This made it easy for him to remove his wrists from the hanging hook.

Kamal knelt next to the burned and tortured body of the soldier and began to search cumbersomely for something to cut through his bindings while Shahin anxiously watched.

"Try the doctor's coat!" said Shahin. "I saw him put a knife in his front pocket."

Kamal bent down and forced his bound hands into one of the large pockets of the torturer's lab coat.

"Here!" he said happily and lifted a knife into view.

Kamal fumbled with the blade, but finally turned it around and began to saw the plastic strap that held his wrists together. Seconds later, the tie fell away. Kamal immediately ran to Shahin. Kamal grabbed him by his torso and lifted Shahin's body up high enough for him to disengage his tied wrists from the hook.

While Kamal was slicing through the plastic binding holding Shahin's wrists, he said, "I don't think we have much time before someone comes in to check on us."

"Yeah, they could come any moment," agreed Shahin.

The tie fell away from Shahin's wrists, and he quickly gave Kamal a gratuitous grin before saying, "Now, let's get the hell out of here!"

"You check outside," ordered Kamal, "while I get their guns and our clothes."

Shahin nodded and hurried to check outside. After peeking through a window in the small front office, Shahin cautiously opened the door and watched the chaotic scene unfolding inside the camp. A fire had broken out, and the place was in disarray. He saw the entry guard and his armed assistant running past the jail to help fight the blaze. The backup generators hadn't turned on, so the only light source in the camp was coming from the increasingly taller flames.

Meanwhile, Kamal quickly rushed over and put on his jeans and boots. Next, he went to the dead men. He searched all three burned bodies for weapons and money. While looking, he found a wad of rials in the doctor's wallet and a second knife and handgun on one of the soldiers. He stuffed the money in his front pocket and jammed the weapons into the back pockets of his jeans.

He was gathering the machine gun and rifle when Shahin tapped him on the shoulder, "We need to go as soon as I get dressed! They're all busy putting out a fire."

Shahin and Kamal peered out and saw that everyone seemed to be battling the blaze. They cautiously exited the building and ran warily towards the vehicles parked near the camp entrance. Suddenly, Shahin noticed that the truck that had transported them to the camp was still parked in the same spot. He recalled seeing the driver take the key out of the ignition and place it under the seat. Excited at the prospect, Shahin opened the vehicle door and stuck his hand into the darkness.

At first, all he felt was dirt and pebbles, but as he continued to search, his hand fell upon a small metal object.

"Got it!" he whispered eagerly, pulling the key out. "Kamal, you go to the other side, and we'll push the truck through the gate."

Kamal heard his directive and hurried around to the passenger side.

The inferno roared as Shahin and Kamal pushed the vehicle past the entrance gate and out into the desert.

"Okay, that should be far enough," said Shahin when they were 20 meters from the camp.

The two quietly slipped into the front seat, but before Shahin turned the ignition switch, he stopped and asked, "You agree, right? It's safe to start the engine."

"Yeah, I think so," said Kamal. "Between the noise of the fire and all the yelling, they're not going to hear the motor."

Feeling reassured, Shahin turned the key. The engine rumbled to life. Shahin hastily put the truck in gear while Kamal watched intently for any signs of pursuit.

Chapter 18 - Searching

Kyra took several minutes to weep and grieve for her dead husband. Even though she had suspected he had been killed, trying to help Paula and her friends escape. The confirmation caused her more of an emotional response than she had expected.

Finally, Kyra composed herself enough to ask Paula to share the details of his death.

"Rostam sacrificed his life for me and my friends," Paula explained gratuitously. "He was a true hero."

"What happened? Kyra asked so softly that Paula felt worried that she might cause Kyra to have another emotional breakdown. Awkwardly, Paula resumed telling her the story leading up to his fatal injury.

"Well, how it happened was... Well, he tried to hide from the bullets. We all did," Paula explained, "but the boat was veering away from the U.S. Navy ship. To get it back on course, Rostam stood up to steer us back toward the ship. That's when the bullets struck him."

Kyra looked at Paula mournfully as tears formed again and slowly trickled down her face.

"I'm so sorry," said Paula. "I wish I could have done more to help him. It all happened so fast. The medical team on the ship did everything they could to save his life, but they said the rounds that hit him were large-caliber bullets, and the damage was too extensive. I don't know what to say except, *I'm sorry*," added Paula, as she, too, became emotional.

Finally, Kyra spoke, "It's not your fault. He knew the risks when he accepted the job. I was angry at first, but I have learned to accept his decision. Zahra has helped me through my grief, and I am finally in a better place these past few months. When he didn't return, I quickly packed a suitcase and left my house. I assumed the government would figure out that Rostam was the one who helped you escape. I knew they might check Zahra's place, but I didn't know where else to turn. She has protected me from them, and I greatly appreciate all she has done."

"Tell me more about Rostam," pleaded Paula. "I'd like to know more about the man who saved me."

Kyra smiled and shared the story of how they met.

"I was only eighteen when I met him; he was thirty-eight. Back then, he was so handsome," she said bluntly. "Shortly after we met, I decided I wanted him for my husband, and I knew he wanted me. Besides his good looks, he was so kind and giving."

"I felt his kindness right away," Paula agreed, "and his love for you was very apparent."

"When he decided to help you, he knew our lives here were over, and I know he was trying to find a way out," Kyra elaborated. "Paula, I'm in a very unsafe situation here, and so is Zahra because of me. We're constantly watching for soldiers, and it's scary and exhausting. They have been here twice, and luckily, I was able to hide from them," explained Kyra.

"I know from experience that it's a horrible way to live," said Paula, empathetically. Even though she had no authority, Paula offered, "Would you want to go with us to the border? I know it's risky, but at least you won't have to live in fear of capture."

"Yes," said Kyra promptly, "take me with you. I promise I will not be any trouble. Plus, I can help Cindy and the baby."

Hesitating only slightly, Paula responded, "You know it will be dangerous, maybe even more dangerous than staying here. Especially now that the authorities know we're in Iran. They'll be hunting us."

"I know, but I cannot continue to live like this, nor can I continue to put my sister-in-law in danger. It's not fair to her."

"I know. She told me she wants to sell the lodge and live with her friend, a widow in the nearby village. She said they can share expenses and live comfortably for the rest of their lives."

At that moment, Zahra walked in. "Please, Zahra, tell her how bad it is here for you and me," Kyra pleaded.

Zahra nodded and turned to Paula, "I didn't tell you everything earlier because I didn't think it was necessary. The truth is that my business has suffered since the revolution, and I am not making any money. Instead, I am losing money every month trying to keep the lodge open. If I sell, my friend and I will have plenty of money to buy whatever we need. Unfortunately, she only has a two-bedroom home, and honestly, it would be no life for Kyra to hide out with us. She deserves a new start."

Paula nodded, saying, "I know she's not safe here. Kyra is welcome to come with us. It's the least I can offer."

Paula went to Kyra and reached out her hand. Kyra responded to her gesture by shaking it and nodding, acknowledging their agreement.

******

It had been two days since Cindy had fallen into unconsciousness. Everyone but Paula was beginning to lose hope that she would ever recover.

"Anything new?" Paula asked optimistically.

"No, dear, I'm afraid not," responded Zahra.

"I think her color is returning," said Paula. "I notice her face has more color even from 4:00 a.m. this morning."

Zahra smiled at Paula, trying to embrace her optimism as she put on her chador. They needed supplies, and Zahra was the only one who could be seen in the village. When she entered the town, she saw a convoy of soldiers pull up in front of the supply store. Zahra quickly turned around and headed back home.

Zahra ran into the house and told the others what she had seen. All took immediate action. Kyra led the way down into the secret wine cellar. Kegger followed, carrying Cindy, while Paula helped Zahra put away any evidence of their existence. When she felt confident that they had removed everything damning, Paula picked up the infant boy and carried him into the cellar. Zahra stayed upstairs in the kitchen to wait for the men to arrive. Moments later, a soldier burst through the back door.

"Good morning, ma'am; sorry to intrude," the soldier said superficially. "However, I need to search the premises," he added, maniacally grinning as he motioned for the other troops to enter the house.

He stood just above Paula and the others in the cellar while he waited for the search to be completed. Zahra stayed with him, all the while trying to make small talk. After searching all the buildings, Paula could hear a soldier enter the room.

"Sir, no sign of them or anyone else. It looks just like the description given to us by the previous team looking for the traitor's wife."

"Did you check the wine cellar?"

"Yes, sir, it was empty except for some jarred food," replied the soldier.

"Okay, then, let's move out," said the sergeant disappointedly.

Just as he began his apology to Zahra for the inconvenience, Cindy began to awake. She was about to scream when Paula covered her mouth and adamantly shook her head, "NO!".

The incident made some slight noises, and a second later, they heard the sergeant say, "Did you hear something?"

Everyone in the cellar heard the sergeant's question and froze.

After a short pause, the soldier standing in the doorway responded, "No, sir, I didn't hear anything except for the guys outside."

"Funny, I thought I heard something," he said questioningly.

Thinking quickly, Zahra said, "I was fidgeting with my fingernails. I know it's a bad habit, but I can't seem to break it. That's probably what you heard."

"Quiet, everyone," he demanded.

They stood in silence for several moments, listening for anything unusual. Nothing could be heard except the distant voices of the men waiting by the truck. Finally, the sergeant's suspicions were sufficiently alleviated, and he and the rest of his squad left the house. Zahra watched them drive away, and when she felt comfortable that the soldiers were gone, she knocked on the floor to notify her hidden guests.

Paula said in Farsi, "You're safe. We'll protect you from the soldiers, but you have to trust us."

Cindy nodded "yes", signaling she was willing to cooperate.

Carefully, Paula removed her hand from Cindy's mouth, saying softly in English, "I wish you knew how much I love you. You'd know I would never hurt you."

Paula looked down at her fragile and lost friend and smiled warmly, trying to hide her deep sadness. Then, uncertainty overtook her, and she thought, "How are we ever going to escape Iran with Cindy so compromised?"

Chapter 19 - Afterwards

"That's the all-clear signal from Zahra," said Kyra. Still whispering, Paula said to Kegger, "It sounds like they're gone. Why don't you head up and check out the grounds? Make sure they didn't leave someone behind to report anything unusual."

Kegger nodded and released his hold on Cindy's arms. Before Paula could say anything else to Cindy, she said softly to Paula, "I, I... understand you. You're speaking English. How do I know this language?" Cindy asked rhetorically.

Surprised, Paula looked down at her in disbelief, "You remember me?"

"No," responded Cindy, "but I understand your language."

"Well, that's a start," said Paula optimistically. "Maybe it means you'll get your full memory back soon."

"My baby! Where's my baby!" Cindy cried, getting her bearings.

"He's here, right here," said Kyra as she brought the infant to Cindy.

"Let me help you," said Paula, taking Cindy with both hands to help her sit up.

"Is he okay?" said Cindy anxiously. "I thought he might not survive."

"He's perfect. Are you sure you were only six months pregnant?" asked Paula.

"Maybe six and a half, but no more than that," answered Cindy.

"All clear!" announced Kegger as he descended the stairs. "Everyone can come up now."

Kyra took the infant from Cindy before Kegger and Paula helped her to her feet. Next, Paula took both of her hands and led Cindy slowly up the stairs while Kegger followed behind, basically lifting her weakened body as they ascended.

When Cindy was settled back in bed, with her back propped up and support pillows on her lap, Kyra returned the baby to her arms.

******

Cindy was still very weak and gladly accepted Paula's help, holding her son while he drank from her breast. Later, after the baby was fed and sleeping, Cindy asked Paula if she would tell her more about their friendship and what Paula knew about Cindy's childhood. Paula had just begun explaining how they met when Cindy interrupted.

"None of what you say makes any sense," Cindy said in bewilderment. "I was told I grew up here, in Iran, and that I am married to Kevah. They told me my name is Yasmin."

"No, like I said, your name is not Yasmin. It's Cindy. You're an American woman and my best friend, and you're not married to anyone."

"I'm so confused," Cindy responded blankly. "When I woke up from my head injury, I was told I was married to a middle-aged businessman."

"Someone has lied to you," Paula retorted.

"Why?" asked Cindy.

"Maybe it was to protect you, or maybe it was to exploit you," reasoned Paula.

"I was told I got married in January, and before that, I was a domestic worker for over a year for a family that moved between Tehran and Shiraz," Cindy told them.

"That's a lie," said Paula. "You were with me up until the fourth of November. We tried to take refuge inside the US Embassy on that day. We didn't know the students had taken it over. A Khomeini soldier saw you near the compound and tried to take you into custody. You fought back, and he struck you with the butt of his gun. They told us all that you were dead, but Darian, a guy who knows you, saw you in the market and told me about it."

"So that's why the soldiers came to the doctor's house," Cindy mumbled.

"What?" asked Paula.

"Sorry," Cindy explained, "when I was recovering from my injury, a group of soldiers came looking for me. A doctor and his housekeeper lied to keep them from finding out that I was there and still alive."

"The doctor must have taken you out of the hospital," Paula concluded. "He must be the one who saved your life."

Cindy digested Paula's conclusion and mumbled, "What you're saying makes some sense to me. It's been confusing and uncomfortable for me since I woke up. I don't feel anything for Kaveh."

Cindy thought back to when she first met her so-called husband. At first, he had been very kind and understanding. However, two weeks after they arrived in Shiraz, he demanded full sexual relations with her. Cindy, politely but firmly, told him that she was still too weak and injured to have sex. Reluctantly, he relented and gave her two weeks to recover fully. On the fifteenth day, he insisted that they have intercourse. Cindy told Paula that whatever sexual feelings she was supposed to have had for Kaveh before the accident had vanished since she awoke. She added that the emptiness and loneliness she endured daily made it hard for her to believe that she had ever felt love for Kaveh.

Cindy momentarily recalled her life in Shiraz. Many nights, she lay awake silently crying. Her lack of love for her husband had left her feeling hopeless and trapped. In the early months of her recovery, Cindy had thought about running away, but then she realized that she was pregnant and it would be impossible for her to leave Kaveh in her condition. Cindy decided then that she must make the best of her situation and accept that it was permanent.

"Now," Cindy thought angrily, "this strange woman is telling me my so-called husband has lied to me about our marriage and who I really am."

At first, Cindy felt overwhelmed with these new revelations, but soon a wave of hope and freedom swept over her. "Can I believe her?" Cindy questioned. "Could it be true?"

As Cindy thought more about her life with Kaveh, anger rose within her, and she blurted out, "Why would he do this to me? So, I could give him a child? That's such an awful thing to do."

"I'm not sure," replied Paula. "Can you remember anything that I've told you?"

"No, I'm sorry, I still have no recollection of my past," she said sadly.

"That's okay, at least you know the truth about who you are. I can tell you a lot more about your life. Maybe it will help you remember, but if not, we'll just start over from here," said Paula as she reached out and gently squeezed Cindy's hand.

Cindy asked Paula to tell her more, so Paula explained who Zahra was and told her the story about their rock-sampling trip and Cindy's deep appreciation for Zahra's convictions. Cindy listened intently and tried to recall this part of her past. She could not raise any image of Zahra in her mind.

"I'm sorry, I don't know who she is," she said regrettably.

Paula smiled lovingly at Cindy as a tear spilled out of her watery eyes and onto her cheek. "It's okay. You don't need to remember for us to love you. I promise I will always be here for you. It doesn't matter if you regain your memory or not. Right now, you just need to trust me. I am your best friend in the whole world, and I will do anything to protect you."

Even though she could not recall her past, Cindy felt an innate kinship with this unknown woman named Paula.

"It may be crazy of me, but I do trust you," Cindy said reassuringly. "As I told you, I never felt any love for my husband. My life with him seemed very unfamiliar and strange to me. With you, I have a different feeling. It's a kind of comfort even though I don't know you. For the first time since I woke up, I feel like things are going to be okay."

"We'll take things one step at a time. You have to tell me if anything I do or say makes you uncomfortable," said Paula. "Please, I don't care how minor it seems. We have to be completely honest with one another."

"Thanks, Paula," replied Cindy. "It's so scary not to know your past. I don't know who to trust, but the fact that I understand you and didn't even know that I spoke English tells me that my husband and his brother have hidden my true identity. They both seemed like such good guys. I'm not sure why they did it."

"Honestly, Cindy, I think the doctor is the one who saved your life. Their deception could have started by trying to protect you, but the bastard saying you were his wife, that sucks. I'm pretty sure he just wanted sex."

"Let's not talk about them anymore," said Cindy. "I want to hear more about my life. How did we meet?"

Paula began with their first meeting in their dormitory at college. As she told Cindy about their lives together and friendship, Cindy asked several questions and voraciously inhaled Paula's words and descriptions. Paula thought it was fascinating as she watched Cindy take in each word and try to imagine herself doing the things that Paula had described. She could see that Cindy was thirsty for the truth and her past. When Paula finished explaining their friendship, she went on to talk about Kamal and Cindy's relationship. Paula continued by conveying the details of the events leading up to their rescue plan and why they took her by force.

Knowing how she acted during her liberation, Cindy couldn't help but make a comment, "I hit the guy grabbing me pretty hard. Kegger, is that his name? I hope he didn't take it personally."

"No, but we didn't know why you were fighting. Knowing about the amnesia would have helped," Paula said almost jokingly.

The levity in her comment made both women smile, giving them their first new memory together.

Finally, Paula told Cindy about her family. She went into great detail about Cindy's mother, father, and siblings. Paula gave a heartfelt account of their love for her and how devastating it had been for them to lose their youngest daughter.

When Paula was finished, Cindy remained awkwardly quiet. She was trying to process the story of her life. Paula understood and politely excused herself.

"I'm going to get us some snacks and drinks. I'll be back in 10 minutes or so."

Chapter 20 - Ride to Shiraz

Shahin drove aggressively through the night while Kamal did his best to scan their surroundings for potential hazards. Both were desperate to create a substantial gap between them and the soldiers from the camp. Finally, after what felt like an eternity, the silhouette of a village emerged in the distance.

"We can hide in that town!" yelled Kamal as he pointed towards it. "This military truck will be easy for them to spot in the daylight. I think we need to get rid of it."

"I agree about the truck, but I think it's better to hide it and head out on foot, not stay in the town," said Shahin. "This area is rocky enough that they shouldn't be able to track us."

As they entered the village, Kamal shouted, "There, that building looks like it has parking behind it! They won't be able to see the truck from the street if we park close to the building."

Shahin nodded and turned into the lot. He drove past the side parking lot and into the back. He pulled the truck snugly up against the back corner of the building so that it was not visible from the street. It was so close to the structure that Kamal had to get out on the driver's side. Before exiting the truck, Kamal locked all of the doors. At the street, the two checked to ensure the truck couldn't be seen before discussing their next move.

"Which way do you think we should go?" asked Kamal.

"I'm a little familiar with the terrain in this area," replied Shahin. "This way is very rugged. A truck can't drive across it."

Kamal approved, and the two men headed out of town on foot. Once Shahin and Kamal were 500 yards from the vehicle, Shahin threw the truck keys over a residential wall.

"With any luck, they won't bring a spare set of keys," said Shahin.

Within a few minutes, they reached the outskirts of the village. They continued to jog into the sparsely populated terrain of the Zagros Mountains plateau. Worried that the soldiers might still be able to track them, the two climbed over the rocky outcrops and used the hardened areas of the semi-arid desert to make their way south towards Shiraz. After hiking aggressively over the rough terrain for an hour, Shahin and Kamal decided to rest for a few minutes.

Still breathing heavily, Kamal finally let out his pent-up emotions and astonishment.

"Did you see her?" he asked Shahin incredulously. "I mean, Cindy, did you see that she's pregnant?"

"Yes, I noticed," Shahin reluctantly admitted to Kamal. "But that doesn't mean anything. Remember, she's a captive here."

"What about her fight with Kegger?" demanded Kamal. "She didn't act like a prisoner. I don't think she wanted to be rescued. I think Cindy wants to stay in Iran," he said agitatedly. "She must be in love with the father. That's why she resisted our help. I'm so stupid to think that she still wanted me."

"I'm not sure why she acted like that, but I know she still loves you," Shahin insisted. "Maybe her captors threatened to kill her if she tried to escape; that makes sense to me. Unless…" Shahin conjectured. "She's trying to protect her unborn baby from something we don't know about. All I can say is that there has to be a good reason for her actions. We just don't know what it is."

"I know you're trying to make me feel better, Shahin, but she acted as if WE'RE the ones doing the capturing," Kamal said defensively.

"They say that pregnant women do crazy things sometimes to protect their unborn child; maybe that's it?" Shahin weakly reasoned. "Whatever it is, we'll be able to find out why when we get to the rendezvous point. Let's just drop it for now and focus on getting the hell out of here."

Kamal understood Shahin wanted to end the conversation, but he couldn't let it go just yet.

"Maybe it is about the baby," he added in frustration, "but look at how she treated me and Paula when we tried to talk to her. She could have at least acknowledged us, but instead, she tried to get away from us!"

"Kamal," Shahin said calmly, "we don't know for sure what's going on. All we can do now is hope they escaped and are at the factory. Regardless, we should stay quiet; people can probably hear human voices for miles out here."

Kamal reluctantly nodded and motioned that he was ready to keep going. They resumed jogging until they came to another village several miles away. Exhausted, the men searched for a vehicle to steal. They needed to put a greater distance between themselves and the military base. Suddenly, they heard several trucks drive into the northern part of the town.

Panic surged through both men, and Shahin whispered forcefully, "Keep searching! We have to get out of here, now!"

The two rounded the corner of a small warehouse and saw a man loading his truck with bundles of clothing. They guessed he was planning to sell them at the open market in Shiraz. However, for them, it didn't matter where he was going as long as it was away from there. He placed the last armful of garments into the back of his truck before pulling down the canvas flap and walking to the driver's door. They watched as he opened it and stepped up into the seat.

"This is our chance," whispered Shahin.

Without hesitation, the two ran toward the vehicle. As they approached the back end, it roared to life. Without hesitating, they opened the cover and jumped into the back. As the driver pulled away, Shahin and Kamal hurried to hide behind the clothing piles.

When they were settled in and felt confident that the driver couldn't hear them, Kamal asked timidly, "Shahin, were you scared back at the camp when they were going to shock us?"

"Yeah, terrified, weren't you?" Shahin replied.

"Yeah, terrified is a good word to describe it," Kamal agreed. "I just wondered because sometimes I think I'm a coward for being afraid."

"What? No, anyone who isn't afraid of being electrocuted is an idiot," said Shahin. "Just because we were scared doesn't mean we're cowards. It means we're not stupid."

Shahin's words made Kamal feel better about his fear and lessened his anxiety about showing it.

"You know, Shahin, I still feel bad about leaving the safe house without telling anyone," Kamal admitted. "I'm not even sure why I did it."

"That's all old shit that's long been forgiven," said Shahin. "We all do things we regret. I still carry around a bunch of guilt for getting you guys into this mess in the first place. I should have stopped the trip sooner, but didn't because I was scared that I would lose Paula. Now, I'm selfishly hoping that by helping rescue Cindy, I can feel less responsible for her capture."

"Everybody knows you blame yourself, but Paula and I know we could have said something and chosen not to. We don't blame you," Kamal added, then reconsidered his statement. "Well, maybe there was a time when we did, but not anymore. We both know we're just as much to blame."

"Thanks for saying that," said Shahin. "It isn't true, but thanks anyway."

There was an awkward pause; then Shahin changed the subject.

"These weapons are really awkward to carry," he said frankly. "I saw a large duffel bag near the tailgate. I think we should use it to carry the guns."

"Good idea," agreed Kamal. "When we're ready to jump out, we can grab it. If we do it now and the guy comes to check on things, he might notice it's missing."

******

Suddenly, the truck slowed. Shahin and Kamal stopped talking and nestled down into their hiding places. The vehicle came to a stop, and the guys heard the driver's door open and then close, but no one appeared at the back of the vehicle. They waited several more seconds and finally assumed it meant the driver was not unloading his merchandise yet.

It was early morning and still quite dark inside the truck. With the dimmest of light showing into the covered truck, Kamal motioned for Shahin to stay put while he went to see what was happening.

Kamal quietly moved the merchandise aside and peered out the rear of the vehicle. He couldn't see anything directly out the back, so he cautiously peered around the truck's corner. He saw the driver standing at one of the few tables in front of a small shack where a man was cooking.

Relief flooded through Kamal as he returned to tell Shahin the news, "He stopped for something to eat. I think this is a good place for us to get out. It looks like we're coming into the outskirts of Shiraz. We can probably walk the rest of the way to the factory."

Shahin nodded and stood up. As he passed two stacks of men's shirts, he grabbed one for himself and another for Kamal. Silently, Kamal opened the duffel and removed the miscellaneous items inside. He placed their weapons carefully, but quickly, into it. Then he turned and took the shirts from Shahin. Kamal laid them on top and closed the bag. Stealthily, the two men climbed out of the truck and snuck away.

Once they were far enough away from the vendor's vehicle, Shahin and Kamal stopped and put on their new shirts. Even though Kamal's shirt was larger than Shahin's, both were too small for the men's physiques, but the tightness didn't matter. Their torn and bloodied shirts would draw much more attention to them, which was the last thing they wanted.

Kamal grabbed their old shirts and shoved them between two large rocks. Unless someone was specifically looking for something small, they would go unnoticed by any passerby.

******

After walking for several miles, the two finally figured out their location. It would take them at least a few more hours to get to the rendezvous point. Feeling hungry and exhausted, the men walked on, stopping only to relieve themselves and to purchase some bread and cheese. They used Shiraz's alleyways and back streets instead of the major boulevards to avoid being spotted by Khomeini's soldiers.

It was late morning when they finally arrived at their meeting place. What they found disturbed them greatly. Besides the note telling them where Paula, Kegger, and Cindy had gone, the back bedroom was filled with blood. It was all over the bed, the pillows, and the floor. It was apparent that someone needed medical attention.

Shahin read the note again, but this time much more carefully, while Kamal looked at it for the first time. It explained in detail what had happened to Cindy and the baby. She did not say explicitly where they were going; however, as Shahin read the note the second time, he knew through Paula's description where she and kegger had taken Cindy and her baby.

"They're at Zahra's," said Shahin, momentarily reliving fond memories of the place.

"Yeah, I know," agreed Kamal. "Hopefully, they made it there safely."

"You know, Paula," said Shahin, trying to alleviate any concerns Kamal may have about Cindy's well-being, "she'll make sure they do."

"How are we going to get there?" asked Kamal. "It's well over an hour from here by car."

"Yeah, we need to take some time and figure out the best way to do it. We can't have anyone following us. It could put all of us in danger if we act too quickly," said Shahin. "I think right now we should rest. They should be safe with Zahra."

"I agree," said Kamal. "I'm exhausted, and if we need to execute a plan that involves running and thinking, I'm not at my best right now."

"You sleep," said Shahin. "I'll stay up in case someone tries to get in. Then, in a few hours, we'll switch."

Kamal didn't argue. He found an extra blanket in the closet and laid it down on the apartment floor. Within minutes, he was fast asleep. While he slept, Shahin nursed his wounds. As he cleaned a cut on his cheek, Shahin smiled at himself in the small mirror above the sink. He felt proud of himself and Kamal for keeping the secret. Then, his thoughts turned to the electricity and the torture it represented. They had been lucky that the tremor hit when it did, and Shahin thanked God and Allah for their escape, believing they were the same type of spiritual being.

******

The sergeant dialed the number to his commanding officer. As it rang, sweat soaked his uniform.

"This is Commander Rashidi, who is speaking?" he asked.

"Sir, this is Sergeant Reza. There's been a major tremor here that was more like an earthquake. The jolt tipped over an oil drum with such force that it poured gasoline several meters into our automotive bay, where one of the men was welding a part together. It caused a fire that took us several hours to contain."

"Was this damage significant?" asked the commander.

"Yes, sir, it burned about a quarter of the camp, and we lost two men," the sergeant responded.

"How's the interrogation going? Did you get the information that I asked for?"

"Well, sir, that's the other reason I'm calling," the sergeant replied.

"What is it? Get to the point," Rashidi said impatiently.

"It's the man you sent to question the prisoners; he...well... he and two of my soldiers had an accident when the tremor hit. It looks like they were just about to use electrocution to force the prisoners to answer their questions, and... well, they ended up electrocuting themselves."

"They're dead?" the commander confirmed.

"Yes, sir, they fell into the puddles of water while the live current was going through it. When we found them, two of my men were dead, plus the man you sent."

"What about the prisoners?" Rashidi demanded.

"Well, sir," the man hesitated again. "They... it was chaos here, sir, you must understand."

"What happened?!" yelled the commander.

"Sir, they escaped. Since everyone with them is dead, we're not sure what exactly happened," the sergeant cautiously explained. "When we discovered our men, the prisoners were already gone."

"You imbeciles," shouted Rashidi. "I can't count on you to do anything right. Do you have an idea of where they are now? Are you in pursuit of them?"

"Unfortunately, sir, we are not," he cautiously admitted. "We had everyone fighting the fire. It could have burned down our whole camp. No one checked on the prisoners until we had the flames under control. By the time that happened, they were gone. I did send soldiers to the two villages nearest our camp, but so far, they haven't found anything except the truck the two men used to escape."

"I don't care how late you need to stay up or if anyone sleeps tonight. I want to know what way they are headed. Is that understood?" Commander Rashidi snapped.

"Yes, sir, I will order the men to keep looking," promised the sergeant.

"I want them found, no matter what it takes!" Commander Rashidi demanded before slamming the receiver down.

Chapter 21 - The Truth Revealed

Dr. Ardehali turned the knob on the back door to his home that led into his kitchen. As he opened the door, there, sitting at his table with a cup of tea, was Commander Rashidi.

The two men stared at one another for a brief moment before Saeed asked, "Commander, what a surprise; may I ask the reason for your visit?"

"I think you know why I'm here," he casually replied before holding up a photo of a woman in a chador with all but her eyes covered by a scarf.

Fear welled up inside the doctor as he stared at the picture. Even though the person in the photo was almost impossible to identify, Saeed knew immediately that the woman was Cindy.

Grinning malignly at the doctor, the commander made a hand motion to one of his soldiers. The man went to the door and ordered another soldier to enter the kitchen. Saeed watched as an armed private entered the room, holding a knife to the throat of his housekeeper. The doctor saw the devastating fear on her face, and his heart sank. He knew her involvement in concealing Cindy from the government was his fault, and he dreaded the idea that she could be harmed because of him.

"She had nothing to do with this!" the doctor declared. "It was me, all me!"

"Too late," the commander chuckled. "She already confessed that she lied to me the last time I was here and was complicit in your cover-up. Did you think I wouldn't ever find out about the American girl?"

Instead of responding to his question, Doctor Ardehali lashed out, "What you asked me to do was immoral and unjust! I couldn't take her life just because you didn't want to admit the truth!" In defiance, the doctor added, "Besides, no one knows who she is. My brother has gone to great lengths to keep her identity a secret. You can see from the photo that he has her almost completely covered when she's out in public."

"Well, that didn't stop someone from recognizing her," the commander argued. "It was only a matter of time before the truth would be known."

"Who told you?" Saeed asked. "Was it his first wife?"

"That would have been my guess also," agreed the commander. "However, it came from a man who knew I would pay good money for this information. You see, Doctor, greed causes many people to turn on their friends."

His comment confused Dr. Ardehali, "Are you saying it was one of her friends? I don't believe you. Plus, they don't even know that she's alive."

"I don't think he's actually one of her friends, but more, a friend of a friend," said Rashidi. "There was a man who went into hiding with the girl and her three friends, but something happened, and he left their hideout and sought refuge with an old high school friend of his who lived in Shiraz."

"I still don't understand the connection," said Dr. Ardehali.

"As you know, most of her friends escaped the country, but one remained in Shiraz," he said pleasantly as if telling a children's story. "When he saw the woman, he told her friends in the US and his roommate. The man here decided to make some money. Mind you, he didn't know the exact details of the rescue, but it was enough for us to..." Commander Rashidi paused before sarcastically saying, "Shall I say, prepare for their arrival. I know it sounds complicated, but it isn't. He had information I wanted and figured he could get paid a nice sum if he told me."

"Okay, so he told you the woman you asked me to kill was still alive; that was all my doing and no one else's," the doctor forcefully admitted. "As I told you, my housekeeper is innocent. Please, let her go! I coerced her into helping me! She didn't want to do it, but I forced her into it!" he pleaded.

"I don't like being lied to," Commander Rashidi said flatly. "She'll have to pay the consequences for that, and so will you."

"What about my brother? He, too, had nothing to do with my decision to save her life. All he did was try to take care of her at my request," the doctor insisted.

"I dealt with him already," Rashidi said smugly. "His first wife is now a very wealthy woman. Of course, we won't actually allow her to have the money or own the assets, but she'll enjoy a very comfortable life."

"What have you done to him? I told you! It wasn't his fault!" cried Saeed as he began to break down.

"Don't worry, you won't have to be sad for very long," Commander Rashidi said with a maniacal snicker, "and your housekeeper, her fear will end soon as well."

Chapter 22 - Stevie

Shahin and Kamal were eating the food their team had stashed inside the factory when they heard a loud knock on the entry door.

"Oh shit! What should we do?" questioned Shahin under his breath.

Before Kamal could respond, they heard a strained voice outside the door.

"Guys, it's me, Stevie. Let me in. I'm a sitting duck out here!"

Kamal jumped up and ran to the door. He unlocked the deadbolt and cracked it open. There, bloodied and bruised, was Stevie. He was dirty from head to toe, and his clothes were torn in several places. He quickly pushed the door aside and hobbled into the factory. Kamal stuck his head outside and glanced up and down the street to see if anyone was watching them. Seeing no one, he closed and locked the door behind him.

"We thought you were dead," said Kamal as Stevie limped across the room to the table. "How did you get away?"

Instead of answering Kamal's question, Stevie asked, "Do you have more to eat? I'm starving."

"Yes," responded Shahin, as he awkwardly helped Stevie sit down at their small table.

Without waiting, the injured man began to stuff his face with food and drink the water sitting on the table.

With a mouthful, he asked, "So, it's just the two of you who made it here?"

"The others were here, but they left," said Shahin. "I'll explain everything after you eat."

Stevie continued to shovel food into his mouth while Shahin and Kamal watched. Once he had eaten several large bites, the guys began their questions again.

"How'd you escape? They called for backup right away after you jumped out. We thought for sure they had captured you," said Shahin.

"This isn't the first time I've been in a tight spot," replied Stevie. "Remember, I do this for a living."

Taking short breaks from eating, Stevie explained what he had gone through after jumping out of the truck. Shahin and Kamal listened intently as he described how he handled each challenge. It was as if they were back in school learning how to play a new sport. After telling them about his trying experience, he asked them about their escape. The last time he saw them, they were in shackles, being transferred to a military camp.

Shahin went first and explained the beginning of the ordeal. Unable to contain his excitement, Kamal interjected his recollection of their experience. The two men continued to take turns reliving their torture and escape. Each mentioned how they had overcome their fear and persevered through the beatings. Finally, they told him about the tremor and their ability to take advantage of it.

"I felt it a little, but it didn't do any damage," Stevie shared while continuing to eat. When satiated, he finally sat back in the chair, "Dudes, you're fucking heroes. Most guys couldn't have handled it. They would have given up their friends' location and probably the whole plan. I'm proud of you guys," he said using a fatherly tone.

Both men blushed slightly before brushing his praises aside as if it were nothing. Still, their faces expressed the pride they felt even if their words did not.

"We have more news," said Kamal. "Cindy, you know, the woman we came here to rescue? Well, as you probably noticed, she was pregnant."

"Yeah, I saw her belly when Kegger pulled away her chador. Did you guys know?" asked Stevie.

"No, none of us knew. It was a surprise to everyone," said Shahin.

"I only glanced over a couple of times, but it looked like she was fighting with Kegger," Stevie said questioningly, "She was, right?"

"Yeah, we saw that too," said Kamal sadly. "We don't know why she acted like that."

"So, that brings us to our next issue," said Shahin as he stood up and motioned for Stevie to follow him. "I wanted to wait until after you ate to show you this. Cindy had her baby here. It must have happened yesterday." He opened the bedroom door, saying, "Check this out."

Stevie walked in and glanced around before stating, "Man, that's a lot of blood. Do we know if she's okay?"

"No, we don't. Paula left us this note that explains some of it," said Shahin and handed him the letter.

"It sounds like she's alive, but something went wrong," said Kamal anxiously. "We need to get to Zahra's and find out what happened."

Stevie read Paula's note carefully before asking for clarification, "I'm not sure what some of this means. Do you know the location she's talking about?"

The three reasoned she had left out the name of the place they were going to in case someone besides one of them were to find it. Shahin told Stevie it was not a problem. He knew by Paula's description where they had gone.

The three decided it was best to wait until dark to make their next move. Plus, Stevie needed to clean up and rest. Shahin and Kamal pulled off all of the bedding and cleaned up as much of the blood as they could in the rest of the bedroom while Stevie showered and dressed his wound. They placed their blankets in the cleanest corner of the bedroom for him to sleep on. He gladly accepted their makeshift bed and lay down to rest.

✳✳✳✳✳✳

Stevie had quickly suggested a plan to safely travel to Zahra's Lodge before falling asleep, but asked Shahin and Kamal to think of some alternatives while he rested. They discussed several scenarios, and at one point, Kamal disguised his identity the best that he could and went out to survey their surrounding area and possible options they could use to help them execute the best plan.

The sun was low in the sky when Kamal finally became impatient.

"We have to wake him," he told Shahin. "It's almost dark, and we haven't even really talked to him about our plan except for his few comments."

"I know," said Shahin, "but he's been shot, and I don't know how long he needs to sleep to be okay to travel."

"I think we should wake him," said Kamal. "We at least need to ask him if there's something we should be doing since it's getting late."

"Yeah, okay, I'll go in," said Shahin.

"I'm coming too," insisted Kamal. "I want to hear what he says."

The guys opened the door to the bedroom and turned on the light. Stevie was awake and shaking. Immediately, the guys went over and knelt next to him.

"Are you okay?" asked Shahin anxiously. "Why are you shaking?"

Kamal put his hand on Stevie's arm, "Oh shit! He's burning up!"

Shahin felt Stevie's forehead and then his chest.

"You're right! He has a high fever. The wound must have gotten infected."

"What can we give him?" asked Kamal.

"Maybe there's something in the first-aid kit," said Shahin as he got up and headed to the bathroom.

Shahin frantically searched their medicine kit, hoping to find some type of medicine that could help Stevie recover. There were several types of bandages and antiseptics for injuries, but no prescription medications.

Shahin glanced around and saw a small medicine cabinet. He quickly opened the door, hoping to find something useful. He didn't find any antibiotics, but there was a bottle of aspirin. Frustrated and disappointed with his findings, Shahin returned to the bedroom. He asked Kamal to get some water while he opened the container and took out four tablets.

Shahin sat them on the blanket next to Stevie before optimistically saying, "Hey man, don't worry. You're going to be okay. This aspirin will drop your temperature."

Kamal heard Shahin's soothing comments as he entered the room and added confidently, "It's just going to take some time for you to get better, and we're here to help. Really, there's no rush for us to get to Zahra's. I'm sure our guys will wait for us. Cindy probably needs time to recover as well. You can rest here while she rests there."

Kamal's compassion touched Shahin, and after processing Kamal's statements, Shahin realized that Stevie's life was in their hands. The two men knelt on either side of the sick and injured man and carefully lifted him into a sitting position. Shahin handed the tablets to Stevie. Unfortunately, he was shaking so severely that he could not hold them. Seeing his difficulty, Shahin took the pills and placed them in his mouth before holding a glass of water up to Stevie's lips to drink. Stevie tried his best to swallow the medication, but the shaking caused him to choke on the liquid and pills. It took two more times, but finally, with help, Stevie swallowed the pills.

Shahin and Kamal looked at one another and nodded. Things had changed, and they would not be traveling that night. Moreover, it would be up to them to help Stevie survive.

******

It was impossible to see out of the filthy upper windows of the abandoned factory, but the light from the sun could still filter through the muddled glass. Kamal was sleeping soundly when the morning sun traveled across his face, causing him to awake. He sat up and looked over at Stevie. He had made it through the night and was finally asleep. Kamal went over and gently felt his forehead. Stevie's fever was still very high. Next, Kamal checked his wound; it looked red and swollen, and pus was oozing out.

The sight caused Kamal's stomach to flip, and for a moment, he thought he might be sick. He realized Stevie needed antibiotics to stop the infection from getting any worse. Luckily, in Iran, as well as many other countries, no doctor's prescription is required to purchase antibiotics. As Kamal placed the bed sheet back over Stevie's leg, Shahin entered the bedroom.

"Hey, I'm glad you're awake," whispered Shahin. "I'm going to have to get him some antibiotics. His gunshot wound is getting worse, and our antiseptics aren't working. I think he could die if we don't do something."

"Yeah, I just checked it. It looks gross," Kamal said as he grimaced. "I'll go to the pharmacy. You're much more valuable to Khomeini than I am."

"Maybe, but that doesn't mean you have to take all the risks," said Shahin.

"He wants you more than me," added Kamal. "That's the reality. Plus, my brown eyes are more common than your green ones. If they ask around, the storekeepers will remember you more than me."

"You always use that excuse," said Shahin. "It's my turn to go. Besides, I could use the fresh air."

"Fresh air? I wouldn't count on it," said Kamal jokingly. "Ask Paula, it might not kill you today, but eventually, it'll get you."

Shahin smiled, and momentarily, the two men felt some comic relief.

"Yeah, anyway, I'm going out to find the pharmacy." Shahin went to the kitchenette and grabbed the money off the counter. "I'll be back shortly," he said before turning to leave. "Come with me and relock the metal door."

Just as Shahin was about to leave, Kamal asked, "Should you get more bandages? We don't have many left?"

"I think it's too risky. If soldiers start asking store owners if they've seen us, buying large bandages would be a giveaway."

"Yeah, you better not do it," Kamal agreed.

Shahin walked casually in search of a pharmacy but kept his head down most of the time, looking up only to check the area around him. It wasn't long before he saw a sign across the street, half a block down. He watched the street traffic for an opening, and when the break came, Shahin darted across and headed quickly into the drug store.

Once inside, Shahin surveyed the people shopping to ensure they were not military personnel. It was a small place. The only patrons were a woman and her young child. A worker was restocking the shelves behind the front checkout counter, and another was sweeping the floor. Shahin looked down again and casually headed to the back of the store, where the pharmacist was waiting to assist customers.

"What can I help you with today?" asked the man.

Shahin smiled and said, "I need an antibiotic for my little brother. He has an ear infection."

"How old is your brother, and does he have any allergies?" asked the pharmacist.

"He's 16, and no, he doesn't have any allergies, just an ear infection," replied Shahin.

"Penicillin should work well for him. I'll need a few minutes to get it ready," the pharmacist responded.

While waiting, Shahin browsed the merchandise on display near the pharmacy window. He pretended to look at the products to avoid eye contact with the worker nearby. It wasn't long before the pharmacist returned with the penicillin, and Shahin was on his way back to their hideout.

As he approached the entrance, Shahin looked around to see if anyone was watching. As Kegger had expected when he rented the factory, the small, dead-end road was empty of pedestrians and onlookers.

"Kamal! I'm back!" Shahin said triumphantly through the door.

Kamal ushered Shahin inside, saying worriedly, "I'm glad you made it. Stevie isn't doing well. He woke up a few minutes ago, and he's hallucinating. I'm not sure what to do."

Shahin followed Kamal into the bedroom. He briefly touched Stevie's forehead. His skin was hot and clammy, with sweat beading around the edges of his hairline.

"Help me sit him up," ordered Shahin.

Together, the two men sat Stevie up to swallow the antibiotic pills. They knew the instructions only called for one tablet at a time, but both felt that the severity of Stevie's infection warranted a double dose.

Chapter 23 - Identity

Zahra rocked the baby while Paula and Kyra made dinner. Six days had gone by, and Cindy was still very weak. She couldn't get out of bed or walk without help. Often, Cindy couldn't even muster enough energy to hold her son while breastfeeding. Her appetite had not returned, and getting her to eat enough food was a struggle. In addition to her significant blood loss, Cindy needed to produce enough breast milk to feed her child and heal her body. All of these things together caused Cindy to have a prolonged recovery. The others had no choice but to remain at Zahra's Lodge until Cindy could travel safely.

In addition to her health, Cindy found naming her child a challenge and agonized over the appropriate name for her son. She felt conflicted between her current life as an Iranian woman, which had turned out to be a lie, and her supposed American heritage as told to her by a woman who claimed to be her best friend. Because of this dilemma, Cindy continued to refer to her baby as "little darling".

While the women cared for Cindy and her baby, Kegger spent most of his time guarding the property from a surprise visit or attack. Paula and Kyra gave him long breaks each day, but protecting the premises was his responsibility. Paula checked on Kegger throughout the day, and they often spoke about Shahin, Kamal, and Stevie. At first, the two ascertained different scenarios of what had happened to their friends and colleagues. Paula thought they were walking to the lodge to avoid being caught at a checkpoint, while Kegger thought all three were injured and laying low until one could get to a phone to contact him or Paula.

As time passed, Paula's and Kegger's confidence that their friends were still alive and not in prison waned. Neither would outwardly admit that their friends may have been captured or killed; instead, they made up excuses for their delay. Kegger told Paula that waiting for Stevie, and maybe Jake, to arrive at the lodge made it easier for him to be patient with Cindy's slow progress. On the other hand, Paula was content with Cindy's incremental improvement. She wanted to give Shahin and Kamal more time to join them at Zahra's.

One evening, after Kegger relieved Paula from guard duty, she was returning to the dining room and heard Zahra mention the baby's age.

"What are you saying, Kyra?" she questioned. "Where did you get the idea that he's three months premature?"

"Well, that's what Cindy told us," she said defensively.

"Yeah," Paula agreed as she entered the room, "I even asked her about it."

"You women don't know much about pregnancy and newborn babies, do you?" asked Zahra incredulously.

"I don't," admitted Kyra. "As you know, Rostam and I could never have kids."

Paula explained, "I'm the oldest in my family, so neither of my sisters have had any kids. Plus, I don't know anyone who's given birth after only six months into their pregnancy. I've heard of women having miscarriages later in their pregnancies, but no one ever talks about it."

"Why not?" asked Kyra.

"I think it's because it makes other people uncomfortable. Everyone just wants them to move on and not mention it. Plus, many people blame the woman, saying stuff like, *If she had taken better care of herself, it wouldn't have happened*. It's just one more thing our society uses to accuse women of things that are often out of their control, and it makes them feel even worse than they already do. That's, I think, why most women are very reluctant to share their grief with anyone, including their friends."

"That's sad," said Kyra. "It seems like it would be a time when she needs support from her friends and family."

"Yeah, it's weird," said Paula.

Deciding that Paula's comments opened the door for additional sharing, Kyra asked, "Zahra, have you shared your story with Paula?"

"No, but only because it never came up in conversation. You can tell her."

Kyra looked sadly at Paula and said, "Zahra's baby died during delivery?"

"Oh, Zahra, I'm so sorry," Paula said compassionately.

"He was a precious little boy," Kyra added. "His name was Majid; it means noble, glorious, and magnificent."

"It was a complicated delivery," Zahra remorsefully explained. "The umbilical cord was wrapped around his neck, and the midwife could not unwrap it in time. It's part of the reason I decided to become a local midwife."

"That's awful; it must have torn your heart to pieces," Paula replied caringly.

Zahra admitted, "Yes, it did."

"Plus, she had complications," added Kyra.

"Do you mind sharing what happened to you with me?" asked Paula.

"No, it's something you should know about, anyway. Right after my son was born, the midwife tried to deliver the placenta. Unfortunately, it had grown unnaturally into my uterus, and they had to do an emergency hysterectomy. I'm lucky I survived."

"That's why she couldn't have more children," Kyra added.

"Yes, but that was a long time ago. Right now, I need to educate you ladies about fetal development. The reason you've never seen a baby born three months premature is because it would not survive outside of the womb. It wouldn't even weigh a kilo."

"So less than two pounds?" confirmed Paula.

"Exactly," said Zahra. "But I don't understand why Cindy thinks her baby is premature. He's small, but he weighs just under three kilos."

"Well, she didn't get married until the end of January. At least that's what her fake husband told her. I thought the baby looked older but I didn't want to press the issue. I thought you knew Cindy's timeline, and since you have a lot of experience delivering babies, I just thought I was wrong," added Paula.

"No, she never mentioned his age to me. I had no idea that she thought the baby was so young," admitted Zahra. "Little darling is a full-term baby. He must have been conceived sometime in early November. That would be my guess anyway."

"If Cindy had gotten pregnant then," Paula mumbled as she said her thoughts out loud, "that would mean she was still with us." Paula quickly relived their last night together in the bunker. Then, the revelation hit her, "That means Kamal is the father!"

"What did you say?" asked Zahra eagerly.

"He's Kamal's!" Paula announced excitedly. "Kamal is Little Darling's father!"

"Are you sure?" asked Kyra.

"Yes, Cindy and Kamal made love the night before we headed to the embassy! That has to be when it happened! I need to tell her," said Paula excitedly.

Without waiting for Zahra or Kyra to agree with her decision, Paula headed towards the bedroom. She was about to open the door when she suddenly stopped. She took a deep breath and then another, trying to think of the best way to tell Cindy the good news.

Sadly, Paula realized that telling Cindy that Kaveh was not the baby's father might make her life even more difficult. Paula knew that Cindy had no recollection of Kamal, and she had no idea of the life they shared before her injury. At least Cindy knew Kaveh, and that might be more comforting than finding out that the father of your child is a stranger, not to mention that he might be dead. Coming to this conclusion, Paula decided to wait until Cindy's physical and emotional health improved before conveying the news about Little Darling. She returned to the kitchen, feeling deflated and disappointed; however, she believed it was the right decision. Paula told the women why she kept the truth from Cindy, and they agreed. For now, Kaveh would be referred to as the baby's father.

Chapter 24 - Outside the City

Shahin and Kamal stressed about staying longer in the factory until Stevie recovered enough to travel. Both men had gone out onto the city streets several times to buy food, medicine, and clothing, and they knew the longer they stayed, the more likely their position would be compromised. Unfortunately, there was little choice but to stay and wait for Stevie's health to improve.

"Stevie... Hey, wake up," said Shahin as he shook him gently.

"Stop..." said Stevie groggily before realizing what was going on. "Oh... It's you, what do you want?"

"It's time for your medication," he said as he handed Stevie two pills and a glass of water. "Wait," Shahin added. "I'll help you sit up. Try not to spill the water."

Shahin awkwardly helped Stevie into a sitting position before continuing his inquiry. "How do you feel today? Your fever seems slightly better, and you seem much more coherent."

"Yeah, I finally have gotten rid of the fever chills. It makes it a lot easier to sleep," Stevie said softly.

"That's good. You still have a way to go, but at least you are making sense today," said Shahin jokingly.

"How long have I been here? asked Stevie. "Things are a little bit sketchy for me."

"It's been a week. I gave you penicillin, and you were allergic to it. Sorry, we saw your bracelet after I gave you the pills," Shahin explained. "You were already out of it before you took the medication, and after I made you take them, you were talking crazy, and your face swelled up like a balloon. Then, you got a rash."

"I vaguely remember something itching," said Stevie.

"Yeah, your rash was pretty bad, but it's better now, and your face is back to normal. I think you still have a fever, but it's a lot better since you've been taking the tetracycline. Kamal went to the pharmacy the second time and got it for you. That's what this is," said Shahin as he handed Stevie the pills.

Stevie popped the pills into his mouth and took a drink of water before saying, "Maybe it's helping, but I still feel like shit, and my leg hurts like hell."

"We've been trying to keep your wound clean, but it's still pussy and bleeding a little," replied Shahin. "For a while, we didn't know if you would make it."

"Thanks, I'm sure you guys have been doing your best. I didn't mean to sound ungrateful," said Stevie apologetically. "I appreciate you taking care of me."

"Are you hungry?" asked Shahin. "Kamal will be back soon with food."

"Fuck yes, I'm starving. Did I eat anything while I was out of it?"

"No, not really. You ate when you first got here, and then you got really sick," explained Shahin. "We got you to drink water, but you didn't want to eat much."

As Shahin finished his statement, they heard a loud knock on the outside door. "I'll be right back," he said as he leapt to his feet.

"Soldiers!" said Kamal urgently as he entered the factory. "They are one street over, talking to the shopkeepers! We need to get out of here!"

"Shit!" said Shahin. "Stevie needs a few more days here before he should travel."

"Well, he doesn't have it!" exclaimed Kamal. "We need to leave now!"

Stevie heard the conversation and got out of bed. He went to the stack of clothes Shahin had purchased for him from a local store. He quickly put on the underwear and shirt before attempting to put on the jeans. When Stevie tried to put on the jeans, he knew immediately that they were going to be tight. Seconds after he struggled to fit into the jeans, Stevie's wound started to bleed.

As he zipped up the pants, he yelled, "Dammit! This fucking wound is pissing me off!"

Shahin and Kamal ran in and saw the blood. The jeans were too snug around Stevie's thighs, and bloody pus had soaked a large area of the jeans.

"They'll spot us for sure if I go out like this," said Stevie. "You're going to have to leave me here."

"No! We are not leaving you!" insisted Shahin. "We'll figure something out!"

"Think!" Shahin ordered himself. "What's another option?" Suddenly, he declared, "Kamal, help him get the oozing under control. Wrap it really tight and use the duct tape if you need to. Give me the money! I'm going to the clothing store. I have an idea."

Shahin didn't wait for a response. He grabbed the cash from Kamal's hand and headed out the door. He walked quickly to the nearest neighborhood general store, where he grabbed the two items he wanted and went to the counter to pay for them. The store owner looked bewildered but said nothing as he took the cash from Shahin.

Out of breath from running back, Shahin declared, "This should work!" and handed Stevie the garment.

Stevie allowed the cloak to unfold. As it did, he questioned Shahin, "A chador? You want me to wear a chador?"

"Yes," said Shahin. "It will cover your leg, and you'll be able to keep the material away from your wound."

"It's a good idea," added Kamal. "Just put it on, and let's go."

"First, tie this hanky around your nose and chin," said Shahin, handing him the cloth.

Stevie did as Shahin instructed before reluctantly putting the chador over his head. He gripped the cloak with both hands to keep it closed. Shahin took hold of Stevie's left arm outside the chador to help guide him while Kamal took the duffel full of weapons and walked a few feet ahead of them. Kamal led Shahin and Stevie away from the factory and the inquiring soldiers.

Stevie soon perfected his role and pretended to be an old woman who needed assistance. Shahin helped him walk while Kamal kept an eye out for the soldiers and cleared a path for his friends to walk. They made it only a quarter of a mile before Stevie had to take a break. He was sweating profusely, and his leg was almost unusable.

"We have to find a new shelter, or at least a place for him to sit down," said Shahin. "He's not going to make it much farther."

"There's a bus stop over there," said Kamal, pointing. "Let's just take whatever bus comes first. At least it will get us the hell out of here."

"Okay," agreed Shahin. "You stay ahead of us and shield Stevie while I help him get there."

It wasn't long before a bus pulled up to the stop. Kamal stepped onto the bus and paid the fare to the end of the route before turning around to help Shahin get Stevie up the steps. The bus was mostly full; however, there were open seats towards the back. As they passed by the other riders, only one woman in the back gave their entry any notice.

While on the road, Shahin and Kamal studied the signage and bus route. They figured out that they were headed south, away from Shiraz. It was the opposite direction of where they wanted to go, but it didn't matter. They just needed to get out of the city.

As the bus approached its final stop, Shahin looked out at the surrounding area. Spread out across the valley and up the side of the mountains were orchards of pomegranates with the occasional pasture mixed in. The houses were modest yet relatively large. Shahin concluded that it meant the people were either successful farmers or wealthy urbanites with second homes away from the traffic and pollution in the larger cities.

When the bus came to its final stop, only one woman was left on the bus with them. She quickly got off but was slow to walk away. Kamal was the next person to exit, followed by Stevie and Shahin. When Stevie came to the steps, he paused. The movements he needed to do to get down the bus steps were problematic for him. As he proceeded to take the first step, it caused him excruciating pain that he could not conceal completely. The woman heard Stevie's groans and stopped to watch him hobble the rest of the way down with heavy assistance from his friends. When Stevie was finally standing on the ground, she could hear his breathing was heavy and labored. She knew the person under the chador was a man and wondered why he was pretending to be a woman. It was obvious to her that something was seriously wrong with this man's leg.

She continued to watch as the three men stood stationary while the bus pulled away. It was apparent that these men needed help. One of the men conversed with the injured man while the other man surveyed their surroundings, seemingly trying to decide which direction to head.

The woman's innate curiosity overrode her fear of strangers as she approached the three cautiously.

"Can I help you?" she said shyly. "My name is Jasmine, and I live right over that hill. I know this area well."

Shahin was honest with the woman and responded, "Yes, we could use your help. Our friend has been injured, and he's bleeding. He needs a place to rest so that we can change the dressing on his leg and allow him time to sleep. Do you have any place on your property where we could rest for a few hours? It doesn't need to be inside your house; any shelter or safe area would be great."

The young woman nodded without speaking further.

"Well, I..." Stevie said, starting to protest.

Shahin interjected, "Please, give us just a moment," he said, disallowing Stevie to make excuses to the kind woman.

Turning to his friends, he whispered, "I know it's risky to let her help us, but Stevie, you need to rest. If you don't, you may lose your leg."

This time, Stevie didn't object to Shahin's comments. He didn't want to be an amputee. Plus, he was already feeling weak and sick to his stomach. The minor exertion and the jostling of the bus had taken its toll.

Without waiting for input from Kamal, Shahin turned back to the woman and accepted any help she had to offer. She told them she had a barn where they could rest. Shahin placed Stevie's arm over his shoulders to prop him up on one side. Stevie grabbed Kamal's shoulder with his other hand to help him limp forward while Kamal carried their heavy bag.

"That's the barn over there," Jasmine said as they crested the small hill in front of her property.

"That will work fine for us," Shahin told the young woman. "Thank you for all of your help."

She escorted them to the barn. As they walked, Shahin tried to make small talk.

"Do you live here with your parents? Are they going to be okay with this?" he asked cautiously.

"It's only me and my mother," said the woman before adding angrily, "Khomeini's henchmen killed my father."

"Oh, I'm sorry," said Shahin. "The government has rushed to execute anyone opposing them for any reason. We've witnessed it ourselves."

"Yes, they murdered him for speaking out against a theocratic government," she said irately. "We know most people thought they wanted it, but many of us wanted a democracy. That's not a crime, and we were hoping Bakhtiar would remain in power as Prime Minister."

"We're very sorry to hear about your father," said Kamal. "I'm not allowed to contact my father, and it feels some days like I've lost him. I know it's not the same, but it still hurts."

Shahin interjected, "Please tell your mother we won't be any trouble, and we're sorry for your loss."

"I will," she said, returning to her more polite demeanor.

She started towards the house but soon turned back and said to Kamal, "I hope someday soon you will be able to see your father."

"Thanks," he kindly responded. "I will see him again, but it may be a long wait." There was a short pause, and then Kamal asked, "What's your name again?"

The woman smiled sheepishly and said, "Jasmine."

"Thanks for your help, Jasmine. We are grateful," he added.

Shahin and Stevie heard Kamal's thanks and chimed in with their appreciative comments. Jasmine nodded timidly before turning back towards her house.

The exchange between Kamal and Jasmine about their parents gave Shahin a pang of guilt. He blamed himself for this whole mess and everyone's unsafe predicament.

"It must suck to have influential people tell you it's too dangerous to contact your family," thought Shahin remorsefully. "Somehow, I will make it up to Kamal."

******

It wasn't long before Jasmine returned with a pitcher of water and glasses. The men thanked her again for her hospitality and immediately drank the entire container.

An hour later, Jasmine stood with her mother at the entrance to the barn. At first, they thought the older woman might insist that they leave. Instead, she quickly introduced herself as Niki and ordered them into the house. Once they got Stevie up and ready, Niki checked to ensure no one was coming down the dirt road to her home. Seeing it was clear, she motioned for them to follow.

Once inside their house, Niki and Jasmine removed their chadors and hung them on a hook near the door. It was obvious that she had been a Westernized woman before the crackdown on women's rights. Both had on a mid-length skirt and blouse. Niki was a fairly tall woman with long dark hair and brown eyes, most likely in her early 40s. Shahin thought Jasmine looked about 20, maybe as old as 22, and her resemblance to her mother was obvious.

"Please help him get onto the mat," Niki said to Kamal and Shahin. On the bed was a plastic mat where she wanted Stevie to sit or lie so she could examine his wound. Together, Shahin and Kamal hoisted Stevie up.

"I am a nurse," she added. "I need to take a look at his injury."

Without hesitating, she cut off the duct tape, pant leg, and bandages before examining his wound. Niki was assessing the damage and infection when Jasmine entered the bedroom.

"I thought you might be hungry," she said, holding a tray of food. "I'll start dinner soon, but for now, I have brought you some bread and cheeses."

******

Stevie stuffed several pieces of food into his mouth while Niki re-dressed his wound. When finished, she told Stevie it would be best for him to remain still for the next few hours. She would bring him a dinner tray when it was ready.

While eating their meal, Shahin and Kamal asked Niki about her husband. She explained that he had been in the Shah's parliament but supported Bakhtiar's democracy movement.

"When things started getting bad in the bigger cities, he thought it best for us to live farther away from the turmoil, so he bought this property for my daughter and me. We were able to live here without the constant threat of violence. Our home in Tehran was one of the first areas to have the demonstrations right outside our door. Jasmine and I lived here full-time while my husband stayed in Tehran during the week and returned here on the weekends."

"Why didn't you leave the country after his death?" asked Kamal.

"The new government confiscated our home and bank accounts in Tehran. They said they were justified because he was an enemy of the state. Luckily, this property was officially purchased in my name only, which helped hide this house from his adversaries. He was a very intelligent man, and I guess he knew this was the best way to protect us. I need to sell it so that I can leave Iran with some money. It will give us enough to start a new life. I plan to hire someone to repair the items that aren't working and then put the property up for sale. I almost have enough money saved to cover the extra expenses."

"She didn't tell you this part," Jasmine spoke up. "I wanted to stay and fight for our country. I was optimistic that the Iranian women would rise up and demand that our rights be restored. Unfortunately, things have only gotten worse. There have been mass layoffs of women in our workforce, and our rights continue to be repealed and outlawed."

Shahin spoke up to verify a suspicion, "We noticed when we got on the bus that all the women were sitting in the back and the men in the front. Is that a new law?"

"Yes," Jasmine confirmed, "women are now required to sit in the back of the bus. It's part of their segregation process."

"That's bloody terrible," added Kamal. "An old lady who's half crippled has to go all the way to the back of the bus while some young guy gets to sit in the front?"

"It is," agreed Niki. "Our new government only cares about male superiority."

The four continued their discussion about the new crackdown on women's rights and the de-Westernization of Iran until Niki decided she needed to check on Stevie.

Chapter 25 - Stevie's Infatuation

Niki attended to Stevie immediately upon returning from her shift at the hospital. Unfortunately, his fever had risen again. She told Stevie that he needed to have surgery to clean out the wound. The antibiotics were not enough to fight the infection. She believed there must be debris inside the wound that continued to cause infection. Even with her insistence, he refused to go to the hospital. Stevie told her he would be arrested and for sure die in prison. Niki and the others agreed it was a considerable risk, but the alternatives were death or amputation at the very least. If he survived, the second option would be a severe life-altering change and a devastating blow to his career. In desperation, Stevie asked Niki to operate and try to save his leg and foot.

At first, Niki told him she could not do it. She had assisted the surgeons numerous times in similar surgeries but never operated herself. She told him the closest she ever got to repairing the artery flow to an extremity was when there had been a serious bus accident where more than twenty people had been injured. Because of the unique circumstances, she was ordered by one of the attending surgeons to proceed with a surgery that he had begun while he went to help with a severe head injury. Luckily, Niki told him that her patient had survived and that she had managed to save his leg.

"But," she added defensively, "I had the expertise of another experienced nurse to help me through it."

"I'm ready to accept the possibility that I might lose my leg and maybe even my life during the surgery," he said forcefully. "We need to figure out a way to operate here, inside your home."

"We can all assist," said Shahin. "I'm ready to study up on the surgery and help."

"Me, too," said Kamal.

"You know I'll do whatever you ask," added Jasmine. "Mom, you have to try."

Feeling outnumbered and emboldened, Niki got out her emergency medical books and searched for a way to perform it without general anesthesia. She found a very unorthodox surgery performed once by a surgeon in a war zone. After reading it three times, she explained the procedure to Stevie. He promptly begged her to do it, and she begrudgingly agreed.

For the surgery to succeed, Niki told everyone she needed additional supplies from the hospital where she worked. She knew of no store where she could purchase these specialty items; therefore, she would need to steal them from the medical supply rooms.

Shahin insisted that he go to the hospital with Niki. He felt confident he could disguise himself sufficiently using Niki's late husband's wardrobe. She had kept his dress clothing as a reminder of his sacrifice for her and Jasmine. Shahin had a similar build to Niki's late husband and was practically the same height, which made it easy for him to fit into the man's clothing.

Another prop Shahin planned to use was one of Niki's wigs. She had kept several of them from her time as a theater actor in school. It was her passion, and she continued to dabble in the arts in Tehran right up until she left the city to move south. In addition to wearing a dark curly-haired wig, Shahin had allowed his beard to grow. Niki trimmed both the wig and his beard to be neat and professional-looking. She felt it would help him pull off the role of a visiting doctor.

******

Soon after Niki and Shahin arrived at the emergency room entrance, they quickly slipped past the security doors and entered the emergency ward. She led Shahin to where the hospital stored generic white coats in case a doctor got blood or stains on his personal coat. Two coats were hanging next to each other on a line of hooks. Niki quickly grabbed one and handed it to Shahin. He slipped it on and followed Niki to the equipment supply room. Luckily, it was a busy time, and all the employees seemed preoccupied with work and appeared not to notice them.

When they arrived at the supply room, Niki began to rummage through the drawers. She pulled out several essential items and stuffed them in a large bag she had brought with her from her home. Next, she went to the shelves and took the larger medical equipment she needed.

Once she had all the supplies for the surgery, she handed Shahin several items she could not carry. Niki left the supply room first and headed down the hallway towards the doors that led outside. Shahin followed her about twenty seconds later. This way, if either of them were questioned, the other would not be associated with the person under suspicion. Fortunately for her, she had left the hospital undetected and was 10 yards away when a security guard and an attending doctor yelled from a distance at Shahin.

"Stop! You there, in the white coat!"

Shahin's heart pounded as he repositioned the bag containing the monitor and other items hidden under the coat. He quickly skirted around an incoming gurney and then darted onto the street. The two men pursued him for a short distance but promptly gave up trying to apprehend him.

Meanwhile, Niki had heard the yelling and ducked into a narrow walkway until she saw the two men return empty-handed to the hospital. When she felt it was safe to continue, she quickly walked the rest of the way to her car. Knowing Shahin had escaped the men, she waited patiently inside for him to return. After only a few minutes, he came up from behind her vehicle and stealthily got in. She quickly started the car and pulled away.

When they returned home, Niki and Shahin joined Kamal and Jasmine in Stevie's room to celebrate.

"Okay, everyone, we have the equipment!" Niki announced triumphantly. "Now, we need to get ready to operate."

"We're ready," said Jasmine excitedly.

"You all know your duties?" Niki asked bluntly. "If not, review my instructions again and ask me anything you don't fully understand." Seeing their assurances that they were ready, Niki continued, "Okay then, let's get our hands washed and gloves on. The sooner we begin, the better Stevie's chances are to survive."

Niki cleaned up first before returning to Stevie's room. She carefully placed the monitoring electrodes on his chest, but before she hooked up the cables to the machine, Niki turned on the heart monitor to ensure it worked properly.

Next, Niki placed an IV in his arm and gave him a dose of ketamine, a drug to induce and maintain his anesthesia.

"We are going to begin soon," she said to Stevie. "The medication is going to cause you to become very drowsy and incoherent. You will still feel me working down there, but you shouldn't feel any pain. If you do, please keep still regardless of how uncomfortable it is, understood?"

"Yeah," he said groggily, "we already went over all of this."

"Okay, everyone, let's get started," Niki said to the others. Jasmine placed a new set of sterile gloves on her mother's hands while Kamal placed the tourniquet tightly around Stevie's thigh.

"It's as tight as I can make it," announced Kamal.

Niki nodded and made an incision into the gunshot wound. She immediately encountered pus and blood. She put her finger in and started clearing out the dead tissue. She saw that the infection had started moving up his leg, and knew there was going to be a substantial amount of dead tissue that needed to be cut out. Niki irrigated the incision with clean water and continued cleaning out the area. Next, she tied off the femoral vein to stop most of the bleeding.

As she reached for the last bit of dead tissue, Niki felt something hard with her fingers.

"I think I feel the bullet! Hand me the tweezers," she told Shahin.

Carefully, Niki entered the wound and pulled out the bullet. Excited about the extraction, she looked up at the others and noticed Stevie's breathing was slowing down, and his heart rate was plummeting. Immediately, she felt for a pulse and couldn't find it.

Niki yelled to Shahin, who was standing beside Stevie's chest, "Start chest compressions!"

"Kamal, hand me the epinephrine!"

"Harder, Shahin!" Niki shouted as she took the syringe and injected it into Stevie's IV.

Shahin continued chest compressions for a full two minutes. When the time was up, Niki ordered him to stop. She quickly checked again for a pulse. Thankfully, she could feel the heartbeat. Quickly, she glanced up at his chest and saw his breathing was picking up.

"Okay, he's back with us," Niki said reassuringly to the group.

They all let out a sigh as they eyed one another with relief-filled gazes.

After taking a moment to compose herself, Niki finished washing out the wound. When finished, she packed the area with gauze and then wrapped it with a large bandage.

Seeing Stevie had stabilized and was breathing normally, Niki suggested that the others clean up while she finished caring for her patient. She went into the kitchen and filled an empty tub with hot water. She tossed a clean washcloth sitting next to it into the tub and carried it back to Stevie's bedside.

Gazing down at the semi-unconscious man, Niki smiled, feeling hopeful that the surgery had been a success. She turned, grabbed the washcloth out of the tub, and squeezed out most of the water before gently wiping the sweat off of Stevie's pale, cool face. She rinsed the rag and moved on to wash his arms and upper body. As she wiped away the perspiration on his chiseled torso, she examined the redness and slight bruising caused by Shahin's punches and compressions to Stevie's chest. Even though he was unaware of her presence, Stevie groaned with pleasure as she soothed his aching body.

******

Niki cautiously returned to the hospital the following day. She heard some nurses talking about the theft, but soon, their patients' needs refocused the employees' attention away from the robbery and back to nursing.

Midday, she asked her shift coordinator if she could take a few days off starting the following day. He told her it was okay if she got others to cover her hours for the two days before her regular days off began. She quickly found replacements for her shifts since many employees were eager to make extra money.

Niki told Shahin and Kamal that Stevie's recovery would be slower than that of other similar surgeries because of her inexperience. She was not a doctor, and she had used simple techniques to perform the surgery, causing the healing time to increase greatly.

In the days that followed, Stevie slowly became stronger. His circulation had improved, but he was still unable to put any pressure on his leg or foot. Niki gave him daily leg massages to keep the blood flowing, which sometimes turned into a full-body experience. During this time, the two often conversed and learned each other's history and personality. They were both grateful for the companionship, and each day, their relationship grew stronger.

Meanwhile, Shahin, Kamal, and Jasmine were busy working on house and yard maintenance and repair. Since her husband passed and Niki had to lay off the gardener, the property landscaping had deteriorated, and the home's overall maintenance was in decline. When everything was done, the three created paper ads to advertise the property for sale. Jasmine then took the flyers and posted them in numerous locations around the city.

For fear of a bleed, Niki decided to keep Stevie in bed longer than she normally would with other patients. Finally, the day came when she allowed Stevie to get up and try to walk. One day, after Niki had helped Stevie take several steps, he stopped, bent down, and kissed Niki gently on the lips. She flinched slightly but did not pull away. This went on for three days until Niki finally took the initiative. She gently bent down and kissed Stevie on the lips while he was sitting up in bed.

"I was wondering when you'd kiss me," he said happily. "I started to think I was forcing myself on you, and I would never want to do that."

She smiled at him broadly and said, "I'm shy," before kissing him again.

Niki and Stevie decided to keep their relationship a secret from the others, and they thought they had succeeded. Each day, their affection for one another grew more robust, and hiding their passion became difficult. Equally, as the days progressed, Stevie grew stronger.

While eating breakfast one morning, they heard a knock on the front door. Immediately, they went into crisis mode. Shahin and Kamal helped Stevie into their hiding place in the back of the bedroom closet while the women cleared the table. Niki yelled to the unknown intruder that she needed a minute for her and her daughter to put on their head coverings before opening the door.

She heard a pleasant, non-angry voice reply, "Please take your time."

When Niki opened the door, a man and a woman with two young children stood patiently waiting.

"Hello," he said warmly, holding up one of Jasmine's flyers. "My wife saw this paper advertising your property for sale. We have been looking for something to buy outside the city. We would like to make an appointment to see your place."

"Of course," said Niki, sounding relieved. "I can show you the main area now, and if you like it, you can come back tomorrow and see the rest of our home."

"Thank you, we would very much like to see it," said his wife enthusiastically.

"Please, come in," said Niki, motioning for them to enter.

Niki showed them the living and dining rooms while Jasmine cleaned the kitchen. When it was sufficiently tidy, she motioned for the family to enter. The wife was very pleased with what she saw and wanted to make an appointment to return the following morning to see the rest.

"I can show them the outside of the property," said Jasmine to her mother. "That is, if you'd like to see it now?"

Excitedly, the kids yelled, "Yes! Yes! We want to see it!"

The parents agreed, and Jasmine led the family out to the barn. Meanwhile, Niki went in and told the men what was going on.

"I could have a buyer! That means I can leave Iran!" she said excitedly. Without thinking, she ran over and embraced Stevie. Shahin and Kamal gave each other a congratulatory glance. Both had seen the couple's chemistry and concluded that something sexual and romantic was happening. This display of affection confirmed their suspicions.

Stevie looked at the two men when they were done celebrating and grinned, "I see you already knew."

Niki was silent, only giving the men a sheepish grin.

"Yeah, it was pretty obvious to us," said Kamal, "especially with us all here. Cindy and I hid our relationship for a while, but we were alone for eight hours at a time. Even then, Paula and Shahin found out."

The following morning, the family returned, and at the end of their tour, they told Niki that they wanted to buy her property and would have a professional draw up the paperwork to complete the sale.

Chapter 26 - The Vines

It had been over a month before Cindy began to show any significant change in her recovery. Breastfeeding continued to drain Cindy's calorie intake, making it more difficult for her to regain her strength.

Finally, by mid-September, Cindy was well enough to travel. Additionally, the soldiers had moved on to other locations, making it safer for them to be visible. Paula and Kegger saw her progress and agreed it was time to go. To prepare for their departure, they needed to retrieve the Jeep Cherokee and bring it into Zahra's shed.

Later that night, Kegger and Paula headed out just before sundown to retrieve the car. The half-mile hike to the vehicle was uneventful, but when they arrived at its storage location, the car was gone.

"Dammit!" Kegger cussed. "This puts a wrench in our plans."

Using the last remnants of light, Paula scanned the ground where the car had been parked. It showed several smeared footprints around the vehicle's parking spot, and they could see tire tracks heading south toward Shiraz.

"It looks like it's been gone for at least a few days, if not a week," said Paula.

"Yeah, maybe even longer," added Kegger. "But I don't think the soldiers took it. If they had, they would have come back and searched the lodge, and we'd have seen more soldiers patrolling the area."

"Whoever it was, it doesn't seem like they're interested in us," agreed Paula.

"Yeah, I think you're right. Regardless, we'd better start back. It's already going to be too dark to walk without using our flashlights," Kegger warned.

The news upset everyone, and they questioned how they would make it to the border without a vehicle. Kegger made it clear that they needed to get another transport. It needed to be a car or truck large enough to easily seat four adults, plus supplies for them and the infant. Getting to the border was just the beginning of their journey to freedom. Another problem would be finding the right vehicle to steal. News of a stolen car or truck would be big news in a small village, and they would not have much time before it was reported to the authorities. The theft would quickly bring the police and possibly the return of the soldiers to the town and surrounding area. Zahra offered her vehicle, but it was impossible to fit all of them in a car that was made to accommodate two people.

******

Paula was preparing for their departure when Zahra politely interrupted.

"Paula, I have a favor to ask."

"Sure, what is it?"

"This may sound insignificant to you, but it is vitally important to me," Zahra admitted.

"If it's important to you, it's important to me as well," responded Paula.

Zahra smiled lovingly at her and said, "Paula, dear, you know Khomeini sent his thugs to destroy my vineyard, and they did come and burn it to the ground. What I didn't tell you is that I prepared for it. Knowing it was inevitable, I dug up a few of my most valuable roots before the arsonists arrived. I have kept them viable in my secret cellar. I was hoping I could replant them in the spring, but it looks like this new government is here to stay with no hope of repealing their intrusive laws."

"I'll take them!" said Paula excitedly. "We can't let 7000 years of your heritage die because of one overzealous dictator."

"That's what I was hoping you'd say," said Zahra.

"I'm sure I can find a spot for them," said Paula optimistically. "Can I see them?"

The two women went down into the secret cellar, and in the corner underneath an old burlap bag lay the roots. They were dry yet in a moist, damp environment.

Paula sized them up and said, "I think I can take all but this big one. Actually," she paused, "if we can cut the growth shorter, I can take it too."

"Of course, I can cut the shoot shorter; it won't harm the root. They keep sprouting because I spray them with a liquid fertilizer. It helps keep them alive."

"Don't worry; I can fit all of them and their food inside my bag," Paula said confidently. "When I get to the States, I'll find a good place to plant them. I have an aunt who lives in California. She'll be able to help me find a good spot for them."

"I'm so happy you're willing to do this, Paula," Zahra said, tearing up.

"It's no big deal. We need to do whatever we can to fight against this bullshit government. I'll get these babies planted in their new home as soon as I get to the US," Paula promised.

******

Kyra finished eating and left the dinner table to relieve Kegger from his watch. She didn't drink alcohol, so it was the perfect time for her to take his place. Zahra had begun a wine ritual with Paula and Kegger to alleviate stress and create some joy in their lives. Each evening, Zahra would pour samples of her wine from two different bottles and encourage her guests to consider the differences in taste. While pouring the wine, Zahra explained how the temperature and rainfall during the growing season impacted the flavor of the grapes from the same vines each year. The education and experience quickly became one of their favorite parts of the day.

When Kegger entered the dining room, Paula immediately told him about the roots. To her surprise, he was very receptive to the plan. She knew he had grown fond of Zahra's wines and seemed enthused to learn more about them. His interest intrigued Paula, and she began to see Kegger differently. When she first met him, she thought he was just a hardline, macho man and nothing more. When she reflected on his transformation, Paula realized she liked this new version of Kegger much better.

Later that night, when it was time for Paula to take over the watch. She quietly snuck out of the house and down the path to where Kegger usually hung out in the evening.

"Kegger?" said Paula softly as she scanned the area for him. "Are you ready for a break?"

"I'm over here," he said in a low voice. "You don't want to be too predictable in this business." She sat down beside him as he continued. "Honestly, Paula, I'm not sure how much more of this I can take. I didn't sign up to be a security guard. I'm really happy we're getting close to leaving."

"I know. We're all exhausted and frustrated, but Cindy's recovery stage is about over. You saw what she went through. We had to allow her the time to get strong enough to care for her baby and herself. There is a pretty good possibility we will run into some trouble at the border. We'll need her to be physically and mentally capable of handling herself. It's not only for her safety but for ours as well," Paula explained.

"You're right," Kegger agreed. "I'm just so fuckin' bored. I guess I should be happy that nothing's going on, but still, this has been torture for me."

"I think, at this point, we're pretty safe. The soldiers have not been seen in this area for a while."

"Yeah, I was going to talk to you about it tomorrow. I think we can move our night surveillance to a dark corner of the porch for the last few nights," said Kegger.

At that moment, they heard a twig snap. Kegger put his finger to his lips, motioning for silence. Paula nodded, took out her handgun, and maneuvered into their defensive stance. Back-to-back, they peered out into the darkness, trying to determine what had made the sound. Suddenly, the moonlight caught the silhouette of an antelope roaming at the edge of the burned vineyard. Relieved at the sight of the animal, Paula and Kegger slowly lowered their weapons.

With adrenaline still coursing through their veins, they turned around to face one another. Instantly, their pent-up physical desire overwhelmed their judgment. Kegger bent down and kissed Paula forcefully on the lips. She eagerly accepted his caress and moved to expand the physical intensity. Paula yearned to release as much of her raw energy as she could.

They enveloped one another uncontrollably. Kegger grabbed Paula by the buttocks and lifted her onto his waist. She quickly encircled his torso with her legs, hungering for more. After a few more moments, Paula broke off the kiss and motioned for him to release her.

"Wait," she said pragmatically as he set her back on the ground. "We need to take a minute and think about this."

"I have thought about it every day since I met you," said Kegger.

"But our situation," Paula said anxiously, "this could really complicate things."

"We're living moment by moment with no guarantee that we'll be alive tomorrow. We have to take what we can today," said Kegger philosophically.

"Wow, that was quite poetic," she said half-jokingly, "but I get it."

Without commenting further, Paula returned to Kegger's embrace and began to kiss him urgently while pulling his T-shirt up.

******

Paula finished re-strapping her holster to her thigh while Kegger threaded his belt strap through the front loop of his jeans.

As he grabbed his shirt off the ground, Paula asked, "Have you figured out a plan to get another car? One that's not going to bring back the soldiers?"

"I have been thinking about it a lot. You know, Paula, it's not just getting to the border. The Iraqis don't like Americans, either. If we make it into Iraq, there's no guarantee we'll be safe there. I can't get us through the swamps and river delta without help from my contacts. With our old plan blown up, I think getting into and out of Iraq without any trouble will be tricky," he said worriedly.

"It is a big concern; you're right about that," agreed Paula. "I've thought about it too, but what choice do we have?"

"Frankly, I've been thinking about contacting a buddy of mine. He's a helicopter pilot who lives part of the year in Kuwait. He's not there in the summer because of the shamals, but he should be back by now since it's September. If we can find a way for me to contact him, I think he'd be willing to pick us up at the Iranian border near the Persian Gulf. He can fly in and out without going into Iraqi airspace. He's got a Canadian passport as well as an American one. I know he used to have clearance to land in that area of Iran."

"So, he'd fly out over the Gulf and back around?" asked Paula.

"Yeah, in and out," said Kegger. "The Iranians probably wouldn't even know he was in their airspace."

"That's a great idea. We can sneak into the village and use a phone," said Paula excitedly. "I think I told you about the store owner who used to take reservations for Zahra before she stopped renting out rooms at the lodge."

"Yeah, I know. Let's talk to Zahra about it in the morning. I need to know if she thinks that's an option for us," Kegger reasoned.

Paula had several general questions about Steelhead's transport business, and Kegger eagerly shared what he knew. When they finished their discussion, Paula asked Kegger a more personal question.

"Does Steelhead know Stevie?"

"Yeah, we all met in NAM," replied Kegger. "Stevie was our lieutenant."

"You mean Vietnam?" Paula confirmed.

"Is there another?" Kegger said sarcastically.

"I guess not. How long were you there?" she probed.

"I did three tours," he said frankly. "Luckily, I made it out without a scratch.

"How old were you when you went in?"

"Eighteen," Kegger replied. "I was the youngest in my unit and knew nothing about warfare. Stevie took me and Steelhead aside and taught us how to survive. He wasn't like most lieutenants. Stevie knew how to get the job done without getting us all killed."

"I can see why you care about Stevie so much. You have a lot of history together," Paula said sympathetically.

"What about you and the guys?" asked Kegger.

Paula paused for a moment, thinking about what to say. She decided to be frank with him and explained in some detail her complicated relationship with Shahin and her friendship with Kamal.

"Even with all that has happened, I know we'll always be friends," she told Kegger. "We've been through so much together. No one else could truly understand what it was like."

"What about Shahin? Do you think you'll ever get back together with him?" he questioned.

"Maybe someday, but for now, I want our relationship to be casual. As I said before, I'm not ready for any major commitment right now," she added.

"I'll take over the watch now. You get some sleep, and after you've had your breakfast, come back and relieve me," she said matter-of-factly.

Kegger pulled his shirt over his head as he stepped towards Paula. Using the moonlight, Kegger gave her a playful grin before bending down and kissing her gently on the lips.

"I'll see you in a few hours," he said suggestively.

"I'll be here," said Paula, returning the smile.

"By the way, what's the key about?" asked Kegger.

"Oh, this..." replied Paula while she re-assuredly fondled the key hanging around her neck. "I'm not sure. A friend gave it to me just before he died. I kept it safe in my jewelry box all these months, hoping to learn its significance; so far, I don't know anything more about it than I did the day it was given to me. Something about it compelled me to wear it for this trip. It may sound stupid, but it makes me feel safer. The guy who gave it to me had some problems, but he was a hero in the end, and I hope his courage rubs off on me."

"Sounds intriguing," he said curiously. "Too bad you don't know what it's for," he added as he turned to head back to the lodge.

He only made it a few yards before Paula called after him, "Don't forget, this stays between us. It was a one-time thing. I don't want things to get any more complicated than they already are."

Kegger didn't look back but waved his hand slightly, motioning that he understood Paula's instructions.

Chapter 27 - The Calls

It was August 17th when Shahin, Kamal, and Stevie first met Niki and Jasmine. The introduction to Niki had been cut short because of Stevie's immediate medical needs, but after she attended to his injury, Niki sat down with Shahin and Kamal to hear why they couldn't take Stevie to a hospital for treatment.

Shahin and Kamal were hesitant at first to explain their entire situation and why they were hiding from the authorities. Niki wasn't fooled by their vague and surface answers and demanded they explain in detail what had happened and why. Feeling backed into a corner, the men shared their story and told Niki how dire their situation had become. Together, they relayed what had transpired over the last ten days, leaving out only some facts that could further compromise their team's safety.

After Niki had asked all her questions and seemed satisfied with Shahin and Kamal's answers, Shahin asked if he could use her telephone. He explained the reason for the call and also told Niki that contacting their team would be slightly complicated because the lodge where they were staying did not have a telephone. He would need to call a store in a nearby village. The owner reserved rooms and took messages for Zahra, the lodge owner. Once Zahra received Shahin's message, she would relay it to their team members.

Niki said Shahin could use her phone on one condition. He must not mention Niki or Jasmine by name or their location. Shahin agreed.

Luckily, when Shahin made his original reservations two years earlier, he made it a point to memorize the telephone number. He asked for a pen and paper, forcing his memory to recall the number. He had associated the number with a silly song and hummed it as he wrote.

Feeling confident he remembered the number correctly, Shahin held his breath while dialing it. The phone rang four times before Shahin heard a clicking sound. A moment later, the store owner's voice boomed over the line.

"Hello, how can I help you?" the man asked.

Shahin let out his breath and responded, "Hello, I want to make a reservation at Zahra's Lodge."

"I'm sorry, Sir, the hotel is up for sale, and she is no longer taking reservations."

"What? But... but..." Shahin stammered.

"Sir, I understand this might come as a shock. Many of her past patrons have been very disappointed about her decision."

Shahin fell silent, unable to think of an appropriate response.

Finally, he politely said, "Thank you for your time. Please wish her good luck."

"Would you like to leave your name?" he asked courteously.

"Ah, no, no thank you," he said abruptly and hung up the telephone.

The call had been a disaster, but Shahin and Kamal were confident that Zahra's decision to sell didn't mean she wouldn't help Paula and Cindy. On the contrary, they believed she would do what she could to protect them, regardless of her current status.

Kamal pointed out that a lack of customers might benefit Zahra and their friends. There wouldn't be other guests who might recognize one of them from the old photo taken at the resort. Shahin happily agreed with Kamal, but the question remained. Did Paula, Kegger, and Cindy arrive safely, and if so, were they still there waiting for them? They had no way of knowing.

******

Another month had passed, and during that time, Stevie had made good progress walking on his injured leg, and Niki had gotten a buyer for her home. The official sale date was set for September 21st, and after that, Niki and Jasmine would finally leave Iran with Shahin, Kamal, and Stevie, hitching a ride with them.

A week earlier, Stevie, on behalf of Shahin, Kamla, and himself, had asked Niki to contact the store owner who used to take reservations for Zahra's Lodge. The three did not want to leave Iran without knowing if their friends were still there. With their departure soon approaching, Niki reluctantly agreed to call and inquire about Kegger, Paula, and Cindy.

Together, the men brainstormed what Niki should say and what she needed to ask the store owner. She willingly rehearsed the questions she was supposed to ask the owner and her responses to his possible replies. She and the others wanted her to be prepared, unlike Shahin's conversation with him a month earlier. Niki's goal was to express her interest in speaking directly with Zahra, knowing she would have to call her back without raising suspicion or causing concern. Finally, the three men came to a consensus on what Niki should say, and once she was finished rehearsing her lines, Niki made the call.

"Good afternoon," she said casually. "I am inquiring about a hotel for sale. I believe its name is Zahra's Lodge."

"Yes, it's still for sale," the man replied.

"A friend told me you know the owner personally and could give her a message for me." Instead of waiting for his response, Niki continued, "Please tell her I would like to speak with her directly about purchasing the property."

Seemingly unaware of any ulterior motive, the owner happily replied, "I will send my part-time errand boy to her place tomorrow if she doesn't come into the store later today."

"Please do. I am looking forward to finding out more about her property. Are you ready to take my information? Do you have paper and pencil to write down my number?" asked Niki politely.

"Yes, I always keep a pad and pen by the phone," he explained.

Niki gave him the fake name, Marmar, and then her number. She enunciated each digit clearly and waited for the man to repeat the integers back to her. He confirmed the number, and Niki politely thanked him before ending the call.

Chapter 28 - Farah

Farah looked back to see if the soldiers were still in pursuit. Not only were they still after her, but they were getting closer. When she turned back to run faster, her face slammed directly into a bulletproof vest. The force of the blow stunned her slightly, and the impact threw her a couple of feet backward. She quickly regained her senses and looked up to see a soldier with full-body gear staring down at her.

Seeing that she had made eye contact with him, he grinned evilly. A second later, the soldiers running after her caught up and grabbed her arms.

As she struggled to free herself, the commander carefully removed the long, dark strands of her hair stuck to the sweat on her face.

"My little lady," he said mockingly, "all that running and flailing around has hidden your young, supple skin from my view."

Without waiting for a response, he took her hand and unclasped it from her chador. The garment quickly fell away, revealing her young, slender, almost girlish figure.

"So young, yet beautiful and dangerous," he concluded. "You gave my soldiers quite a run. I guess if they can't catch a girl in a chador, they need more exercise, but that's a subject for another day. Right now, I need to ask you a few questions."

The officer turned around and headed to the truck waiting nearby. The soldiers secured Farah's hands behind her back and escorted her to the same vehicle. The men holding Farah maneuvered themselves and her into the back seat while the commander settled into the front passenger seat. The driver began moving slowly through the numerous people in the streets, stopping to allow pedestrians to pass in front of them.

"Make them move!" his boss demanded. "They can get out of our way."

The soldier did as he was ordered and stepped on the gas pedal. People were visibly startled by the change in the vehicle's speed and quickly jumped out of the way. Soon, the truck pulled onto the open highway towards their military camp.

Once inside the temporary base, the commander brought Farah to his private office. She stood defiantly before him, trying to present her bravest face and posture.

"What do you want with me?" she asked angrily. "I'm just a student exercising my right to protest. There are thousands of us. Why me?"

"Yes, but not all of them have a brother who has killed one or more of my soldiers," he said flatly.

"Kamal?" Farah asked in surprise. "That doesn't sound like my brother. If he did kill your soldiers, I'm sure it was in self-defense. He's not a murderer, but I know you were after him and his friends. My family and I have heard rumors that he has escaped to the United States. I bet that makes you look bad," she said smugly.

"You don't know," he said, slightly taken aback. "That's interesting. I thought he might have told you he was returning to Iran."

His statement shocked Farah, who was speechless for a moment. The commander could see an expression of surprise on her face and knew she was unaware of his return.

Finally, she spoke up, "So this is about my brother, not about protesting. You don't want me; you want Kamal and think you can somehow lure him into a trap by arresting me. Is that the plan?"

"Now, why do I want him when I can have you?" he said maniacally.

The words caused chills to run up her spine. She hadn't considered that she, as a woman, was part of his conquest. Farah was alone with a commander in the Iranian Army and vulnerable to whatever he wished to do. Trying to be strong and defiant, Farah narrowed her gaze and stared directly at him.

"You think you can have me," she said coolly, "but it will never happen."

The commander laughed a hearty, full-bodied bellow. Then he stopped abruptly and gave her another evil stare.

"I will have you," he said as he walked directly up to her. Without any warning, he grabbed both sides of her blouse and tore the garment open. The buttons flew off and landed noisily on the wooden floor. "You are a little old for me," he said callously, "but you'll do."

Reacting to his violence, Farah turned to run. She only got a few feet before he grabbed her arm and turned her back around.

"You're mine now," he said definitively, gripping her arms tightly.

"Guard! Help me!" she yelled.

The commander covered her mouth with his hand and laughed, "Do you think they don't know what's happening in here? They are hoping to be next."

With that, the man forced Farah down onto his sofa and continued to tear away her clothing. Helpless to stop him, Farah fought unsuccessfully as he thrust himself into her. Immediately, she forced her mind to treat this intrusion as an act of violence and nothing more by reassuring herself that this moment would not define her.

"Millions of women have endured this same fate," she thought, "and like many, I will not suffer quietly." Defiantly, Farah shouted, "You weak, inferior man. Does this boost your ego? Are you hoping this shows the other men how powerful you are against a helpless woman?"

"Girls are my preference, not women," he responded while continuing to gyrate.

Farah became enraged by his comment. The thought of him doing this to a young adolescent woman or girl ignited the fearless portion of her character, and she began to laugh at him. Soon, her laughter turned to words outwardly mocking his physique and performance.

"Stop it!" he yelled. "You need to stop talking! I demand it!"

"You will never control me!" she said defiantly. "You can stick your dick in me, but I will never give in to you. I am my own person, and you are nothing to me but a worthless little man trying to make himself feel important."

Her words incensed him, and he slapped her hard on the face.

"I will!" he yelled. "I will control you!"

"With what? Your tiny little limp dick?" she said tauntingly.

That's more than the commander could take. Enraged, he swung a fist sideways into Farah's temple. Almost instantaneously, she fell unconscious.

Chapter 29 - A New Plan

It was mid-morning when Kegger groggily entered the kitchen.

"You're up early," said Paula sarcastically while she and Zahra continued to clean up after breakfast.

"I guess I needed the sleep," he replied.

Ignoring his statement, Paula announced, "You'll be happy to know that Zahra and I have a plan."

"What are you talking about?"

"Our call to your friend, Steelhead," she responded curtly. "Zahra said it's okay for us to use her car. Plus, she and I figured out the best way to make the call to him without the owner knowing about it."

"Okay, let's hear it," Kegger said as he sat down at the table.

"First, I'll drop you off at the opposite edge of the wooded area behind the general store," she said excitedly. "Then, while you're walking through the patch of forest to the back of the store, I'll park the car at Zahra's friends and walk back to the front. You know, it's pretty easy for me to go unnoticed with my chador on."

"How are we getting into the store without the owner seeing us?"

"When I get there, I'll distract the store owner's son while you go in and make the call."

"Where's the owner?" Kegger wondered.

Zahra interjected, "He's recuperating from an illness, so his son is still going to be there tomorrow."

******

Paula ingeniously lured the owner's son outside by noisily knocking over the newspaper stand. The distraction allowed Kegger to slip in the back door unnoticed as planned.

"Hey, it's me, Kegger," he whispered to his friend. "I only have a minute. Listen, I need a big favor. Can you pick me and a few friends up near the Gulf by the Iran/Iraq border? It's going to be difficult for us to get into Iraq, and we need to get the hell out of Iran."

"Sure, I can handle that," said Steelhead. "I can use the helipad of one of my customers in Khorramshahr. Can it wait until September 22? If not, I can change my schedule."

"No, that date works," replied Kegger. "We should be able to make it there by mid-morning. Will that fit your schedule?"

"Yeah, I'll plan on 11:00. You'll see and hear me coming, so it should be easy for you to find it," said Steelhead.

"Okay, we'll see you on the 22nd," replied Kegger.

"You know I owe you one, buddy. I'll be there," he stated just as Kegger was about to hang up.

"Thanks," he whispered back.

Kegger slipped out the back door and made his way to a location where Paula could see him, but the young man could not. When Paula saw the all-clear signal, she quickly finished picking up the mess, thanked the son, and suggested they go inside. She hurriedly bought two items and returned to the car. Meanwhile, Kegger went back to the drop-off point and waited for Paula.

Minutes later, Kegger opened the car door, saying, "We're good! Steelhead will meet us on September 22nd."

"That's awesome," replied Paula. "I think this is a much better plan."

"Yeah, trying to cross several borders with people who have no papers or ID can be tough, especially with an infant in tow," Kegger admitted.

As they approached the lodge, they saw Kyra give the safe wave. Paula quickly drove the car into the shed while Kegger took over the watch.

Once inside the house, Paula shared the excellent news with the women. She explained their plan and added a short story Kegger shared on their way back. Kegger had saved Steelhead's life a few years earlier, and Steelhead had been looking for a way to repay Kegger. Paula figured it was that debt that convinced Steelhead to put himself and his chopper in danger for them with no other type of reward.

******

The following morning, after Kegger had made his call to Stealhead, Stevie was working with Shahin and Kamal to load Niki's trailer and vehicle with supplies and memorabilia. Without knowing each other's plans, both groups were planning to leave Iran independently of one another.

Shahin stopped working momentarily to watch Niki walk up the hill towards the bus stop. She was on her way to sign the official sale documents while he and the others stayed there to finish packing.

A knot formed in Shahin's stomach as Niki crested the mound. They were getting ready to leave for the border in the morning, and still, there had been no return call from Zahra. Shahin's mind raced as he tried to justify the additional trip to the lodge. It would take them hours out of their way, just so he could check and see if Paula, Cindy, and Kegger were still at the lodge. Niki had opposed the detour earlier that week, and Shahin knew Niki was right about the additional risk it added to their departure. The extra travel would put all of them, including her daughter, Jasmine, at a higher risk of being detained by soldiers or police before they could safely leave the country. The decision had tormented Shahin, but he knew he had to do it, with or without the rest of them. Accepting his assessment of the situation and his resolve to move ahead with his plan one way or another, Shahin stopped lamenting and went back to loading.

Niki had insisted on taking numerous containers of sentimental items with them, saying that the objects were important to Jasmine, but the guys knew the stuff was as much for Niki as for her daughter. It became evident as each day passed that Niki found leaving her present life behind much harder than she had anticipated. Understanding her state of mind, Shahin and Kamal honored her request with only some slight grumbling.

Stevie, however, argued against the trailer. He warned her that it could be highly problematic for them to take items across the border, but he promised to do what he could to get her things through Iraq and into Kuwait.

While Shahin and the others got ready to leave the country house, Paula and her group were proceeding with the first step of their alternative plan for leaving Iran. Zahra was on her way to the village. She was doing what Kegger called reconnaissance to ensure no soldiers or police were patrolling the streets of her town and the surrounding vicinity. It would make it easier for them to steal a car.

******

At Niki's house, Jasmine was still inside filling boxes while the men were loading them into the trailer. Shahin came in to get another box when he heard the telephone ring.

"Hello," said Jasmine cautiously.

A soft, unfamiliar voice echoed over the line.

"Hello, I was given this number by my friend who owns a store near my home. Did you inquire about the sale of Zahra's Lodge?"

"Yes, my mother called," Jasmine said excitedly. "Are you Zahra?"

"Yes, I am," she said, sounding surprised. "I am sorry it has taken me so long to return her call. The owner was ill. I only received her inquiry today. Is your mother available?"

"No, she's gone into Shiraz, but she'll be back later," she said nervously. Then, panic surged within Jasmine, "Please don't hang up!"

Shahin had heard the conversation and immediately rushed to Jasmine's side. He was anxiously awaiting his chance to speak when he heard her plea.

Shahin reached over and grabbed the receiver.

"Zahra, it's me, Shahin. We'd given up hope you were going to call. I know you can't talk openly, so please listen to what I'm about to tell you."

Just as Shahin finished his sentence, the store owner walked by Zahra. Even though he was a good friend, she didn't trust him to keep quiet about Shahin's whereabouts.

"Okay, dear, I can answer all of your questions," Zahra said evenly, "but there is no need to yell. This receiver is emitting the sound of your voice several feet away from me."

Shahin understood and took a deep breath. In a calm, low voice, he began, "Me, Kamal, and a guy named Stevie are okay. Stevie is one of the mercenaries we hired. He got shot, and he was in terrible shape for a while, but he's good now. We've been staying with a mother and daughter several kilometers south of Shiraz. We're leaving tonight for the border and are wondering if Paula and Cindy are still waiting for us at your lodge. Please say *yes* if they are still with you."

"Yes..." she said, pretending to answer a question about her property, "They're available, and I also have one more," she added, hoping Shahin knew she was talking about Kegger. "All are ready and waiting for someone like you."

"Are they okay? Is anyone hurt?" Shahin asked urgently.

"Everything is in good shape," she said cleverly. "It's just time to move on."

"We'll be there as soon as possible," he conjectured. "The mother has a car, and right now, she is in Shiraz finalizing the sale of her house. We all plan to leave later today." Then Shahin asked, "Do they still have their Rover?"

"No," Zahra said sadly. "That's no longer available."

"Oh... this complicates things. We have a car that can fit six, and there are five of us," said Shahin while trying to solve the problem. "I know. We can steal another from the city on our way up. That's probably better than you guys trying to steal one in the little village near you."

"Yes, I agree," Zahra concurred. "So you will be able to do that?" she confirmed."

"Yes, we can, but we'll be there early tomorrow morning instead of tonight," he replied confidently.

"I am looking forward to meeting you. I'm sure you will like my lodge," Zahra said happily.

"I understand," he said quickly. "We'll see you soon. Thanks, Zahra, for helping us."

As he set the receiver down, Jasmine asked, "So that was her, right? The lady you've been waiting to hear from?"

"Yes, it was, and my friends are still with her. So, we need to go there first before we drive to the border. There's one problem. They don't have a car." Smiling, Shahin added casually, "But that's okay; we'll get one on our way up to the lodge."

Jasmine saw Shahin's smile and wondered why that seemed like no big deal to him. Feeling uneasy, she grinned awkwardly back at him as she considered the consequences of car theft. It was a significant offense and would land all of them in prison for many years if they were apprehended.

Moments later, Kamal and Stevie came in from the outside. Shahin excitedly told them about Zahra's call. Jasmine watched Stevie's facial expressions as Shahin told him they needed to steal an additional car. The look on his face was indifferent to the news; even jovial would describe it. At that moment, Jasmine realized their casualness meant that they had experienced much greater dangers and risks than grand theft auto. It also brought into focus the reality and danger of their impending journey to a safer country and the perils they should expect to encounter.

Chapter 30 - The Art of Thievery

Jasmine ran to her mother, yelling, "She called! Zahra called us!"

"What did she say?" asked Niki anxiously. "Are their friends still at her lodge?"

"Yes! We're going to meet them tomorrow!" declared Jasmine. "It's great news, except for one thing."

"What is it? What's the thing?" asked Niki curiously.

"Well, we're going to steal a car," Jasmine said indifferently, trying to downplay the danger, "but the men act like it's no big deal. I think they've done it before and know what to do."

Niki's face filled with concern as she tried to process the news, especially the statements about car theft.

"I need to speak with Stevie," she said angrily. "Is he in the house?"

"Yes, he was just coming in to get a drink of water when I came out," she replied. She saw her mother's cross look and added, "He's been working very hard to get everything done so we can leave later tonight."

Niki ignored her comments and strode into the house. She found all three men casually sitting at the kitchen table.

"I heard the news," she said, trying to sound upbeat and cover up her obvious concern. "Zahra called, and we're leaving tonight to get there by morning. Is that right?" But before she allowed anyone to answer, her façade fell away, and she said curtly, "Plus, we need to steal a car!"

"Yeah, I can explain it all to you," said Stevie, ignoring her attitude. "But first, how did the closing go? Is everything finalized?"

"Yes, the money has been transferred to my account in London," she said abruptly. "Can I talk to you privately?"

Shahin and Kamal knew that was their cue to leave the kitchen. They congratulated Niki on the sale and hurried out of the room. Niki and Stevie argued for several minutes about the risks of stealing a car, not to mention the additional time it would take to accomplish this goal. She wanted to go directly to the border, citing the additional risk it posed to her daughter's safety.

Stevie understood her concern but ultimately won the debate. He told Niki that he would not leave Iran without helping the other team members, who were stranded at Zahra's Lodge. Niki gave in, feeling like she had no other choice but to accept Stevie's decision.

******

"Okay, that's all the boxes," Niki announced as she entered the house. She continued her optimistic update as she plopped down on the nearest living room chair. "Stevie and I moved things around inside the trailer and got everything in."

Jasmine walked in from the kitchen, saying, "Shahin helped me with the food and drinks. It's almost ready." Glancing around, she asked, "Is Stevie still out there? Isn't he supposed to be resting?"

"Yes, he insisted I let him and Kamal finish hooking up the trailer to the car," said Niki. Seeing Shahin appear with the large cooler in hand, she added, "I should have come in and asked you to help. He had no business lifting so much."

"How's Stevie's leg?" asked Jasmine.

"Not great, he's pushing himself. I asked him to slow down, but he won't stop," Niki grumbled.

Shahin heard her concern and was headed for the front door when it swung open.

Stevie entered and announced, "Okay, that's it! Everything is packed except the cooler."

******

Around 2 AM, the men left the house first, giving Niki and Jasmine time alone. Outside, the three rechecked their handguns and made sure they were loaded and the safeties off. They needed to be ready to use them at a moment's notice. The rest of their stolen weaponry was still in the duffel bag on the floor in the back seat.

For Niki and Jasmine, leaving took on a whole different feeling. The last happy memories of Niki's husband and Jasmine's father resided inside this home, and the women knew this was the last time they would ever be in this place. Jasmine hugged her mother tightly, hoping it would help her say goodbye. Both women teared up but didn't cry. Overall, it was a good thing they were leaving and had gotten a fair price for the property.

Niki hugged her daughter back and said softly, "It's time we made a new life for ourselves. Your father would have wanted it this way. Now let's go and make him proud."

"I know, Mom. It's going to be okay."

Without saying another word, the two women, still in an embrace, turned and walked out of the house.

Once again, Kamal was the driver. He looked the most native, and everyone felt that anonymity was important. To help him alter his identity, Niki used her theatre makeup. She carefully placed additional facial hair on Kamal's short beard and made the hair longer, with a few streaks of gray mixed in. It made him look at least 15 years older, which would help fool anyone looking for a younger man. Niki also had him wear a turban on his head. It created a different image of him and hid the fact that he had no gray hair on his head. She dressed him in a shirt she had bought while in Shiraz and completed his outfit with an altered pair of her husband's dress slacks. This final façade was the finishing touch to help them go unnoticed.

******

It was early morning when Kamal drove into the outskirts of Shiraz's northern border. Stevie decided it was the best area to steal a vehicle. The authorities wouldn't know if the thieves were heading out of the city or into it. Plus, it was closer to their destination.

They scanned the streets and parking lots for unattended vehicles. A few cars were suggested as possibilities, but Stevie quickly said "no". Then, Jasmine noticed a Jeep Cherokee with a "For Sale" sign on the windshield.

"This's it," Stevie announced. "It could be that the owner has parked it here because he's having trouble selling it. He may not report it stolen immediately, hoping the thieves will get away and the car will never be found. That way, he gets to collect the insurance."

"I agree," said Shahin. "Plus, it's an older car that won't attract much attention. It will blend in with the majority of cars around here."

With the decision made, it was time to execute their plan. Kamal drove past the vehicle and turned onto the next side street. He parked the car and gave the key to Niki. The men got out while Niki and Jasmine waited.

They walked cautiously back to the car. As they approached the Jeep, Stevie nonchalantly surveyed the area for witnesses while inspecting the vehicle. The doors were locked, but he told Shahin and Kamal that it was an easy car to break into. The street was dimly lit, and the sidewalks were empty. A vehicle passed but didn't slow down. Kamal and Shahin stood 20 feet away and pretended to have a meaningful conversation. The plan was to draw the attention of passing drivers to themselves and not to the vehicles parked next to them on the street.

Stevie quickly pulled out the hook he had made from a piece of wire. It looked similar to the altered coat hanger that many people used to break into their cars in the US. Stevie expertly maneuvered his wire through the top of the window and down onto the door lock. Within seconds, he had the lock lifted and the door opened. Shahin and Kamal jumped in the back while Stevie broke the steering column and hotwired the vehicle. A moment later, they pulled up behind Niki and

Jasmine. Quickly, Shahin got out and grabbed the duffel of weapons out of the trunk. He threw them in the backseat of the Jeep and then returned to Niki's vehicle. Shahin opened the front door and got into the driver's seat while Niki and Jasmine got in the back. Stevie scooted over to the passenger seat of the Jeep to make room for Kamal to drive. Shahin waited while Kamal passed him before pulling away himself.

******

It was just after daybreak, and everything was going smoothly until they drove through the small village nearest Zahra's Lodge. They were moving slowly through the main street when a woman's grocery bag blew out of her hand onto the road in front of Shahin. The woman accompanying her ran out to grab the bag. Shahin slammed on the brakes to avoid hitting her. Startled, she spilled her tote bag all over the potholed road, making it necessary for Shahin to wait while she picked up all of her belongings. The commotion caused a group of soldiers to take notice. They had just pulled up to the intersection adjacent to Niki's car to set up a temporary checkpoint. Kamal and Stevie saw what was happening but could not do anything about it.

"Bloody hell!" yelled Kamal. "Soldiers are stopping Shahin!"

"Oh shit!" cussed Stevie. "We have to go back! Pull off the fucking road!"

Kamal followed his order and came to a halt on a side road. Instantly, Stevie was in the backseat, pulling out the guns. He threw one to Kamal and stuffed an additional handgun into his belt. He grabbed a third and took off the safety to have it ready. Next, he handed Kamal some zip ties and handkerchiefs for gags. Stevie stuffed more of these items into his pocket. Together, they headed back towards the checkpoint. When they got close enough to see it, they saw Shahin shoved up against the hood of the car with his hands on top of his head. The women, with their hands held high, had been stripped of their chadors and were being forced at gunpoint over to one of the soldiers' trucks.

232

"Once we get the two soldiers at the checkpoint subdued," said Stevie. "You focus on the soldiers who have Shahin, and I'll go after the two arresting Niki and Jasmine." He looked directly at Kamal and said, "Remember your training, and do it like we practiced. If you do, we can overtake these amateurs," said Stevie forcefully.

Kamal nodded and raised his weapon. They easily snuck up on the two soldiers guarding the makeshift barrier. The two men had been intently watching the arrests and were oblivious to their surroundings. Kamal and Stevie simultaneously covered the soldiers' mouths and ordered them to be silent, threatening that they would shoot them if they alerted their fellow soldiers. Within seconds, they gagged the men, stripped them of their weapons, and put them on the ground behind the main barrier.

Once they were secured, Kamal's mission was to subdue the soldier holding Shahin while Stevie took the two holding the women. As Kamal approached him, the man caught a glimpse of him in his peripheral vision. The soldier glanced over his shoulder to see who was coming. When he did, he was met with an uppercut from the butt of Kamal's rifle. The hefty blow caused the soldier to stumble backward, losing all his ability to defend himself. Without hesitating, Kamal drew his handgun from his waist belt and handed it to Shahin, who immediately pointed it at the dazed soldier.

Knowing Shahin had that soldier under control, Kamal ran to help Stevie, but it wasn't necessary. When he arrived, both soldiers holding the women were on the ground, moaning in agony.

Stevie, Shahin, and Kamal quickly rounded up the downed men and zip-tied their hands behind their backs. They marched the men off the road and into one of the military transport vehicles. The local people watched in awe but did nothing to stop them.

Inside the truck, they found some shackles and handcuffs. Stevie watched for reinforcements while Kamal and Shahin chained the men together in a circle with their hands cuffed behind their backs before fastening them to the cast iron ring they used to transport prisoners.

After the soldiers were securely locked up, all five got into Niki's Rambler and drove to the Jeep. As he approached it, Shahin slammed on the brakes just long enough for Kamal and Stevie to jump out.

"We have to move fast!" Stevie blurted to Kamal and Shahin. "We're done trying to stay incognito! Get there as fast as you can!"

Shahin pulled ahead, and the two cars raced north across the province before stopping a hundred yards from Zahra's Lodge.

"Stay here and shoot anyone who approaches the car with a weapon," said Stevie to Niki.

"I will," said Niki. "I'll do whatever it takes to save my daughter."

"You, too, Jasmine. Shoot if you have to, and then you and your mother must leave here and go to the border."

The women stayed inside their car with the guns cocked and ready while the men headed towards the lodge. As they made their way up the road, all three took turns covering the leader like they had practiced, ensuring no one was flanking them or coming up from behind.

Kegger saw them coming and yelled, "You crazy bastard. I thought I might never see you again."

"Who me?" Stevie yelled back. "You know it takes a lot more than a few soldiers to kill me."

They gave each other a hearty hug and several pats on the back before returning to the business at hand. Stevie explained the latest situation, and Kegger instructed Shahin and Kamal to get the women inside the house out and ready to step into the vehicles while he and Stevie retrieved the other women and the cars.

Shahin and Kamal went to the back door and yelled their presence before asking to be let inside. Zahra was in the kitchen when she heard their cries. She quickly went to the door and unlocked the deadbolts.

"Where is she?" Kamal demanded as he frantically glanced around the kitchen.

"Kamal, dear, Cindy is doing fine, but there's something I need to tell you before you see her," said Zahra. "Please sit down at the table."

"Is everyone okay?" asked Shahin. "Did something happen?"

"No, no, but I didn't have the opportunity earlier to tell you about Cindy," she said solemnly.

"What! What's happened?" questioned Kamal.

"You know she was struck on the head."

"Yeah, of course!" yelled Kamal.

"Well... She has amnesia," Zahra said flatly. "She cannot remember anything from her past. She does not remember either of you, and you must be prepared to accept this when you see her."

The news caught both men off guard, and it took them a moment to process what they had been told.

Kamal was still grappling with this new information when Shahin mumbled, "That's why she ignored Kamal and Paula. It's not that she's in love with some other guy; it's because she can't remember us."

"Yes," Zahra agreed, "she doesn't know anyone."

"I don't care. I want to see her now. Is she with Paula? I promise I won't scare her," said Kamal.

"Yes, me too. Can you take us to them?" asked Shahin eagerly.

"I can, but there's one more thing you need to know. You're aware that she's a mother now."

"Yes! We know!" Kamal yelled impatiently. "It's not her fault if she doesn't remember me."

"That's not it," Zahra said, becoming annoyed with Kamal's impatience.

"What then?" demanded Kamal.

Deciding there was no gentle way to tell him, Zahra exclaimed, "You're the father!"

Her statement stunned Kamal, and his reaction was like that of someone unable to speak or move.

Seeing his shock, Zahra started to apologize, "I didn't plan to be so direct, but you left me no choice," she said defensively. "Also, because of her amnesia, we HAVE NOT, she emphasized, told her yet that the man she thought was her husband is not the father of her child. We didn't know if you were dead or alive, and we couldn't risk telling her that an unknown stranger was the father of her child. We decided it would be better to give her more time to recover and then tell her the truth."

Chapter 31 - The Introduction

Zahra wanted the men to wait a bit before rushing into Cindy's room, but both men insisted on seeing her immediately, mentioning the need to leave quickly. Understanding the urgency, Zahra led Shahin and Kamal into Cindy's room. She opened the door to see Paula packing a bag and Cindy dressing the baby. They both looked up expectantly when the door opened.

Seeing them, Paula immediately raced towards them. She jumped into Shahin's arms and hugged him tightly before kissing him frantically on the lips and cheeks. Then, trying not to diminish her love for Kamal, Paula went to him and hugged him tightly. Meanwhile, Cindy watched curiously while continuing to wrap her baby up in a light traveling blanket.

When Paula was finished hugging and kissing the men, she cautiously brought them over to meet Cindy.

"Cindy, this is Kamal Ahmad, and this is Shahin Ali. They are the friends I've told you about. The ones who were with us on the day you were injured."

"Hi..." said Kamal awkwardly. "We've been told that you wouldn't remember us. It's okay. We can start over."

"I'm sorry, I don't recognize you," Cindy shyly admitted, "but I would like to get to know you."

"Please, don't be sorry," Kamal said lovingly. "It's not your fault. Maybe someday you'll get your memory back, but if not, our friendship begins today."

They shared an awkward smile, and then, without warning, Kamal asked, "May I hold your son?"

Cindy looked over at Paula questioningly. Paula nodded affirmatively, giving her some reassurance that his request was safe. Cindy looked down at her baby and hesitated slightly before stepping forward and gently handing him to the strange man.

Finally, Shahin spoke to Cindy, "It's great to see you. We were all ecstatic to find out you were alive."

Cindy appreciated his enthusiasm but didn't know how to respond to his statement. Therefore, she gave him an awkward grin and then looked down at the floor. Paula saw her struggle and stepped in to move the conversation in a new direction.

"We're so happy you made it," she said quietly to Shahin. "We have…"

"Look, I want to hear everything, but you can tell me later," he finally said with urgency. "We need to leave now. We stole a car but got into trouble with some soldiers on the way here. Grab your stuff, and I'll explain all of it on our way."

Shahin and Kamal began ushering Paula and Cindy out of the bedroom when Paula stopped them.

"Shahin, wait! We have an extra passenger. I need to tell her it's time to go. It's Rostam's wife, Kyra. She has been hiding here with Zahra the whole time. That's why the CIA couldn't find her. She can't stay here, so she's coming with us."

"Is Zahra coming, too?" asked Shahin.

"No, she's staying."

"Okay then, you go and tell Kyra to meet us outside," ordered Shahin. "Kamal, give Cindy back her son. You need to carry their things outside, and I'll get Paula's stuff. The others will be here any moment."

As they waited on the porch, Cindy went to Zahra.

"Paula told me about your son," she said compassionately. "I hope you don't mind, but I've decided to name Little Darling after your child. His legal name will be Majid in honor of your son and your bravery." A tearful smile formed on Zahra's face as Cindy added, "I am so very grateful you were willing to risk so much to help us. Thank you."

Cindy, while holding Majid, gave Zahra a one-armed hug that lasted for several seconds. When she released her embrace, Zahra smiled broadly, and tears of joy streaked down her cheeks.

Kegger and Stevie pulled up to the group moments later. Stevie, Niki, and Jasmine stayed in their car while Kegger and the others quickly thanked Zahra for her help and friendship. Their goodbyes were quick yet emotional.

With Paula's input, Kegger decided that even though the number of people in each car would be unequal, it was the best situation emotionally to keep the two groups together as suggested. His only rule was two men in each car, with him and Stevie in separate vehicles.

Kyra wanted to stay with Cindy to help her with the baby, and Stevie did not want to split up Niki and Jasmine. Therefore, Niki's Rambler held Kamal, Niki, and Stevie in the front seat. Shahin would drive Paula and Kegger in the Cherokee.

Chapter 32 - Invasion?

They were two hours out of Shiraz when Shahin flashed his lights at the Rambler ahead of him. Understanding his signal, Kamal turned onto the next dirt road. Shahin pulled in behind him and jumped out of the Cherokee. He went up to Kamal's window and said, "The Jeep won't make it to the border. We have to stop for gas."

Stevie leaned over Kamal and asked, "Do you think you might have another half-hour before you run out?"

"Yeah, I think so, but we need to start looking for a gas station," replied Shahin.

"We have a small container of gas in the trailer," said Kamal. "Do you think that's enough?"

"No, we're going to need more than that to make it to the border," replied Shahin. "I know these Cherokees. They don't get a lot of miles per gallon."

Fifteen minutes later, Stevie saw a gas station. Kamal drove slowly past it, and he and Stevie decided it was safe for them to stop. A few hundred yards down the road, both vehicles pulled off onto a side dirt road and stopped. Kegger and Shahin decided they would be the ones to walk back to the station for the additional fuel while the others waited.

Unable to sit still, Paula got out and walked over to hang out with the people in the other car. Kamal got out to stretch his legs while the others waited in the car. Cindy was breastfeeding the baby in the backseat, and Kyra stayed with her to care for Majid after he finished eating. It was hot inside the car, and everyone rolled down their windows to bring in some cooler air.

Cindy had just handed her son to Kyra and was adjusting her clothing when Paula told Kamal, "Remember what Cindy would say in this situation: *live free, fast, and fearless.*"

Without thinking, Cindy repeated the motto to herself a couple of times. A moment later, she gasped out loud. Kamal and Paula heard the sound and turned to look.

Kamal asked fearfully, "Are you okay? You look…"

"I remember," Cindy interjected as she frantically worked to open the car door. Once out, Cindy grinned widely at the two, "Guys, I remember, I know everything… every fucking thing!"

For a brief moment, Paula and Kamal just stared at Cindy in disbelief. Without waiting for a response, Cindy flung herself into Kamal's arms while pulling Paula in to join their embrace.

Tears of joy trickled down Cindy's face as she hugged and kissed them uncontrollably, all the while murmuring her thanks.

When she was done, Cindy looked up and said proudly, "Ask me anything! Go on, test me!"

Shahin was walking up to the cars when he saw Cindy launch herself at Kamal. He knew something important had happened, but he didn't know what.

"Shahin!" Cindy cried when she saw him. She ran over and squeezed him tightly before blurting out her news. "I finally got my memory back! I know everyone. I remember all of it, every bit!" She looked at all three and said, "You guys, you're so fucking awesome. Thank you so much for coming to get me!" Her friends blushed and dismissed her gratitude, acting as if their rescue mission was no big deal.

Kegger understood that this was a big moment for the four of them. However, they had a schedule to keep, and it was time to leave.

"Guys, we need to go. I understand you want to keep talking, but we have to leave now."

"Please, Kegger, I want to be with my friends. Can we ride together?" asked Cindy imploringly, "Please!"

Because of her request, Kegger withdrew his gender rule and allowed it. His only requirement now was that he and Stevie be in separate cars, and both of them would take over driving. This meant Paula, Cindy, Shahin, Kamal, and Majid were in one car with Kegger while Stevie drove Niki, Jasmine, and Kyra.

An hour into the drive, Niki noticed that Stevie's wound had begun to seep again. She knew his stitches had broken open and he was going to need them repaired as soon as possible. She asked him to pull over and let her drive, but he refused.

After riding together for a while, Majid woke up from his nap. Cindy picked him up from his makeshift bed and began to comfort him by commenting on what a big boy he was becoming. As she finished her comments, she thought about Zahra's remarks about her son's age. She hadn't given the words much thought until that moment. Suddenly, her memory went to the night before her capture. The images of her and Kamal making love flashed before her eyes.

"Oh shit, I just realized something," Cindy concluded. "Kamal, do you remember our last night before we went to the embassy?"

"Of course, it was one of the best nights of my life," he said proudly.

"I was just thinking... I know I told you Majid was my fake husband's son," she rationalized, "but Zahra had mentioned several times that he was the weight and size of a full-term baby when he was born. I think that she was trying to make me realize he couldn't be Kaveh's son. Kamal, I don't want to shock you, but... I think Majid is your son."

"He is!" exclaimed Paula. "We all wanted to tell you, but didn't know how to. Especially since you couldn't remember any of us."

"I knew too," said Kamal. "We were eventually going to tell you, but not right now, not with all this happening."

Cindy didn't need any further explanation.

She lovingly smiled at her man and handed him his son, saying, "Majid, this is your father. His name is Kamal."

******

When they entered the outskirts of Khorramshahr, people were yelling and running in every direction. Immediately, they knew something big was happening. As they continued toward the helicopter pad, Kegger stopped the car to try to understand what was going on around them.

At first glance, Paula thought the large number of soldiers coming towards them in the distance were Iranian men. However, it quickly became clear that the soldiers were Iraqi forces. Within seconds, she saw small groups of Iranian soldiers heading toward the invaders. Suddenly, there was an explosion in the distance.

"What the hell is going on?" yelled Kegger.

"I think Iraq's invading Iran!" yelled Paula. "We need to get to the helipad now!" she insisted. "We're under attack!"

"I think it's this way!" shouted Kegger and hit the gas. Ahead, he saw the corporate headquarters of a big oil company. Next to it was the helipad.

It was clear now that Iraq was storming the city of Khorramshahr. In the distance, they could see hundreds, if not thousands, of soldiers coming up from the river, and artillery munitions continued to explode in the distance.

Suddenly, Paula heard an unfamiliar noise overhead.

"Get out of the vehicle and take cover!" yelled Kegger as he heard the sound of a bomb flying overhead.

A moment later, Kamal was out of the backseat, cradling his son in one arm and dragging Cindy out with the other. Together, they ran for the nearest shelter.

Paula, Shahin, and Kegger were in the front seat and got out with their weapons ready to fire. Luckily, the ordinance exploded well behind them, and the group breathed a sigh of relief.

At the same time, Stevie ordered his group out of their car. As he exited, he pulled Niki with him. Kyra and Jasmine were in the backseat and followed quickly behind them.

A few seconds later, another mortar came down. This time, they weren't so lucky. It struck Niki's trailer and sent a giant fireball into the sky. She and Jasmine watched in horror as their most precious possessions exploded.

Surveying the scene, Paula told Shahin she was going to help Cindy and dashed over to where she and Kamal were huddled with Majid.

Within moments of Paula taking cover next to Cindy, another bomb hit Niki's Rambler. Instantly, flames towered over the vehicle, completely engulfing the car. Shrapnel from the explosion flew high up into the air and landed only a few feet from where Paula and her friends were hiding.

They were still trying to assess the situation when the sound of a helicopter overpowered the distant noise of gunfire.

Kegger ran to the helipad to guide Steelhead down onto the ground. Shahin ran to his friends, yelling, "Follow me! We have to get you guys out now!"

Paula nodded before helping Kamal and Cindy toward the helipad. As they arrived, Paula turned back and saw Kyra running to them. Behind her, Niki and Jasmine were helping Stevie hobble to the helicopter. His wound had opened up, and a steady stream of blood was trickling down his leg.

Shahin ran to help them, and while he and Niki assisted Stevie, he yelled, "Niki, I need you to call my father when you get to Kuwait! Not all of us can get on the helicopter. Me and the others are heading to Gürbulak, Turkey."

"I know it. It's Turkey's northernmost border town across from Bazargan," she shouted back.

"There's a small café in the village," Shahin continued, "My father knows the place. Tell him we'll need a car. Tape the key to the front tire."

The aircraft landed just as a group of soldiers opened fire on their position. Everyone crouched down until it was determined that the men were still out of range.

"Hurry, get in!" shouted Kegger. "The Iraqis are gaining ground fast!"

Kegger was standing next to Stevie, Kyra, Niki, and Jasmine on one side of the open helicopter, while Paula, Cindy, Kamal, and Majid were on the other. Shahin was a couple of meters away, firing back at the Iraqis.

Steelhead looked at the group and yelled to his friend, "I can't take everyone!"

"I know, not all of us are going with you," Kegger hollered back. He looked at the women and yelled, "Ladies, hop on! He needs to leave now, or it'll be too late! Kamal, you too! You're a dad now, and your son needs you!"

Kegger quickly helped the women on his side into the chopper. Paula grabbed Majid from Cindy while Kamal lifted her inside. When Cindy was settled, Kamal took his son from Paula's arms and handed him to Cindy. Kamal stepped inside before holding his hand out to help Paula get in. Instead of taking Kamal's hand, she suddenly yelled across the open chopper to Kegger, "Send Stevie instead of me. He's bleeding. Besides, they need someone to defend the helicopter. He's the right person to do it."

Stevie began to argue, but Kegger knew he needed medical attention and wouldn't get it if he remained in Iran. He looked over at Paula, and she reaffirmed her decision.

"You heard the lady, get in!" Kegger demanded as he lifted his friend into the bird.

"Be safe, you guys! We love you!" Cindy shouted as Paula stepped away from the copter to join Shahin.

Paula didn't waste any time. She lifted her machine gun and fired at the oncoming soldiers, trying to give as much cover as possible to the exiting chopper. As the helicopter lifted into the air, Paula could hear Cindy still yelling words of encouragement.

"Give them hell, Paula!"

The chopper was barely off the ground before it began to fly away from the invasion. Within seconds, it had gained altitude and was speeding quickly towards the Persian Gulf.

After the helicopter was safely away, Paula felt this was her cue. She stopped firing and ran to the Cherokee. Paula jumped into the front seat and grabbed the ignition wires. She hastily twisted the ignition wires together with the pliers. The car roared to life as she stepped on the gas and put the car in gear.

Paula slammed on the brakes as she pulled up next to Shahin and Kegger.

"Hop in!" she yelled.

The men didn't hesitate. They leapt into the backseat an instant before Paula slammed the car into reverse and sped rapidly away from the gunfire and bombs exploding around them. When she came to the T intersection for the main road, she swung the car around 90 degrees and forced the shifter into drive. The car jolted forward, and the three raced away from the invasion.

"Wow! That was some driving, Paula," said Kegger after he could sit up in his seat. "Where did you learn to drive like that?"

"I didn't. I saw it in a movie and decided it was the quickest way to get the hell out of there," she said smugly. "I have to say, it went better than I expected."

"The woman never ceases to amaze me," said Shahin, smiling proudly.

A few miles down the road, with the immediate threat diminished, Paula relaxed her grip on the steering wheel and headed north towards the border with Turkey.

Part Three

Chapter 33 - The Real Reason

Farah awoke with a start. It took her a couple of seconds to realize that she had gone unconscious and was just coming out of it. An instant later, her head began to pound. Trying to fight through the pain, Farah forced her eyes to focus. She glanced around the room and realized that the office was empty. She didn't know where the commander had gone or when he would return, but that didn't matter now. The only thing on her mind was escape. She swung her legs down and quickly stood up. For a brief moment, she felt dizzy but promptly recovered and refocused on the mission.

Farah's eyes darted around the room, searching for a way out. Excitement rose within her when she noticed the office window was slightly ajar. It was a small, low-framed window just 30 inches from the floor. She hurried over to it, her hands trembling with anticipation. She turned around and gripped the bottom of the pane with her fingers. With her wrists tied together, Farah did not have the mobility she needed to lift the window easily. It resisted her force and was getting stuck every few inches. She was strong, but the window was proving to be a formidable obstacle.

Farah turned around to view her progress. The opening was still several inches too low for her to slip through it. Frantic, she forced herself to think of a way to open it wider. It came to her an instant later. Farah lifted her leg and foot and positioned them into the small opening parallel to the bottom of the window pane. Quickly, she slid her foot to the edge of the frame. Once it was firmly in place, she began to shift her weight forward while bending her knee upward. The strength and leverage of the large muscle groups and bones in her leg forced the glass upward. She ignored the pain and continued her upward thrust until the opening was just high enough for her body to squeeze through it.

Suddenly, Farah heard the commander outside the office door. She panicked at the sound of his voice. There wasn't time, she thought, to get out of the window, not with her hands tied. Scanning the room, she saw a space behind the sofa where she thought she could hide. Farah rushed over and quietly wedged herself between the wall and the sofa.

"Where's the prison uniform?" he growled as he began to open the door. "I thought I told you to have a uniform ready when I returned."

"Corporal Ahad has gone to get one, sir," the soldier replied.

The commander was about to walk in when the corporal hurried up to him, holding the garment.

"Sorry, sir," he said apologetically. "It was difficult to find a small enough uniform."

"Just give it to me," the commander said impatiently as he waited to take it with him into his office.

The extra moments gave Farah time to quiet her breathing before she heard the clicking of his heeled boots cross the room to the sofa. There was a short pause before she heard him run to the window.

"She's gone!" he shouted angrily. "Search the base and bring her to me. She couldn't have gotten very far."

His soldiers jumped into action and began searching the camp for any sign of Farah. Meanwhile, she could hear the commander mulling around his desk, rustling papers while waiting for word from his staff. A few minutes passed before she heard him get up and return to the window. She could hear the framed window squeak loudly and imagined he had opened it most of the way.

"Have you found her yet?" he yelled out.

"No, sir, she's not around here. We're now looking throughout the camp and outside of it," a voice responded.

"It's already dusk. You need to find her before it gets fully dark!" Commander Rashidi bellowed before storming out of the room and slamming the door.

"Corporal, I'm going to be at my residence," she heard him roar. "When you find the girl, bring her to me there!"

"Yes, sir, we will continue to search for her until she's found," his assistant assured him.

Night fell quickly, and Farah heard the Corporal leave the building.

Feeling relieved, she thought, "The dark will make it easier to get away. It's time to make my move."

She quietly pushed the sofa away from the wall and gave herself sufficient room to maneuver out of her hiding place.

Once she was free from the confines of the sofa, she went to the commander's desk. Using the camp's searchlights to help her see, she rifled through the drawers to find something to cut the ties holding her hands. It wasn't long before she found a small knife; most likely, it was the commander's letter opener. It didn't matter. She only needed something sharp enough to cut the zip tie into two pieces.

Gripping the knife with her left hand, Farah sawed the restraint until it broke apart and her hands were released. She rubbed her wrists for a moment to bring back the circulation. Then, she shoved the knife into the remaining parts of her skirt and headed to the office door. She listened for a moment but heard nothing. Believing all the men had gone home for the evening, she opened the door. Immediately, a light turned on and blinded her eyes.

"Well, I see you've decided to come out from your hiding place," she heard the voice say.

Farah's heart sank. The commander had been waiting for her to reveal herself. He was playing a malicious game at her expense. A soldier switched on the overhead light, and Commander Rashidi turned off his flashlight. A grin of victory covered his face while he waited for Farah to speak.

"So, you knew the whole time that I had not left through the window," she said irritably. "You maniacal pig!"

He just laughed at her outburst, reveling in his cunning.

"What now?" Farah asked. "What are you going to do with me now?"

"First, you can hand the soldier next to you my letter opener. Then you can put this on," the commander said, throwing a prison uniform at her feet.

Farah handed over the knife while looking down at a black smock with an emblem representing the Tehran prison system embroidered on the upper left side of the front panel. At that moment, she realized that the threats of her imprisonment for speaking out against Khomeini could be real.

"I haven't done anything wrong, so why do I need to put this on?"

"The charge is conspiracy against our government," the commander answered. "You have been outwardly condemning the new policies put in place for our women, even after you were warned to stop."

"I have the right to express my opinion about the changes to our laws and the oppression of the women of Iran," Farah insisted.

"No, you don't, it's illegal. In addition, your brother, Kamal, is considered an enemy of the state, making your rhetoric even more dangerous to the general population. I have the authority to arrest you and hold you in detention indefinitely or send you to prison."

"Did they also give you the authority to rape me?" Farah said defiantly.

"That's at my discretion," said the commander, smiling. "One of the perks that goes with the job." He took her by the arm and pulled her closer. More serious now, he looked directly at her. "There is one more thing that I wanted from you, but you fell unconscious before I could get it. It took me a while, but I finally figured out that you are Little Sis." He let go of her arm before pacing several feet away. He turned around and continued with his story. "You see, I found a note from your buddy Charles. He must have written it just hours before his untimely death."

Farah's defiance reignited.

"I don't know what you're talking about," she replied, trying to sound innocent.

Unfortunately, his statement had caught her off guard, and her voice sounded noticeably shaken.

"That's hard to believe. It's addressed to you and references a previous meeting together. It details information about the Ali family jewels. He mentioned that he didn't give you all the information. However, he did say that he shared with you the name of the city where they are hidden." He turned away again and said, "I need you to tell me the city's name. If you do not..."

Suddenly, a soldier burst into the room, "Sir, I just got word that we have a credible sighting of Shahin Ali and Kamal Ahmad. They are still here inside Iran!"

"A sighting? When?" Commander Rashidi demanded.

"The man is holding on the line, Sir. He wants to speak with you directly."

"We'll finish this discussion later," said the commander. "Corporal, take her to the jail and make sure she's secured."

"Yes, Sir, I'll take care of it," the man responded as he stepped to attention and saluted.

The commander walked hurriedly past him without acknowledging the salute and closed the door behind him.

The other two soldiers stepped to either side of Farah as the corporal ordered her to strip off her torn clothes and put on the smock. Farah was exhausted, and she knew that continuing her battle with the underlings was worthless, so she followed his orders.

After she had changed clothing, Farah calmly allowed the men to take her to their makeshift jail and handcuff her to a chain attached to a cast-iron loop cemented into the floor. It looked to Farah like it had recently been poured, most likely, she thought, after they had made the building into a jail.

Immediately after the soldiers left, Farah tested the strength of the chain and anchor. Sadly, both of them were strong and secure. She sat down on the hard concrete floor and pulled her knees up to her chest. Feeling emotionally exhausted, Farah placed her forehead on the back of her hands, which she had placed on top of her bent knees.

While resting, Farah thought about the day and replayed the arrest, trying to figure out if there was something she could have done to escape. Suddenly, the door opened, and the corporal came in with a small plate of food and a carpet on which Farah could sleep.

He handed her the items, saying, "Get some rest. Commander Rashidi wants to see you first thing in the morning."

He abruptly turned and walked out without waiting for any questions or comments from Farah.

After she ate, Farah waited for sleep to come. Lying on the mat with her eyes closed, Farah's mind returned to the assault. She smiled as she recalled the commander's anger and frustration while she mocked him. The words she had inflicted upon him had caused his penis to soften and shrink, and he could not finish. That is when he struck her.

Even though she was his prisoner, Farah felt she had achieved a small victory over the commander. She momentarily considered telling the other soldiers of his impotence, but decided it was in her best self-interest not to infuriate the commander further. The satisfaction of knowing she had caused his failure would have to be enough.

Chapter 34 - Good and Bad News

Mr. Ali was placing the receiver onto the phone base when Mrs. Ali came into his study.

"Who's calling so late? I heard you say something about Turkey," she asked anxiously. "Was it news about Shahin? Is he safe?"

"Yes!" said Mr. Ali with exuberance. "Except for Jake, he didn't make it."

She ran to him and hugged him tightly. Joy and relief flooded through her, knowing that her son was okay.

While still in his embrace, Mrs. Ali asked excitedly, "Where are they now? When will they be back here?"

"Well, things are a little complicated," he replied hesitantly.

Pushing away, Mrs. Ali looked her husband poignantly in the eye and demanded an answer, "What exactly does that mean?"

"It means," he paused before adding, "Kamal, Cindy, and some others were all flown to Kuwait by a friend of Keggers, but Shahin and Paula stayed in Iran with Kegger for the time being."

"So, Shahin's still in danger!" she shouted. "Why did they stay?"

"Like I said, a lot is going on. I got a call from the helicopter pilot. His name is Steelhead."

"What did he tell you?" she asked impatiently.

"Please, this is a complex situation. Let's sit down, and I will tell you everything I know."

Mr. Ali took his wife's hand and gently led her to his sofa.

"Stop stalling!" insisted Mrs. Ali. "What's happened?"

"I'll explain everything about Shahin, but before I get into all the details of what has transpired, I need to tell you some other news." Mr. Ali took a deep breath and said flatly, "Iraq has invaded Iran."

✳✳✳✳✳✳

Kamal and Cindy walked out of Steelhead's front door to enjoy the early morning weather. The wind had died down, and it felt pleasant in the shade.

They arrived safely in Kuwait the day before after a turbulent flight out of Iran. Luckily, it had been early enough in the conflict between Iraq and Iran that Iran's local artillery was in transit when their helicopter flew over the military troops and machinery headed to Khorramshahr.

"I hope Paula and Shahin made it out of that fucking mess," Cindy said softly as she sat down on the porch step. "Oh shit, I meant to say, darn mess. I guess it's going to take me some time to clean up my language."

"Majid is too little to know what you're saying," Kamal said lovingly. "Eventually, you'll have to stop, but right now, just let it all out."

In her arms, Majid stirred slightly as Cindy repositioned herself closer to Kamal.

"Thanks, Babe. Did I ever tell you why I started cussing?"

"No, why?" asked Kamal.

"It started when I was in junior high. I felt the adults, not so much my parents but others around me, were constantly trying to restrict my behavior and mold me into what they wanted me to be. Cussing was something they couldn't stop me from doing. I felt like it gave me the freedom to express my frustrations and escape the confines society puts on teenagers," Cindy reminisced. "Now, I use it not only as a way to voice my frustrations, but also to accentuate my passions. It makes me feel free and empowered."

"I like that you don't worry about what other people think," interjected Kamal.

"Sometimes I care," replied Cindy, "but not as much as most people. The ones that piss me off are the group that thinks they have the right to judge me for my choice of words. They aren't listening to me and what I'm saying, only how I say it."

"Yeah, I'm sure that's frustrating," said Kamal. "Just so you know, I like it when you cuss out of passion. It adds that extra edge to your point."

"I don't really care about the judgy ones' opinions, but I care about our son, and I don't want my cussing to make Majid's life more difficult. I'm never going to stop cussing altogether," stated Cindy, "but around Majid, I am going to try to tone it down."

"Hey, speaking of other people," he said optimistically, "I have a good feeling that Paula and Shahin are doing okay."

"I think you're right," agreed Cindy. "The Iranians have their hands full fighting off the Iraqis right now. They're probably too fucking busy to care about our guys."

"I hope so," said Kamal. "Shahin and Paula need a break. It's going to be tough to cross the border without anyone finding out who they are."

"Yeah, and it doesn't help that Turkey had a military coup ten days ago," Cindy added. "Steelhead said it's been nonviolent so far, but everyone knows things could change in an instant."

At that moment, Steelhead opened the front door and whispered, "Hey, Mr. Ali just called me back. Even with the crazy shit happening, he thinks he can get them into and out of Turkey successfully. He knows the men who are now in power."

"Does he know how?" asked Kamal.

"Not yet, he's still working on a plan," responded Steelhead. "I told him I would help if he needed me."

"He'll figure something out," said Cindy. "He knows how to get things done."

"Yeah, I agree," added Kamal. "All our guys need to do is get to Turkey without getting caught. I think Mr. Ali will take care of the rest."

Chapter 35 - The Note

Almost a year earlier, on November 1st, 1978, Charles, the Alis' head butler, sat down at his desk and wrote a note to Farah.

Dear Little Sis,

First, I want to explain why I am using Shahin's nickname for you. If this note were to fall into the hands of someone other than yourself, I want your identity to be protected. We must both be extra careful during this time of great uncertainty.

There has been a new development since we last spoke. I got a call earlier today from Shahin! It came as a great shock and surprise, and I did not handle the call well. After my conversation with him, it took me several hours to consider this new development and what it might mean for us moving forward.

I have concluded that Shahin will most likely return to the estate to retrieve his passport. If he does come here, I plan to explain why I hid the jewels and tell him of my unspeakable behavior over the last several months. I hope to have an opportunity to express my deepest regrets and offer him my sincerest apologies. I do not deserve to be forgiven.

I must try everything to redeem what little dignity and honor I have left. Therefore, I thank you again for agreeing to assist me in my efforts to return the Ali family jewels to their rightful owners. I greatly appreciate the risks you are taking on my behalf.

If you are required to make the journey, beware that it will be convoluted with some surprises, but I will explain it all to you if necessary. If, for some reason, you cannot make the trip, I feel confident that you will find a way to relay the information I have shared with you to someone in the Ali family. If Shahin does not return within the next ten days, I will resume my plans to give you the key to the safety deposit box. As I mentioned in our first meeting, my situation here has become even more complicated, and it is impossible for me to collect the jewelry myself. Khomeini's soldiers are watching my every move.

Sincerely,

Charles

******

Charles had carefully folded the letter and tucked it under some clothing in the top right-hand drawer of his dresser before his death. After he and the lieutenant were killed, a lengthy investigation followed. During this time, the investigators insisted that nothing be moved or changed until they had completed their report. The entire estate was considered a crime scene. When the report was finally released, Commander Rashidi noticed something of great interest to him. Within Charles's list of personal items was a letter addressed to an unknown source. The investigators had decided it was not pertinent to the murder case, so the note was not considered evidence. It was packed with the rest of Charles's property and would be temporarily stored for six months to see if anyone claimed his belongings. Commander Rashidi immediately contacted the storage facility and demanded to see the items.

For a couple of weeks, the commander studied the note, trying to discern who the person was that Charles referred to as "Little Sis" and what exactly "sis" meant. Finally, he discovered that "sis" was an English term. It was short for the word sister. That, however, didn't make any sense to him. Shahin Ali was an only child, and thus, he had no sisters. It wasn't until the commander met Yousif, Darian's roommate from Shiraz, that he was able to identify the person named Little Sis.

Yousif had heard that the Khomeini Regime would pay money for information about Americans hiding inside Iran and decided to turn informant. Yousif began his betrayal by meeting with Commander Rashidi. First, he offered what intel he knew about Darian's American friend. Yousif shared the knowledge given to him that the woman named Cindy Stetson was alive and living in Shiraz.

Next, he told the commander that Kamal Ahmad, the boyfriend of the American girl, and Shahin Ali, a friend, had planned to return to Iran as part of an extraction team. They were coming to Iran in early August.

During the meeting, Darian's roommate added an anecdotal comment. In addition to Shahin and Kamal's concern for the American woman, both men also felt guilty for not helping Kamal's sister get out of Iran. Yousif had heard that even though the woman wasn't related to Shahin Ali, he considered her to be part of his family.

Rashidi listened to his statements and put two and two together. He quickly concluded that Kamal's younger sister was the one he had been searching for; she was Little Sis.

Within minutes after the meeting, Commander Rashidi began making plans to find both women. Simultaneously, he worked to identify and locate Kamal's sister while surveilling Cindy Stetson and devising an ambush to capture Shahin Ali and his team.

******

It didn't take Commander Rashidi long to learn that Kamal's little sister was named Farah. She had already been arrested twice by the police for protesting against the new government's policies toward women.

The first time Farah was detained, she received a stern warning of imprisonment if caught demonstrating again.

The second time Farah was officially arrested, she was held for a week and subjected to mild torture. It was reported that the punishment did not produce any results. Even though Farah did not comply with her captor's demands, the officer in charge decided to release her with a second warning because of her youth and gender.

After talking to the police who had questioned her in the past, Rashidi learned that Farah was an extremely obstinate person, and while in custody, she was a very uncooperative detainee. Even with threats of torture and imprisonment, she refused to reveal anything about her fellow protesters or the locations where they met.

Understanding it might be slightly complicated to get the information he wanted from the young woman, Commander Rashidi decided not to arrest her unless it was necessary. Per the letter written by Charles, he believed the Ali boy had the key and knew where the jewels were hidden. Farah wouldn't be required if he had him.

******

To the commander's chagrin, his soldiers had bungled the capture of Shahin Ali and Kamal Ahmad. Therefore, to lure the escapees into another trap, he would have to arrest Kamal's sister.

Rashidi wanted his trap to be believable, which meant he needed to make Farah voluntarily break the law. To accomplish this task, the commander organized a rally, ensuring that Farah and her circle of friends were given the necessary reasons and avenues to protest publicly at the event. He called the media to confirm they would cover the demonstration, no matter how small it might be.

As he had intended, Farah and her friends showed up. The commander ordered his soldiers to purposely provoke Farah into taking her chador off her head before chasing her through the streets of Tehran. The newspaper photo of Farah uncloaked and in custody was perfect for the commander's hidden agenda. He made sure that her face was on the front page of the largest newspaper in Iran. It looked like Farah was detained in what seemed to be an unplanned event.

Unfortunately, his plan to entice Shahin's team into rescuing Farah had not worked. More weeks passed, and there was no sign of Shahin, Kamal, the American women, or the mercenaries. He was about to release Farah when he got word that Shahin Ali and Kamal Ahmad were still in Iran.

The intel came from a store owner who positively identified Shahin and Kamal. His store was located in a poorer industrial area of Shiraz. Sadly, the soldiers leading the investigative team reported that the two men they sought had already left the vacant building where they believed the men had been hiding.

Again, weeks went by, and Rashidi contemplated releasing Farah a second time. Fortunately for him, before he made his final decision, Rashidi received new information about the escapees. Three men had been spotted the previous day on a property outside Shiraz. Two of the men fit the descriptions of Shahin Ali and Kamal Ahmad, and the third man was assumed to be the mercenary who had been shot and then escaped.

The house belonged to the wife of an executed politician, and the dead man's pro-democracy beliefs caused Commander Rashidi to question the loyalty of the politician's wife and daughter. Therefore, he had ordered a team to do monthly surveillance checks on the two women and the property. During the September inspection, the investigators saw the unknown men packing up a storage trailer.

Immediately, the commander had the newspaper rerun with the article about Farah on the front page. Even more enticing, Rashidi ordered this edition to be free to the public. In addition to the paper, the commander dropped free flyers throughout western Iran in hopes of notifying and persuading Shahin and Kamal to take the bait. He felt confident that the two men would not leave Iran without Farah if they knew she was in serious trouble.

In addition to the notice, Commander Rashidi made it easy for them to plan a rescue by describing the army camp in detail and highlighting that there would be a skeleton crew at the camp for the next two weeks. He made sure the article stated that she was being held indefinitely, with a thorough investigation underway that would most likely produce more charges being added to the other charges already brought.

Chapter 36 - The Choice

Paula, Shahin, and Kegger were once again stranded in Khorramshahr, Iran. Thanks to Paula's quick thinking and driving, they had eluded the soldiers from both Iran and Iraq and were on their way north. Once the three were away from the fighting, Paula stopped to let Kegger drive. At the stage of their journey, he was the least recognizable of the three.

The road going south soon became flooded with Iranian military vehicles carrying troops and equipment to the war zone. Paula hoped the invasion would move the focus of Khomeini's military away from them and onto Iraq, and so far, the troops' movements seemed to confirm this to be true.

After a few hours on the road, they again had to stop for fuel. Paula wrapped herself in her chador to hide her identity from the attendant while he filled their tank. Shahin put on the sunglasses Jasmine had given him and went into the small store to buy snacks and drinks. At the checkout, he noticed a stack of newspapers sitting on the counter with a sign saying, "Free Papers, Please Take One". Curious about what was happening in Iran, Shahin grabbed the top paper and folded it under his arm. He paid for his items and headed back to the car. As they pulled away, he began to read the paper.

"It looks like the Iraqi government pulled off a surprise attack," he said soberly. "The front page doesn't even mention a potential invasion."

"I think that is obvious by the lack of Iranian troops in Khorramshahr," said Paula. "Speaking of border security, I hope our friends made it safely to Kuwait."

"Steelhead is an excellent pilot," replied Kegger. "I'm sure they've already landed and are drinking a beer on his porch."

"I hope so," Shahin added before returning his attention to the newspaper. The headline was talking about the people arrested for speaking out against the oppression of women and how the government's crackdown on protesters was justified. When he was finished reading the story, Shahin looked closer at the photo accompanying it. To his horror, in the center of the picture was Kamal's sister, Farah. She was handcuffed and being led away by Khomeini's soldiers.

Shahin immediately read the photo description: "Farah Raja Ahmad is being held at the temporary military camp outside of Tehran until a further investigation is completed."

"Dammit!" he said vehemently. "They've got her! The government has Kamal's sister."

Alarmed by his statement, Paula asked anxiously, "Farah? Why? What did she do?"

"She was protesting new laws restricting women's rights. It says here she has been taken to a military camp just outside Tehran," said Shahin. "I wonder why they took her there and not to the police station. Something's wrong about this; they're holding her there while investigating something."

"Are they making an example of her? You know, showing the other would-be protestors what could happen to them?" questioned Paula.

"Maybe," replied Shahin, "but it seems like she's been unfairly charged. It also sounds like she's been there for a while. The article says in small print that it's a repeat photo of an arrest that took place well over a month ago. It says they reran the article because of newly discovered information. I know it's risky, but I think we have to break her out. Farah's association with us might be the reason they're holding her for so long. She could be in real trouble."

Paula and Shahin agreed that Farah was targeted and likely jailed because of her friendship with them. Therefore, they concluded that it was their responsibility to free Farah from her imprisonment.

A lengthy discussion ensued between Paula, Shahin, and Kegger about Farah's arrest, the danger she might be in, the possible consequences to them if they were caught, and how much time and money it would cost to plan and execute her prison break.

To help make their decision, Shahin reread the article numerous times to assess the feasibility of successfully breaking her out of a jail cell. Each time, the three took the slightest bit of information and discussed how they could overcome a specific obstacle or use it to their advantage. After much discussion, they determined that the camp and prison didn't sound overwhelmingly complex. Plus, Kegger added that his personal experience in this area was a huge benefit to their risk analysis.

Ultimately, after an exhaustive discussion and a hefty bonus was attached to Kegger's pay, the three agreed that with their training and Kegger's experience, it would be a relatively easy task to sneak into the camp and free Farah.

Chapter 37 - Breakout

Paula's eyes darted back and forth as she searched for any sign of movement towards her or acknowledgment of her presence. She watched intently as the soldier guarding the perimeter of the small building they had determined to be the jail continued to follow his earlier pattern of guard duty.

"So far," she thought, "it looks good. Hopefully, Farah is inside."

It was dark out, but Paula could still see pretty well with the help of the stationary lights hastily installed inside the temporary camp. It was apparent that the camp was built around a few permanent buildings and that the jail was nothing more than a regular building designated as a holding cell.

The trio arrived at the camp just after dark, the day following the start of the invasion. They spent the first night and day observing the camp's procedures and learning about the guards' schedules. During the day, they noticed one or two soldiers entering the building with food and exiting empty-handed. It became clear that the men were guarding someone inside.

At night, one soldier was stationed in the front of the assumed prison and one in the back. After serving the evening meal, the day soldier locked the door behind him, and the night guards took over the watch. Every 30 minutes, the guard in the front would walk around to the back of the building and check in with the other watchman. It was the best time for someone to slip into the structure unnoticed.

Excitement and anxiety rose inside Paula as she saw the night guard check the time.

"This is it!" she told herself as she watched him turn the corner and head around to the back. When he was out of sight, Paula darted to the window next to the door. She had noticed the guard peering into it occasionally for a moment or two, most likely to ensure his prisoner was still secured. A dim light illuminated the room, and Paula saw a small human figure lying on a piece of cloth on the floor. Paula quietly stepped over to check the door. As she expected, it was locked. She returned to the window and tried to open it. Luckily, it was unlocked. Paula sprayed the frame with silicone, making it easy to slide the glass pane upward. Paula quickly squeezed through the opening before gently closing it. As she turned around, the figure on the blanket stood up and stared warily at Paula.

"Don't be afraid," Paula whispered. "It's me, Kamal's friend, Paula."

"Paula? What are you doing here? How'd you find me?" Farah asked in disbelief.

"There's no time to explain. The guard will be back soon. He usually chats with the other guy for only a few minutes."

"I'm handcuffed to this chain that is cemented into the concrete floor," Farah said as she lifted her wrist. "I've tried numerous times to open it or pull it out, but nothing's worked."

"Don't worry. Most cuffs use this universal key," explained Paula as she pulled a key from her pocket. "Give me your hands."

Paula hastily inserted the key and turned it. The shackles clicked open and fell away from Farah's wrists. Paula quietly laid the chain on the concrete before taking Farah's hand and leading her quietly to the exit. Paula released the deadbolt and cracked open the door. She listened for any movement close by. When she heard none, Paula turned and nodded silently to Farah, who knowingly nodded back.

Shahin watched anxiously as Paula and Farah ran towards him. Suddenly, Farah tripped and fell forcefully onto Paula's back. The impact caused Paula to fall flat onto the hardened dirt just past the slightly raised slab of concrete, which had caused Farah to tumble.

As Paula fell, her top boot lace slipped through one of the large circular eye hooks anchored into the mold at ground level. The three-inch-high iron loop held Paula's boot motionless while her body hurled forward. The additional thrust and sudden stop caused Paula to release her grip on the knife she was carrying. Without it, she was able to use both hands to save her face from directly hitting the hard surface. Immediately after the impact, Paula felt the tug on her foot and ankle. The pain associated with the awkward position was minimal, but the contortion made moving it difficult. Farah's entire body weight lay on Paula's torso. Before Farah knew what had happened, Paula urgently turned sideways to see if Farah was okay.

"Are you hurt?" Paula asked anxiously.

"I'm startled more than anything," she responded, trying to get up.

Paula squirmed vigorously around, ignoring the strained and awkward pressure it placed on her ankle and foot. She forcefully took Farah by the shoulders, pulled her close, and whispered, "Stop! Listen to me. You need to run to that man," Paula said as she pointed into the shadows. "It's Shahin. He'll take you to safety! Now, go!"

"But what about you?" Farah asked worriedly.

"I'll be fine. They're after you, not me," Paula urged. "There's no time to waste. You need to go!"

Farah nodded obediently and started for the silhouette of a man that was supposed to be Shahin. As she got close, Shahin grabbed her into a quick embrace before directing her towards Kegger.

"Go to that man crouched down by the fence. His name is Kegger, and he'll get you to safety. Do everything he tells you. I'll help Paula."

Again, Farah began to argue, but Shahin cut her off, "Do it now!" He said forcefully, "Go!"

This time, Farah obeyed his command and ran toward Kegger. He saw her coming and put down his weapon to grab her hand.

"Keep a hold of my hand. Don't let go," he whispered, pulling her towards a small opening in the fence.

When Shahin got to Paula, she was outstretched as far as she could go, trying to retrieve the knife she had dropped. It had sailed out of her hand and landed several feet from her body.

"Get my knife!" she demanded when she saw him approaching. Shahin saw the blade, quickly picked it up, and handed it to Paula. She bent down and cut the lace of her shoe.

"Let's go!" she said while Shahin helped her to her feet.

They had just taken cover behind a building 50 feet away when a soldier yelled, "She's escaped! The girl has escaped!"

Farah and Kegger had just made it to the Jeep Cherokee when sirens blared over loudspeakers. Luckily for them, the noise covered up the sound of the Jeep's engine, and they headed away from the camp undetected.

As the sirens echoed through the night, additional searchlights began to pan the military camp. Soon, more lights beamed outside of the fenced compound, but it was too late. Kegger and Farah were too far away for them to be seen by someone inside the camp.

While the chaotic search unfolded, Paula and Shahin stealthily made their way to the other end of the camp. They knew the opening in the fence would be found and hoped the camp's resources would be allocated to search outside the confines of the compound.

Soon, the siren quieted so the troops could hear the orders from the highest-ranking officer. Instead of hearing the officer's voice, they heard the cry of a soldier near the perimeter, "Here! The fence is cut, and I see footprints in the dirt going through the opening!"

Another soldier yelled, "They're on foot!"

"Follow them and bring her and whoever helped her escape back to me immediately!" demanded the officer.

Several soldiers raced through the fence while others got the keys to their trucks. It wasn't long before distant yells from the soldiers on foot echoed through the night air. They were flagging down the trucks. Paula and Shahin assumed they had found the Jeep tracks. Orders to get into the transport were heard, and seconds later, the vehicles resumed their pursuit.

When the camp settled, Paula and Shahin quietly headed to the motorcycle parking. Several were lined up, and they cautiously inspected each one, hoping to find one with the keys still in the ignition. Shahin's heart pounded with excitement when he saw a key sitting on the seat of one of the bikes.

"Get on!" he motioned to Paula.

Without hesitating, she swung her leg over the back seat and wrapped her arms tightly around Shahin's waist. He started the engine, put the bike in gear, and headed to the opening in the fence.

The soldiers who were left, heard the engine roar, and ran towards the sound. The guard in the tower opened fire, hoping to hit the riders and halt their escape. The men running pulled out their guns to assist him. Fortunately for Paula and Shahin, the searchlight couldn't keep up with Shahin's erratic driving. Even with the soldiers doing their best to bring down the bike, their aim proved unsuccessful. Angrily, they watched as the motorcycle sped out of the opening and into the darkness.

It wasn't long before Paula and Shahin heard the other motorcycles rev their engines. The sound was distant at first but quickly became louder and louder.

"You have to turn off the light!" exclaimed Paula. "Go slow, and we can use the moonlight to get us far enough away that they won't be able to see the beam when we turn it back on." Shahin did as Paula insisted, knowing the light would give away their position. "See that shadow of a hill to the far left? Head for it; we can use it as cover. They can't hear our engine over their machines."

"But it's the wrong way," said Shahin without thinking.

"It doesn't matter," argued Paula.

"No, you're right," agreed Shahin. "It's the only way to lose them."

Shahin flicked off the beam and slowly headed towards the hill. The engines grew even louder, and Shahin decided it was best for them to take cover until the soldiers passed them. He pulled in behind a low ridge, and they jumped off the bike to hide. Shahin laid the cycle on its side, hoping the hill was high enough to conceal it.

"They're getting close," Paula whispered, pulling out her handgun. "I'll shoot them if I have to, but I'm pretty sure I can't hit all of them before they shoot back, especially in the dark. Give me yours. I'll probably need more firepower since I won't have time to reload."

Shahin handed Paula his weapon as he said, "By the sound of it, they have slowed way down. I think they're following our tread marks. If they find us, be ready to jump on when I say *go*."

The motorcycles were almost upon them. Suddenly, the lead bike went silent. A moment later, a second motor turned off. A voice mumbled something inaudible as a third cycle stopped. One of the bikes began to scan the hillside using its headlight like a flashlight. As he slowly turned the handlebars over the terrain, Paula and Shahin saw the light approaching their position. Just before it shined on them, Shahin whispered, "Go!"

Shahin yanked the machine up to an almost vertical position while Paula fired into the group of men. The actions startled the three men, and they immediately tried to take cover to avoid the oncoming bullets. In his panic to survive, the soldier, panning his light, pulled his motorcycle down onto himself while the second man knocked his bike down, trying to get away from the oncoming gunfire. The third man shot wildly into the air as he ran to the back of his machine for protection.

By the time he was in position to take aim and fire, Shahin had spun the bike around and created a cloud of dust. Paula jumped on the back, and Shahin hit the gas. Within a second, they were behind the small hill, safely out of the sight of the one soldier able to return fire. This time, Shahin kept his light on and used his childhood skills to maneuver through the rugged landscape. Paula checked every few moments to see if the soldiers were following, but there was only moonlight behind them.

After an hour of twists and turns to confuse anyone trying to follow their trail, Paula and Shahin made it to the outskirts of Tehran. Shahin pulled onto an unlit side street and stopped.

"I think we're safe for now," Shahin whispered and turned off the engine. "It would be tough for them to track us inside the city unless someone reports us."

"I agree," Paula concurred. "We need to find a cheap hotel for the night and let the soldiers think we're headed straight for the border."

"First, we need to make the bike less identifiable," replied Shahin. They got off the motorcycle, and Shahin started to remove anything that could help identify it as a government-issued machine. As he stripped it, he asked, "Do you think Kegger and Farah got away?"

"Yeah, I think so. He's a pretty resourceful guy, plus he has a lot of weaponry with him," replied Paula.

"It's a good thing we made a rendezvous point," said Shahin.

"Yeah, getting split up must happen a lot. This is twice for us."

Shahin added nervously, "I just hope Kegger is right about waiting until tomorrow to meet up, but it does make sense that one of us could be captured or followed."

"Yeah, by waiting, the others have a better chance of seeing an ambush," agreed Paula. "What scares me is his comment about the guy who grabbed Farah. I hope he's not as cunning as Kegger thinks."

"Let's hope not," Shahin said optimistically. "All I know is that I gave his guys a tough path to follow. It's going to take them more than just a few hours to find us." Finally, he yanked the license plate free, saying, "There, that looks better."

"Give them to me," said Paula. Shahin handed her the identifying items. She walked to an existing pile of trash and threw them onto it. "Okay, let's find a hotel."

Chapter 38 - The Key

While Paula and Shahin raced through the nighttime desert, Kegger and Farah were busy losing the trucks following them. Using the engine's strength, Kegger maneuvered the vehicle up steep slopes where more timid drivers would hesitate to go. When he was high enough to see for miles, Kegger stopped and walked back to the other side of the mountain to look for his pursuers.

Kegger could see the distant glimmer of three sets of headlights in pursuit. Luckily, the soldiers were far behind them. He had expected them to respond quicker and was ready to take a stand if necessary. To his delight, the trucks seemed slow and cautious. He concluded they were not used to driving on dirt tracks at night.

Kegger was about to return to the Jeep when he saw the lead truck stop. He stayed and watched as the other two trucks paused. This was good news, he thought, and ran back to drive down the other side of the ridge. The distance between them widened, and before long, the headlights of his pursuers faded into the darkness.

Confident he had lost them, Kegger made his way to the main highway leading out of Tehran. It was around 3:00 AM, and the highway was empty of traffic. He pulled onto the road and headed for the city of Qods. On the way, Kegger saw a forested area on a hillside. He pulled off the road and into the trees. He found a location where the ground cover was thickest and pulled the car in behind the shrubbery.

"Well," he said to Farah, "this will be our hotel for the night. We might as well get as much sleep as possible before heading to the rendezvous point in the morning. I'll sleep in the front seat, and you can sleep in the back."

"I'm sure it'll be more comfortable than a rug on a concrete floor," said Farah as she climbed over the seat. There was a short silence, and then she added, "Thanks again for saving me from that monster."

"No thanks necessary, it's my job," said Kegger. He paused momentarily, then inquired, "Can I ask you a question?"

"Sure," replied Farah, "what's on your mind?"

"I'm just curious. Why didn't you leave Iran a long time ago? You knew your family would be targeted."

"It wasn't that simple. We tried to leave after we figured out that Kamal was in the United States, but the government said we needed new passports. They had to have the Islamic Republic of Iran listed as our country of origin. I don't think this was necessary for everyone, but we had no recourse. They told us it would take a few months to process them since they had so many earlier applications. We waited for months with no response from the passport office. Finally, my father began to push for some answers. He was told that our applications were held up due to questionable intentions. Therefore, the process was going to take much longer."

"So, they wouldn't let you leave?" he confirmed.

"Yes, that's the reality, and we're not the only ones being held here. They're not issuing new passports to most, if not all, of the Jews in Iran, either."

"So, they're keeping you and them hostage in your own country," stated Kegger.

"Yeah, I guess it's similar to the people living in the USSR," added Farah.

"Well, that's one mystery solved. I know Kamal has questioned why you and your family didn't leave months ago," said Kegger. "He'll be happy to know you've been trying to get out. He misses you a lot."

"I miss him too," replied Farah. "I'm glad he was one of the people who made it on the helicopter you mentioned earlier, but honestly, why did he go and not Paula? She seems like more of an easy target than him."

"I wasn't going to bring this up because I thought it would be a nice surprise," Kegger explained, "but I don't want you to think he was being selfish for no good reason."

Baffled, Farah uttered, "I don't understand."

"I'm saying your brother had a good reason to get on the helicopter instead of Paula," Kegger said, trying to find the right words. "I'm just going to say it. Your brother is a new father."

Farah sat upright, "What! My brother's a dad? He has a baby? Who's the mom?"

Kegger explained the best that he could the chain of events leading up to and including the birth, Cindy's amnesia, and her recovery.

Farah continued to pepper him with questions, and Kegger did his best to respond. Finally, he told Farah that the conversation was over because he needed to sleep. Reluctantly, she agreed and lay back down to rest.

******

Paula and Shahin happily entered their motel room, both covered in dirt and sand from riding through the semi-arid landscape. They desperately wanted to take showers and rinse out their clothes. Shahin went first while Paula vigilantly watched the parking lot to guard against possible threats.

Even though it was September, the night air remained warm. Shahin returned to the room wearing only a towel around his waist. Paula looked at him and smiled sensually, unable to hide her desire for him. Shahin responded with a devilish grin and said casually, "I know you don't want to have a serious relationship, but under the circumstances..."

"I'll think about it while I'm in the shower," said Paula, returning a suggestive smirk.

When Paula opened the bathroom door, she was naked. The stress and uncertainty of the day had unleashed her raw desire to release the immense pressure she had endured only hours earlier. She silently walked to the bed and smiled down at Shahin before gracefully slinking in next to his freshly washed skin.

******

The telephone rang at camp headquarters, and the ranking officer leaned over and lifted the receiver. A voice boomed over the line before he could ask who was calling. "Are they convinced they've gotten away?" asked Commander Rashidi.

"Yes, sir," the man responded with calculated confidence. "However, things didn't go exactly as we planned. Three of my men were shot at, Sir, but luckily, no one was seriously hurt."

"I don't care about that. They have the girl and believe we have given up finding them, right?"

"Yes, but two stayed in the camp, then stole one of our motorcycles. Our trucks followed their other vehicle for several minutes and then made it look like the lead truck had engine trouble. It allowed our targets to widen their gap enough to think they were safely away. The two on the motorcycle were also allowed to escape."

"Good, I don't want them to suspect anything," the commander added. "I need them to lead us to the jewels. Trying to capture them without killing them has proven difficult, and forcing them to talk has also been a disaster."

"Yes, sir."

"I'll notify my men that they should be arriving here within the next day or two."

Without saying anything further, Commander Rashidi ended the call.

******

When Paula awoke, it was mid-morning, and Shahin was still asleep. The night's exploits had drained away her stress, leaving Paula emotionally and physically satisfied. It was something she hadn't felt in a long time, and she wanted to soak in the feeling. The encounter had allowed her mind and body to relent, giving her the deep sleep she so desperately needed. Shahin opened his eyes and looked at Paula with the faintest of grins.

She smiled back and said, "I don't think I've slept that well in a long time." Shahin put his hands around Paula's waist and drew her closer to him as she continued. "You'd think I would be super stressed and unable to sleep after the chase and our close getaway, but being with you last night must have allowed my mind to rest finally. Usually, it's replaying the day's events over and over, trying to analyze what I could've done differently or better."

"I'm glad I could help," Shahin beamed. Then his face turned serious, and he said, "Maybe for the first time in months, you're feeling that Cindy is safe."

"Yeah, that could be it," replied Paula. "I watched the helicopter in the rearview mirror, and it was far away from the fighting and close to the gulf when it flew out of sight. I do think they're all safe. Maybe it's just foolish optimism, but I sense they're okay."

"Me too," said Shahin happily. "Hey, are you hungry?"

He asked as he propped himself up on one elbow.

"Starving," said Paula.

"I'm going to run out and grab us some food."

Shahin quickly got dressed and went to the mirror. He ruffled his hair and pulled the front curls down into his eyes and around his face. "It was a good idea for me to keep my hair long. With it like this, I don't look anything like the photo taken on Kish."

"You do look different with your hair that way," said Paula, boosting Shahin's confidence.

Shahin leaned down and gave Paula a peck on the cheek. "I'll be back."

When the door closed, Paula jumped up and went to the window. She carefully moved the drapes to watch him leave and to ensure no one noticed his presence.

It was hot in the hotel room, but Paula didn't want to risk opening a window. Instead, she decided to stay in her bra and underwear until it was time to leave. She took the map from the back pocket of her jeans and got back into bed. She opened the map and began to study the roads leading north and west of Qods.

Shahin returned minutes later with some street food from the nearby vendor and a headscarf for Paula. As they ate, Paula continued to examine the map, and Shahin joined in once he finished his food. Together, they mapped the best route to the rendezvous point. When it was time to go, Paula got up and started to get dressed.

Shahin watched admiringly as she stepped into her jeans. His gaze continued to linger on her as she buttoned up the lightweight blouse. He was about to look away when he saw Paula reach down and pick up a necklace that had been hidden underneath her pile of clothes. He watched as she placed a gold chain around her neck. Hanging from it was a small key.

"I haven't seen that necklace before," said Shahin, "and what's with the key?"

"Oh, the chain's mine. I've had it for several years but never wore it. The key, well, it was given to me by Charles. The thing is, he didn't tell me what it was for or why he was giving it to me," she explained. "He slipped it into my pocket in the bunker just before you guys went up to get the weapons. You know, before he... before it all happened."

Staring at Paula, he said in disbelief, "Paula, that key, I'm sure it's the key to the jewels Charles mentioned in his letter."

"What letter?" she probed.

"The letter in the bunker. You know, the one he was writing to me when I punched him in the face."

"Oh…" said Paula knowingly, "that letter. Yeah, I remember."

"I thought it got lost, but when I got out my duffel bag to pack for this trip, I found it stuck in one of the small inside pockets."

"So, you had it all this time?" she questioned.

"Yeah, now I remember that I saw it lying on the floor, and without thinking, I picked it up and crammed it into my bag as we headed down the tunnel. All I was focused on was the dogs coming to find us, remember?"

"Of course I do. That was one of the scariest things that has ever happened to me."

"And you've been looking for the key this whole time?" Paula asked.

"Well, no," replied Shahin. "I never read the whole letter. I didn't realize there was writing on the back, and everything about the key was on the other side. When I got home, I didn't want to think about Charles or any of it. I dumped everything out of the bag and threw it in the back of my closet. I told myself, *the past is in the past, and it's time to move on.*"

"Do you have it?" Paula asked. "I mean the letter. Do you have it with you?"

"It was in my bag," he replied. "The one I left in the Range Rover. I assumed it was still in the car when it got stolen."

"No, we unloaded the Rover before that happened. Kegger put it in the Cherokee while you and Kamal were in with Cindy. That means we should have it," said Paula excitedly.

"Even if it's not there, I remember a lot of it," said Shahin before suddenly contorting his face.

"What?" Paula asked, seeing the expression.

She watched as Shahin worked out something in his head.

"Now, it all makes sense," he mumbled before looking up at her.

"I'm not following you," stated Paula.

"Back when Kamal and I were arrested, the men questioning us kept asking us about a key. They searched both of us more than once, trying to find it. We didn't know what they were talking about, so, of course, we didn't tell them anything. I didn't think about Charles's key because I didn't have it, and how would they know about it anyway?"

"That would have been awful if they thought you were keeping something like that from them," said Paula without thinking.

Hearing her statement, Shahin's facial expression changed to alarm, "Yeah, we knew they wanted to know where we were meeting, but we had no idea what key they were talking about. Luckily, we got away before the real torture started."

Paula realized she had elicited the fearful emotions Shahin had wanted to suppress. Slowly, she walked over and gave him a long, silent embrace as she searched for the right words to ease his worry. She wasn't trying to erase his past experience, only diminish the possibility of torture in their future.

Finally, she pushed herself away and said, "We're not going to let that happen to us. We're going to meet up with Kegger and Farah and get the hell out of here."

"Yeah," said Shahin as he regained his composure. "Let's head out."

He started to open the door and then closed it. A second thought surfaced regarding the message in the letter. He turned back and looked knowingly at Paula.

"That's it! I don't know why I didn't think of it earlier," he exclaimed.

Confused by his outburst, Paula gave him a strange look.

Again, she had no idea what Shahin was talking about and curiously asked, "What's it?"

"Farah, it's why they wanted Farah. I call her Little Sis, and in Charles's letter, he uses her nickname. He said it was for security reasons. The commander must have found out somehow that she's the one who knows the city where the jewels are hidden."

******

Shahin and Paula pulled over and got off the bike. He walked it to the back corner of an office building, hoping to hide it from the authorities. Together, he and Paula walked the short block to the perimeter of their rendezvous point. Being extra cautious, they watched intently for several minutes to catch any type of movement around the structure. Knowing Commander Rashidi was most likely using Farah to help him find the jewels, they felt he might have followed them to this location. After studying the grounds, they concluded that it was safe to check out the inside of the building.

They entered the building cautiously, with their handguns drawn. They found Kegger and Farah sitting together on the floor in the corner. When they saw Paula and Shahin, Farah jumped up and ran to Shahin.

"Oh, thank God you both got away," she said as she embraced him.

"Luckily, we only had one confrontation. It was intense, but once I shot at them, they stopped following us," said Paula.

"It was easy for us, also," said Kegger, "almost too easy."

"Yeah, I have a bad feeling about it all," added Shahin.

"It's probably because of me," said Farah. "The commander asked me about Charles. Somehow, he knows that I met with him and that he told me the name of the city where the jewels are hidden. I'm sorry, Shahin, but I had to tell him. He was going to hurt my parents if I didn't."

"I understand," replied Shahin. "No necklace is worth someone's life."

"Does this mean we're not going to try and find your family's jewels?" asked Paula.

"It's useless to try anyway," Farah interjected. "Without the key, we don't know which bank they're in, and there are hundreds of banks in Tabriz. I read an article recently saying that our financial system has over 8000 bank branches. Plus, even if we knew the location, we need the key to open it."

"We have the key," said Paula. "Charles gave it to me the day before we left Iran last November, but he didn't tell me what it was for."

"Is that the key you have around your neck?" asked Kegger.

Shahin glanced at Kegger, momentarily wondering how he had known about the key.

Paula ignored the look and replied, "Yes, that's the one."

Shahin considered asking about it, but quickly shrugged off his curiosity and refocused on Farah, "So, the jewels are in Tabriz?"

"Yes," she replied.

"Do you think the commander has enough manpower to surveil every bank in Tabriz?" asked Paula. "I wouldn't think so, especially now with the war happening."

"I agree," confirmed Kegger. "There's no way he could have troops at each location."

"I think we should try to get them," agreed Farah. "I'm not ready to give up yet."

Paula made a suggestion.

"Let's sit down and talk about what we know and don't know. Then we can have a better understanding of our odds."

The others agreed, and Paula began the conversation. "First, Shahin has a letter from Charles that talks about the jewels. It's in his bag," she said to Kegger. "The one we brought into the lodge from the Rover. Do you know where it is?"

"Yeah, it's in our pile of supplies and stuff. I'll get it."

Kegger got up and went to the corner of the room where everything was stored. While he searched for the duffel, Paula took off the necklace.

Kegger returned with the bag and handed it to Shahin. Without hesitation, Shahin reached inside and pulled out the letter. He read the note aloud, and when he was finished, Paula read the part of the inscription on the key that gave the address of the bank. Then she asked the others to look at the other symbols to see if anyone knew what they meant. They took turns examining the key, but none of them could make sense of the markings.

The four briefly discussed the letter, the key, Farah's intel, and why the pieces of information were somewhat conflicting and confusing. After several minutes of discussion, Kegger decided it was best to start their drive to Tabriz and talk more about their plans along the way. They would need to pass through the city on their way to the border, even if they weren't planning to retrieve the jewels.

Chapter 39 - Sharing the News

To avoid any misunderstanding or confusion, it was decided that Paula's parents should be the ones to break the exciting yet awkward news about Cindy's status to the Stetsons. The reason for this decision was simple. Cindy's parents were already acquainted with Harry and Mary Jane Williams. That familiarity would help the Stetsons believe that what they were being told was the truth. The more difficult part of their conversation and explanation would be why the Williams' and others kept Cindy's potential existence from them until now.

******

Harry and Mary Jane were on their way to the Stetsons' home a few hours after learning that Cindy was, in fact, alive and well. On the way there, Mary Jane made a request to her husband.

"Dear, I know it's unusual for me to ask you this type of favor," she said cautiously, "however, this is important to me, and I want you to consider my request."

"What is it, Mary? We don't have all day. We'll be there in five minutes," Harry responded.

"I'm getting to it," she said defensively. "It's about Cindy. I want to be the one to tell the Stetsons she's alive."

Surprised, Harry replied, "Darling, I am the head of this family, and it should be me who tells the Stetsons about their daughter. After all, Mr. Ali contacted me, not you."

"I'm not challenging your position in our relationship," Mary Jane said amiably. "It's well... I feel strongly that I am the better person to present the news about

Cindy. You hardly know the Stetsons, but I have spoken to Mrs. Stetson several times and we've met on occasion to talk about our daughters."

Harry took offense, "You don't think I can relate to how they're feeling?"

"It's not that you can't relate to them," she replied dubiously. "I just think Mrs. Stetson would be more comfortable hearing the news from a friend. Please, let me tell them that their daughter is alive."

"I think I can make it comfortable," Harry argued.

"Well," Mary Jane added, "Cindy's going to call them in a few hours, and I think I can help them get over the shock more easily. Plus, we don't want Mr. Stetson to have another heart attack."

This time, Harry paused to consider his wife's logic. Without arguing further, he replied, "Okay then, you can tell them. It's not that important who gives them the news anyway."

It was the first time Paula's mother didn't back down after her husband initially rejected her proposal. It gave Mary Jane a deep sense of satisfaction when she realized she had finally gained the courage and initiative to stand up for her beliefs.

Similarly, it was unlike Paula's father to yield to his wife's wishes. He had always been able to halt his wife's suggestions with little resistance.

The encounter had caught him by surprise, and before he knew it, he had given in to Mary Jane's wishes. The idea of relinquishing some of his superiority to his wife caused him some consternation.

Within seconds of granting her request, Harry regretted his statements and thought seriously about changing his mind. With every passing second, Harry felt his option to rescind his approval was becoming increasingly problematic. Yet, uncharacteristically, Harry remained silent. He knew his reason to rescind his approval needed to sound justified, but he couldn't figure out what to say. Everything that came into Harry's mind made him sound like a spoiled child demanding his toy back after allowing a friend to play with it.

Finally, Harry found the words to use to regain his prominence, but just as he was about to speak, Mary Jane said, "Harry, I want to thank you for understanding. I know it took a lot for you to concede your position to me for this particular moment, and I love you for being so understanding."

The statement took Harry by surprise, and he quickly reconsidered what he was about to say.

"Now," he thought, "it's going to be impossible for me to tell her *no*, she can't tell them about Cindy, without me, sounding like a complete asshole."

Feeling defeated, Harry reluctantly accepted that his wife would be the one to convey the exciting news about Cindy. Mary Jane cracked the faintest smile as she realized her comment had quelled any further discussion about it.

As they pulled into the Stetsons' driveway, Mary Jane felt empowered as a woman for the first time in her life, and the feeling was incredible. It gave her a new sense of identity, and she hoped she could incorporate this newly found assertiveness into other parts of her daily life in the future.

******

Carefully, but with some visible emotion, Mrs. Williams shared the recent news about Cindy with Mr. and Mrs. Stetson. She explained clearly and with as much detail as she could how Cindy had been mistakenly labeled as deceased when, in fact, she was living in Iran under an assumed identity.

She went on to explain about the rescue and how the team safely got her out of Iran and into Kuwait. The news caused all four parents to become emotional as tears of joy surged through Mr. and Mrs. Stetson. They hugged one another, and Mrs. Stetson briefly sobbed uncontrollably before regaining her composure and addressing her guests.

"I'm sorry, I'm just so happy. Please tell us more," Mrs. Stetson said as she wiped the tears from her face.

Paula's mother continued to relay the thirdhand details told to her by her husband, who had gotten them from Shahin's father, who was told of the situation by Stevie and Steelhead. Not knowing the Stetsons well, Mr. Williams awkwardly interjected additional details into the narrative to try to clarify parts of the story he felt were not accurately explained by his wife.

When Mrs. Williams finished the part about Kuwait, Mrs. Stetson interrupted.

"What about Paula? Is she with Cindy in Kuwait? You haven't mentioned her."

The question caused Mrs. Williams to falter. A lump formed in her throat, and her voice cracked as she tried to continue speaking. Seeing his wife's distress, Mr. Williams quickly took over and told the Stetsons Paula's status.

The joy and delight for Cindy's return were swiftly clouded with concern for Paula as Mr. Williams described what little they knew about their daughter's whereabouts. When he finished, an uneasy silence momentarily fell over the room.

Realizing he had to lighten the mood, Mr. Williams said optimistically, "I'm sure she'll be out of Iran soon. She and Shahin are with a very capable mercenary. In fact, he's the head of the whole damn team."

Mrs. Williams found her composure and assured Cindy's parents that Paula would be home within days. It was just a minor adjustment that the team had to make. Her statements sounded more like a confirmation to herself than an explanation to the Stetsons.

******

In Kuwait, Kamal led Cindy and Majid outside to Steelhead's front porch. He held his son while Cindy sat down on the steps. Once she was situated, Kamal handed Majid back to his mother before plopping down next to Cindy. She was talking about the latest weather forecast when Kamal suddenly jumped up and told Cindy he'd be back momentarily.

"Cindy," Kamal said as he returned with Kyra. "She's going to take Majid inside. I need to talk with you, and I don't want to be interrupted if he wakes up."

Cindy gave Kamal a concerned look but uncharacteristically refrained from commenting. Instead, she carefully handed Majid to Kyra.

"I'll take good care of him, don't worry. Just enjoy your free minutes while you can," she said sympathetically to Cindy.

Once they were alone, Kamal sat back down. She could see by his mannerisms that he had something important to discuss. He apprehensively took her hand and said, "I have something to tell you."

The tone of his voice was serious but without urgency. Cindy felt slightly uneasy, yet curious about what he planned to say.

"Okay, I'm ready," said Cindy. "What is it you have to tell me?"

"Well... when I returned to the United States, I... well I, I asked Nousha to marry me," he announced anxiously. "I thought you were dead, and I was so lonely. I didn't love her! I never did! It's you, only you, that I have ever loved!"

Cindy sat silent, trying to digest Kamal's confession. While living with Kaveh and his first wife, she had learned to be less reactionary and more even-tempered. Unaware of her newly found self-control, Kamal felt desperate for a response.

"Did you hear me? It was always you that I loved," he pleaded. "Please understand that I didn't know you were alive."

Finally, Cindy broke into a smile. A little part of her enjoyed watching Kamal plead his case, but she didn't want to make him suffer any longer.

"It's okay. That's in the past," she said magnanimously. "What matters now is that we're together. I love you, Kamal, and I'm happy that you love me," she said before planting a light kiss gently on his lips.

Kamal's expression turned into exhilaration as he realized he had been forgiven for his mistake. He took Cindy into his arms and zealously kissed her while thanking her for understanding.

A minute later, they heard a helicopter in the distance. Cindy broke off the kiss, and she and Kamal listened as the sound grew louder.

"It sounds like Steelhead is returning," said Kamal eagerly.

"Let's go to the pad!" replied Cindy.

The two ran to the waiting area for the helipad. Moments later, Steelhead's copter hovered above the landing site. Niki and Jasmine had also heard the humming of the engines and ran to join them. The four waited impatiently as they watched him touch down.

Once the engine was turned off and the rotors slowed, the four ran up to greet Steelhead. Everyone shouted at once, eager to learn how his mission had gone.

"All right, everybody," said Steelhead. "At least let me get out of my bird." The group settled down and waited while Steelhead unstrapped himself and removed his headset. He jumped down from the cockpit, saying, "The trip went well. I only broke about 25 international laws, and who knows how many other laws in each country."

"So, you didn't have any trouble?" asked Niki.

"Nope, but you'll have to excuse me. I gotta take a leak," said Steelhead as he hurried to the house.

Relieved and happy the news was positive, the four headed back to the house to hear the whole story.

Chapter 40 - Opening the Box

At the bank in Tabriz, Iran, Kegger kept watch while Paula, Shahin, and Farah followed the bank manager into the vault. Once inside, he took the key from Shahin and examined it closely. After reading the code, the manager went to a box approximately three feet above the floor in the center of the safety deposit boxes.

He returned the key to Shahin and watched as Shahin inserted the key and turned the lock.

"Please do not open it until I have left the vault," said the manager. "I am required to give you complete privacy while you examine the items inside. I will lock the door behind me for additional security. There is a latch right there," he said as he pointed at a lever on the large metal door, "to open the vault from the inside if necessary."

Just as the manager was turning to leave, Commander Rashidi and two other soldiers, holding Kegger at gunpoint, entered the small room.

"How did you find us?" asked Farah disbelievingly. "I only told you the city."

"Silly girl, I had lookouts at all of the roads heading into Tabriz. Honestly, there aren't that many to surveil. Once you were identified, I had my people tail you to this location," Rashidi boasted.

Understanding he may be taken into custody and not see the items inside the box, Shahin pulled the container out enough to open the top. To his surprise, it looked empty except for a tiny sliver of paper. Immediately, Shahin covered the remnant with his thumb. A second later, the commander pushed Farah aside to see the contents inside the container. Thinking quickly, Shahin took his other hand and pulled the drawer completely out of its holding place. Using the distraction, he slid the scrap to the edge of the box, and when the commander ripped the container from his hands, Shahin slipped the paper into his pocket without anyone noticing.

"I don't understand!" yelled Rashidi. "Where are they? Where are the jewels?" Enraged, he turned to the banker, grabbed him by the collar, and started choking him. "What have you done with them? I know they were here! Where have you hidden them?"

The general's grip around the manager's neck was so tight that he could not respond. Realizing the man needed to breathe to respond to his questions, Rashidi released his grip enough for the man to explain.

"Sir, I don't know," he replied. "No one else has a key to this box. It is under surveillance 24 hours a day, and we have never had an issue with our security."

"That's impossible. They have to be here," he insisted.

Unable to comprehend that there were no jewels, the commander turned the box upside down and shook it in frustration. He then searched every crevice of the box for something that would give him an indication of where the treasure might be.

"Looks like Charles fooled us all," said Farah. "He always did have a quirky sense of humor."

"Shut up, you little whore!" demanded the commander as he swung his hand back towards Farah's face.

Knowing his temper and demeanor, Farah stepped back, and his hand missed her completely. This maneuver enraged Rashidi even more, and the spectacle he created diverted his soldiers' attention away from Kegger. The mercenary saw his opening, grabbed the barrel of the first soldier's gun, and yanked it out of his hands. In the same motion, Kegger whirled around and caught the second soldier with the butt of the pistol. In the chaos, Paula threw her chador over the head of the commander. As he struggled to remove the cloak, Farah saw her opportunity to scissor-kick him forcefully in the groin. He yelped loudly upon impact, and just as he bent over in pain, her second foot landed in the exact location. Down he went, lying in the fetal position on the floor.

Paula grabbed the commander's gun and pointed it at him while Kegger and Shahin finished subduing the other two men.

"Let's go before reinforcements arrive," said Paula.

Her friends agreed and followed her out of the vault, leaving the three soldiers on the floor, injured and incapacitated. Shahin locked the door while Kegger jammed one of the rifles into the vault's latch mechanism, making it impossible for the soldiers to exit the room.

Shahin pulled the bank manager close before making his demands.

"Lead us to your back entrance, and don't yell for help!"

The man nodded and motioned for them to follow him. He led them through a maze of hallways until they reached a small reinforced door.

"Open it and check to see if there are soldiers outside," said Shahin.

"Don't respond if they are out there," added Paula. "Just motion silently to us, *yes* or *no, and if yes, how many*."

The man hesitated, seemingly unaccustomed to a woman giving him orders.

"Do as she said," Shahin added firmly.

Intimidated by Shahin's demand, the man quietly opened the door just enough to peer outside. He saw two soldiers conversing with their backs to the door. The manager turned to the group and raised two fingers. Kegger stepped up and mouthed, "How far away?"

The manager whispered back, "About three meters past the entrance. They're turned away from us right now."

Hearing their positioning, Kegger bulldozed past the manager, burst out of the door, and ran up to the unsuspecting soldiers. The other three followed his lead, and together, they quickly subdued the two men without anyone firing a shot.

Chapter 41 - The Crossing

Paula and Farah had laughed and joked about the fight inside the vault for almost an hour while Shahin drove the women and Kegger to the border town, Bazargan. The guys joined in the conversation occasionally but didn't find the crotch kicks as funny as the women. Finally, Paula and Farah settled into a more sober frame of mind as the four contemplated how best to retrieve the jewels and get out of Iran.

Everyone agreed that by now, their faces were known to the Iranian military, so Shahin drove while Kegger laid out his ideas. He made Farah part of the team and insisted that everyone, as a team member, must understand each segment of the two missions for them to be successful.

Back at Khorramshahr, when Shahin told Niki and Kamal of their plans to head north away from the fighting, he had a good reason for choosing this particular border town. Charles's late grandmother was buried in the town's cemetery. The letter Charles had written to Shahin before his death alluded to his grandmother's grave as the place where Shahin's family jewels might be hidden, but other parts talked about a safety deposit box. The note they found inside the box at the bank was vague, but it concurred with Charles's letter. Now, Shahin was confident the jewels were stored at the gravesite.

It was mid-afternoon when Paula, Shahin, Kegger, and Farah entered the village. It was a remote border crossing located in the very northwestern corner of the country. Cautiously, Shahin drove through the town to the small cemetery north of the village center. They hadn't planned on entering the site until dusk, but wanted to check it out ahead of time. Their main task for the afternoon was to head back to the border station to do some reconnaissance.

It was warmer than usual when they stopped on a side street near the center of the village, but the team couldn't wait for it to cool down. Paula and Farah needed to complete their portion of the job before sundown. They needed to gather as much information as possible about the border crossing setup, the support buildings, the lay of the land on either side of the river, and, equally important, a reliable estimate of how many guards and soldiers were stationed there. The intel would help the team determine if their plan was even viable.

At the drop-off point, Paula and Farah placed their chadors over their heads and around their bodies. It would be hot, but necessary, to cover themselves. The garments not only helped the women conform to local customs; they also aided in hiding their identities. The women were about to exit the vehicle when Paula pulled Farah back onto the seat.

"Just a minute," she said. "I have something for you. It's not very big, but it can do some damage, and it's small enough to fit in your pocket." Paula pulled out a medium-sized knife from the weapons bag and handed it to Farah. "Here, hide this; I'm not sure what to expect at the border crossing or the cemetery. If you need to use it, use it without hesitation. Don't threaten the person with it first."

"I will, Paula. I know our lives are at stake," said Farah categorically.

Paula and Farah walked side by side toward the river, taking in as much of the station setup as possible. There was a lot of security, but less than they expected. Timidly, the women entered the buildings and cautiously observed what services were in each one. Paula took particular notice of the small jail near the village entrance. She and Farah concluded it was a temporary detention facility used mainly to hold criminals before being transported to Tehran for prosecution.

Shahin and Kegger parked in the village near the local general store while they waited for the women to return. Because of the vast amounts of goods crossing the border daily, many strangers often visited the town center. This helped the men's presence go unnoticed by the locals.

To pass the time, Shahin told Kegger what he knew about the two border towns.

"Both are Kurdish settlements," he announced, "and for some reason, both governments discriminate against the Kurds. I'm not sure why because the people that I've met here with Charles seemed like good, hard-working folks."

"Yeah, I've heard that," agreed Kegger. "I think it's an ethnic thing."

"Charles and I witnessed it first-hand when we came to Bazargan years ago. He had known about it from his grandmother, and when I came with him, we brought extra money and gifts to give to the locals. I even took money out of my own savings account. I wanted to show Charles I approved of that part of his heritage and was sympathetic towards his grandmother's people."

Kegger listened with interest but told Shahin it was difficult for him to imagine.

"Being a tall, large, white man," he said flatly, "I don't know what it's like to be discriminated against. I have always gotten preferential treatment everywhere I go, and I mean everywhere throughout the world."

Shahin nodded in agreement and added, "Being male and wealthy used to grant me special treatment by pretty much everyone as well, but since the hostage crisis, that stuff doesn't seem to matter much. If people find out I'm Iranian, they make snide comments under their breath and avoid me if possible."

After finishing their scouting mission, Paula and Farah returned to the waiting vehicle and reported what they had seen.

"I expected more guards," said Shahin, "but that's good news."

"Do you think it's because of the war with Iraq?" asked Paula.

"No," Kegger responded. "I think it's because it's the afternoon, and most of the grunts are planning to guard throughout the night when it's easier for people like us to cross.".

"What are grunts?" asked Farah.

"He calls the low-ranking soldiers grunts," interjected Paula.

"It's a distinction between the haves and the have-nots," Kegger said sarcastically.

"Sorry, I didn't know what that word meant," replied Farah.

"Ignore him, Farah," said Paula dryly. "It's his own personal slang. Most people just call them soldiers."

"I like the word. It makes me think of pigs," Farah added pointedly. "Most of the soldiers smell and grunt like them. The name fits them perfectly."

Completely out of context and ignoring the banter between the others, Shahin said frankly, "I think it's going to be difficult to cross the border and stay out of trouble in Turkey. Hopefully, my father got the message about the car, but there's no way of knowing," he added somberly.

Shahin's comments destroyed the bit of levity the three were enjoying and returned the group to the seriousness of their situation.

"We'll figure out the best area to cross," said Paula. "If we have to wait a day or walk a long way, we're all up for it, aren't we, guys?"

Kegger and Farah mumble their agreement, hoping to shift the mood to a more positive vibe.

Then Kegger said, "Hey, Shahin, if shit goes wrong, it's not your fault. I'm the boss of this operation. I'm to blame, not you. Besides, we'll be fine. It would be nice to have a car waiting, but if not, we're resourceful. We'll make do without it."

Shahin nodded, attempting to accept Kegger's declaration, but he couldn't fully shift all of the responsibility to someone else. This time, he felt even more determined to ensure their safe exit from Iran.

Chapter 42 - The Grave

As a young boy, Shahin had gone with Charles to visit his grandmother's resting place. The journey had made an impact on Shahin, and the location of the grave was forever etched in his mind.

Dusk was just beginning when the four returned to the cemetery. The nearby houses had just started to turn on their lights for the evening. Shahin, alone, made his way through the headstones to where Charles's grandmother was buried. It was a risky endeavor because the grounds of the cemetery were vacant of trees or other types of shrubbery that could have provided Shahin with some cover. His friends watched intently from behind a rocky outcrop as he casually walked past numerous grave plots. Finally, he stopped at one of the larger headstones.

When Shahin arrived at the spot, he noticed that the size and type of stone differed from what he remembered. He surmised that Charles had replaced the old stone with a new one when he decided to hide the jewels inside.

The others waited anxiously while Shahin knelt beside the granite marker and began to feel for the outline of a rectangular box. As described, the geometric cutout was there. He carefully applied inward pressure on the shape. After two seconds, Shahin removed his fingers to allow the stone to rebound. The rock responded to his touch and recoiled a few millimeters past the outer perimeter of the headstone. Hastily, Shahin tried to pull it out. Unfortunately, his fingertips were too large, and he could not get enough grip on either side. Paula saw he was struggling and motioned to the others that she was leaving her hiding position to assist Shahin. She knew every second he was out in the open added significant danger to all.

"Shahin!" Paula whispered forcefully as she squatted next to him. "Let me try!"

Without waiting for an answer, Paula muscled in to get a better angle on the stone. Her strong yet slender fingers could easily grasp the section of rock.

"It's coming!" she exclaimed under her breath.

Another second passed while Paula jiggled the granite to dissipate the friction holding the treasure in its hiding place. Finally, she gave it one last pull. It came loose, and a moment later, she held a lopsided metal container awkwardly in her hands. The medium-sized box was heavy and cumbersome. It was made of finely finished stainless steel with a large, heavy piece of granite glued onto one side.

"Here, you take it," said Paula as she handed it to Shahin.

"Okay," Shahin mechanically replied, taking the container clumsily from Paula's grasp.

Shahin and Paula stood to leave, but before they rushed away, Shahin reached out and held Paula back.

"I just need a second," he whispered.

Shahin repositioned the box to hold it with just his left hand. Then, he placed his right hand on top of the headstone.

"Your grandson was a good man," Shahin said lovingly. "I hope he is with you and can hear my words. Thank you, Charles. You are my second father, and I still love you."

Instantly, Shahin felt a heavy burden lift off of him. He stood still, taking in the feeling as if he were possessed. Paula was touched by his sentiment but also aware of the urgency for them to take cover. She gently slipped her hand around his left arm and pulled slightly to remind him of their mission.

Shahin did not respond to her touch, so she whispered, "I know you'd like to stay longer and show more love and support for Charles and his grandmother, but Shahin, we need to go. It's too dangerous for us to be out here in the open."

Her words got Shahin's attention. He nodded and took his hand off the headstone.

"I'm ready. Let's get back to Farah and Kegger," he said, refocusing his concentration on the moment.

Paula and Shahin quickly headed back to the rocks where the others were waiting. Paula was slightly ahead of Shahin when they rounded the corner of a large boulder protruding past the other rocks. Suddenly, she stopped. Shahin knew instantly that something was wrong. He grabbed her arm to pull her back, hoping they could turn around and run, but it was too late. A soldier had snuck up behind them and had his machine gun raised and ready to shoot if they tried to make a move.

"So nice of you to retrieve the treasure for me," Commander Rashidi said gloatingly to Shahin. Then he looked at one of his men, "You," he said, "bring me the box."

"How did you find us?" Paula asked, being honestly curious. "When we left the bank, we made sure that no one was following us."

"Yes, you did outsmart my soldiers at the bank, but you couldn't hide from my lookouts here," explained the commander. "You see, when we considered recruiting Charles years earlier, we did a thorough background check on him. We were aware that he had an Iranian grandmother of Kurdish descent who was buried somewhere near the western border. This being a Kurdish settlement, it was simple to assume this was the town and a perfect location to hide the jewels. One could easily grab the treasure on one's way out of the country. In case I was wrong, I also sent scouts to the other crossings farther south. Finally, even if the jewels weren't here, this is the most likely place you would choose to leave Iran. The USSR isn't easy to get into, or out of, if you know what I mean," the commander joked. "And Iraq, well...I think you know that would be impossible now."

"Why didn't you just take the jewels before we arrived?" asked Shahin.

Commander Rashidi rolled his eyes before saying, "You probably didn't notice, but there were no identifying words on many of the gravestones. My troops looked through the cemetery several times but couldn't determine which grave was the old woman's."

Commander Rashidi fumbled with the awkward box, working to position it so he could find out how to open it. His heart was pounding, and it was evident that his excitement was building. He moved his fingers over the surface of the metal until he felt a latch that should have opened the chest. He tried to move the small button-like mechanism up and down, left and right, and nothing happened. He looked closer at it and could see a space for the button to move toward the back of the box, but as he forced it backward, the button refused to move. Finally, he took a deep breath and simultaneously pushed the button in and back. It moved with the force. When it was as far back as it could go, the commander released the control, and the top of the box popped open. He peered inside, there was one large cloth bag and two small ones. He assumed the smaller bags held loose gems, so he focused on the large one. He opened the cinch and allowed the treasure trove of exquisite pieces of jewelry to be revealed.

The first item he pulled out was a very ornate necklace with large groups of diamonds and rubies set in platinum. The next item he grabbed was a large solitary diamond set in a gold facet with a slender, delicate chain.

"Now, this is more like it," he said happily. "This diamond alone will bring a pretty penny."

Unable to wait, he continued to pull out the jewelry, one piece after another. He was almost done when something really excited him. It was a man's ring, and he held it up high to admire its magnificence.

"This ring is exquisite," he said admiringly. "I must keep this for myself as a reminder of my hard work."

Mr. Ali had promised Shahin the ring when he turned thirty years old. It was a tradition passed down from father to son. Shahin never thought of himself as owning it; only the next person given the privilege to wear the ring before passing it on. Mr. Ali's fingers had thickened over the years, and he didn't want to risk having the ring resized. Therefore, it had been put away ten years earlier until Shahin was of age to wear it.

The ring was encrusted with one massive round, brilliant-cut diamond and many smaller ones, highlighting the outer rim. In between were gold and platinum designs. Commander Rashidi examined the ring further with a flashlight and saw an inscription written inside. It read, *Wear With Pride.* He mumbled the phrase first before saying it louder as he placed the ring on his finger.

"I'll gladly honor the inscription's request," he said as he repositioned it. He held up his hand to admire it, making sure Shahin could see it clearly on his finger. "I wear it well. Don't you think?" he said smugly before grinning maliciously.

Shahin had watched angrily but calmly as Commander Rashidi mused over his family's jewels. It wasn't until the commander put on the ring that he lost his cool.

"Take it off!" yelled Shahin as he tried to free himself from the soldiers' grip.

The commander immediately drew his handgun and pointed it directly at Shahin, "Give me a reason," he said evenly.

"Shahin," said Paula coolly, "don't give him the satisfaction. He's not worth it, and neither is the ring."

Regaining his self-control, Shahin stopped resisting his bondage.

"It's time I got back to headquarters," said Rashidi. "You four," he motioned to his soldiers. "Take the men down to the station jail. I'll deal with them later. And you," he said to a fifth man, "drive their vehicle to my headquarters."

"Yes, sir," replied the men before shoving Shahin and Kegger towards their truck.

"The women will be coming with the rest of us," Rashidi stated manically. "I have plans for them."

As the four soldiers headed for the village with Shahin and Kegger, the commander turned and smiled evilly at both women. Without saying a word, he walked smugly over to face Paula. He looked her up and down and then walked around to check out the rest of her body.

"She'll do," he said to the remaining soldiers as if Paula were a piece of meat to be purchased from the market. Then, he went over to Farah. He opened his mouth and licked his lips just inches from her face, but said nothing. Mohammed Rashidi slowly raised his hand. Paula thought he was going to strike Farah, but instead, he stuck out his pointer finger and lifted her chin to meet his gaze. "You, my dear... well, we have some unfinished business, don't we. You'll be first."

"I'd rather die than allow you to touch me again," said Farah defiantly.

"You may get your wish, but it will be after I'm through with you," he mused.

"Don't do something stupid," said Paula to Farah. "He's just taunting you."

Dusk was quickly turning to darkness when suddenly, Stevie, bandaged leg and all, stepped out from behind a boulder.

"Drop your weapons, boys, and no one has to die today."

The soldiers glanced at the well-armed man and quickly did as he instructed. Both guards recognized him from his earlier escape on the way to their camp, and they knew he was a seasoned mercenary.

"I repay my debts if I can, Paula. I hope this makes us even," Stevie said as he gave her a whimsical smirk. Then he turned to Farah, "It looks like you gained a friend since I saw you last."

"You guys made it?" Paula confirmed happily.

"Yeah, we're all good," Stevie replied.

The commander saw his opportunity. With one quick movement, while still holding the bag of jewels, he wrapped his left arm around Farah's torso and pulled her into his body. With his right hand, he pulled out his knife and placed it firmly below Farah's chin.

"Stay back, or I'll slit her throat," said the commander calmly. "You men," he demanded, "pick up your weapons."

"I wouldn't if I were you," said Stevie to the soldiers. "I don't know the woman he's holding hostage, and if I need to, I'll lay down several rounds and kill all four of you within a second. She'll just be considered collateral damage."

"You won't do it!" yelled Commander Rashidi. "Now drop your weapon, or she's dead."

While the two men were conversing, Farah had slowly and carefully reached into her front pocket. Without warning, she swiftly pulled out the knife given to her by Paula. She wheeled around and stabbed the commander in the chest.

Unfortunately, the wound was in the meaty part of Commander Rashidi's upper body, causing only a minor injury. He had begun to laugh and was already pulling out the knife when Paula lunged forward. Deep into his neck went her blade, completely severing his carotid artery.

Commander Rashidi stared at Paula as he dropped the bag of jewels and put his hand on the neck wound to try to stop the bleeding. Simultaneously, he swung his knife wildly to cut Paula. Farah saw his movement towards Paula and grabbed his forearm with both hands. She pulled the limb to her mouth and bit down hard into his flesh. He instantly let go of the knife and tried to cry out in pain, but the gushing blood muted his cries.

Commander Rashidi stumbled backward as he succumbed to his injury. The excessive bleeding had weakened his body. The commander dropped to his knees for a brief moment before collapsing forward onto the ground.

Both soldiers looked on in horror as they watched their commander die. Neither man made any attempt to go to his side. Instead, they stayed still with their hands raised.

"Well, ladies, I came here to rescue you, but it doesn't look like you needed my help," Stevie said glibly.

"There's no time for jokes," said Paula hastily. "The other soldiers have Shahin and Kegger. They're taking them to the village jail. If we don't break them out, they'll be moved to a real prison. Then, it'll be impossible to free them."

"You," Stevie said, pointing to one of the soldiers, "get down on the ground belly first. "And you," he waved his gun at the second man, "you get on top of him. I want you back-to-back with your arms out." The two men did as he ordered, and when they were in position, Stevie stood over them and asked Paula to take out their handcuffs. He had Paula cuff one of each man's hands together. "Now tie their shoelaces together as tight as you can."

"I'll stuff their mouths," said Farah. "We don't want them yelling for help."

Farah lifted her smock and tried to tear off pieces of it, but she was not strong enough to break the seams. "Let me hold the gun on them while you tear my dress," she said to Stevie.

The comment took him by surprise, and he hesitated for a moment. Then he smiled and handed her the weapon. He picked up the hem and tore two strips off the bottom. He handed the pieces to Farah, and she gave him back the gun. While Farah gagged their prisoners, Paula went over to the body of the commander.

Paula knelt and picked up the commander's right hand. Angrily, she began to wiggle the ring off the commander's finger, saying out loud, "You don't deserve to wear this ring. I'll make sure it gets back to the rightful owner." She gave Rashidi's body a disgusting look before stuffing it into her jeans pocket.

"I'll take this bag as well," Paula told the corpse. "The devil can adorn you with a necklace made of fire and a ring of sand spurs." She picked up the bag and stood staring down at the fallen man. A calmness fell over her. This man had hunted her and her friends for over a year, bringing in dogs, soldiers, and gunboats to try and kill them. Now, it was he who lay lifeless at her feet.

Farah walked over to confirm for herself that he was dead. Farah took Paula's hand and squeezed it gently. Paula returned the gesture before saying, "He won't be raping women or torturing men ever again."

Paula released her grip and put her arm around Farah's shoulders. She turned them away from the corpse and walked up to Stevie.

"Let's go get our friends."

Paula bent down and picked up the soldiers' weapons. She handed one rifle to Farah while Stevie gave the two soldiers one last set of instructions.

"Be still, and don't try to cry out. Don't make me regret my compassion."

With the mood changing, Paula asked Stevie, "By the way, how the hell did you get here?"

"Not in front of the soldiers," he replied. "I'll tell you once we're out of earshot."

"Sorry, I didn't think about that," said Paula. "I have a lot to learn."

Chapter 43 - Village Jail

The soldiers shoved Shahin and Kegger through the door of the border station holding cell. A man sitting at a desk in the middle of the room looked up at them as they entered.

"I need these men held until our commander arrives," the ranking soldier said. "I'm not sure how long it's going to take. It could be a few hours, but it will most likely be tomorrow."

"I'm here until midnight, then the night watchman takes over. If the commander hasn't arrived by the time my shift ends, I'll tell my replacement what to expect. In the meantime, I need some questions answered for my official ledger," he told the soldier. "Let's start with you," the jailer said to Kegger when he was ready.

After the mercenary answered all of his questions, the man turned to Shahin and said, "Your turn."

Shahin decided to give his real name. He figured they would find out anyway, and there was no sense in lying at this point.

"Shahin Ali," he said proudly.

The man immediately looked over at the soldiers. They were talking amongst themselves, paying little attention to the questions he was asking and his prisoner's responses.

"Shahin Ali," mumbled the man writing the notes. Then he looked diretly at Shahin. "Do I know you, son? Your name sounds familiar to me."

"I was here years ago when I was a kid," said Shahin while studying the man's face. "Now that you mention it, I do remember you."

Suddenly, the man recognized Shahin and whispered, "You were with Charles! Right?" he confirmed.

"Yes, I was here with him to visit the grave of his grandmother," responded Shahin softly, "I think I was 14 at the time."

"Okay, men, I'm finished," the jailer yelled to the soldiers. "You can put them in the cell now. I'll guard them until your commander arrives," then he added. "If you're hungry, the restaurant at the edge of town is open late, and they give soldiers a discount."

The ranking soldier watched the jailer lock his prisoners inside the cell before turning to his men and motioning for them to exit the building. He thanked the watchman for the advice, and the group left the station.

After the soldiers were gone, the jailer walked up to the cell bars and said, "I know your friend Charles well. He comes here at least once a year. Come to think of it, it's odd; he hasn't been back since he purchased the new headstone for his grandmother," he said ponderingly. "That was about a year and a half ago."

"I hate to tell you, but you won't be seeing him ever again. He was murdered by Khomeini's soldiers last November, and I'm pretty sure that's what's going to happen to us if we don't find a way out of here," explained Shahin.

A grief-stricken expression fell over the man's face as he said, "What happened?"

Charles died protecting me from a soldier's bullet, and all I was trying to do was leave Iran," Shahin replied.

"The new regime's military is no better than the Shah's Savak, maybe even worse," the guard offered. "Khomeini's men killed my brother for a minor issue that wasn't even his fault!"

"We know their tactics, and they don't care about human life," Shahin agreed.

"Charles was a good man, and he spoke very highly of you, Shahin. He showed me photos of you each time he came, but now you look different. I didn't recognize you with your long hair and beard."

"I did it to change my appearance. I guess it worked," Shahin explained.

"I owe Charles a lot," said the jailer. "My wife and I will miss him. He helped us on more than one occasion with our bills. He was a very generous man."

"Yes, he was. I miss him, too," Shahin added. "What about you? What will happen to you if we escape on your watch?"

"Nothing good; that's why we've got to make it look real. I'll say you overpowered me and took the keys from my belt. I'll tell them you wanted some water, and when I handed a cup to the big guy, he pulled my entire arm into the cell and slammed my face into the bars."

"Do you think they'll believe it?" Shahin questioned.

"I think so, but he's going to have to bang my head on the metal bars. Otherwise, it won't look authentic," he said to Shahin. "I'll tell them you grabbed the keys and unlocked the door while the big man continued to hold me against them."

"It sounds like a good plan," said Kegger, "but it's going to hurt."

"I know, so let's get it over with," he said flatly. "You're going to need as much time as possible to figure out how to get over the border. It's crawling with additional soldiers besides the regular border patrol."

******

Paula, Stevie, and Farah crouched behind a parked truck while the soldiers who had brought Shahin and Kegger to the jail stopped to talk to three other troops on the street just outside the entrance. They could vaguely hear what the men were saying, but it sounded like the two were telling the others how they had captured four of the wanted fugitives and brought the mercenary and the rich boy to the jail.

While they waited for the men to leave, Paula whispered to Stevie, "So, I have a million questions. Again, how did you get here? The last time we saw you, you were bleeding badly and headed for Kuwait."

"Steelhead had a doctor come to his house and patch me up. Then we called Shahin's dad and told him the news. He immediately went to work. He got permission from the new Turkish government that allowed Steelhead to land in Turkey. I'm not sure how he did it, but we landed in Gaziantep, Turkey, a day later."

"That's a long way from the Iranian border. How'd you get here?" she persisted.

"There was a car waiting for me at the helipad when we landed. Mr. Ali must have some excellent connections," said Stevie.

"That explains how you got into Turkey, but how did you know we'd be at the cemetery?" asked Paula. "We didn't even know we were going there until after we went to the safety deposit box in Tabriz."

"Mrs. Ali found a copy of Charles's letter in an envelope with a short note from Shahin. I guess he left it on his desk for her to find in case he didn't return," replied Stevie. "Anyway, she knew all about Charles's grandmother and where she was buried. She figured you would look for the jewels there if you were going to be in Bazargan. We all agreed that it was the logical place to look for you," he added. "So, when I got into Bazargan, it made sense for me to go there first to try and meet up with you."

"You have great timing," said Paula.

"Now I have a question," said Stevie. "Who's your friend?"

"This is Kamal's sister, Farah," responded Paula, but before either could say more, the two soldiers announced loud enough for them to hear, "Well, we'd better get going. Otherwise, we won't have enough time to eat before we need to report back."

The group said their goodbyes, and the soldiers went their separate ways. Stevie was about to make his move towards the building holding Kegger and Shahin when he saw Kegger open the border station door and peer out. It was now close to 11:00 PM. The stream of trucks and cars had slowed, but there were still a few coming across. Kegger motioned for Shahin to follow him, and they slipped quietly out of the door before scurrying to the next closest building for cover. They were deciding what to do next when Paula ran up to them.

"How'd you get out?" she asked and hugged Shahin.

"It's a long story," he said. "What about you? How'd you get away from the commander?"

"We had help. Stevie showed up, and, well, together, we took care of him and his soldiers," said Paula.

"Stevie?" asked Kegger.

"How'd he get here?" asked Shahin.

"It doesn't matter…" Paula began, but Kegger cut her off.

"Where is he? Is Farah with him?"

"Yeah, they're waiting across the street," replied Paula.

Kegger glanced around before saying, "Okay, let's go!"

The three crouched and ran to where Stevie and Farah were waiting. Without even a "hello," Kegger said, "We need to move now. The troops could be back any minute."

"I came over north of the village about a half mile away. I think we should head up there to cross. There are fewer soldiers, and the river is narrower up there."

"So, you waded across the border?" asked Kegger.

"Yeah, I called Mehmet when I got to a phone. He told me about a spot where there's much more vegetation on both sides of the river, like a small flood plain," described Stevie. "Anyway, I parked my car nearby and waded across, using the foliage to help hide me most of the way. I'm hoping we can get back the same way." Then he added. "Oh, there's one more thing. Did you hear about the military coup in Turkey? It happened September 12th."

Paula was the first to respond, "A coup, oh no, is it safe for us to enter?"

"Yeah, so far, it's been peaceful. The military took over, and now Kenan Evren is Turkey's new president. I guess it had to do with the right and left fighting and killing each other and the rise of communism. Being a NATO country, the military didn't want it to get out of control. Anyway, there's a curfew, so we'll have to be extra careful."

"We knew a coup had been brewing for a while," said Kegger. "It's just too bad it had to happen right now."

"What does it mean for us?" asked Farah. "Are we going to able to get out of Turkey once we get in?"

"Don't worry," said Kegger. "I have friends in Turkey who can help us. People and companies like mine have a kind of unofficial network in many countries. We support each other when one of us gets in a bind."

"Like I said, I already contacted Mehmet," said Stevie. "He has gotten us two rooms in Dogubeyazit. It's only about 20 miles from the border. We'll stay there and rest until morning and then head towards Istanbul."

They cautiously headed north to the less guarded part of the frontier where Stevie had crossed. It would be a risky journey because the light from the moon was bright. It had been a full moon only a couple of days earlier. In addition to the lunar intensity, the reflecting surface of the sand added to the landscape's luminescence.

Chapter 44 - At the River

The five stopped every fifty feet to reassess their position and listen. Finally, they were close to where Stevie had crossed, but it was impossible to know if the river was now under surveillance. As an extra precaution, they watched intently the surrounding area to see if they could detect soldier's movements on either side of the river. After minutes of observing and listening for any type of movement, they heard one vehicle drive past on the Turkish side of the border.

"Do you think it's safe to cross now?" asked Farah. "We haven't heard or seen anyone on the Iranian side."

"That doesn't mean they're not there," said Kegger. "Sitting and watching doesn't take a lot of movement or noise."

"What worries me as much as the patrols is the rising water level," said Stevie. "There was a huge rainstorm to the north, and the extra water has finally made its way down here. I can see the river is already a couple of feet higher than when I waded over. If we wait much longer, we may not get across."

Paula asked optimistically, "We just need to make it to the center of the river, right?"

Kegger cynically replied, "Don't count on it. I've heard stories of border guards dragging bodies back to their side. Not at this one, but in general." Just then, the faint sound of a siren echoed through the night air. "Damn it!" Kegger cussed. "Rashidi's soldiers must know we've escaped."

"What now?" asked Shahin.

"I say we should go now," said Paula. "Soon, this area will be crawling with soldiers."

In the distance, but coming fast, was the sound of motorized vehicles on the road paralleling the river.

"She's right!" declared Kegger. "Let's go! There's no time to waste!"

The five entered the water with everyone but Farah holding a rifle or machine gun above their heads. Kegger was in the lead, with Farah directly behind him and Paula behind her. Next was Shahin, and Stevie brought up the rear. Farah struggled to keep up with Kegger as the water got deeper, and soon, she was several feet behind him. Paula was only a few feet behind Farah when she noticed Farah teetering. A moment later, Farah lost her footing and was swept downriver by the current.

Paula reacted instinctively, "I'll get her!" she yelled.

She dropped the gun and allowed the current to help her catch up to Farah. Paula had grabbed Farah's arm and was pulling her up when men's voices transcended the sound of rushing water and the sirens. A foot patrol neared the group's position just as a large cloud passed between the Moon and Earth, temporarily darkening the night sky. It wasn't enough to completely obscure one's vision, but it hampered everyone's ability to see accurately.

Kegger and Stevie heard the threat and brought their guns down into a firing position. Without any warning, the soldiers began shooting, and a split second later, Kegger and Stevie returned fire. The patrol panicked and stopped shooting momentarily to find cover.

Shahin had seen Paula go after Farah and decided to help. Instead of firing at the soldiers, he also threw his gun into the water and floated towards the women. Farah was still trying to regain her footing when Shahin took Farah's other arm. Together, the three continued to traverse the river's ever-stronger current.

They were in the middle of the river when the full brightness of the moon returned. At that moment, a male voice boomed through a megaphone on the Turkish side of the river. He ordered the Iranian forces to stand down, and Turkish troops quickly lined the shore with their weapons drawn. The man told the Iranians that the group of people crossing the river were now on their side of the river and legally within Turkish jurisdiction. Being outnumbered and intimidated by the large number of Turkish forces, the Iranians stopped firing. All they could do now was watch as the escapees made their way to the shoreline. The chase was over, and they had lost.

Chapter 45 - Going Forward

Cindy burst into the room just as Kamal was putting Majid on the bed to nap. "Kamal!" she said loudly before realizing Majid was sleeping. She immediately lowered her voice before continuing to tell him about the call with her parents. "Sorry, did I wake him?"

"No, he's still asleep. How'd it go?" he asked.

"It felt so good to hear their voices. Believe it or not, I was a little nervous at first," Cindy admitted. "I'm just so glad to have them both still here, and they're really excited about having another grandchild. They said they can't wait to meet Majid."

"That's great, it's cool that things went so well," said Kamal, trying to sound supportive.

The tone of his voice made Cindy realize that her joy and enthusiasm to talk with her parents must have been hard for Kamal. His parents were still in Iran, and he was unable to communicate with them for safety reasons.

As Kamal listened to Cindy, the thought of losing her again and going through life without any family support caused Kamal to blurt out his feelings uncharacteristically.

"Marry me!" Kamal exclaimed.

"What did you say?" asked Cindy, wanting to make sure of his proclamation.

"Marry me, Cindy," he said more calmly. "I love you, and I love our son, and I want us to be a family."

"Okay," said Cindy, sounding unsure.

"You don't sound very excited," questioned Kamal. "Do you want to marry me or not?"

"Yes," Cindy said awkwardly. "It's just, well, it's that you sprung it on me so suddenly. I wasn't expecting it." Before Kamal could respond, Cindy continued, "Do you think we're ready?"

"Ready?" Kamal said, sounding slightly annoyed. "We love each other, and we have a child together. How much more ready could we be?"

"You're right. It's just that things are happening so fast. I haven't really had time to fantasize about being a happily married woman. Remember, I just got my memory back," Cindy tried to explain.

"I know. I'm not trying to pressure you. I was going to wait and make a whole date of it when we got back to the States, but I couldn't stop myself," Kamal added.

Cindy grabbed Kamal and pulled him to her. Smiling broadly, she said, "I will be your wife. Now kiss me!"

Happily following her orders, Kamal eagerly pressed his lips hard against Cindy's mouth, and together, they passionately explored one another while their infant son contentedly slept nearby.

After several minutes of necking and professing their love, Kamal and Cindy began discussing some basic ideas for the wedding. Then Kamal thought of something, "Babe, I'm wondering. Are you going to be Mrs. Ahmad or stay with Stetson?"

"I don't know, I'll have to think about that some more," said Cindy, her tone becoming distinctly defiant. "Just because I'm getting married doesn't mean I'm going to become someone else," she insisted. "I plan to be the same fucking person I've always been."

Kamal smiled devotedly at her and said adoringly, "And so it begins."

******

"Paula," said Shahin tentatively.

"Yeah," she replied, not looking at him or even acknowledging the tone of his voice.

"What do you think is going to happen to us?"

"I think we're safe," replied Paula. "There's really no threat to us here in Turkey."

"No, that's not what I meant," said Shahin cautiously. "I'm talking about our relationship."

"Oh, sorry," Paula answered politely. "I guess I misunderstood what you were asking."

Paula knew this conversation with Shahin was inevitable. He had given her many signs that he was ready and willing to pick up their relationship where they had left off.

Stating the obvious, Shahin said, "I know I'm the one who broke up with you, but I miss you so much, and I want us to be together."

"I missed you too, but so much has changed, Shahin," said Paula pragmatically. "Our breakup still hurts some, but it gave me a chance to see a different future for myself. I see something that I never considered when we were together as a couple. Now, I can see a future where I'm more in charge of my life."

"What exactly does that mean?" asked Shahin.

"If we had stayed together," Paula explained. "I might have worked in my career for a while, but then, as your wife, and maybe later as a mother, my career would take a back seat to yours. I'm not saying that's a bad thing or that someday I may not want to do it. It's just that, well, that's not what I want right now."

"I thought you might say something like this," said Shahin. "I could feel things were different between us. Especially the last couple of times we've been, you know, together."

"Yeah, I felt it, too," she agreed. "That's why I need to be on my own for a while and figure out what it is that I want to do next."

"I get it," said Shahin. "You're ready to explore new options and experiences, which don't include me."

"I wouldn't say they that," she said, giving him a sensual look. "But you're right. I need to *broaden my horizons,* as they say."

"So, do you have any ideas of what you want to do?" asked Shahin.

"Well, I'm thinking that I'm pretty good at keeping it together in a crisis, and I like helping people in trouble. I want to see if this *gun-for-hire* lifestyle is right for me. Plus, we both know the money is really good."

Shahin smiled proudly at Paula before gently stroking her cheek. "I know you'll be great at it," he whispered. "But remember, if you ever want some normal in your life, I'll be here."

Without saying a word, Paula smiled sensually back at Shahin, and before he could react, she hungrily pulled him into a kiss.

Epilogue

The wedding day finally arrived, and the courtyard gardens were bursting with color. The immaculately trimmed grass in the open space of the clubhouse grounds silenced the footsteps of the waiters as they quietly brought cocktails to the wedding guests.

When Cindy and Kamal first returned to the US, Cindy told everyone she didn't want a big wedding, saying that it was too late to have one since she was already a mother. Mrs. Stetson, Cindy's sister, and Paula disagreed and pleaded with Cindy to reconsider.

"Wow, the Cindy Stetson that I knew was known for breaking social norms. Now she believes she has to adhere to these made-up rules," said Paula sarcastically.

Cindy quickly responded, "Well…" then stopped as she thought about Paula's comment.

Paula finally broke through to Cindy when she pointed out one additional rule. "So, are you saying that because the current standards in the US *prohibit* women who are already mothers from wearing the traditional white wedding gown, that you're not going to wear the dress you want? I know it was originally meant to be worn as a sign of virginity, but come on, Cindy, most women aren't virgins when they get married. It's an outdated and stupid custom. It's only meant to intimidate and demean women, that's all."

Cindy immediately realized that she had been unknowingly influenced by the "establishment". Happily, she recanted her earlier decision by electing to have a big wedding, but with a few unconventional elements sprinkled in.

Cindy quickly rejected the traditional wedding venue and the ceremony. She and Kamal had different religious upbringings, and she felt a church or a mosque would be inappropriate. Cindy wanted something relaxed and enjoyable for her, Kamal, and their guests. The wedding would take place in the outside courtyard at the Stetsons' country club, and cocktails would be served to their guests before the ceremony began. The club manager questioned the idea at first but quickly saw the economic benefits and agreed to serve alcohol.

In contrast to the unconventional wedding venue, Cindy decided to wear the traditional white wedding gown. The dress she chose provocatively highlighted Cindy's curvy figure and prominent breasts. It was a white satin material with a V-shaped neckline off-the-shoulder and wide straps of lace instead of sleeves that hung loosely just above her biceps. From the waist up, the dress was covered in a large-patterned lace that was lined with intricate beadwork. The bottom portion of the dress was elegantly simple and full, with a short train in the back.

Cindy thanked Paula for making her see the discrimination and expressed her pride in breaking with the customary protocols. Both women felt it was time for all women to stand up for one another, and together, they might be able to stop American society's criticism of those who make non-traditional choices.

******

When everyone was served and the waiters had retreated, Cindy, with her father as her escort, prominently walked down the aisle with the white train of her wedding gown flowing beautifully behind them.

Kamal was beaming from ear to ear as his soon-to-be wife stepped up onto the low platform next to him. Cindy smiled mischievously back at him before turning to hand Paula her floral bouquet. As she passed Paula the flowers, Cindy gave her a thankful grin, and Paula responded with a wink and a smile.

Kamal's parents sat proudly in the front row with their grandson, Majid. Once they found out Farah had escaped Iran and was safely in the US with Kamal, they decided to risk leaving Iran without the proper paperwork. At the southern border crossing with Turkey, the border patrol looked at their passports and allowed them to go through without questioning their documentation.

At that moment, Mr. Ahmad realized that either they never needed new passports as purported, or the war with Iraq had drained the government's resources enough to diminish its capacity to monitor all of its citizens.

Cindy's sister, Debbie, who was the first bridesmaid, became emotional during the vows and gently touched Paula on the arm. Paula slyly turned to check on Debbie. When she glanced into her eyes, Paula knew Debbie was silently thanking her again for saving her sister.

A moment later, Farah, who was also a bridesmaid, looked gratefully at Paula before nodding her appreciation. When she saw her expression, the hesitancy Paula had been experiencing about her new career choice melted away, and she finally felt completely comfortable with her decision.

The following morning, around 10:00 AM, Paula headed for the airport lounge. She saw an open chair at the end of the bar and quickly weaved through the tables to the stool. Once seated, Paula ordered a Bloody Mary with an extra lime. She still felt a little drunk and hoped the cocktail would extend her relaxed feeling, at least until she was comfortably sitting on the plane. She figured she could sleep off the hangover during the flight.

As Paula sipped her drink, she thought back to the night before. She and a small group of friends stayed very late at the after-reception party, laughing and reminiscing about their experiences together.

"It was really nice to see everyone," she said to herself. "I'm so happy Shahin's found a new career. He needed to find something that excited him, and now he has. And Kyra, she looked great. Freedom has really given her a new lease on life."

Paula vaguely heard the telephone ring behind the bar as she reminisced. The sound had no significance to her, and she ignored the bartender's voice as he yelled out her name. It wasn't until he said Paula Williams a third time that his words made an impact on her thoughts.

"I'm Paula," she said, raising her hand slightly.

"There's some guy on the phone who says he needs to talk to you. He says it's important."

Paula got up and walked around the bar to the phone. The bartender handed her the receiver and walked away.

"Hello?" said Paula questioningly.

Kegger's voice boomed over the line, "Hey, I have a job for you."

"How'd you know I'd be here?" asked Paula.

"Hair of the dog," said Kegger, "especially after last night."

"Yeah, it was quite the party, wasn't it?" added Paula.

"Anyway, I got a call from an influential businessman from Santiago, Chile. He has a daughter who needs outside security protection. It's an immediate assignment. He's insisting on a woman. His daughter is seventeen, and he doesn't trust men. Plus, you'll need to shadow her everywhere she goes. He's trying to keep things normal for her under some tough circumstances. His wife has been missing now for two weeks. He's not sure if she's fled the country, been killed, or is part of the group that wants to take him down."

"It doesn't sound like a very happy marriage," said Paula sarcastically.

"No, it doesn't," agreed Kegger. "There are going to be a lot of moving parts and uncertainty in this job, but it shouldn't require direct combat. It's going to be more like babysitting. Are you in?"

"I guess," replied Paula. "You've worked out all the contract details with him?"

"Yes, he is willing to pay our price," said Kegger. "He's waiting for me to call him back with an answer and wiring instructions."

"Okay, then," said Paula. "Do I have time to fly home and repack?"

"You have today," replied Kegger. "I'm booking you on a flight out tonight."

"I'll call you when I get home, and we can go over the details then," said Paula.

"Sounds good," responded Kegger and ended the call.

As Paula handed the receiver back to the bartender, she nervously said with excitement in her voice to no one in particular, "Well, I guess it's showtime!"

About the Author

Trish has traveled and lived in many places in the world and draws on her own knowledge and imagination, as well as actual historical events, to create her exciting and challenging novels. The books transport the reader back to a place and time where real-world events have reshaped the future of millions of people and their cultures.

Trish has embarked on a new lifestyle, and it  began by moving out of Austin, TX, to become a traveler once again. She will be visiting and living in various places across the globe, but her home base for the immediate future will be Charleston, SC. Her upcoming experiences will enhance her knowledge of remote and popular places that exist on our diverse and interesting planet, called Earth.

RETURN TO IRAN is the sequel to ESCAPE FROM IRAN, and it is the second book in a series that highlights the life of a young woman, Paula Williams, beginning in the late 1970s and continuing on into the 1980s and beyond. The series is going to take the reader all over the world in a series of exciting adventures, sexual encounters, and life-threatening circumstances.

www.ingramcontent.com/pod-product-compliance
Lightning Source LLC
Chambersburg PA
CBHW021533250626
47154CB00006BA/2103